I0712982

Rustblind and Silverbright

Edited by David Rix

www.eibonvalepress.co.uk

...You are yourself a railway track, rusty, stained, silver, shiny, beautiful and uncertain. And you are divided into sections and bound between stations. And they have sign-boards whereon is written women, or murder, or moon. And then that is the world.

You are a railway -rumbled over, cried over -you are the track -on you everything happens and makes you rustblind and silverbright.

You are human, your brain giraffe-lonely somewhere above on your endless neck. And no one quite knows your heart.

-Wolfgang Borchert (1921-1947), from *Railways by Day and by Night*, translated by David Porter

Contents:

Act 1

Act 2

Contents:

Act 3

Act 1

Introduction

It is 11:15 PM. You stand on a deserted railway platform – the only traveller, it seems.   Around you, the lights of buildings twinkle and the haze of sodium fills the world – but down the tracks there is nothing but darkness, pierced only by the red and green stars of signals and the gleaming threads of the rails. Out of the darkness, your train arrives – at least you think it's your train. It's hard to ever be quite sure. You scramble on board and the doors hiss closed behind you. Somewhere up front is a driver – maybe. One assumes so. In this carriage, you are still the only traveller. Always relaxing to be alone as you roll gently onwards. You look around warily for security cameras, wondering if you are being watched and by who – but you can't see any. Not in these older carriages. Out of the window, you can see little except vague hints of passing trees, brick, tunnel, fence. You have no idea where you are because as you ride the train, you are a helpless passenger in a world that you never see any other way save as brief glimpses – a world isolated and cut off from any other paths people tread.

I suppose it is possible to make some comparisons between the train and the book – after all, both take you on a journey and show you sights, which you follow with a certain degree of helplessness. In the case of a book, you run on the rails of language and the writer's imagination. In the case of a train, you follow the narrative of the railway construction and the driver. But for me at least, such intellectual musings pale a bit in comparison with the thing itself. After all, trains occupy a special place in the human psyche. The twin threads of the rails forge ahead from place to place, the ultimate symbol of travel and connection and all the hopes, fantasies, fears, reasons, romance and excitement that come with that. The links between points, the bridges and tunnels, are always so much more profound than borders or walls. And yet you travel these links through a world that is isolated from normal life and unique to itself. The railways are so mundane and taken for granted, passing through the backs of your cities and towns, yet they are worlds that cannot be visited, cannot be known. Worlds that can only be glimpsed from blurred windows or from the far end of the platform. Hidden places. Private places. Places where the ordinary and the secret meet. For me, living in London, riding the train is more like a kind of urban exploration than anything else. And when in the right mood, one could almost wonder – are there branch lines somewhere towards other places or states of being? Are there lines that run through no ordinary stations? Are there stops occasionally where you really shouldn't alight? Or really *should*? Are there train tunnels with no exit or end?

This was the mood in which Rustblind and Silverbright came into being – a book of railway stories that aimed to look far beyond what you might expect from classic horror or sci-fi. Like any good journey, the scenery of this book is ever-changing. You will ride the rails of language and imagination through many and varied places – some almost unendurably disturbing, some bleak and miserable, some surreal and strange, some touching and moving, some absurd and comical, some exquisitely beautiful. This is a collection that ranges widely from the almost-familiar double-track line of slipstream fiction to the grungy metro of sci-fi and the dark and sparsely served branch line of pure horror, while the squawking locomotives of absurdism jostle with still stranger trains that ride to – other places.

When you look at a railway line, the possibilities seem endless. It sometimes seems as though, if you put your ear to the tracks, you can hear the entire world talking.

David Rix, London, 31 May 2013

Tetsudo Fan

Andrew Hook

Saturday morning Kazuo packed his camera and lunch into his rucksack and headed down to Tokyo Station. The day was bright. Sunshine bounced off the sides of glass buildings like the metallic sphere in a pinball machine. Kazuo's mother had waved as he left their apartment, and Kazuo had ducked his head as though he wasn't her target. At fifteen he considered that he was coming into his own as an individual. That morning his mother was the only shadow on his thoughts.

He rode the bus, his knees pressed close together, the bag on his lap. Other passengers were quiet. Two girls whispered together on the back seat, but their voices were no more than susurrations in the air. Some men clutched briefcases. Women held shopping bags that dangled from long straps over their shoulders. Kazuo took all this in as though he were capturing it on film. One day, he thought, he might feel part of it, but currently despite his best efforts he remained an outsider.

At Tokyo Station he hurried to the Tōhoku Shinkansen line. He had many photos of the various 'bullet' trains in his collection, but he hadn't long been a tetsudo fan and there were always new pictures to be taken. Some of his friends collected stamps, others photographs of wildlife, some of them even collected girlfriends, but what Kazuo liked most about the trains were that whilst they had the permanence of stamps they weren't static, and in spite of their movement they were not as transitory as birds or girlfriends.

He laid his rucksack on a surprisingly empty bench and removed the camera. Checked the settings for light. Then sat and folded one leg over the other, waiting for the musical announcement of the train. He was expecting to catch one of the 200 series, the first type that had been introduced on the Tōhoku Shinkansen line in 1982. Whilst most had been withdrawn, some were still in operation as 10-car sets. Unlike the more modern N700 or E5 series, the 200 series couldn't maintain speeds of 300km/h but still ran at an impressive 240km/h. Besides, Kazuo wasn't in it for the speed. There was a beauty to the design of all of the trains that spoke to something inside him. Something that favoured travel, exploration, excitement, and the thrill of the sounds of metal upon metal.

The earlier 200 series Shinkansen trains didn't have the shark nose of the 100 series, and they were lighter and more powerful than the 0 series. Kazuo wished he had been around to see those that were originally painted in ivory with green window and lower bodyside bands, but those still in existence had been revamped and refurbished, and he satisfied himself with sight of the white upper, dark-blue lower scheme with the wrap around cab windows.

Either way, they were sleek. Kazuo stood as one entered the station, slung the rucksack over a shoulder, and then bent at the knee to get his best shot.

His camera clicked repeatedly. He knew that if he flicked through all the images one after the other he would create the illusion of movement like an old-style flicker book. He could video the train, of course, but he wanted the static image. In some respects, the flicker photographs created a more staccato sense of movement than the real-life video image. For Kazuo, it was a more realistic movement.

Once the train left the station, he returned to the bench and opened his rucksack. His mother had packed some *bocchan dango* together in a clear plastic box. Each of the types of dumpling, one coloured by red beans, another by eggs, and the third by green tea, were skewered together, three on a stick. There were five sticks in total. He placed the first in his mouth and pulled all three off simultaneously, the mix of flavours odd yet pleasant on his tongue.

14

After lunch, Kazuo intended to catch one of the E4 series. These were double-decker cars, similarly painted to the 200 series although the nose dropped at the front as though diagonally sliced. As he chewed on the dumplings he imagined the kind of photograph that he wanted to take. Preferably a face front shot, then moving to one side to capture the length of the train. Some of the websites he frequented mentioned hotels with 'train-view' rooms where you could get a good view of the rails, trains and stations in one shot. The rooms also afforded guests overhead views of trains that ordinarily could only be seen from the side. Yet Kazuo had no expectations of being able to frequent such places, just as some of his friends had fantasised about going to love hotels they remained just that: a fantasy.

The lid on his lunchbox popped back with a satisfying click. Kazuo replaced it in his rucksack and, camera in hand, made his way to another part of the station.

Light filtered through the building, reflected off the trains, illuminating the faces of pedestrians angelically. Suddenly for Kazuo all seemed right with the world, despite his overbearing mother. He was outside. He was with trains. There was a niche to be had and he squeezed inside it.

As he approached the platform, an E4 series Shinkansen was ready for boarding. He would have to satisfy himself with photographs of it leaving the station rather than arriving, and whilst he always found something more exciting in an arrival he uncapped his camera and prepared his shot all the same.

Taking his first photo, a shadow distorted the light, and just for a moment he thought of his mother. Looking up he saw a man in casual dress, also with a camera, also pointed at the E4.

Kazuo stood. The man regarded him briefly. Then they both looked back at the train as pedestrians boarded.

"Two eight-car sets have been coupled together," the man said, his voice low. "That sixteen-car E4 series formation can carry a total of 1,634 seated passengers. It's the highest-capacity high-speed rail trainset in the world."

Kazuo nodded, unsure what to say.

The man looked at him again. Then raised the camera and took Kazuo's picture. "Always good to meet another tetsudo fan," he said.

Kazuo remained standing, dimly aware of his own camera held tight by his right hand.

"My name is Kunihiro," said the man, "I come here every Saturday and Wednesday when my wife is at her pottery class."

He looked at Kazuo expectantly.

"Kazuo," Kazuo said, at last. "My name is Kazuo."

Kunihiro nodded. "Someone young like yourself interested in the trains is important," he said. "After the E4 leaves, maybe I could take you somewhere."

Kazuo felt the aftertaste of the *bocchan dango* at the back of his throat, the green tea flavour over-riding the others.

"Ok," he said. Then he raised his camera and snapped the E4 in its static position.

The sun was still beating a ferocious rhythm as they left Tokyo Station. Early afternoon was bathed in stark light, like the difference between a digital photographic image and traditional film. Faces seemed pockmarked, teeth serrated. Smiles burnt themselves right into the corners of mouths. The blue and white of schoolgirl uniforms captured light and dark simultaneously.

Kunihiro beckoned a taxi and before Kazuo knew it they were travelling away from Tokyo Station and towards Akihabara.

The inside of the taxi felt like a vacuum, the unyielding light barely penetrating. Kazuo had the sudden thought of being in a cave. His rucksack sat between him and Kunihiro, an unspoken barrier. Briefly it crossed his mind to wonder what he was doing there, but then Kunihiro answered that question for him.

"Have you heard of Shin Akiba Denki Tetsudou?"

Kazuo shook his head.

"Then you are in for a treat." Kunihiro steepled his fingers in front of his face. "It's a fictitious railroad company, also known as the New Akihabara Electric Railroad. You sure you haven't heard of the Little TGV Bar?"

Kazuo didn't know whether to feign knowledge. His lack of understanding concerned him, but in the end he simply shook his head again.

"Perhaps you are too young," mused Kunihiro. Then he unsteepled his fingers and turned his gaze outside the window.

Kazuo slipped one arm through the strap of his rucksack, anchored himself to the present. He wondered how old Kunihiro was. Surely in his early to mid-forties. His jet black hair should be speckled with grey streaks but Kazuo suspected it was dyed. He realised that Kunihiro was of similar age to his father.

When the taxi stopped, Kazuo thought about making an excuse to leave, but Kunihiro touched him by the elbow and together they looked up at the sign of the bar.

"This way," Kunihiro said.

Inside, the bar was decked out like the interior of a train. Young waitresses were dressed as railroad clerks, complete with caps. Their uniforms stopped above the knee but they weren't improper. Even so, Kazuo couldn't help but become transfixed by the sight of their long red and white striped socks. As they entered they were approached by one of the girls.

"How many passengers for today?"

"Two, please," said Kunihiro.

The waitress smiled. "You may have to share a table with others, is that ok? It will take an hour to reach your destination."

They were handed two train tickets and the waitress beckoned them to follow her down the aisle. Either side were seats as if on a train, memorabilia decorated the walls, somewhere out of Kazuo's sight he could hear a model train racing round a track, the familiar *shoo shoo* noise settling him.

As they made their way further into the restaurant, the waitress called out 'two more passengers on board.' Kazuo glanced at Kunihiro to see if he were smiling, but his expression was fixed. So was his gaze, also at the socks of the girl leading them to their table.

"So," Kunihiro said, as they sat, "tell me about your interest in trains."

Kazuo recovered some of his composure. He explained how from an early age he had been fascinated by trains, from his first train set to his first journey. He omitted the fact that he had chosen trains over stamps, birds and girlfriends and he omitted the reason why. Kunihiro only appeared to be listening to half of what was said. His eyes moved from side to side of the room as though he were looking at the scenery. The drinks on the menu carried railway related names. Kunihiro had ordered Hanzomon Line for himself and Ginza Line for Kazuo. Kazuo sipped his drink softly. He had refused food as he was still full of dumplings, and anyway he did not want to impose too much on Kunihiro's generosity, but the man had ordered *omuraisu* for himself, and when the omelette and rice arrived he had the waitress write the name of Takasaki Station on the side of his plate using tomato ketchup.

"Next Saturday," said Kunihiro, "I want to take a trip to the Hara Model Railway Museum. Will you accompany me?"

Kazuo found himself nodding. Today seemed a day for nods.

"Good," said Kunihiro. "We will meet at Tokyo Station at ten o'clock sharp."

With that, their encounter seemed to be concluded. Kunihiro dropped his head to his meal and Kazuo found himself rising and making his way back out of the train. As he left one of the girls caught his eye and beamed at him.

"Thank you for riding our train!"

Entering into the sunshine Kazuo had the feeling he had emerged from a tunnel.

During the week Kazuo found himself wondering about Kunihiro. It seemed he had found a kindred spirit, but the circumstances of travelling to the Hara Model Railway Museum troubled him. Whenever he had imagined a companion he had shyly considered it would be a tetsuko, a female railroad enthusiast. Sometimes whilst riding the trains he would look at the girls reading *Tetsuko no tabi*, a travel manga about a female manga artist with no particular interest in trains, who travelled the country by train with a travel-writer who is an enthusiast. That dissociation yet immersion appealed to him. Despite deciding to choose trains over girlfriends, he knew it wasn't a real choice. Truth was, he had not yet met a girl who he could feel comfortable having a relationship with.

His mother was pleased with this. "You have no need to rush into anything, Kazuo," she might say, as she dampened the corner of a tissue and cleaned dried toothpaste from the side of his mouth. "Besides, whoever you find will have to match up to me."

Kazuo would nod, almost blush with embarrassment, and then flee to his bedroom with his railway magazines and the soothing hum of his Plarail model trainset.

Unlike the previous Saturday, rain fell in torrents when Kazuo awoke. The drumming of the rain had infiltrated his dreams as the hum of train tracks, and when he awoke he had an obscure feeling that he had been travelling.

In the kitchen he sidestepped his mother's questioning over his plans for the day. Shortly after nine he found himself on the bus, its wheels creating mini-tidal waves at the edges of the pavement as it winded its way towards Tokyo Station.

Kunihiro greeted him with a slight nod. Before Kazuo knew it they had taken the Tōyoko Line and then the underground Minatomirai Line to Yokohama Station, following which they made a short walk to the museum.

"A special treat," Kunihiro said.

Kazuo was well aware of the Hara Model Railway Museum. It had opened only the month before and housed an extensive display of model trains built and collected by the model railway enthusiast Nobutaro Hara. Even so, the museum could house only one sixth of his collection. As they walked around the exhibits, Kazuo marvelled at the dedication.

Kunihiro also seemed obsessed. "Imagine," he said, "if something should happen to this collection. An earthquake, maybe. Imagine how the exhibits would fall apart, buckle under pressure, how these little figurines would fare in such a scenario."

"And yet," Kazuo intercepted, some of his shyness evaporating like the rain on the streets, "consider how during the Shinkansen's 45-year, 7 billion passenger history, there have been no passenger fatalities due to derailments or collisions."

Kunihiro tilted his head. "There is that," he said.

At the centre of the exhibit they paused for some time before 'Ichiban Tetsumo Park', a 310 square-metre diorama featuring model trains from all over the world.

"Imagine," Kunihiro said again, "that this landscape is the real world. We would be like Godzilla if we were to mount this display and crush it beneath our feet."

Kazuo looked at him, to see if he were joking, but Kunihiro just repeated 'like Godzilla', and he lifted each foot in turn, stamping the ground underneath him as if to emphasise his point.

"Godzilla," he said.

As they were leaving the museum Kunihiro's eye seemed to linger on a woman with a girl around Kazuo's age following in her wake.

"A *mamatetsu*," he said, and went over to speak to her.

Kazuo leant against the wall of the museum, hunger pangs affecting his stomach. He hadn't eaten all day, despite the dumplings in his rucksack. He had felt embarrassed to offer one to Kunihiro and therefore had had nothing himself. Equally, he didn't want to embarrass Kunihiro by having him pay for his food. As he mused over his position, he became aware of the girl standing beside him.

"I'm Neko," she said, extending a hand which was soft, cold and limp to his touch. "Your father is talking to my mother."

Kazuo saw no reason to contradict her. In any event, words caught in his throat. Neko had a bobbed fringe haircut, which extended long at the sides and spiralled in two ponytails at the back. Her eyes were accentuated by black mascara, and her lips were highlighted with soft pale pink lipstick. When she smiled, something tugged within him.

"Are you *tetsuko*?" he asked.

She smiled again. "Sometimes. I have an interest, but often I have to hide my boredom. It's my mother's hobby. She still thinks of me as her little *kotetsu*. But, of course, I'm too old for that."

Kazuo noted calmly how the front of her blouse pushed forwards as she stood, one leg casually against the other. She wore a large pink bow at her neck, one that matched her smile.

"And you," she asked. "Are you tetsudo?"

Kazuo felt inexplicably challenged, as if she were mocking him. He shrugged off her attention and began walking towards Kunihiro. "Yes," he said, "yes, I'm tetsudo. It's what I am."

When Kazuo reached Kunihiro he saw he was talking animatedly with Neko's mother, yet his gaze kept sliding away to a corner of the room where a party of schoolgirls were congregating. Kazuo glanced at them himself, thought he recognised one, then realised Neko was at his side again, her eyes wide open with curiosity.

"Are you rude?" she asked.

Kazuo was taken aback. "Sorry?"

"I said, are you rude? I wouldn't have walked away from *you*."

But try as he might, Kazuo couldn't express his feelings.

"Come," Kunihiro touched his elbow. "It's time to go."

On the train back to Tokyo Station Kunihiro said, "There's something I want to show you."

Kazuo almost rolled his eyes. "The bar again?"

"No," Kunihiro said, "not the bar. Would you come to my apartment? It's just a short journey from the station."

Kazuo looked out of the window. It was no longer raining and the summer sun had dried the landscape. There wasn't a drop of water to be seen against any of the buildings, even in the areas that were shadowed.

He looked at his watch. "Only if it won't take long," he said.

Kunihiro smiled. "Of course. Just for a moment."

They completed the remainder of the journey in silence.

Entering Kunihiro's apartment Kazuo found himself looking out for his wife's attempts at pottery. Kazuo's mother had undertaken a similar creative course herself, and for a while their house had become littered with misshapen lumps of clay, before his father had finally suggested that they would make better use in the garden. But in Kunihiro's apartment there was no indication of his wife's hobby. Instead, there was much to illustrate that Kunihiro himself ruled the roost in his own home.

Railway memorabilia decorated the walls. Train tickets preserved behind glass. Uniforms on hangers. Pamphlets yellowing with age.

"My goal," said Kunihiro, "was to ride every line of every railway company in the country. Of course, we have approximately 160 different railway companies and the largest alone has over 20,000 kilometres of track, but I was sure it was possible. I used to colour in blank route maps to show where I'd been, but of course this has now moved onto the internet which automatically calculates the travelled distance just by entering the name of the railway line. For me, this takes the fun out of it, so I abandoned my challenge."

The entrance to the apartment was narrow. In the silence which followed Kunihiro's admission Kazuo could clearly hear his breathing.

"In here," said Kunihiro.

Kazuo followed him into a room crammed with a model trainset layout save for an approximate six foot by two foot gap in the middle of the floor. Stations, tiny people, trees, hedges, tunnels, barriers: the full set-up like a miniature but still impressive centrepiece similar to the Ichiban Tetsumo Park at the Hara Museum.

"Lie there," Kunihiro said, pointing to the space in the floor. Kazuo looked at him expectantly, querulously.

"Lie there," Kunihiro repeated.

Kazuo became aware that intentionally or not Kunihiro was blocking the door.

"It's ok," he said. "There's just something I want to show you." Then he lifted Kazuo's rucksack from his shoulder. "Just in case," he said.

Kazuo felt himself carried as if by a dream over the tracks and into the centre of the room, tiptoeing through the display. Dropping first to his knees, he edged himself into position. It was only as he lay down that he noticed the flat-screen television face above him on the ceiling.

"Wait there," said Kunihiro.

Kazuo heard the flick of a switch and the trains which had previously been stationary came into life. Models of all sizes and descriptions began to circumnavigate the track. It was unclear from his position, but he estimated at least twenty trains began to run faster and faster, approaching his body from all angles then turning away, the noise in his head cumulative as the trains met in an arc and then sped tangentially in all directions.

The effect was soporific. The swish of the wheels on the track, the hum of the engines, the breeze that was created by their movement. Kazuo felt at home, probably for the first time in his life. A sanctuary was created within the cocoon of the tracks. Within the niche that was his world he had found another niche: a refuge within the whole.

It was then, just as he felt he might settle into sleep, that a film began to play on the television above his head.

It started innocuously enough. A young girl walked in and around a model railway set much as the one that surrounded him. She was wearing a schoolgirl uniform, although it was obvious to Kazuo that she was too old for school. Then she bent over one of the stations and he realised he could clearly see her white panties.

He tried to sit with a start, but a pressure seemed to hold him down, as though a centrifugal force from the trains that circulated him were able to pin him to the floor.

The image changed. A woman in black PVC boots, tight pants and a rubber top was gyrating over the model railway. She wore stockings, and Kazuo became open-mouthed as she extended a gloved finger to caress the top of one of the trains. The shot panned further back to reveal her high heels. Suddenly, without warning, she lifted a foot and stuck the point of one of the heels into the top of the train station.

Kazuo heard a gasp in the room, but couldn't turn his head from the screen. The girl raised her leg again, the camera angle affording a glimpse of her thighs, then she rammed her shoe onto one of the tiny plastic figures standing by the station. Its body broke in two, one arm crushed sideways like an insect.

The camera remained focussed on her heels as she trampled across the set. Grassy hillocks were crumpled, carriages broken underfoot, each step marked with a sickening crunch and forced laughter. After a while the woman was joined by the schoolgirl and they set about decimating the diorama together, linking arms, with their hands round each other's waists. Kazuo was aghast yet consumed simultaneously. He remembered Neko at the museum, replaced the schoolgirl with her image. He remembered Kunihiro speaking of Godzilla crushing the exhibits. As the PVC-clad girl stood on a railway bridge at the exact moment a train crossed it, Kazuo closed his eyes and shivered deep inside his being. Not only was he home, but he had found his heart.

The image ceased and the whirr of the trains came to a halt. In a daze, Kazuo finally managed to turn his head to one side where Kunihiro was standing, leaning against the wall, breathing hard, looking as if he were about to collapse.

Kazuo closed his eyes again. Replayed his memory. He realised he had made a jump from being *tetsudo* into adulthood. He pitied his friends who had chosen stamps and the arbitrary fluctuations of birds. They could never know the simple pleasure of a train.

Platform Alteration: Animal Station Masters, Japan

As an admittedly inexperienced Japanophile, I am still trying to get to grips with one of the basic dichotomies between Japanese culture and what we call the 'west': why does cute work so well in Japan but not here? Is it really just the sense of the exotic that makes it slip down the throat more easily, or have they genuinely found some mysterious secret that we are lacking? Although trains and cute don't often coexist in the same sentence, this does apply to the Japanese railways as well. By no stretch is it possible to really call the Shinkansen bullet trains cute – they are more the cartoon spacecraft of the train world. It is the smaller local lines where this comes to the fore. The Japanese countryside regularly faces the intrusion of trains with cute cat faces or pop-culture designs, trains covered with autumn leaves or cherry blossom, gaggles of cartoon girls or even mecha robots – and I am left somewhat bemused. On the one hand, it is maybe nice to stamp one's culture and aesthetic so enthusiastically on mundane objects and maybe we could learn a lesson or two from it over here in our world of rather uninspired corporate branding – on the other, I am thinking of our own miserable efforts at 'cute' and thinking I might just shoot myself if I lived in such a world. The closest we have managed in the UK was the bizarre and pop-arty rainbowstriped Thameslink trains (Google it) that used to crawl 'cutely' through the murky depths of London – and it's just not the same!

This is the backdrop of cuteness against which a cat called Tama sparked a cultural revolution among the minor and not so minor stations of the Japanese railways.

It happened more or less by chance when a stray cat turned up at Kishi station and soon began being fed and fussed over. Since she was so popular, someone got the bright idea of making her an official stationmaster, complete with official stationmaster cap. And by that I mean officially official – she is now the world's only feline corporate executive. Everybody loves cats, and it seems just about everyone loved Tama and wanted to see her – but I dunno if anyone was expecting her to end up as famous and successful as she did. The company that took her on was certainly delighted with the massive boost to both themselves and the economy that this stationmaster cat caused. She now has her own office and is the highest ranking female executive in the company – make what you will of that. There is even the Tama Densha (densha = train) – one of the quaint little local multiple unit trains especially done up in honour of this most famous stationmaster. As one would expect, it sports whiskers on the front, has vaguely cat-themed decor inside and more cartoon cats on the flanks than should ever be allowed to congregate in one place. The station at Kishi was even rebuilt in the form of a cat face. What started with a stray cat wandering in has ended with a bloody theme park!

The old cliché that Japan can never have too much of a good thing may or may not have had anything to do with what happened next. Maybe it was just human nature. More cats were predictable enough. If you want animal stationmasters, cats were easy. Cats were everywhere. Dogs too – Ajigasawa and Oku-Nakayama Kogen both have dog stationmasters. Unomachi Station in Seiyo has a rabbit stationmaster. But it gets stranger. A tortoise stationmaster presides over Ibusuki station – Uzen-Komatsu station has a goat – a penguin works part time at Kashikojima Station and Shishikui Station even has an aquarium of official lobster stationmasters. All wear the official caps (ok, in the case of the lobsters, it is just perched on top of the tank) and as far as I can tell, all perform their duties admirably and are as pampered and fussed over as any animals you will find.

In Japan, someone somewhere must have the fun job of designing these official caps. Someone somewhere has to get up in the morning and go to work driving the Cat Train or the Strawberry Train (Google it) or the Pink Ninja Train (Google it) or the Kitaro Train (Google it) or Tadanori Yokoo's Eyeball Train (Google them all!). And suddenly I am getting the feeling that we are a long way from home . . . and that, whatever your feelings about 'cute', just maybe home is very boring!

DR

On The Level

Allen Ashley

As a boy, I always loved level crossings. I was never scared on them. I used to look both ways – up the line and down the line, you might say. I never saw anything coming. You never do.

Of course, sometimes you might see a local service slowly *departing*, if it's been sitting at the station maybe fifty yards along, picking up passengers and heading away from this danger zone.

Lisa lived near the railway. We were friends since the start of secondary school. Her real name was Alissa but during the early days she dropped the first syllable and changed the pronunciation of the other two. She was always headstrong. Tomboyish with her short dark hair and tigerish at sports but as puberty properly hit she became quite beguiling to my eyes.

I recall walking home in the drizzle most days but I also have strong impressions of stopping off on many occasions with a couple of other mates to play cricket in Lisa's scruffy back garden. Trains to the coast and commuter specials rolled past her high back wall with a frequency that belied the regular jokes about the British railway system. We lost a lot of tennis balls to wild slogs and cover drives into the blackberries and hedgerow. After a while, we started using yellow sponge balls which flew hawk-like for a few feet then died due to air resistance. Later still, we dispensed with games and just sat jawing around the kitchen table. Condensed to a tight knit group now; four of us – me, Lisa, Terry and Dave – always on good behaviour, no cuss words or dangerous opinions. Her mother was a fine hostess, plying us with hot drinks, cold drinks and light refreshments as if this were the buffet carriage on the Anglian ride to Ipswich. Sometimes when the express rattled by, it set the cups and plates to rattling as Mrs Jones prepared tea and cakes; the loose crumbs were being shaken like tiny grains of gravel on the rails. Mr Jones worked a night shift as a security guard at a local factory and was constantly moaning above his *Evening Standard* that the blasted 4.10 was late again. Lisa used to raise her eyebrows at his minor bitching and I always wondered when her father had last caught a train anywhere and why should he care?

I don't know who first mooted the idea of starting a band. It's a typical teenage thing, I suppose. Maybe it was me raving about my late uncle's vinyl collection fetching a small fortune on eBay. Perhaps it was Dave unwittingly auditioning for percussionist by absentmindedly drumming on the empty biscuit tin. Lisa had some intense poems that she could turn into lyrics. Terry knew how to 'borrow' equipment from the school stock room. Alissa Jones and Whitchurch Junction were born.

I had this idea of collating a definitive CD of train songs through the ages. From the Blues up to the modern day. Not forgetting *Oh, Mr Porter* from the music hall days. Other random selections kept coming to mind such as George Hamilton IV, who once had a big hit with the slightly saccharine *Canadian Pacific*. It's a decent enough sing-along; but whatever happened to George the first, George the second and, crucially, George the Third?

Terry was the first to drop out of our regular little late afternoon gang. He started to hang out with some of the 'lads' at the shopping centre, troubling the constables with his lip and unwillingness to "Move along, sonny." Dave left us next. He had been struggling with his studies for some time and his parents decided to engage a tutor four evenings a week. Poor sod.

Which left just me and lissom Lisa wending our casual way home from St Petrifa's, not hand in hand but physically close and comfortable in an old pals manner. We weren't an item; in fact, our GCSE choices meant that we spent most of the day in separate classes. At three-thirty, though, she would always seek me out. Quietly, I considered that I had landed in clover. All those machinations that might lie ahead of me: learning ways of chatting up girls, getting the nerve to speak to the opposite sex in the first place, surviving the scrum in pubs and nightclubs – maybe I could be excused them. I was shy as fuck, after all. The strong possibility presented itself that Lisa and I might just gradually become inseparable.

A two-carriage job trundled by virtually empty just beyond the embankment. Lisa had loosened her tie and undone the top buttons of her regulation white blouse. Smooth skin and hints of fledgling feminine roundness.

"Lift your eyes, Tom," she laughed before giving me a little peck on the cheek. No cake or tea today.

I was well into my train songs search now. I learnt all the call and response lines in *Midnight Train to Georgia* by Gladys Knight and the Pips. Someone put me on to *Morningtown Ride* by The Seekers. Catching it on You Tube, I was immediately transported back to a forgotten memory: my Year 3 teacher, Miss Croft, who used to strum it on an old Spanish guitar at the end of the day. For all its locomotive references, it's essentially a lullaby meant to send kids to sleep. That's probably why she never played it at 9.30 in the morning.

Nothing wrong with a train being a metaphor, of course.

Lisa bumped into me on her way out of French. Her short dark hair sported a butterfly clip and her breath smelt pleasantly of spearmint.

"Old Hinton's off sick," she announced. "They can't get a supply. So, how about study leave this afternoon?"

"I'll see you two trees beyond the main gate," I grinned.

"You and your secret agent stuff," she laughed, heading for Sociology A' Level.

She was off the premises five minutes earlier than I managed. She stayed ahead of my black brogues pursuit like an elfin creature teasing a mere mortal. She paused at her door, made a disparaging remark about my athletic ability, then dragged me upstairs to her bedroom.

"Mum's at work. Dad's gone to Watford. It's your lucky day, Tom."

Her window was slightly open, as if the chill air from outside might season the heat within. She slipped out of her school trousers, pulled down her white cotton knickers in the same movement. She had hardly any pubic hair, as if a work crew had come along and clipped back the undergrowth surrounding my destination. She was slightly dry and I was quite clumsy. It was all over very quickly.

I lay my head against her bare bony shoulder and listened to the clatter of unfamiliar trains rattling along some twenty yards away. I wanted to shout the good news to the harried commuters, tell them that wherever they were going, I was already at the place I wanted to be. Wanted to stay.

"Shall we try again, Tom?" she whispered.

This time we took a little longer, letting the clattering shuffle of the nearby wheels on tracks guide our thrusts and groans. The bedsprings wheezed beneath us like a relic from the Victorian era. The conflicting rhythms formed a sweaty mash-up and I came like a pale pink stallion.

Old Hinton had heart trouble so we had several free afternoons that half term. I got to anticipate the passage of the express trains and local services beyond Lisa's sash window, imagining that we were aboard that rolling stock, fucking our way to the fertility of East Anglia and the frothing North Sea beyond.

If my later employers, Techno Solutions, had been in the time machine business, those are the moments I'd want to return to.

Her dad had 'gone to Watford' again. I was all for spending the afternoon in the musky blankets. However, Lissa, as she was now styling herself, wanted to work up some new music.

"I've got these train songs," she announced. "Little regular rhythms going through my head. Lyrics about arriving and departing."

I smiled, already seeing *Lyrics about Arriving and Departing* as the title of our debut CD. "I'm cool with train songs," I answered. "Although stuff like *Trans Europe Express* is tediously hypnotic."

"It's meant to be, Tom. Most rail journeys are pretty boring. Anyway, I want to record. Did you bring the gear?" I shrugged. "You just thought we were going to shag all day, didn't you?" she added.

"A boy's gotta have dreams."

"Go and get the mikes and the box. Sex can wait but my songs can't."

It took me twenty minutes to do the round trip, my jacket unhooked and held tent-like to protect the equipment from the metropolitan drizzle.

"Shouldn't we tell Terry...?"

"I'm fucked off with him! Just tune up, will you, Tom?"

Her playing and chord-choice was as scratchy as ever. Her voice whispered like a nurse bringing your bedtime medicine. I tried to keep up with the awkward changes. Soon we were so in the throes of playing that we didn't make the usual decision to stop when a train rattled by noisily at the foot of the garden. In fact, I think it had been Lissa's intention all along to incorporate the cross-rhythm into the song's background, thus creating a unique texture. Neil Young did something like this donkey's years ago with a crackling fire and the effect was pretty mesmeric.

At last, she was finished. There were tiny beads of perspiration on her forehead, echoing the raindrops clustering on the outside of the window.

"Come on then, big boy," she ordered, resting her second hand acoustic against a chair.

My hands were cupping her small breasts beneath her soft white bra when her mother's voice called from the hallway, "Hi, darling, I'm back. Are you hungry?"

*

There are surprisingly few genuinely British railroad songs. I've had to reluctantly discount Lonnie Donegan's *Rock Island Line*; even though it's a top performance by the King of Skiffle, it's still a cover version of an American original. Ah, heck, put it on the compilation, anyway. This song, as much as anything by Elvis, inspired the young John Lennon to pick up a guitar in a thrift store.

The Who, though. Different case. Their raucous *5.15* has their mod hero out of his brain on a commuter train and its insistently rhythmic exploration of paranoia is a keynote of the *Quadrophenia* album and film. No one's writing stuff like this these days and more's the pity.

We had to put the band mostly on hold when I signed up for university. We hadn't got any further than a few nights at local pubs playing for beer money and the forced adulation of school and college mates. With Dave off the scene we went through drummers like steam through a whistle. We had a couple of reunions during the summer break but they went off the rails after one fateful Sunday.

I was signed up for an engineering degree. It seems odd to me now but as a youngster I was a 'right Meccano kid', as my granddad used to call me, always building and fixing things. If only my fingers could have slid up and down the guitar neck with such grace and skill. I thought that I wanted to construct buildings or create useful artefacts, maybe move into design at some point, be some sort of 21st Century Brunel. I don't apologise for having hopes and dreams.

Uni. was a disappointment. Dull lectures and tedious assignments. Despite the albatross of student debt hanging around my neck, I was still expected to go out on the lash with my hall mates every night, living off curries or takeaway pizzas when, realistically, I could barely afford beans on toast. There was too much drinking, too much horseplay next to the railway line or in otherwise quiet residential areas. Everyone was in a band, everyone was a Mixmaster DJ, everyone was young and foolish.

I was missing Lissa like crazy. I got back home a couple of weekends but these always seemed to be on occasions when she had other matters to attend to – such as mediating in another potential reconciliation between her parents. The closest I got to her was a demo recording that arrived one morning in a brown jiffy bag. It was just Lissa on guitar, burrowing into my head with her hypnotic whisper and strum:

> *The tracks are long and it's a narrow gauge,*
> *I feel encumbered by this age,*
> *I'm only whole when I'm on the stage,*
> *The rest of life is shadows.*

I was thousands of pounds in the red, I was drifting away from the girl I loved, and I was obliterating my problems with Strongbow and Stella Artois. Then something unexpected changed my whole perspective.

I entered a story in a competition run by the world's top science fiction magazine. Stumped up the postage to send the manuscript to America. Had largely pinched the love story part of the plot from Shakespeare – hey, if you're going to steal, do it from the best. Didn't really have the proverbial snowball's chance… Except that, SF being an ideas-based genre, my *Rails across the Ocean* hit a nerve with the sponsors and I was awarded first prize. The dollars were welcome but beyond this came an invitation to complete my studies with the help of a sizeable grant and a guaranteed work placement when I graduated.

What had interested Techno Solutions was my concept of cities built on artificial islands in the world's main seas; these self-sustaining environments running their own greenhouses and wind turbines and being connected by computer controlled locomotives running on suspended rails that used the ionic charge of seawater to maintain their position above the waves. It was all baloney, background detail for my tragic romance, but the company felt I had stumbled upon a workable idea for the post-oil age. I finished my desultory studies. I wanted to spend some time drinking coffee and strumming the chords to Lissa's epic *cris de couer* such as *Off the Rails* and *Can't Stay on the Right Track*; instead, I found myself in a scratchy suit going to meetings to practise the unholy arts of blue sky thinking and thought showering. My course had been full of Neanderthals with greasy thumbs; my office was full of Cro-Magnon wankers with manicured fingernails. And I became one of them for far too long as we worked on our billionaire oligarch chairman's pet project of a transatlantic tramway linking Britain and New York without the need for jet engines or deep sea tunnels. What's that story about how water swirls one way in the Northern hemisphere, another way in the South, but goes straight down the plughole at the Equator? Think finances and hold onto that final image.

Lissa called me a corporation monkey and much worse. I had a vague impression, though no actual evidence, that she was occasionally seeing erstwhile pianist Terry on a fairly intimate basis. He'd graduated from petty crime to a more politicised pattern of disorderly behaviour. I saw him in background shots on *Stop the Cuts* and *Save our NHS* marches. To my old band-mates, I was a class traitor. So be it. The years passed.

Please be aware of the following Station Announcements:

> *The 14.18 will be travelling from Teenage Depression Terminus onto Young Adult Junction; stopping at Skint Alley, Existential Despair and Hopeless Corner. A limited buffet service is in operation on this route.*

> *The 18.21 University Transfer has been delayed. We now expect this Inter-City shuttle to run from 19 years to 22 years.*

> *The Alissa Jones Special has been cancelled. All passengers intending to use this service are advised to seek a refund.*

Most people assume that level crossings are a rural phenomenon. Wrong. Look around the outskirts of major cities and you'll find plenty of them. Unmanned and computer controlled these days, with their poles, barriers and signs patterned in the usual red and white repetition indicating danger. Warning lights will start to flash. This is the time to stop. Don't risk jumping across. Even most of the locals – on foot or in cars – will stay cautious. Death traps or romantic throwbacks to a pre-Beeching dream of the golden age of steam? Make your own choice.

Just seeing the rails embedded in the tarmac instead of resting on a bed of gravel gave me a thrill.

The level crossing closest to us had only half barriers. Sometimes it kept you waiting there for nearly a quarter of an hour. Just as you thought to yourself – heck, it's only ten yards or so over the tracks, finally some blue and yellow liveried diesel tramp would come chugging along from right to left with a waft of grime and fumes. Then at last the all clear could sound and the safe mundanity of British life could resume.

One time Lissa and I accepted a wager from Dave that we couldn't keep our lips locked throughout the whole sequence at Inn Road level crossing. We began snogging as soon as the stop lights started to pulse. My hands wanted to explore further than denim jacketed shoulders but by now we had an appreciative audience of stalled motorists catcalling and tooting horns. That was one long ten minutes. Lissa moaned afterwards that my stubble had irritated her chin but as the express sped off towards East Anglia and the wooden gates began to rise, I was already stretching out my left hand for Dave's grubby fiver. A sustained hoot from a van driver served as the full stop on our breathless endeavours.

Heads were about to roll at Techno Solutions. Marketing were shitting themselves. We had lost out big time in the rail franchise bidding wars against Richard Branson's Virgin, First Capital Connect and even some bunch enigmatically styling themselves as *One*. Legal were calling 'Foul' and mounting an appeal but the writing was on the wall for the whole company. In truth, I was bored. I had a mortgage and an overdraft but I liked to tell myself that any sort of redundancy deal would be welcome. I had done more pitches in the past decade than a journeyman footballer. My Italian suit and striped shirt had probably absorbed enough business verbiage that they could have run the show without me. Yet still we had only a toehold in about one percent of the country's railway stock and just two or three loss-making, no-mark routes to our name. The great trans-marine monorails seemed a mere sci-fi pipedream.

What made my blood run truly cold was my line manager's quiet talk at the washbasin in the men's urinal.

"It's a vanity project, Tom," he stated. "A Russian oil billionaire laundering his money by playing big boy train sets. Word is that he's going to wind this up and pump his money into a Premier League club. Like the sheikhs or Abramovich."

"Perhaps I should get my old band back together and fill in those audition forms for *The X Factor*."

"As good a bet as any. My advice is: get off at this point before the whole business gets derailed."

This trains songs CD project might run and run. Every time I thought I'd made the definitive list, something else would turn up knocking against the buffers in my memory.

Casey Jones, steaming and a-rolling. He certainly is. How about that old spiritual that Woody Guthrie did – *This Train is Bound for Glory?* Add in Gordon Lightfoot's epic *Canadian Railroad Trilogy*; don't forget Glenn Miller's camp and somewhat questionable *Chattanooga Choo-Choo*. As for Johnny Cash, he had probably left a whole album of them tucked away in the vaults. His first hit *Hey Porter*, along with *Orange Blossom Special* and *Wreck of the Old 97* were all contenders but the one for me was *Folsom Prison Blues*. You know, that classic Cash song with the lyric about having shot a man in Reno purely for the sensation of watching him die. Genius. At the very end, the narrator is bemoaning his fate and listening from his jail cell to the distant whistle of the engine. He imagines the rich – more pertinently, *free* – passengers drinking coffee and smoking cigars. The passing train represents the liberty that he has sacrificed. Terrific stuff.

I haven't mentioned the old rockabilly classic *Mystery Train*. It features on Elvis Presley's era-changing *Sun Sessions*. I used to play it on guitar – in fact, it was our sound check song. I haven't listened to it in years, though, because of Lissa. We'd just finished one of her plaintive ballads to scattered applause at *The Dog and Shunt* when I slipped into the riff. Our drummer at the time – Kev? Kyle? – picked up the rhythm and Terry glided in Ray Manzarek style by wibbling out a bass line on his electric keyboard. I took the vocal on the first verse. By the end of it, Lissa had stormed off, leaving her Fender to create a low hum of feedback. We finished our truncated set ten minutes later. Terry cleared up the gear and I went in search of my wayward muse. I found her by Inn Road level crossing, leaning on the white painted wooden half-barrier cursing and swearing to the empty railroad track. In a nutshell, she had the hump because we'd slipped in a cover version instead of staying truly original.

We argued on and off for three days. We were teenagers. Idealistic.

I quit the band before the next no hope gig. Lissa sent her dad round to return a few books, CDs and, embarrassingly, pairs of underpants that had made a temporary home at her place.

We were nineteen. Stupid. Unworldy.

J. K. Rowling knew what she was doing when she invented the Hogwarts Express. Hook the kids with boarding school wizards but get the grown-ups and the grandparents all nostalgic for the age of steam. The many heritage lines around the country are still reaping the benefits.

The future of trains, though, is high-speed links. Services running on a wider, more appropriate gauge than the one that 'Rocket' man Stephenson bequeathed us. Eurostar. Pendolino. Aerodynamic bullets encouraging us that in the time your video caller looks away from their screen in order to froth up a cappuccino, you could actually have arrived in the flesh rather than simply the pixel.

Techno Solutions shouldn't have failed so dismally. I should still be looking at thirty or forty K a year instead of Jobseeker's Allowance.

Alissa Jones and the Whitchurch Junction shouldn't have failed so dismally. I should have practised harder. I should have got a manger or producer in to take Lissa's nuggets of song craft and polish them into gleaming jewels. We should have stuck with Dave on drums and Terry should have limited his lager and coke intake.

A friend of a friend was putting on a local music festival. Could I get the old band back together for a show or two?

One of the gigs was at the recently refurbished *Dog and Shunt*. I should have known better. But it was an excuse to reconnect with Lissa, Terry and, hopefully, Dave. My unemployed ego wasn't going to turn this opportunity down.

Of course, the best level crossings are Stateside. You see them in movies with their weird signals pointing to two, four, eight and ten o'clock. American trains can be half a mile long and take thirty minutes to brake safely. Sometimes a programme like *Road Wars* will show one of these sinuous beats hitting a stalled vehicle on the tracks. There is always the possibility of a derailment but most times it's a case of jump out of the Chevy, stand clear and watch the mayhem as your car is smashed back into its pre-industrial state. Watch that mother smack you back into the mother lode, brother!

She'd been through a couple of difficult relationships post-us. Maybe I'd now retrospectively be seen in a better light. She'd moved into her own flat for a while but was back at her mother's temporarily. Her father had 'gone to Watford' or gone to hell permanently, she was a little vague on the details. They were euphemisms. Synonyms.

We sat on her old bed as she strummed her way through our underdeveloped back catalogue. Her voice was stronger, slightly deeper during the slower sections, although there weren't that many of those. She was wearing torn jeans, a scruffy black halter top and a Marks & Spencer bra that didn't flatter her bust line. I couldn't help looking, though. Her right arm was decorated with a couple of really rubbish tattoos. I mean, abysmal. Unintelligible, amateurish shit that you might get done in a hurry to cover up track marks. I didn't enquire.

Above the scratchy songs, I was listening out for the usual percussive interruption of passing trains. Half an hour passed and I heard none. Was there a rail strike? Were they subject to that curse of modern transportation – the replacement bus service?

"Mother had triple glazing installed," Lissa muttered as she placed a capo at the third fret. "Can get a good night's sleep for the first time ever." She laughed, wiped a droplet of Red Bull away from her lips. "Alone, in case you were wondering, Tom. Staying that way, too."

It was the morning of our comeback gig. I should have been checking through the changes for our nostalgic set list. Instead I was noodling on the internet. Amongst the usual slew of distant wars, footballers shagging wannabe Page 3 girls, and ministerial obfuscation something truly troubling caught my attention. MSN was running a trailer for the big new Hollywood blockbuster *Motion City* and a lot of the iconography seemed chillingly familiar. Directed by the guy who did *Giganticus* and that movie about blue people on a green world, this was near-future Earth with trains crossing the surface of the Atlantic and linking the new marine metropolises standing proud of the ocean. There even appeared to be something of a Romeo and Juliet type story involving Matt Damon and Keira Knightley. Someone once told me that there's no copyright on ideas. Someone else once told me how much lawyers charge per hour. They'd stolen my story wholesale and I just had to swallow it. At least, the tale had done me all right for a while. I hoped this movie flopped like a dead whale's dick.

I was somewhat preoccupied as we sound checked. Likewise Lissa, who was constantly hunched over her Smartphone, scrolling through Facebook or some such shit. At least Terry was holding it together; now charged with playing keyboards, bass pedals and drum pattern sequencer in our cobbled-together trio. Without intending to, we had developed something of a 1980s sheen that made us sound curiously on trend.

The lunchtime crowd consisted mostly of old school friends and their new partners and sprogs. At times I felt like I was seventeen again. We played two short sets with a break in between. I'm not sure exactly where the arguments began because, although I can highlight a particular incident, maybe all we were doing was picking at old scars. An undercurrent of anger and discord ran through both performances. I freely admit that I suggested early doors that we should slip in a few cover versions to keep the punters happy. Lissa went off on one.

"I want to play the whole demo tape that we sent to John Peel before he died."

"He never got back to us. Nor did Jo Whiley or Mark Radcliffe, Liss."

"Those are the songs that matter."

"Sure, I understand that they mean a lot to you. To all of us. But we could fit them around something a little more familiar to the audience."

She threw her guitar down, stood on tiptoe to yell right in my face, "Fuck the audience! What do they know about anything? Fucking morons."

"Not so loud, Liss," I said, touching her pristine arm as gently as I could.

She turned to face Terry. "You agree, don't you, Tel?"

He shrugged beneath his habitual ragged knitwear. "You two should sort this out by yourselves," he muttered. "I can program anything you want in terms of rhythm tracks –"

"Oh, you're as useless as each other! Men, why do I bother with them?"

For a time I thought she'd blow out the whole show. Luckily, she only went as far as the pub toilets. She emerged five minutes before show time, necked a bottle of Becks, said nothing to either of us, just plugged in and began strumming.

You hear a lot of platitudes on TV talent shows about 'owning the stage', 'smashing it', 'singing like your life depended on it', fill in the rest of the clichés yourself. Lissa sang and played like she wanted to leave an indelible mark on all of us. It was all I could do to keep time and watch her shine. Like the proverbial shooting star – perfect and lambent in the sky for brief moments then extinguished and crashed.

I tried to talk to her after the encore but she was wrapped up in her phone again, whispering to someone in that private, involved way that lovers do, as if there was a boyfriend on the other end who'd let her down by not turning up. My heart tore with the memory that Lissa and I had once been like that. However, her aura told me to stay distant. Today was not the time to reconnect and reignite.

She swigged some more lager, tucked her purse into the waistband of her skinny jeans and sauntered out of the pub.

As a boy, I always loved level crossings. I was never scared on them. I used to look both ways – up the line and down the line, you might say. I never saw anything coming. You never do.

*

The emergency services recovered her phone. The last call was to an automated train timetable service.

The song I keep playing is not one by Alissa and the Junction; that would be too painful. No, I finished my CD compilation and gave it its crowning glory, which was Neil Young's *Southern Pacific*. It's a story of a guy – Mr Jones, wouldn't you know? – forced to retire from his job driving the diesel trains when his eyesight starts to fail him. His work meant everything to him and his life is effectively over. He's living on his memories.

It's a song about trains. But mostly it's a song about loss. What else is there to write about?

The Wandering Scent

Aliya Whiteley

She drives the train around the park, sitting behind the engine on a seat that is far too small, booted feet dangling from the cabin, nearly touching the track. Her waistcoat is the green of peppermint, and she smells of it, too; she has always considered it the duty of a miniature train driver to make the customer think of sweets, sunshine, all kinds of escape. And that is why she named the engine Cappie, short for Escape, even though the official name painted on the side, the name by which it is known up and down the county, is *Spirit of Littletown*.

She is Tina T Driver, working on her thirty-fifth year in the village, with retirement drawing ever closer, glimmering like the last section of track at sunset on a long bank holiday Monday.

Today is only an April Thursday, and Cappie has a long weekend ahead of him, but right now he must take the last load of children for the day through the thatched cottages and Ironcast figures, past the working waterwheel and windmill, around the carousel, slowing down for the replica of King Ludwig's castle, speeding up for the downhill stretch into the valleys and farmlands with mooing and baahing on the loudspeakers to boot. And then Tina begins to slow Cappie down in earnest, judging the speed for the return to Littletown station where the children will be reunited with parents who hold their mobile phones outstretched for final photographs before bedtime.

Cappie breathes out, exhales slow steam, warm into Tina's face and legs. She is already thinking of the spit and polish she must apply once he is returned to his snug shed, but first they must pass through the Mystic Forest - the only part of the journey that regularly punctures her perfect peppermint armour. Not in the morning, and not early afternoon, when the sun casts short shadows through the overarching leaves and makes the plastic jewels set into the trunks gleam with the fervour of imagined riches, but only in the last hours of the day. Then the Mystic Forest reminds her of something else, something she would rather forget.

It starts with the tunnel. The valley farmland leads into a stone archway, and then there is darkness, just for a moment, long enough for the smaller children to whine out nervous breaths that Tina feels rather than hears, and then there is the carpet of plastic grass below the real ash trees with the jewelled trunks, like eyes, deep-set, dull, now that the sun is on the wane. And the orange-red set to the sky, like a memory of blood, is that what it is? At this point, passing the plastic mushroom ring and the fairies on strings, Tina always closes her eyes, and thinks of nothing but the small, sharp pain of memory in the centre of her, willing it gone, willing it dead. It lasts only for the length of the forest, and then the last tree is left behind and the station is ahead, with the parents and their flashes and their smiles. Welcome back to the real world of Littletown.

The children disembark and Tina waves and smiles them goodbye, until the station is empty and the bunting over the ticket stile hangs still. She switches the points on the line and climbs up to Cappie's tiny seat, squeezing her bottom into the leather with a familiar squeak. She releases the brake and guides him to the shed, quarter-speed, where the chamois and the soap are waiting for him, along with the bucket and the sponge and a long, cosy night tucked up like an obedient dog after a muddy walk. She strokes his engine as she washes, and plucks the mess of the children from the carriages: torn pink and blue ticket stubs, lolly sticks, forgotten purchases from the gift shop and an abandoned cuddly toy with a mournful expression and a drooping beanbag body. She walks this little bundle to the front gate, hoping it won't end up abandoned in the cardboard box under the ticket office, and there finds Mr Mannfred, staring into middle-distance through the iron railings, watching the last of the cars reverse and drive away.

"A little stowaway," says Tina. Mr Mannfred turns, and gives her an empty, forlorn look, then rearranges his face into pleasantness.

"Oh dear," he says, and takes the soft little body from her hands. "There'll be one sad little girl or boy being tucked up in bed tonight. How's Cappie? Running like clockwork?"

"Running like a steam machine," says Tina, as she always does to Mr Mannfred's enquiries. The world skims along on the tracks of such automatic responses; he asks, she replies, he supplies the coal, she feeds it to Cappie, and Cappie follows the route that he has been given. Why is it, then, that this time around Mr Mannfred must change the direction?

"Such a reliable one, but they all have their time, don't they?" he says, and then hums, his eyes to the sky, as if he has said too much and is hoping she hasn't noticed.

"Everything has a time," she agrees. "Cappie reminds people of a golden age."

"Do you know, I really think there never was such a thing," he muses, "not in the way people think, and we shouldn't let such ideas cloud our judgement, should we?" He raises his thumbs and eyebrows at her. How very ridiculous he is, with his projections and expectations. He's been running Littletown for four years now, and the family business has become a cash cow, milked and timed and timed and milked with no thought of enjoying the green of the grass that surrounds them.

"I was alive back in the Golden Age," she tells him, with the unexpected appearance of bravery in her repertoire, "and our judgement was all the better for it, I think."

He nods twice. "Well, how long have you got to go?"

"Three weeks."

"You must be counting the days. Retirement is the second golden age, right? Right? I'll never be able to replace you, you know." He gives her a smile, and with a flash of foresight she realises that he has not attempted to replace her. Cappie will be driverless once she has gone. He will be left in the shed, or maybe sold, scrapped, substituted for some monorail or cable car. Something electronic, that beeps and plays tunes and doesn't blurt out smoke or whistle at a volume that attracts complaints every year from the sensitively stupid. This is progress; this is the age where gold is only worth what you can get for it when you melt it down.

In this moment Rita T Driver decides to liberate Cappie from his future. She has no idea how, but she is certain she will take the miniature train with her when she goes. That gives her three weeks to plan.

Three weeks is not long. It's the kind of length of time that disappears in a moment of starshine.

Rita finds herself in the last hour of her last day. She turns around; who stole her time? Where did it go? But behind her there are only small children, waving Littletown flags, jumping up and down on Cappie's bottom-shined seats. There has been no brainwave, no great plan. And Cappie approaches the dark tunnel that leads out into the Mystic Forest, trusting her, taking her commands. She has let him down. She has let her whole life down, and the sunset is upon them; as they emerge from the tunnel there will be the eyes of the trees, staring, making her think of it, leading her towards the worst thought, the one that hurts inside.

She stops the train.

That moment of black, where the children draw their breaths, stretches onwards as Cappie pulls up, and snaps into whimpers and cries, a soft cacophony of fear. Rita tries to ignore it, but there is no way to think of anything but straight lines – the track, the past, the future, all so very ruler-drawn in regularity. How can she become a heroine, when her whole life has been a tightrope of schedule and steadiness? Her aging arms and legs, her peppermint waistcoat, her well-polished cowboy boots, all shout out against it.

But she must.

The children cry on. Minutes, and minutes, and the track is so dark. Then, the voice. Mr Mannfred, of course; an outline at the mouth of the tunnel, up ahead, from the mystic garden, asking her if everything is all right, if Cappie has broken down.

"Not Cappie," she shouts. "Me."

"What's that?"

She considers expanding her statement to: *I'm having a thing. A breakdown. I'm a danger to myself and others. Don't blame Cappie. It's not his fault. I'm holding the children hostage. I want you to relay the track. To my house. Make it run to my house and let me keep Cappie, and you can have the kids back.*

"Rita, come on now," says Mr Mannfred. "Just bring Cappie out and stop mucking about, please."

No, he's right. That won't work. Stupid idea, she castigates herself.

"He's stopped working, Mr Mannfred," she calls, hating herself. "He's just stopped and he won't go any more."

"Typical. I'll get some staff to come and lead the kids out."

How could this be typical, she wonders, when it has never happened before, not in thirty-five years? It was as if it was always waiting to happen, always a certainty, as if everyone else had been given binoculars to see the way the tracks were heading.

"Sorry," whispers Rita, and puts her hands on Cappie's barrelled engine. Instead of feeling the warmth of him, the reassurance of his steam and power, she feels only the shock of ungiving metal, and it comes to her that Cappie is not alive, and does not care what happens next.

It's all her. She has made Cappie a person, a standard, a personal motto, and all she has for her investment is a miniature train. A very nice example of a miniature train, but no more than that. Her emotions belong only to her, and she can carry them with her, wherever she chooses to go.

She gets down from the train, says to the children, "There now. You'll be back home soon," and walks out of the tunnel, into the last light of the day, where the Mystic Forest glows. She is alone, and that is good; solitary, standing on the tracks, aware of the memory she has tried so hard to keep at a distance. It comes towards her, out from the trees, through the fairy ring, over the plastic mushrooms, and wraps itself around her. It is here. The past was here, all the time, in this very forest, and it is not golden at all. It is green, the colour of peppermint, and the smell of it is not sweet and comforting, not any more.

She steps from the track, walks away. Goodbye Cappie. She follows the scent of her grandfather, who built toy trains in his shed and sucked endless peppermints, through the garden, down to the orchard that looked like a forest to her, until she comes across a wooden hut with the rough door ajar, and inside, inside, there is Cappie, on the floor, clutched between old hands that have folded in on themselves like petals closing at the end of day.

A golden age, thinks Rita.

She crouches next to the body of her grandfather and prizes Cappie from his grasp. The tiny train is perfect, the barrel of the engine warm and welcoming. This time around, Cappie is alive and real and he belongs to her. This is a golden age for the two of them.

Once before, she sat on this floor, with only death for company, and waited for someone to find her. She was certain that they would know what to do, what to say, what track to follow to make her forget.

This time, Tina gets up, and leaves the shed. She does not return to the track. She weaves her way between the trees, and leads Cappie in a new direction.

Platform Alteration: Der Breitspurbahn

You have to imagine a locomotive that is longer than a normal entire commuter train. Over 300 feet. With 72 wheels. And capable of travelling at 155mph. And a carriage that is like a small row of terrace houses granted the gift of movement – 138 feet long. Or rather a whole string of them of course – for that is what a train is. That was the Breitspurbahn. Or rather wasn't. And if it had been dreamed up by anyone other than Adolf Hitler and his crowd, it would probably be much better known.

It has to be said, the top fruitcake and other high-up fruitcakes of the 3rd Reich came up with some wondrously bizarre plans as they put together their fantasy land of Grossdeutschland – the future 'unified' Europe ruled over by Welthauptstadt Germania ("World Capital Germania" – though we still call it Berlin). This was a place of buildings so grand that it is debatable whether they would ever have stood in the real world – and a transport system equally ambitious. The autobahn, the first ever motorway, was largely down to Hitler *et al* – and you can see the legacy of that every time you take a drive on the motorway today. But what about rail? What trains would serve this larger-than-life world? The answer is kind of obvious really – larger than life ones. Hitler's pet railway that never was. Maybe shouldn't have been. Maybe couldn't have been. Maybe *should* have been. Running on tracks twice as wide as ours, these vast cities on wheels would thunder through the countryside, linking a unified Europe from Paris to Rostov, Hamburg to Istanbul. And who knows whether such a thing would ever have been practical or even possible. It was never tested – never progressed beyond the planning stage. The war was lost and, unlike the Autobahn, the Breitspurbahn died with it, along with Grossdeutschland, World Capital Germania and all the other crazy plans.

Looking round the world today though, there is a strange irony to be observed – because what do we see? Marvellous high-speed trains do indeed streak through a unified Europe without border controls (Schengen, not Welthauptstadt). It's not the Breitspurbahn, but the TGV, the ICE etc. that race from Stockholm to Malaga and from Napoli to Calais (not London since the UK seems incapable of letting anything through its borders without waving sticks at it). A very different kind of fantasy with a strangely similar result. And long may they remain and grow.

DR

To the Anhalt Station

John Howard

Berlin in November can be depressing. It is often damp and cold. In the evening twilight, mists gather in the streets as if bonfires had been lit nearby. I worked in a renovated and refurbished office block in a street running southward from Unter den Linden. At dusk, in these older parts of the city, it seemed to me that the most time-worn of the buildings that had survived war and redevelopment drew themselves in like old people contracting their limbs and huddling deeper into their overcoats. Facades faded into the fog and roof lines merged with the low brown clouds. Streetlamps and windows shone out, holding their own but with little effect, and pavements seemed to grow more uneven and risky to walk on. As the darkness draws on, sounds became muted, as if the city centre were falling into its nightly dream and preparing itself to send away anyone who shouldn't be there.

I had lived in Berlin for just over a year. Despite having experienced a full cycle of the city, I never felt quite sure whether or not I was accepted. On late afternoons in autumn, as the darkness gathered, the deep mournful reverberation of the bells of the Protestant cathedral on the other side of the Spreekanal being rung for the evening service always seemed to perfectly fit my mood.

And yet after work I often liked to take my time walking to the S-Bahn station at Potsdamer Platz to catch a train home. I frequently varied the route I took to get there. The streets between Unter den Linden and Leipziger Strasse are almost entirely a network of squares and rectangles. After leaving the brightly lit office I sometimes made my way to Potsdamer Platz by a zigzag progression, crossing the road at each corner before walking along the street again, changing direction briefly, and then again, but always in the end heading west.

One murky Friday evening when work had ended for the week, a small group of us went to a new bar just off Stresemannstrasse, across the road from the ruin next to Askanischer Platz. That ruin – a stark pile of brickwork, clearly the jagged remnant of a very large building – had intrigued me when I first came across it not long after having made the move to Berlin. The yawning arches and broken walls seemed so out of place until I remembered that only a short time earlier I'd gazed at the preserved ruin of the Kaiser Wilhelm Memorial Church, its remaining tower a broken fang shooting up above the packed pavements and traffic of the Kurfürstendamm. So I'd stopped at the second ruin of the day and read the small information display, which informed me that it was all that survived, above the ground, of the Anhalter Bahnhof, once one of Berlin's main railway termini as well as one of the largest stations in Europe. It was an architectural and engineering marvel, but had been badly damaged during the Second World War and eventually demolished, except for a tiny fragment of the entrance façade. Beneath Askanischer Platz the Anhalter Bahnhof S-Bahn station still remained; and now I travelled through it every day on my way to and from work.

I don't know why it is, but in every office where I've ever worked, whether in Berlin or anywhere else, there has been a colleague who is fascinated by railways, locomotives, trains, and all the paraphernalia, and who will take the least opportunity to talk at length about them. Over the years I have noticed this. The romantic old days of steam are an obsession with these people. To me, a train is something to get on at the beginning of a journey, and off again at the end, with the least amount of time as possible having been spent in between.

Our railway enthusiast, Rainer, was in the group that went to the bar. As we entered it, going from cold dimness to warm dimness, I heard him gasp. As soon as the mist cleared from my glasses, I saw why. Perhaps

I should have been ready: the name of the bar should have told me all I needed to know. The Anhalter Barhof was railway themed, and seemed to have made a concerted attempt to capture something of the ambience of the late nineteenth century – of the lost Anhalter Bahnhof. The interior walls had been faced with genuine brickwork, rendered dull and dirty (so I assumed) in order to enhance the atmosphere. What light there was came from fittings resembling oil lamps and flickering gas lights. There were old photographs, timetables, and reproduction posters, all framed and covering up every last square metre of the lower parts of the walls. Rainer rushed over to a set of photographs and started to examine them closely.

In the noisy gloom someone gently nudged my shoulder. "Let's get some drinks and leave him to it, Hannes," Karolina said. "He can look at that sort of thing for hours. I should know." She smiled. "I will get my chance for his attention later!" Karolina was Rainer's girlfriend. I led the way to the bar and ordered beers for us both.

Eventually Rainer joined Karolina and I and the rest of the group at our crowded table. "Anhalter Barhof," he said, smiling. "Ha, I suppose that's funny, isn't it?" He looked around. "They have made a good job of this place, though. The fixtures are quite accurate. And it's certainly very atmospheric."

After a couple more drinks Rainer and Karolina left to go home. The rest of us soon went on our ways. Outside, a sharp breeze had sprung up, clearing the mist. A faint frost was forming on the pavement. Cars swished past on the wide Stresemannstrasse. Overhead, the sky had cleared: I could make out one or two of the brightest stars. There was an almost full moon. It was still cold, but refreshing rather than numbing. I felt wide awake. My breath flowered briefly into clouds and dispersed. We wished each other a good weekend and shook hands all round. I looked at my watch and decided to walk a large stretch of the way home, possibly stopping for another drink along the route and catching the train at Schöneberg. On the other side of the river of traffic, the ruin of the Anhalter Bahnhof stood like part of a set of broken and holed dentures.

I was about to cross the road when I sensed someone approaching on the pavement from behind me. My shoulders tensed, and I began to turn away, getting ready to stride out into the street. Then I thought that perhaps one of my colleagues had forgotten to ask me something and had returned, although I was pretty sure they must have all been gone for several minutes by then.

"Excuse me, please."

I turned back to find myself looking at a man of about my own age and height. His hair was blond, neatly trimmed and parted. He was dressed very much as I was except that over his suit his coat was unbuttoned to the night air. The collar of his shirt was open and his tie was loose. I remembered what time it was, and without thinking I performed the ritual that I hadn't yet done and undid the top button of my own shirt and loosened my tie. After all, this was fully my own time now.

"I saw you in that bar just now, and I thought —"

I began to turn away again. If it were money he was going to ask for I wasn't going to allow him the chance. I wasn't going to give a complete stranger anything to buy himself more drinks.

He grasped my arm. "No, please, it's not what you think."

The expression on the man's face let me rule out the possibility that he might have been about to proposition me. And I couldn't smell alcohol or anything else on his breath. I had probably had more to drink than he had. The man didn't seem to be drugged-up either. As I looked at him in the harsh street lighting he just looked rather — lost. He made me think of a child who has arrived in the big city and lost his way.

"OK."

"Listen," he said. His eyes were rimmed by dark patches and the skin of his face was pale in the harsh artificial light. "I asked the way to the Anhalter Bahnhof and everyone told me to go to that bar. It's not the right place." It was as if he were making an appeal. "I mean, it's not the railway station, is it? There are photographs, but I don't want photos. It was all right when I got off the train underground. Everywhere had all been cleaned up and the train was new as well. But when I came up into the street there was nothing… How can I catch my train when the station has gone? Can you answer me that?"

I shook my head. "I'm very sorry, but I don't know. I'm new here myself." That didn't seem too far from the truth.

He gave no sign of having heard me. "It was the same with the Potsdamer Bahnhof. Under the ground at Potsdamer Platz it was all shining and clean and new. Above ground – the station had gone. Perhaps I must try for one of the others. Yes, that's it. There's the Anhalter, Potsdamer, Lehrter, Stettiner, Görlitzer." Suddenly his voice changed, and became forceful and decisive. "Very well, Lehrter Bahnhof it is." He smiled and shook his head slowly. "But thank you."

Then he was gone.

The following Monday morning, as soon as I had the opportunity, I went over to Rainer's desk. "Tell me about the old Berlin railway stations," I said.

Rainer showed no surprise at what I'd asked. Then he and Karolina exchanged glances. "I told you, Rainer," she said. "I thought it must've been him, Friday night, didn't I?"

"But I wasn't in the mood," Rainer said. Then he looked at me. "Lutz. You met Lutz, didn't you?"

I shrugged my shoulders and described the man who had spoken to me in Stresemannstrasse. Rainer nodded. I listed the names that Lutz had reeled off as we stood in the street. Rainer seemed to be ticking the names on a mental list.

"So you know this man?" I said.

"Yes, but only a little. Like me, he's a railway enthusiast. He visits some of the web forums and discussion areas that there are for people who share our interests. And he attends the same railway fairs as I do and writes little articles for the railway-lovers' magazines. I've heard it said that he's writing something about the old railway stations of Berlin, the ones that have gone. He has, well, something of a reputation, if you see what I mean."

I shook my head.

"Well, he can be rather intense, but he's harmless. That's the consensus. Lutz is serious about the big old railway stations. I expect that what he doesn't know about them can't be worth knowing, but he takes it all so seriously – so personally. That's the only way I can describe it. I've overheard him talking to people. It's as if it's his whole life, and it depends on those stations."

We had to get back to work, but arranged to talk further over coffee at lunch time.

*

I bought Rainer a coffee and sat down opposite him.

"Like most big and important cities, Berlin had several large passenger railway stations," Rainer said. "They were built as the Berlin termini for the different lines serving different parts of Prussia and then the old Empire and beyond. They were huge and magnificent buildings, meant to show the quality and power of German engineering and the great future of the railways. Those stations were glorious palaces of steam. Take the Anhalter Bahnhof. It was gigantic! Forty thousand people could have fitted in under the glass roof, which was over thirty metres high!"

"But it got bombed during the war," I said.

"Right. The Anhalter Bahnhof was badly damaged, but most of the walls were still standing. No amount of bombing and shelling could have smashed those walls down, they were too well built. The station could've been rebuilt, a new roof provided. It could've been used for something. I was looking at the old photos of the Anhalter Bahnhof in the bar. The ones showing it being blown up in the 1950s. Tragic. A complete waste! There's just that little bit of the entrance façade left now."

"So why wasn't the Anhalter Bahnhof rebuilt and used again? People still travelled by train."

Rainer sipped his coffee. "Same reason all the other main stations were eventually pulled down. When Germany was divided between the Soviets and the Allies, Berlin was marooned in the middle of the Soviet Zone. To get out of Berlin and to the Allied Zones or the Federal Republic as they became, one had to travel along certain routes through the Soviet Zone, the Democratic Republic when it was formed. Four out of the five great old termini were in what in effect became an island: West Berlin. The railway lines couldn't go anywhere without going through the East. So the railways stopped running those routes and the station buildings were closed. They were all demolished. Decades of Berlin's history all just – blown away. Boom!"

*

That evening I took a long detour on the way home and walked to Unter den Linden. There were several tourist souvenir shops there. Now that I tried to regard myself as a Berliner I naturally avoided them, but I remembered one of them stocked a lot of books on Berlin history, facsimile editions of old street maps, and collections of old photographs.

It was another damp and misty evening. Throughout the afternoon the mist pressing in against the windows of the office had grown darker. Once out in the street I felt cold and disheartened. There were still a few weeks to go to the winter solstice, and the return of daylight after that seemed a very distant prospect, all but impossible to imagine. Berlin was settling into its winter; the lights and laughter of all the various Christmas markets that would soon be springing up, and the Glühwein, would only make it worse. Streetlights were haloed in yellow mist, matching the grimy patched-up walls of the buildings lining the street. As I walked vaguely in the direction of the Roman Catholic cathedral figures loomed out of the darkness, coming into sight and passing without touching or acknowledgement. Their voices lingered as the last twilight drained away. No-one could now hurry through the dusk to gain the smoky warmth and tumult of one of the railway cathedrals – these days only the tiled burrows of the underground stations led anywhere. As I skirted the Hausvogteiplatz shutters came down with a crash. I realised I was alone in the street.

On the train I turned the pages of one of the books I'd bought: a collection of 'then and now' photographs. On one side of the page the 'then' photos showed parts of the city as it had been during the first half of the twentieth century: views along streets, landmark buildings and monuments, that sort of thing. Facing them were photos of the same places taken in the present from as close as possible to the original viewpoints. In some cases, where tremendous changes had occurred, that had clearly been very difficult. So many entire streets had vanished, not just because of bombing but due to the radical reconstruction that had sometimes taken place later, whether or not as a result. Often it was a small and seemingly insignificant part of the cityscape that had endured to provide the clue: a drop in the smooth line of the kerb, a lamp post, a drain cover.

Because they had been close to where the Berlin Wall ended up being built, the sites of some of the demolished stations had remained empty and overgrown for years. Others were turned into parks or were eventually built over, wholly or in part. According to the book it had been possible, into the 1990s, to find rusting nuts and bolts from the vanished railway tracks that had led to where the Anhalter Bahnhof had stood. Bricks from the destroyed station had still littered parts of the waste area where the platforms and sidings had been and had been sought-after by souvenir hunters who spent their spare time grubbing around in the earth beneath the grass and bushes that had grown over the place where millions of people had travelled. And all this so recently in what I now regarded as my city.

On Saturday I decided to take a walk around the Anhalter Bahnhof site. Emerging from the underground station there during daylight for once was a strange experience. It was cold and overcast. The sky pressed down: the giant red and white spike forming the top section of the Television Tower would be hidden by swirls of grey cloud. By day the old station's ruined façade was no more than that, but the circular windows were gaping and vacant eyes. I strolled into the portico through the central arch of the three. Opposite, in front of me, there were three more large doorways, yawning like the windows. Stepping through one of them led me back out into the open air; back out into the space of the city again.

I knew what to expect. Tennis courts had been set up where the station concourse had been. Further on, the flowing curves and sharp edges of the tent-like Tempodrom filled the rest of the space that had once been enclosed by the massive brickwork of the station's walls and the iron web of its roof. I walked around the outside of the tennis courts and up the steps to the entrance of the Tempodrom, where I sat down and surveyed the site. It looked as if the whole area had long since been cleaned up, and there would be no chance to pick up any relics of the past. As the weak November sun gradually forced itself through the overcast sky, I imagined where I was sitting being suspended in the air within the vast volume of the station, with the swarming passengers and the slow movements of the trains and serried lines of carriages beneath me, the whistles of the engines and the combined mutterings of the crowds and the announcements echoing amid clouds of smoke and steam.

I walked back towards the ruined entrance. Absorbed in thought, I almost collided with someone. It just had to be Lutz. He looked much the same as when I'd met him before: utterly ordinary, the sort of person whom I would've expected to stop and simply ask for directions rather than to reel off a list of railway station buildings that had all vanished decades ago.

"Anhalter Bahnhof, this is Anhalter Bahnhof," he said, a look of wonder on his freshly-shaved face. Without thinking I touched my Saturday stubble. "High in the air the smoke rises all around you, the walls hold you in. The sun can get in through windows and roof but you can't get out. I know that. I know what you're thinking. This is Anhalter Bahnhof, the terminus."

"What are you on about?"

"I know what you're thinking, in the smoke and crowds of the wonderful stations. Yes, there are the Anhalter, Potsdamer, Lehrter, Stettiner, Görlitzer – we all terminate in the termini, don't we?" Lutz spoke hurriedly, but with no special emphases or anything to indicate that he wasn't speaking in anything but a normal way for him. Once again for a moment I considered his drunkenness or being on drugs, but I didn't think so, not really. "Here I am, here are all the people. I see the trains, hear them, I see and walk those tracks. They are gone but I still walk them, those shining metal paths." Lutz pointed towards the Tempodrom, and somehow I thought he meant through it.

Patiently I offered to buy him a cup of coffee and to show him one of the collections of old Berlin photos I'd bought, and which I had with me. We walked to the Potsdamer Platz and found a café. He took the book out of my hands eagerly and started turning the pages, looking at the pictures as if scanning them.

"Yes, these photos are correct," Lutz said.

I laughed. "But of course. Cameras cannot lie. They record what's in front of them."

Lutz looked up sharply. "But they need not show all," he said. "None of these photographs show everything. They don't show what's there now."

"Of course not," I said, trying not to show my exasperation. "These are old photographs, aren't they? The buildings have gone. The people have gone too."

He shook his head. "Oh no. That's just what I mean. They don't show what's there now. Where the stations were I see the trains, the tracks, the walls – the people too, all those myriads of people."

"You see them? You see, ah, ghosts, are they?"

"Yes." He pointed at one of the photos. It was one I'd actually seen before. I remembered it from one of my school history textbooks. The photo had been taken in early 1945. The wide façade of the Anhalter Bahnhof loomed in the background, partially obscured by clouds of smoke and dust, but nevertheless still standing firm and dominating the rubble-strewn street. The ornate statuary surmounting the smooth and elegant curve of the roof was hidden; it might already have been destroyed. In the aftermath of an air raid people scurried past clutching their suitcases, heading towards the station entrance, while others wandered around, apparently aimlessly, in the middle of the destruction and confusion.

Lutz lightly touched an old woman in the photo, who had stopped and was staring, resigned, into the camera. She wore a black coat and hat. "That lady never left her city," he whispered. "Grete Meyer survived in the cellar of her apartment block. She was a widow. Her sons never returned from the fighting in East Prussia, but she lived to see peace and the division of Berlin. Of course, she was raped several times by Soviet soldiers and her watch was stolen. I stop seeing her in the street outside after about 1949. I see the trainloads of refugees and deportees from those years as well. The lines of carriages arriving at the stations are endless, repeating themselves. Sometimes they depart again, sometimes they don't. The railway officials shout and the announcers call out the platforms and destinations. Police are standing there, watching. Steam rises into the great heights of the roof. It's all clamour, clamour…"

"And this happens all the time? These – these bad dreams? These endless nightmares?"

Lutz looked up at me and smiled. "Bismarck left Berlin after his dismissal and President Ebert departed in a coffin draped with the flag of the Republic that barely survived him. But no, it's not all bad. I see the sunlit stations full of holiday crowds, or the statesmen assembled to greet an important visitor. In my turn I like observing the poets and writers as they observe the scene, thinking about what to write. They think they are the only ones looking, but it isn't so."

"What did you mean about all terminating in the termini, or whatever it was you said?"

"Yes, there are the Anhalter, Potsdamer, Lehrter, Stettiner, Görlitzer – we all walk along the shining lines of the tracks, like they do and the trains running. In Berlin we were fenced in. When the railway lines were cut it was like chopping out the centre of a beautiful spider's web. Removing the railway lines didn't cover up the tracks. I know where they were – and still are. When the stations were destroyed the termini remained. I walk them, I see. This morning it is the Anhalter Bahnhof. Now I must go to the Potsdamer Bahnhof. It's simple enough. I walk down to the Landwehrkanal and along to where the bridge once was and make my way back to the terminus through the new park. It wasn't as grand as the Anhalter, though."

Lutz got up from his seat. I muttered something conventional about perhaps meeting him again on our wanderings around the city. I followed him out of the café. Suddenly he turned to me as I was buttoning my coat.

"I see you and others like you, wandering too, endlessly... No, it's not a nightmare for me, not what I do – I just have to be there. It seems to be my job, like an office I hold. That makes a difference. And I don't mind the endings and won't mind my ending. One day when I find my way to one of the stations I'll find it's the terminus, where the tracks end. Anhalter, Potsdamer, Lehrter, Stettiner, Görlitzer – it'll be one of those. I walk until I find it and get there."

He rushed away before I could think of anything else to say.

I didn't want to catch the train back home. I walked around the bustling Potsdamer Platz and into the Arkaden, wandering up and down the rows of brightly-lit shops. Then I went to the Tiergarten and strolled slowly along the paths and across its hidden meadows. I didn't notice my shoes getting wet and muddy; I just walked without any destination in mind and breathed in the smell of decaying leaves and mist rising from the damp grass. Towards sunset the sky cleared and it caught fire in the west. As the lemon afterglow flared up over the bare trees I left the park and made my way home on foot and by bus.

Spending the evening alone at home didn't appeal to me, but neither did phoning around friends and arranging to meet at a club or bar. I had dinner in the small restaurant on the ground floor of my apartment block. It was quiet and I had a table to myself, but there were other diners and I wasn't totally on my own. I sipped beer and in the dim light I studied the photos in one of the books I'd bought. There was still a lot of evidence of the past in Berlin if one knew where to find it: traces of violent and harrowing events recorded in the street and still visible to those with eyes to see. Or a book to follow. I wouldn't have believed it in the restored and united city. But when that city is Berlin…

Upstairs in my flat I opened another bottle of beer. Surrounded by images of the city from over the decades I got to thinking about how I'd ended up where I had, what tracks I'd followed or been driven along. I had made some departures and missed others. I'd switched tracks at certain points. I thought about Rainer and Karolina. Perhaps she had kept him from moving on to the track of obsession that seemed to be where Lutz was. I smiled grimly. Perhaps if I'd had a woman in my life for any length of time I'd be moving along a different – and better – path even now. But then, we might both have crashed or still be travelling inexorably, even unknowingly, into disaster.

One afternoon I went to the derelict railway bridges in Yorckstrasse, saw the marks of the bullets on the supports and examined them, touching the cold wet metal, the scarred and pitted surfaces rough under my fingers. I often hear the squeal of brakes and the hissing of steam, the clanking of carriages over the tracks and the laughter and the crying. Grimy brick walls rise up on either side to the clear heights of glass. And always there is movement.

What was it that happened to Lutz? He must be no older than I am. I wonder who or what he encountered. When did he stand on the wrong platform and make his departure? Or perhaps he survived his derailment or crash. Does he wander because the station terminus is gone, and there is no end of the line?

This is enough. It's as far as I want to go now. The books are gone. And as for Rainer and Karolina… It's more than likely the laughter is theirs and the crying mine.

I turn away from Lutz if I glimpse him among the cloudy faces.

These station termini are so vast as to be boundless. On the platforms and concourses the travellers come and go, but their number never decreases. The announcements are indistinct, but they must surely be obeyed before they fade away. Like the crowds, they too are endless, as is the city and the dank grey November outside.

Death Trains of Durdensk

Daniella Geary

As any secondary-school geography student knows, Durdensk is the capital of the middle-European state of Rezkadova. Less well-known however is its notoriety as home of 'Poyezd Smerta', or 'Totenbahn', 'Train du Mort' or 'The Death Trains', as the foreign tourists variously call them.

This peculiar cult was born back in 1994, four years or so after the Soviet withdrawal when the ensuing period of poverty and social upheaval was at its height. Around this time, a man of around 65 years of age, relatively well-dressed, was found sitting upright on an underground carriage with his eyes closed, apparently asleep. Sergé Voltonizk, as his name later turned out to be, had actually been dead for four days, his dead body apparently touring the underground system unnoticed by the numerous commuters that must have brushed against him and even sat beside him.

His niece Petrova Mulneska was distraught upon learning the identity of this mystery corpse, whose discovery had by then been plastered all over the newspapers for a week. Apparently her uncle Sergé had fallen upon hard times and been very short of money, not even having enough to pay for his own funeral, and being a doctor himself by training: had been at least partially aware of his own impending demise and decided to die quietly in a busy train carriage. The 5.40pm Sarenjsko Circular Express had therefore in a sense been his funeral cortege of choice, and the ordinary citizens of Durdensk, beloved strangers and friends alike: all his unwitting mourners. In that sense, a train carriage is a rather beautiful and moving sort of coffin, when you think about it. Not such a cold and lonely place in which to face eternity, but a busy bustling place full of people of all ages, laughter and nervousness, the usual human gamut. Also by including living people in your choice of coffin, one is in a sense reminding them of their own ultimate destination: the station from which no traveller has yet returned. All in all, after the initial horror and shame had subsided, the citizens of Durdensk felt touched and enlightened by the singular gesture and statement that Sergé Voltonizk had made with his remarkable death.

But it didn't end there. Durdensk has long been famed for its sub-culture of unorthodox artists, beatniks and bohemians, and among those was Petrova Mulneska's young nephew Marko Dvjizktla who began a series of drawings and installations inspired by the death of Voltonizk, which gathered quite a lot of international interest. Buoyed up by this success and various grants from the Guggenheim Foundation the European Cultural Fund he founded a company called TotenbahnCentral© and began to solicit, as it were, bereaved relatives for the use of their recently deceased as passengers on a 'Death Train' which he had purchased from the archaic gothic bureaucracy of the Durdensk Railway Authority. After much local controversy and several failed lawsuits, work on the Death Train began in earnest in late 1998. It seems incredible now that the objections were so numerous and vociferous, given the considerable tourist revenue and international artistic credibility that the Totenbahn has brought to the City. The logistical difficulties in procuring an actual workable railway route and timetable slot were, however, substantial, and it wasn't until mid-2002 that Dvjizktla's grand project was finally unveiled.

Tourists visiting Durdensk between the years of 2001 and 2011 were treated to the extraordinary spectacle of a train and two carriages filled to the brim with perfectly embalmed corpses that could sail sedately through any underground station without the slightest warning, to eerie effect during rush hours. The exact timetables of the Death Train were kept carefully secret and random, to produce maximum awe, reverence and even a little terror among the dazzled populace. The bizarre spectacle was less popular among the locals (particularly the more senior citizens) than it was with the tourists, and things came to an unfortunate head in 2011 with the now infamous train collision in the tunnel between Moulplzjha and Jylchza Brdna Stations. The traumatised rescue services found themselves expected to differentiate between the body parts of living and embalmed human beings, blood and embalming fluid, in conditions of flickering half-light and total darkness amid the cries of the injured and the horrified. Understandably, a brief international outcry ensued, before the ever-fickle media moved on.

Today, visitors to Durdensk will find an altogether more practical arrangement has been arrived at, and ultimately perhaps a more artistically satisfying one. After a brief period in the wilderness, the star of the city's artistic hero Dvjizktla has risen again, and with renewed inspiration and funding he has constructed no less than three new Death Trains over the last year, all of which are on show at the usual unpredictable times and locations. It has been calculated that those using the Durdensk underground can expect on average to see one Death Train for every eight 'normal' ones, and the fact that this appears to in no way interfere with or slow down the efficient Durdenskan rail system is a feat of organisation to be marvelled at. Today's Death Trains do not contain embalmed corpses seated upright in clothes as before, but perfect white skeletons in a variety of commuter poses. The sight of the skeleton driver in his cab as a Death Train approaches is said to be the most dramatic spectacle of all, often featured in tourist brochures and postcards.

In fact, this arrangement has a surprisingly long and noble heritage in Europe, as students of Thanatology and Archaeology can doubtless attest. Our ancestors often practiced 'excarnation' whereby corpses would be exposed to the sky on mountain tops so as to be stripped of flesh by birds, and many ancient chapels in places such as Austria, Portugal and Italy, particularly in areas known to flood or where excavatable soil is scarce, are adorned with, or even built out of, human bones that have been dug up after putrefaction has run its full course. In such cultures, the skeletons of our grandparents are viewed with awe and respect, as indeed they should be, and as they are being again, through the death trains of Durdensk. The waiting list to have one's dead body accepted to be prepared for inclusion in a Durdensk Death Train is said to currently be anything between 3 and 13 years, and the rich and famous have taken to jumping the queue by paying well over the already not-insubstantial fees. Thus Marko Dvjizktla is said to be on the way to becoming a very wealthy man. Of course, in Durdensk of all places the adage "You can't take it with you" may not now necessarily hold true!

His aunt Petrova Mulneska is now an old lady, and talks proudly of what Marko has achieved for his city and particularly for its deceased citizens. Her own husband died ten years ago, and of a Sunday afternoon she likes nothing better than to go to a nearby park where one of the rare 'overground' sections of the Durdensk railway runs for a quarter of a mile before heading back down towards the numerous twists and turns that pass under the Vlchzja Docks district. Dressed in her Sunday hat and dress she likes to sit on a park bench amid the Gladioli and Gardenias and wait for the chance apparition of a Death Train going by, occasionally one bearing the skeleton of her husband, discreetly pinned upright to his seat, reading his favourite morning newspaper. She claims to have seen him on several occasions: "It is a great comfort to me... to think of Vaslav like that, enshrined in a kind of everyday immortality along with his fellow men and women. People brush the dead away too much like dust in other countries, right out of their minds, but here in Durdensk we live alongside them and are always being reminded of what we owe them, what they mean to us, and how we must live up to their example or try to. Some people think it's ghoulish, but I'd say it's a really beautiful thing."

Petrova hopes in time to be 'enshrined' next to her husband in his carriage on the Death Train, but demand is high. Ever inventive, Marko Dvjizktla has ambitious plans to answer this issue too: whole caverns underground of dead stations and dead waiting rooms, filled with skeletal commuters waiting, as it were, for the end of time. He imagines that these new stations would be ones that commuters would be unable to stop or get off at, but would catch mysterious glimpses of as they passed through on their way to work in the mornings, or on the way home after a stressful week. "We need to stop thinking of the dead as something sad and threatening..." -he muses wistfully, "I think seeing them the way I have arranged them can remind us not of our mortality, but, paradoxically, of our immortality. All our greatest writers and artists and musicians are dead after all, and yet we communicate with them through the miracle of their art. Life goes on, round and around like an underground train on a circular route, history repeats itself, and we are all in this together, part of a big team. Every moment contains a choice to be happy or sad. I know which one I'd always choose, and which one my Art is designed to lead people to. Just follow the signs and the crowds and join the party. And mind the gap of course."

Vivian Guppy and the Brighton Belle

Nina Allan

1: My Uncle the Child Killer

Families are funny things. Funny peculiar is what I mean. All four of my grandparents were a bit gaga in one way or another. My parents are OK, and I love my brother Michael – there's not one friend I wouldn't give up for him on the spot, even if he is a data analyst – so I suppose you could argue that family weirdness tends to balance itself out in the end. My aunt on my mother's side is great, I really like Aunt Ronnie, but the guy she married is a complete arsehole and both their kids show every sign of following in their father's footsteps.

I should have had an aunt on my father's side, too – my Aunt Rose, she would have been – but my Uncle Clive accidentally killed her. The killing of Aunt Rose is just about the most exciting thing that's ever happened in our family, but in true British bulldog form it was the one subject my grandparents never talked about openly. Michael and I weren't even supposed to know about it when we were children but of course we did.

"Perhaps Rose is our aunt still," I said once to my brother. "Technically, I mean. Would your father's sister still be your aunt, even if she died before you were born?"

"Come off it, Marian, who cares?" Michael said. "She's still dead."

Trust Michael to cut straight to the chase. He was only twelve when we had that conversation (I was eleven) but his basic inclination towards sensibleness was already well formed. Michael's not prudish, he's just private. The discussion of other people's misfortunes embarrasses him, and he hardly ever discusses his own, not even with me.

I don't think I'm any more prurient than my brother Michael is prudish. Being fascinated by the details of people's lives doesn't make me a gossip, and I can keep a secret if I have to, no problem. The only reason I'm telling you this at all is because I'm puzzled and (if I'm honest) a bit scared. The business with Vivian Guppy still preys on my mind.

I'm telling you about it now because I thought it might help me work out what really happened.

My paternal grandparents had three children, of whom my Uncle Clive was the eldest, a year older than my father (Kenneth) and three years older than their little sister, Rose. When Clive killed Rose he was eight. Rose was just three weeks short of her fifth birthday.

What happened was that my Uncle Clive threw a model railway locomotive at my Aunt Rose's head. It was a Hornby, one of the Dublo models, die-cast and very heavy. Even so she was extremely unlucky. Ninety-nine times out of a hundred she'd have been OK – scared and hurt, but not permanently injured and definitely still alive. As it was, the engine hit Rose in just the wrong spot – the side of her head, just below the temple – and that was that. I knew the basics because our parents told us, me and Michael together, when we were still quite young. I suppose it was one of those Important Subjects – like sex, or menstruation – they wanted to put their own spin on for us, before we picked up the Penny Dreadful version in the school yard. I suspect they'd have preferred us not to learn about it at all, but at least this way we wouldn't put our feet in it in front of our grandparents. And the potted version was what I had to make do with, until I happened to overhear my dad talking to my mother about it a year or so later. I didn't mean to eavesdrop – I'd gone to ask my mother if I could have a pound from her purse to buy a magazine with and didn't even know my father was with her – but once I realised what they were talking about there was no way I could resist stopping to listen.

"She went down like a rag doll," Dad said. "There was blood everywhere."

I had that image stuck inside my head for a week. In the end I cracked and asked mum if it was true, that Rose's blood had been all up the walls and everything. My mother tut-tutted a lot, but in the end she told me there might have been blood, but she didn't know, and my dad couldn't have known either, not really, because he wasn't even there at the time.

"It was probably just his imagination about the blood," she said. "It must have been very scary for a little boy. Your dad was younger than you are now when his sister died. Sometimes people make things up because it helps them. It's better to think of *something* than not to know."

When I asked her what she meant about dad not being there she said he'd been at a birthday party, at another boy's house in Cooden.

"Your Uncle Clive was supposed to go too," she said. "Only he had a nasty cold, so your grandma thought it would be better to keep him inside."

That cold was what stuck in my mind, more than the blood even, which didn't seem so exciting now that I knew there might not even have been any. My Uncle Clive had a cold, and so he stayed at home. If he hadn't had a cold, he'd have gone to the party in Cooden and everybody's lives would have turned out differently. It seemed such a small thing, a cold, but it helped me get to grips with what had happened. I hated having colds myself – still do – and so I understood at once that Clive would have been feeling cranky and unwell, short tempered and irritable, not his normal self. Wouldn't it be logical that a not-normal Clive might do not-normal things?

I thought it would. It was that cold, more than anything else, that made me feel sorry for him.

People who've come into contact with murderers often go on about how nice they seemed, how *normal*. I think there are plenty of times when this is bullshit – it's easy to mistake quietness for normality, and I've seen plenty of programmes on TV about people who've killed (you know the sort of thing) where no matter how much their friends and neighbours insist how great this guy was, how much fun he used to be at barbecues, there's always something. Something behind the eyes, something *greedy*. But in the case of Uncle Clive it really was true. It's not greed you see behind Clive's eyes, or rage, or madness or even emptiness. What you see there is sadness. Not sadness for himself even, but for his sister Rose. What I think is, he still misses her. He can't quite figure it out, that this person he once loved isn't in the world any more.

He dwells on that thought, not trying to reverse it or deny it but just feeling sad.

He accepts the blame for what he's done as squarely and matter-of-factly as he would if you complained at him for forgetting to post a cheque.

Clive Lawler never left home. He didn't go to college either, though everyone had assumed he would, he was very good at maths, my father said. Instead of going to university, Clive took a job with a local accountancy firm in Bexhill, caring for my grandparents as they became older and more frail. When they died he stayed on, living in the house, sleeping in the same bedroom he'd had as a boy, leaving everything the way it was when Rose was alive.

When we came to visit as a family, Clive always stayed in the background. Sometimes, if Michael or I happened to enter a room he was in, he would quietly stop what he was doing and leave that room, not making a big thing of it or anything, just... going.

It was almost as if he believed he might do us harm just by being present.

As well as the birthday party he never went to, the other factor that sealed Clive's fate was his love of model railways. As a boy, my father said, Clive was crazy about model trains. He had a large track layout set up permanently in his room, which he didn't like anyone going near unless he was there. He spent every penny of money that came his way on railway stuff – sections of track, new rolling stock, model station buildings and houses and figurines to make the model landscape his model trains ran through more realistic. Some of the engines in his collection were rare and quite valuable.

On the day of Rose's death, Clive leaves his room briefly to go to the loo or something, and when he returns he finds everything in chaos.

Somehow his little sister has got in there. Somehow she's managed to lever five or six sections of track free of the layout board. Several of the little buildings are on the floor, and she's divested one of Clive's favourite engines of its funnel and wheels.

Clive's head, aching and heavy with cold, begins to hum. He feels sick in his stomach, and there's that awful sense of tiredness, of an irritation so profound it defies all logic.

"Oh, for God's sake, Rosie!" (Clive never swears – mild blaspheming is the best he can manage.) There are tears in his eyes, tears of frustration and of sorrow for the ruined train. The little girl stands there, grinning sheepishly, her rounded milk teeth gleaming like pearls. She knows she's done something wrong but she's not sure what. She drops the metal train to the floor. It bounces back up from the carpet and lands on her foot. She begins to cry, more out of confusion than from any real pain, and Clive's had enough. "Go away, Rosie," he says. He's breathing heavily through his mouth and each indrawn gasp of air chafes his inflamed throat like a strip of sandpaper. Tears prickle at the back of his eyes. He just wants his sister to be gone, so he can get on with repairing the damage she has caused, but Rosie is just standing there, not moving. He picks up the engine closest to hand and hurls it at her. He hates himself the moment he's done it – his action will scare his sister and will probably damage another engine, too. Serves you right for being a pig, he thinks. But it's already too late.

I've seen photos of the four-year-old Rose Lawler. She's a chubby child, all russet hair and dimples. She's soft and smiley and seems very different from both of her brothers. The two Lawler boys, Kenneth and Clive with their neat side partings and school blazers, both look rather serious.

"It shattered our family," Dad said to me once, years later. "Things were never the same afterwards. How could they be?"

Clive Lawler had no boyfriends or girlfriends and he sired no children. His life effectively came to a standstill at the age of eight.

The story enthralled me. I feel ashamed to admit this now – what was the story, after all, but a tragic accident, barely a story at all – but as a child I was obsessed with it. I went over the chain of events leading to Rose's death time and again, logging the facts, checking them for loopholes and inconsistencies, cross examining history as if determined to prove that time was a liar. Perhaps it won't surprise you to learn that I am a lawyer now, a specialist in conveyancing and property law just like my grandfather. The work pays well, and it's not without interest. It isn't fashionable to admit this, I know, but I like my job. It's hardly as glamorous as some other sections of the legal profession, but there are compensations. It doesn't take over your life, for a start, which is an important factor to consider if – like me – you have other hobbies or interests that are important to you.

Looking at it from the outside, my obsession with Clive was probably natural – my child's way of coming to terms with the idea of death, perhaps – but I'm still not proud of it. I fixated on detail: the name of the boy whose birthday it was (Adrian Wimmer), where he lived (Barron Road, Cooden) and what my father had taken him as a birthday present ("I have no idea, Marian – how do you expect me to remember something like that?") Who else was in the house at the time (just my grandmother, Ellen, who was actually outside weeding the garden – my grandfather Leonard was at work, at the solicitors' office in Haslemere Road where he was a partner). How Rose happened to be in Clive's room in the first place (no one knows – just ten minutes earlier she was taking her nap in the small nursery adjoining my grandparents' room, Ellen swore she had checked on her). More than anything else, which train my uncle had thrown at my would-have-been aunt hard enough to kill her.

Clive still had all his trains. They weren't set up or anything – I went into Clive's room at my grandparents' once, by mistake, and it was as neat and uncluttered as a monk's cell: a bedstead and a wardrobe in that dark, heavily varnished wood that seemed to take over the world in the 1930s, a shelf or two of books, a bentwood chair, his dressing gown – burgundy, with a black silk collar – hanging sadly on the back of the door. But all Clive's railway stuff – the hundreds of yards of track, the trackside buildings and many dozens of other layout accessories, the beautiful miniature locomotives and rolling stock, some of them still in their original packaging, even the large green-painted plywood board Clive had once used as the base for his layout – was in the attic, packed into boxes in one of the small rooms up on the third floor of my grandparents' house that no one ever went in. Mostly the rooms were used to store junk – you know the kind, no one needs it but no one seems able to pluck up the courage to chuck it out – and were pretty cluttered (there was one room you couldn't get into, it was so stacked with crap). The room with Clive's trains, like Clive's bedroom on the first floor, was at least tidy. There was an old Parker Knoll dining chair by the window, a drop-leaf table and an Anglepoise desk lamp. Everything looked recently dusted. (The other attic rooms were grey with dust, so much dust it made you cough, especially in summer when the heat puffed and bagged like old net curtains under the eaves.)

"D'you reckon he comes up here, you know, *secretly?*" I said to Michael. I was eleven or twelve by then, in the full throes of my Clive obsession, and we had just stumbled upon the train room for the first time. Neither Michael nor I had ever been that much into toys. I suppose we must have had all the usual kids' stuff – teddy bears and building blocks and dolls that pissed themselves – when we were toddlers, but I don't have a clear memory of it. What I remember is Michael's fetish for thousand-piece jigsaw puzzles, then later his chess computer. I was into chemistry sets for a while (generating crystals from copper sulphate, blowing things up). Also I had a kit for growing a bonsai apple tree. I dabbled in these things, but none of them took me by storm. It was as if I was looking for something to sell my soul to and in that third-floor attic bedroom in Bexhill I finally found it.

"Why should he do it in secret?" Michael said. "It's his stuff, isn't it?"

"It would be weird, don't you think? Considering."

"Considering what?" Michael gave me a look. He didn't like talking about the Clive thing, and for once in my life I was happy enough to let the subject drop.

"Look at all this stuff, though. There's aeons of it." Aeons was my word of the moment and I applied it at every opportunity, regardless of semantics.

"Oodles," Michael said (ever the pedant). "You mean oodles, not aeons."

"No I don't," I said, but distractedly. I felt too excited, at that moment, to get annoyed by minutiae. There were marvellous objects, right in front of me, demanding attention. "Let's see if it still works." The words, I thought (and I felt pleased with myself for this) were well chosen. They had about them the ring of usefulness, of giving us permission to do as we wanted – but in the name of science.

We lifted the green painted board carefully away from the wall and laid it down on the ground. There was just enough space for it to lie flat, and still leave us room to move around it on our hands and knees. Neither of us had ever encountered a train set before but that didn't matter. We were both – like all children – born and dyed-in-the-wool natural construction engineers. We quickly worked out how to snap sections of track together to form an oval, and within less than half an hour we had a basic layout. We found an engine (a gorgeous mint condition Class 52 'Western King' in maroon livery, if you're interested) and teamed it with four DMU passenger carriages in the post-1970 British Rail blue-and-white paintwork. Our choice of coaching stock wasn't strictly correct (isn't hindsight wonderful?) – most Class 52 locos were already out of service by the time the blue-and-white DMUs came in – but it looked good to us. We set the little assemblage on the rails. We still hadn't worked out how to connect the power supply, but even like this, gently immobile, the sight of that shiny red engine and its waiting carriages gave me a thrill.

Perhaps it's the same for all scale models, the studied perfection of them, I'm not sure, but looking at that locomotive and its tiny entourage gave me a spooky feeling. It was as if *another whole world was waiting*, just out of sight.

"Nice," Michael said, which was high praise from him. He reached out to take hold of the train, gently tugging the loco forward along the rails. He felt a similar sense of wonder, I could tell, or maybe that was just wishful thinking on my part. Either way, we were so caught up in what we were doing that neither of us noticed we had company.

"Would you like me to show you how it works?" said Uncle Clive.

He was standing outside on the landing, gazing in through the half-open doorway with a look on his face, I can't describe it really, a kind of longing so acute it seemed to pierce my heart. What Clive was doing there, how he came to be up on the third floor in the first place, I have no idea. Perhaps he followed us up there. Perhaps he had simply wanted to have a visit with his trains. I didn't give any of this much thought at the time, I was just freaked out to see him. Michael was too. When he first heard Clive's voice he jumped a mile. I could feel it, like mental feedback.

We were gaping at him like lunatics. If someone didn't say something soon it was going to get seriously embarrassing.

"Thanks," Michael said at last. He even managed to sound as if he meant it.

"That would be great," I added. It was a couple of seconds before I realised that it would be great, actually, because getting that loco to run along those rails was pretty much my biggest ambition at that moment.

The next hour was weird. Uncle Clive joined us in that upstairs room, settling himself beside the layout board on his hands and knees as if he'd done so a thousand times before, which of course he had. He showed us how to wire up the terminal section, and how to connect the control unit to the transformer. Within ten minutes of Clive's arrival we had the trains running. Clive didn't comment upon my wrong choice of coaching stock, except to say how fine they looked, those blue-and-white carriages, but that he never really liked them as much as the more usual British Rail blue-and-grey. Or the old Southern Region green that had been in service before the network was nationalised.

"They were mostly all gone by sixty-five," Clive said. "Although you still saw them every now and again, here and there. Before Beeching got to them, anyway. I can't stand that man."

I'd never heard of Dr Richard Beeching or his notorious axe, but the way Uncle Clive spoke of him – the closest I'd ever heard him come to an emotional outburst – caught my attention immediately. I thought I might ask him about Beeching later, though in fact I forgot. We saw Uncle Clive at supper time as usual, but none of the three of us said anything and when Clive passed me the plate with the corned beef on he glanced downwards and away without meeting my eye.

For some reason, I felt like crying. I could not avoid the thought that for an hour that afternoon I'd had a proper uncle. That uncle had got down on his hands and knees to enter our world. Having entered it, he had changed it, forever. There was no sign of that person now. He had reverted to the Clive-of-before, a weak, rather pathetic man who lacked the courage to stand up to his demons.

We all have demons, after all, even twelve-year-old children.

That should have been it, but it wasn't. We broke up the track, put the Bakelite buildings and the tiny stationmaster back in their boxes and tidied them away, but when I went to bed that night I found myself thinking of the brave little loco, the Class 52 in her maroon livery, snaking around the oval track like the proud and feisty workhorse she was. In the tightening of rail joiners and points switches, in the handling of the models (so lifelike, and yet so much stranger, at the same time) it was as if I'd been granted access to some other realm of existence, a realm where anything was possible – all I had to do was to imagine it.

There had been several times during that hour he spent with us when I'd felt Clive looking at me, noticing me with pleasure and with surprise and with that eerie longing that had nothing to do with anything except model trains.

I think he forgot who he was, for a time, forgot the terrible thing that had smashed his life and remembered who he had been before it happened.

I like to think so, because I know I did. By the time Uncle Clive straightened up from the floor and stepped back into his accustomed persona of washed-out wariness, I had stopped thinking of him in any context other than the one we were in.

Clive Lawler, train man.

It's a sad story, one that still makes me sad, even today.

2: How I Learned to Forget My Dead Aunt and Love Model Railways

Michael thought the model trains were cool, but for him that afternoon building the layout had been a one-off. The following day he returned to his chess books and coin collection, his impossible jigsaw puzzles. I snuck back up to the attic to visit Clive's trains.

I'd like to be able to tell you that the experience with Clive and the train set made me grow up a little, that it made me see my uncle in a whole new way and realise how cruel and how intrusive my earlier speculations had really been. But if I'm honest, although my attitude to Clive changed significantly, it wasn't because I'd suddenly become a better person. In fact, I more or less stopped thinking about Clive at all. From being the pivot point of my imagination, he shifted sideways and fell away. In my mind he became simply my uncle, a rather colourless character who'd had his moment of glamour once but who was now faintly boring, in the way of all semi-distant relations who form a part of the background of your life but have no starring role.

A once-great tragedian now reduced to playing walk-ons.

I went back to the third floor two or three times during that visit, not to set up the layout again (too risky, too likely to draw unwanted attention from my grandparents) but just to look at the locos, to feel their weight and examine their workings, to peer in at the tiny windows and imagine whole worlds. Michael kept out of my way. He always knows (as I do with him) when I need to be private. After lunch on the day before we went back to London, my grandmother asked Michael and me to pop to the newsagents to buy matches for granddad (his usual brand, Swan Vestas, in their flat yellow box). As we stood queuing at the till I spotted a magazine on the rack beside the counter, *Model Railway World*. I picked it up and began to flick through it, excited by the many colour photos of Hornby and Lionel and other makes I had yet to come across.

"Mr Evans doesn't like customers to handle the merchandise," snapped the shop woman. "Are you intending to buy that?"

"Yes I am, actually," Michael said. He snatched the magazine out of my hands and thrust some of the small change from his own pocket over the counter. "Present for you," he said to me quietly as we left the shop. Once we were outside he shoved the rolled-up magazine into my hand, like a relay baton.

"What's that for?" I said.

"Chuck it away if you don't want it. I can't stand that woman."

He meant the woman in the newsagent's, who always was a bit of a bitch, now I came to think of it. I'd already forgotten about her.

Model Railway World featured a cover photograph of the Hornby EDL 12 'Duchess of Montrose', locomotive and tender, in British Rail green. I thought I'd never seen anything more beautiful in my life. That night, by the light of the pink-shaded lamp beside the narrow black-wood bed I always slept in at my grandparents' house, I read the magazine from cover to cover.

As to what it was that hooked me, I can't really say. A lot has been written on the subject of collecting – the anatomy of control, the psychological likeness of obsessive model-makers to dictators and mass murderers – but I don't find it convincing. People have always collected things – it's more normal to collect things than not. All I know is that I thought they were beautiful, those model trains, and part of what made them beautiful was that they were small. I liked the idea of a perfect little engine that could be fitted inside my desk drawer, or carried in a pocket, or made to stand guard on my bedside table while I slept at night. Such a train seemed like a miracle to me, a cheeky little miracle that did no one any harm and gave only pleasure.

I guess I just liked the idea of something lovely that could be all mine.

The first train I acquired was a model of a GNR steam locomotive 69567, designed by Nigel Gresley for the Doncaster works in the early to mid 1920s. I found it at a town hall jumble sale, of all places, which made it all the more surprising that it was in such good condition. My mother was fond of jumble sales and would find one to go to most weekends. I usually tagged along with her on her scavenging trips, mainly because I liked to browse the book stand but also because I was nosy about what other people kept in their houses. The white elephant stall, with its endless minor variants on the theme of Monster Vase and Orphaned Fish Knife, was a reliable source of enlightenment in that direction. I didn't often feel moved to buy anything, but when shortly after that fateful visit to my grandparents' in Bexhill I spotted the little black steam loco on the toy stall (on top of a thousand-piece jigsaw with '3 pieces missing' scrawled in red marker pen across the lid of the box and in between a Girl's World that now resembled a bag lady and a particularly hideous bright pink piggy bank) I knew I had to have it. It wasn't expensive either, just a pound, a price I thought not only reasonable but ridiculously cheap, given how much I wanted the thing, which was a lot.

"Should we get this for Michael, do you think?" my mother said. She was looking at the jigsaw puzzle (a Landseer stag, rather handsome). I shook my head. Michael couldn't bear a jigsaw to have missing pieces, not even one, not even right at the border. (It was a shame though, because he would have liked that stag – all that complicated purple heather would have kept him busy for half a morning.)

"I'm going to get this," I said. I reached out (finally) for the train. My mother made no comment. The last time we'd been to a jumble sale I bought an EPNS salt cellar in the shape of Queen Victoria. The loco must have seemed quite ordinary by comparison.

It was heavy, like one of the old fashioned brass scale weights Mum still used for measuring out baking ingredients. It felt cold to the touch, satisfying to hold, and it seemed to be in perfect condition.

I could not imagine who had sent it to its doom. Maybe, I thought, it had been placed here deliberately, for me to find.

I still kind of believe that, actually. Go on and laugh. I'm used to it.

I was given a basic Hornby train set for my birthday, a simple oval of track with transformer and controller, an R2879 Class 55 Deltic 'St Paddy' diesel locomotive in the old cobalt blue British Rail livery and a set of four coaches, including the R4468 buffet car. My new train set was a miniature duplicate of the locos and coaching stock I was used to seeing in action on the Southern Region on a daily basis, but the train's familiarity only seemed to add to its fascination. It took me a hour or so to build the layout and get the train running. I called Michael in to see 'Paddy's' first lap of honour. I was already saving my pocket money so I could buy more track. For Christmas I asked for Hornby vouchers. The mechanism of lasting enthusiasm had been set in motion.

I was tall for my age right through school. I had knobbly knees and sticking-out elbows. My school jumpers always ended just above my wrists. I usually wore my hair in two long pigtails, and the guy who sat beside me in form room – Matthew Bannister – was forever attaching clothes pegs to the ends of them. I never tried to hide the train thing. If I had done, people would have found out anyway and ragged me about it. As it was, no one cared. All kids are freaks in some way. My particular brand of freakery was no big deal.

Everyone in model railways has their own specialism. Some are mines of stats and other info, some are amazing at creating scenery and planning track layout. (There are computer programmes for that now – they're extremely popular.) Others can fix any electro fault or repair any set of corroded points you care to throw at them. There's a niche within the hobby for everyone, and in due fullness of time I discovered mine.

I'm good at finding things that are hard to find. The business term is 'sourcing'. I prefer to think of it as tracking stuff down.

What I mostly do is seek out rare trains. American imports (all those beautiful observation cars and Pullmans with the period detailing), pre-1960 Hornby, tin-plate Bing Brothers rolling stock from the early 1900s, expensive limited editions by specialist firms. Anything someone might want but cannot find. Friends and colleagues have called my talent for sniffing things out uncanny, but I doubt it. I'm good at it, I think, because I enjoy it so much. I like writing letters to down-at-heel model shops in Morecambe that aren't on the internet. I get a kick out of tracking a passing reference from one forum thread to another and then back again. I don't mind spending hours going through back issues of *Hornby Magazine*, searching for an ad once placed by someone who's dead now, but who had a nephew who moved to Gibralter or Shanghai.

It's a kind of detective work, isn't it? I started out finding things for people I knew, either in person or from the internet, fellow enthusiasts. I did it because it was fun, and because it satisfied something in me, an instinct for problem-solving that is a little like Michael's, only not so abstract. I like to find something concrete at the end of my search, not just a number but an object I can look at and touch. Some might say my need for such literal gratification is an indication of woolly thinking but I'm stuck with it. Anyway, word spread as word does, and in the end I began marketing my skills as a train tracker for actual cash. I ran adverts in some of the magazines, then later online. I have my own website now, and a blog where I post news and updates several times a week. From the comments I get, the train fraternity seem to like it.

It was through my website that I first came into contact with Vivian Guppy.

3: *Vivian Guppy Contacts Lost Property*

I assumed 'Vivian Guppy' was a pseudonym, though it turned out not to be. Vivian Guppy wanted me to find him a Brighton Belle.

The Brighton Belle was famous, a named train on the Southern Region, a five-car Pullman that ran the line from London Victoria to Brighton from the early part of the twentieth century until the 1970s. The 5BELs were a byword for luxury. The original 'Southern Belle', as the train was first called, was the first to utilize electric lighting, and the Brighton Belle's named carriages – 'Vera', 'Doris', 'Hazel' and 'Audrey' – were fitted to the highest standards of comfort and opulence. The regular Pullman service from London to Brighton quickly became popular, especially with the theatre crowd, many of whom had pied-a-terres in Brighton, or simply enjoyed going there for the weekend. There were many on-board parties, not a few scandals, even the odd murder. When British Rail announced the demise of the Brighton Belle, her regular commuters were outraged. They fought a hard campaign to save her, but it sadly failed.

You'll find the collectors' catalogues listing several models of the Brighton Belle. The earliest (and possibly the rarest) is the 1923 Bing clockwork 'Southern Belle', originally manufactured in both O gauge and OO gauge. Either model is now extremely hard to find – I've only ever seen one example of the OO gauge, and that was in a closed case at the Brighton Toy Museum on Trafalgar Street. Wrenn produced two commemorative Brighton Belle sets in the early 80s, the 3051 and the 3052. (The 3051 set – with 'Doris' and 'Hazel' as the centre cars and the distinctive and much rarer white buffet tables – is the more sought-after. The 3052 – with 'Audrey' and 'Vera' as the centre cars and brown buffet tables – was one of Wrenn's most popular lines, and continued in production until the Basildon factory finally went out of business in 1991.) There are the newer Hornby sets of course, the R2987 and the R2987X, both with functioning table lamps, and there's also an amazing set by Goldenage Models, a work of art with a price tag to match at £2,000.

The model Vivian Guppy asked me to find was none of these. When I saw his email in my inbox, my first feeling was one of dismay, closely followed by a secret shiver of pure excitement. The dismay was because the thing he wanted me to get hold of was very scarce and so super-expensive and I honestly wasn't certain that I could find it for him. The excitement was for that same reason.

I do love a challenge.

The subject line of Guppy's email read: *Barstein Belle.*

Gerhard Barstein was born in Oberammergau in 1933, the same year that Hitler (who actually attended a performance of the famous passion play there in 1934) took up his elective position as German chancellor. Three years later, Gerhard's father Otto moved the family to Sheffield, where his twin brother Martin (who had married an Englishwoman) worked as the foreman of a factory specializing in the manufacture of Sheffield steel cutlery. Otto Barstein didn't trust Hitler. He liked even less the way large numbers of his friends and neighbours seemed to be warming to him. He thought his son (and later his daughter) might be better off enjoying a Nazi-free childhood. The family settled well in the north of England. Gerhard spoke German at home with his parents and sister, but grew up with English as his primary language and the art and craft of metal running through his veins. When Otto retired, Gerhard inherited his post as foreman at the cutlery factory. His knowledge of the job and his efficiency in carrying it out meant he had ample time left over for what he called his 'hobby factory', the small-enterprise craft workshop known simply as Barstein and that specialized in the making of quality model railway locomotives for the serious collector.

Unfashionable though it was, Barstein preferred the old German I scale (10mm to one foot as opposed to the 4mm to one foot that was the standard British OO gauge) because it allowed him to indulge his passion for meticulous detailing. Barstein locos are rare for one reason: few were produced. Each limited edition issue consisted of one hundred locos only, one hundred and fifty at most. Even at the time, they were expensive, and (in spite of the non-standard gauge size) eagerly awaited. Many issues were sold out prior to manufacture.

I'd seen a few Barstein models – there's a Barstein 'Flying Scotsman' in the Science Museum, for one – but not many. Most are in private collections. I'd never seen the Barstein 'Belle', not in the flesh anyway, although I had once seen an auction brochure for one, the #37 of the original hundred, pre-BR brown-and-cream livery. From the dozen or so photographs supplied, both the exterior and interior detailing were quite extraordinary. There were individually sewn cloth-moquette seat covers, for a start, velvet curtains and working carriage lights, starched white table cloths and crystal champagne flutes on the buffet tables. There were people, too, finely detailed lead figurines, each painted by hand. The photos of the GB5BEL0X1/37's buffet car 'Hazel' showed close-ups of four different passenger figures: a soldier in uniform with a miniature canvas kit bag stowed under his seat, a young couple in evening dress, an elderly woman wearing a pince-nez and reading a newspaper. There was also a dog, a tiny Jack Russell, which I think was supposed to belong to the old lady. It was amazing, how lifelike they were. Looking at them in the photographs, I kept thinking that the figures looked not so much inanimate as *waiting*.

The young couple planning their honeymoon.

The old woman, completing her crossword then ordering lunch.

The soldier, gazing out of the window, dreaming of home.

The Barstein 'Belle' in the auction catalogue had had a guide price of £5,000. And that was ten years before I'd even heard of Vivian Guppy.

Beneath the attention-grabbing subject line, Guppy's message managed to be evasive and up front at the same time. The strangest thing was that he wanted to meet – 'to discuss the particulars,' was the way he put it. I often travel long distances to visit dealers, particularly if I feel it necessary to check the authenticity of something, but most of my business with clients is conducted online. There are some I've known for many years, and never met. Guppy's request was certainly odd, but it didn't worry me, or not especially. He was hardly going to supply his personal contact details (a landline telephone number and an address in West London) if he was some kind of train-obsessed serial killer, was he?

(*The Hornby Maniac.* I could just see the headlines.)

When I called his number later that afternoon it seemed to take him a couple of moments to register who I was. His voice was educated – rather posh, actually – but there was a hesitancy in the way he spoke, a nervousness almost, as if he was afraid his phone line was being tapped.

"Could you come here, do you think?" he said. "It would be more private."

I said I could, and we agreed a time. I didn't think of it until I'd put the phone down, but the way he spoke – that mournful hesitancy – reminded me of Uncle Clive.

"It's not as simple as I made it sound, I'm afraid," said Vivian Guppy. (That was a laugh, for a start – as if there was anything remotely simple about tracking down a Barstein 'Belle'.) "It's not just *a* Barstein 'Belle' I want you to find, it's *my* Barstein 'Belle'. She was given to me by my father, for my fourteenth birthday. Fortunately I know the serial number. I've written it down for you."

We were having tea in his living room, a bright, well-proportioned room on the first floor of a semi-detached Georgian townhouse about five minutes' walk from Parson's Green tube station. It was an imposing building of the kind that is sure to arouse instant domicile envy in any Londoner, and Guppy's flat occupied the whole of the first floor. Glancing around the spacious rooms with their idiosyncratic but well chosen furnishings left me convinced that Guppy's quest for a Barstein 'Belle' was no idle fantasy. The guy certainly had a bob or two, no doubt about it.

He told me the house had been in his family for seventy years.

"I had it divided into flats when my father died," Guppy said. "The place is far too big for just me on my own. The basement flat's rented out now. And I sold off the attic flat completely. Anthea was anxious to buy it and she's been living up there so long it seemed only fair."

Who Anthea was – relative, friend, lover, mad old aunt – I didn't enquire. Anthea was none of my business. Vivian Guppy was my business – at least he had made himself so – and he was enough of a surprise to be going along with. From his voice on the phone – that odd hesitancy – together with the rather formal way he'd expressed himself in his original email I'd been imagining him as old or getting on towards it, slow-moving and absent-minded, horn-rimmed glasses.

In fact, he was fifty at most – not much older than I was. He was wearing baggy brown corduroys with worn knees, a grey pullover and Nike trainers. He looked like an overgrown schoolboy on a long detention.

Once again I found myself thinking of my Uncle Clive.

I'd been expecting Guppy's place to be stuffed with railway paraphernalia but there wasn't a train-related object in sight. There were books (plenty of them, history mainly) a stuffed tawny owl under a glass dome, an ornate-looking carriage clock, a large and rather beautiful oil painting (of a woman holding a globe) over the fireplace. A Chesterfield sofa covered with a tartan throw-rug, a coffee table stacked with magazines (*The Economist*, *New Scientist*, *History Today* – once again, no train interest), a slightly out of place-seeming le Corbusier-style chrome and leather armchair. The room was tidy, but looked pleasantly lived-in. The room of someone who would always rather take care of the things he owned than buy something new.

I liked it, and (I realised) I liked Guppy, too. But he presented a mystery. If he didn't collect model trains himself, why was he so intent on procuring the Barstein 'Belle'? Was he a dealer, perhaps? I didn't think so – he lacked the shark's face and the greedy fingers. I gazed at the picture over the mantelpiece. The woman holding the globe was fair-skinned, with pale, wispy hair that fell to just below her shoulders. Her expression seemed strained, as if the whole idea of sitting for her portrait had been an ordeal.

She looked vaguely familiar. At first, I had no idea how this could be. After a moment or two I realised it was because she looked like Vivian Guppy.

"That's my mother," Guppy said, seeing me looking. "She and Tania were so alike. Everyone said so."

First Anthea, now Tania. The man seemed to specialise in mysterious females. I noted his use of the past tense. If Guppy's father was dead, his mother was likely to be, also. Tania was less of a known quantity.

"Could you tell me something about the train, do you think?" I asked hopefully. Following his initial disclosure about the 'Belle' and her provenance he seemed in no hurry to return to the subject. If I didn't make some headway soon I might be there all night, drinking tea and reminiscing about his mother. Not that this was an unpleasant prospect, exactly, but I had stuff to do.

"Actually it's very simple," Guppy said. "I sold the train, and I shouldn't have done. I would like you to buy it back for me. Do you think that might be possible?"

"Well," I said. "I'm assuming you know the Gerhard Barstein 'Brighton Belle' is very rare. Finding any example would be very difficult. Tracking down a numbered model would be even harder."

That wasn't strictly true – in fact the opposite was true. With only one-hundred-and-fifty Barstein 'Belle' sets in existence, finding a specific individual should theoretically have been easier than if there were a thousand, or ten thousand. But it was still one hell of a job and I was playing for time. "There's no guarantee your set will even still exist, as a set, I mean," I added. "Some dealers split them up deliberately. They put some of the carriages on the market, then hold the others back and wait for the price to rise. It's not a practice I admire, but it happens a lot. Your carriages might be scattered all over the world by now. There's a lot to consider."

What I really meant was: this is going to cost you. To his credit, Guppy seemed to understand this immediately.

"Don't worry about the money," he said quietly. "And I don't actually need the whole train, though I'll pay you for it if you find it's intact. What I'm looking for is the centre car, the buffet car. 'Hazel' GB5BEL0X1/37/3H."

It was impossible to deny that I was intrigued and I acknowledged to myself with a sinking heart that the job had hooked me. I wanted to know where Guppy's 'Belle' had got to, and I wanted to find her. I wanted to see the look on Guppy's face when I brought her back to him. I was going to take this thing on, no question. My lunatic inner twin (is it just me who has one of those, or do they come as standard?) had as good as shaken hands on the deal.

"I can have a go, I suppose," I said. "See where we end up." I told him my rates, which were mainly just to cover expenses, plus a finder's fee, payable whether the client decided to go ahead with the purchase or not. "The Barstein trains are pretty special, I have to say. I can understand how people must get attached to them." I was just making conversation now, the kind of idle small talk we all go in for at times. On this occasion it was mostly to cover the embarrassment of having to talk about money.

I was totally unprepared for what came next.

"Not me," Guppy said. "I hate the thing. But I have to get it back because my sister's inside it."

Try to imagine what you'd do if someone said something like that to you. I bet you a hundred pounds – a thousand – that you see yourself backing away, cutting short the conversation and getting the hell out of there. But I think that kind of reaction is actually rarer than you might care to think. Partly because (for us Britishers, anyway) it doesn't seem *polite* to run – unless the nutter has a gun you'll most likely do him the common courtesy of hearing him out. But it's also because human beings are naturally curious. Given the chance, there's nothing we like better than a good story. If it's a crazy story so much the better.

So what I actually said to Vincent Guppy was: "Oh." To be honest, I might not even have said that. I might have just laid my custard cream back in my saucer and goggled like a goldfish on valium.

"I know you'll think I'm mad," said Vivian Guppy. Again, that sadness of his, that resigned stare, so like my Uncle Clive. The look of a man who's given up on his place in world. "But it's true. My sister Tania is trapped inside that model railway carriage. She's been there for thirty years, and it's all my fault."

He showed me a photo of her – Tania. He had one in his wallet. It made me feel weird to look at it, not just because the young teenager in her green school cardigan and her hair done in bunches really did resemble the dreamy, somehow absent woman in the oil painting above the fireplace (they were mother and daughter after all – that they would look alike was hardly rocket science), but because at the time the picture had been taken Tania Guppy had been thirteen years old, just a year younger than her brother Vivian. Now Vivian was, what, forty-six? Forty-eight? Whereas Tania, in Vivian's mind at least, hadn't aged a day.

Just as Uncle Clive's life had been thrown irrevocably off course by one ill considered action, so Vivian Guppy believed – on some level at least – that he was responsible for the supernatural disappearance of his sister Tania.

As to what really did happen? I think it's safe to say it's complicated.

It's hard to stop crazy people once they get started, and Vivian Guppy didn't need much encouragement. The basics of his story go like this: Vivian Guppy was given a Barstein 'Brighton Belle' for his fourteenth birthday and not surprisingly the engine and its carriages instantly became his pride and joy. His younger sister Tania – not remotely interested in model trains before that – developed a kind of crush on it and kept trying to steal it away from him. The brother and sister, who from the sound of it had been pretty close up till then, began to argue over it more and more, until Vivian finally lost his rag. He bought a curse from a passing witch (as you do) which resulted in Tania getting trapped inside the (comfortably appointed if you don't mind me saying) buffet car of GB5BEL0X1/37.

"The 'Hazel' carriage was her favourite, you see," said Vivian Guppy. "You know the way all the passenger figures inside Barstein's trains are supposed to be different? Different for every model, I mean? One of the figures inside my 'Hazel' buffet car was a little girl, and the strange thing was she looked exactly like Tania. Probably that was what attracted Tania to the train set in the first place. She had a book open on the table in front of her – the passenger figure, I mean. Tania was always desperate to know what that little girl was reading. I told her not to be stupid, that the book didn't have a title because the covers had been moulded flat to the table – you couldn't take it out and look at it, even if you wanted to. Tania would never accept that. She always insisted that even if you couldn't pick the book up, whoever had made it would have *imagined* it with a title, and the right number of pages, so that was all that mattered. 'I bet it's *The Magician's Nephew*,' she was always saying. 'Or *Chocky*.' Those were her favourite books at the time. Tania was always reading. She adored books more than anything – except that train."

He looked so distraught as he said this that I felt like crying. I took a tissue out of my bag and blew my nose. I tried to concentrate on the facts. I believed Vivian Guppy was wrong about the figurines, for a start. I remembered the photos in the auction catalogue perfectly well – the soldier, the elderly lady, the honeymoon couple. There had been no little girl. Of course there could have been other figures, not shown in the photographs, but I was pretty certain none had been listed. Vivian Guppy was either remembering it wrong, or he was letting his imagination get the better of him. The look on his face when he talked about Tania though, there was nothing made up about that.

"I don't even know now what made me so angry," he said. "Tania and I were thick as thieves when we were younger, we told each other everything. If she wanted something of mine I gave it to her gladly. It was just that damned train. I should have felt happy, knowing she loved it so much, but I didn't. I felt jealous, and so *angry*, tight inside with rage. It was such an ugly feeling, as if someone were trying to reach inside my mind and twist my thoughts."

He took off his glasses (Armani, as it happened – no manky NHS frames for fast-stream civil servant Vivian Guppy) and began to polish them on his pullover. He looked completely defeated. "Tania used to take 'Hazel' out of my room and use her as a night light," he said. "Each carriage had its own internal battery, so you could turn on the table lamps without having to connect the train up to the power source. I would sometimes come home from a walk, or from the additional maths classes I used to go to after school, and find Tania sprawled on her bed, reading one of her ridiculous fairy books with 'Hazel' glowing away beside her like a lit-up shop window. I used to yell at her for running down the battery. As if that mattered when it would recharge itself straight from the mains the next time I ran the train around the track. I must have been mad."

Going through puberty, more like, I thought. Michael and I had some appalling rows in our middle teens, and all over nothing. We soon grew out of it, and I felt certain that Tania and Vivian Guppy would have grown out of it also, given world enough and time. I didn't have too long to think about that though, because it was right around then that Guppy's story stepped off the just a bit weird path and took a sharp left towards the district of bonkers. He told me how on that particular day – the day Tania had gone missing – he'd snatched up 'Hazel' from his sister's bedside table and locked her inside his wardrobe. He banged out of the house, and went to sit on the swings in the partially overgrown recreation ground at the end of their road. He'd been coming to that park since he was a toddler and knew every inch of it. It was the place he always went when he was feeling upset or pissed off or when he just wanted to be by himself for a bit.

Only that day, he wasn't alone there. Vivian would normally have expected to find the park empty at that time (especially since it was drizzling) but it wasn't. A tall figure in a long black mackintosh was shifting along by the straggling, rain-shiny privet hedge that formed the boundary of the park along its northernmost edge. There was a dog, too, a nondescript grey thing. Vivian was wary of dogs, unless he knew them. He glanced towards this one uncertainly but it ignored him. He sat down on the centre swing, still raging inside over Tania, determined to pretend he was alone in the park, that the figure in the black raincoat did not concern him.

"You'll get cold, sitting there like that."

Vivian jumped, his hands clutching at the swing's upright chains and making them rattle. The chains were wet and slippery and had a rusty smell. (Afterwards, when he got home, Vivian would notice that both his palms were streaked red with iron oxide.) The voice was a woman's, which for some reason surprised him. When he thought about it later, he told me, the thing about her he remembered most apart from the black mackintosh had been her ankles, stalky and thin and straight in their dark woollen stockings. The ankles, and the woman's hair, poking out from under her hood in damp swatches, curly at the ends, and grey, the same colour as the hair on her bedraggled-looking dog.

"Didn't you bring your coat?" she said. This second question made it impossible to ignore her. Up till then, Vivian had been doing his best to pretend that he hadn't heard her, or that she hadn't been talking to him at all but to someone else – her dog, maybe – but to carry on with the charade any longer would be rude.

Perhaps the woman was a friend of his mother's.

And it was true, what she said, about forgetting his coat. The dampness – not really rain yet, there wasn't enough of it – was seeping inside his school pullover, and he was (the woman was right) getting cold. He felt surprised he hadn't realised it until now.

"I'm all right," he mumbled, and then (regretting his candour almost at once), "I live just over there."

Still holding on to the swing chain with his left hand, Vivian raised his eyes and saw the woman properly for the first time. She seemed ordinary and at the same time terrible, grey and spindle-limbed as one of the monster spiders that lived in the outside toilet, and he found that looking at her gave him the oddest feeling, a feeling he could only describe as being in danger. He could see no reason why he might really be in danger – it was broad daylight after all, and (as he had said to the woman herself) he was close to home. The woman was old – older than his mother, anyway. She was tall, but surely not strong enough to overpower him. But still there was that feeling when he looked at her, that sense (there was only one word for it) of *dread*. Looking at her made him remember things, awful things he'd seen and tried to forget (the legless boy in the Underground, balanced on some kind of pushchair, his lank brown hair cut straight across his forehead in the kind of cripple haircut you wouldn't give your worst enemy, the news report about the old hunchbacked woman set on fire by a group of teenagers at her home in Barking).

The knowledge that the world was pitiless, bottomless in its horrors, and that so far – *so far* – he had been lucky.

All the badness he could ever imagine, not just in the world, but in himself.

He felt his insides contract, his prick shrivel between his legs like a lump of spent gristle.

Like staring into a space where nothing was, only terror and shivering.

Like stepping off the kerb in front of a bus, even though you knew the bus was coming, you could see it plainly.

The woman's mackintosh was glistening and wet, and Vivian realised he was wondering what it might be like to have sex with the woman, to hitch up her raincoat and pull down her panties and stick it right in. He'd never seen a woman's pussy, not for real, except (once, accidentally) for Tania's.

Tania's pussy didn't have any hair yet.

"She doesn't know you saw," the woman said. "She doesn't think about things like that yet, she lives in a dream world."

"I wish she'd bloody well stay there," said Vivian. He heard his own voice as if from outside – the grumpiness in it, the lack of charity (charity, which really meant love – Miss Cuthbert who taught RE had explained it to them), the petty tantrum of a much younger child.

Suddenly, he hated himself. What was all this shit, anyway? He loved his sister.

He could feel the blood rising in his cheeks, as much from saying 'bloody' and thinking 'shit' as from wondering about Tania's hairless pussy and the spidery old woman.

"If you say so," the woman said, "then she will."

Vivian glanced up, with a start. He felt like he'd been miles away. It was a shock to discover that the woman was still there.

"Will what?" he said. The feeling he'd had before – that feeling of dread – was ebbing away now. There was nothing weird about the woman really, that was obvious. Only that she was standing out here in the rain, talking to him.

Her eyes, he noticed, were grey too. Grey as her hair and grey as her dog. Grey as the English Channel on a cloudy day.

How old was she, really? Not that old at all. She was, Vivian thought, completely different from how he had imagined her.

"Stay there," the woman said. "In her dream world. She's there already."

He didn't like this. He felt the urge to say 'you're mad' or even 'piss off', the way the tough kids did to the teachers on Grange Hill, but he knew it wouldn't be real, that even if he managed to get the words out they would be TV words and not his own, not really what he was thinking at all. And then he'd feel worse.

"I have to go now," he said instead. He jumped down from the swing, almost slipping over on the rain-dark tarmac. Both his hands were filthy with rust. He could feel a small but painful cut near the base of his right thumbnail.

He stepped past the woman without looking at her, then ran down the street right to his house, where he changed out of his wet school things and went back to working on the signal box he was making for his Weymouth layout.

(The tracks at Weymouth were unusual. The trains came all the way through the town, at street level, down to the harbour. The whole set up was amazing.)

He forgot about the woman in the park. He even forgot about 'Hazel', locked away in his wardrobe amongst his clothes. (When he took her out later, he found he'd left the battery on. The carriage lights gleamed at him feebly, like dying glow worms.) Gradually, he began to feel more normal. When his mother poked her head around his door just before six and asked him where Tania was, he said in her room.

"No, she isn't," said Clairmont Guppy. (The whole family had peculiar names, apart from Tania. It was as if they were playing a joke against themselves.) "I've just looked."

"That's when I knew," Vivian Guppy said to me. "That's when I realised what I'd done. And the worst thing about it – my punishment – was knowing I could never tell anyone, that never in a million years would I be believed."

*

The way I saw it, there were two ways of approaching the problem. One (the sensible option, the option I decided more or less at once that I would have to follow) was to ignore all Guppy's guff about a missing sister and simply concentrate on doing what I was paid to do. Just find the damn train, in other words. What Vivian Guppy did with it once I'd found it was up to him.

If his sister wasn't inside, he could always sue. (If he could find a lawyer to take the case, he deserved to win.)

The other way – which I of course rejected – was to involve myself in his madness. I couldn't see that this would help Vivian, much less myself, and so I ignored the voice inside me – that lunatic twin again – that told me I couldn't leave it there, that I had to know.

What I had to know seemed much less clear. The one thing I did know – that I felt I owed it to myself to find out – was that Vivian Guppy really did have a sister called Tania. It was easy enough to confirm. I already knew from Vivian that he (and so presumably his sister also) had been born in the Parson's Green house, that he'd lived there all his life. I now had Vivian's date of birth on file (he was forty-eight) and from there all I had to do was track forward through the records from him to Tania.

Tania Bethany Guppy. Born Brompton Maternity Hospital, 19th January 1972.

She definitely existed. I spent some time searching for a date of death for her, but I couldn't find one. On the one hand this was a relief (I didn't even know the woman – wishing her dead would seem a tad over the top) but on the other it did make things more puzzling. In the days following my meeting with Vivian Guppy I found myself dreaming up a scenario in which Tania Guppy died in childhood – following a long illness perhaps, or in a tragic accident. It was easy to imagine Vivian – who was clearly a sensitive soul – being unable to come to terms with his sister's demise, perhaps even blaming himself for it. (Clive had blamed himself for what happened to Rose, after all, he blamed himself his whole life.) His feelings of guilt – bingo – had found their outlet in his bizarre act of make-believe. But if Tania was still alive, the theory fell flat.

I was intrigued, I have to admit it. My lunatic inner twin was egging me on to take it further. It was only the logical me putting her foot down that brought a stop to it. How was discovering the truth about Tania going to help me find the missing 'Brighton Belle'? Short answer: it wasn't. There was also a good chance that a still-living Tania might actively resent my investigations. People who went missing often wanted to stay missing. Tania's whereabouts were none of my business, and if you wanted to be brutal about it they were none of Vivian's business, either. I resolved to concentrate my attention on the matter in hand.

The first useful thing I did was to look for the auction catalogue, the one with the listing for the Barstein 'Belle' that I remembered seeing some years before. I wasn't sure I still had it – I do hold on to auction catalogues when they're of particular interest but you can't keep everything – but I thought I remembered seeing it about, and locating it seemed like a good place to start. In fact, I unearthed it quite quickly – it formed part of the ever-increasing pile of randomly assorted magazines and other detritus on top of the filing cabinet in the spare room. The discovery was accompanied by a shock: the serial number of the 'Belle' in the brochure – GB5BEL0X1/37 – turned out to be the same as the number that had been given to me by Vivian Guppy.

I was looking at a picture of what I was looking for. Not only that – I'd actually seen this image of the thing I was looking for about a decade before I knew I was going to be looking for it.

I don't think I can ever convey how strange that felt. A bit like going to answer the doorbell and finding yourself staring back at you from the outside porch.

But weirdness aside – and if there was one thing about this case I was discovering, it was that putting weirdness aside was more or less essential – it was the most amazingly absurd of lucky breaks, the kind of lucky break that comes once in a lifetime, and cuts your workload more or less in half at a single stroke.

When I asked Vivian Guppy what caused him to sell the 'Brighton Belle' in the first place he shrugged, looked sheepish, and said his father had made him get rid of it. When I probed a little deeper, it turned out that Vivian had needed money for his gap year in Australia (he based himself in Perth, at the home of his mother's closest schoolfriend Hellen Wade, nee Hellen McNair) and Guppy Senior (Leyton, in case you're wondering –

Tony to his friends) had promised that if Vivian would agree to put some cash in the kitty by selling off his model railway stuff he would make up the difference.

"I wasn't really interested in trains any more," he said. "And I could see it was true what dad said, that they were just taking up space." He paused. "I think there was a part of me that thought getting rid of the trains might make me feel better."

"And did it?"

He shook his head. "It was fine while I was in Australia – nothing felt quite real to me there. But when I came home there was this horrible gap."

"Do you happen to know," I asked hopefully, "who bought the Barstein?"

He shook his head again. "By the time the things were sold I was already abroad. My father organised the sale. Afterwards he sent the money out to me by travellers' cheque. I'm sorry, but that's all I know."

It was a blow, but not a huge one. Tony Guppy had put the Barstein 'Belle' up for auction in the August of 1990, and I'm sure that with a little fishing around the various auction houses I could have discovered who had bought it and what they had paid. But now, with the lucky auction catalogue in my hand, I didn't need to know – the catalogue told me that GB5BEL0X1/37 had definitely come on the market again in the June of 1995, not through a London house this time but as one of the lots in a specialist toy and models auction in Harrogate.

Auction records can be tricky things to get your hands on. Naturally all reputable auction houses keep detailed records of individual sales – apart from anything else they need them for tax purposes. It's getting to see them that poses a problem. Even if you attend an auction in person there's no guarantee you'll be able to discover the identity of a particular buyer. Many, especially the high profile ones, prefer to remain anonymous, and what with proxy bids and telephone bids and now online bids there's a lot of secrecy involved. Finding information on a sale you never attended that took place years ago? The guarantee on that would be even less.

My usual first approach is simply to write to the auction house. If you're polite and don't come across as a stalker they'll usually forward your enquiry to the buyer at the very least. I actually did get as far as emailing the manager of one of the big salerooms in Harrogate (the actual firm that auctioned the 'Belle' had gone bust, but I felt certain the guy I wrote to would know who to contact) but the day after sending that message (which was eventually answered in the negative) I had a second lucky break that bypassed the need for it. I was searching online for more information about Harrogate toy fairs when I stumbled across an archived newspaper article from 1995 that not only mentioned the auction house but the Barstein 'Belle' too. The article, which was rather touching, described how a model railway enthusiast from Bradford (apparently he was something of a local celebrity) had bought the 'Belle' as a future investment for his twelve-year-old grandson. The buyer's name was Ernest Sales. His grandson was Harry Feathers. Mr Sales was intending to keep the train in trust for Harry until he turned twenty-one.

Harry Feathers was now a marketing manager for an IT company. He lived in Edgbaston. I contacted him by email through his firm, and told him I had a few questions I wanted to ask him about his grandfather. He said he was in London almost every week on business, and we arranged to meet in one of the bars at St Pancras Station.

I'm sorry to say I took an instant dislike to him. I had the feeling he didn't care for me, either.

He had no interest in model trains, he told me that straight off. "I mean, they don't actually do anything, do they? They just go round and round. I could never see the appeal, personally." He was chewing gum, which distorted his voice, and made it hard for me to place his accent, an odd mixture of English public school and Hollywood brat. When I asked him about it he explained he'd spent most of his childhood in Minneapolis. "My dad hooked a contract out there and we just stayed," he said. "I never really knew Grandpa all that well. He died when I was sixteen. My mom came back here for the funeral and to pack up the house, but Jacqueline and I were in the middle of a school semester, plus the flights were expensive. We stayed home with Dad."

Jacqueline, he informed me, was his younger sister. I have to say that by this point I was feeling pessimistic. Harry Feathers was clearly bored by our conversation and eager to leave. But when I asked him what had happened about his grandfather's bequest his whole manner changed.

He went very quiet, taking one quick sip after another of his Jack Daniels. When he'd drained the glass he called the barman over for a refill.

He seemed nervous.

"My mother brought the train back to the States for me, after the funeral," he said finally. "I kept it in my room for a while. It was kind of cool, I suppose, the way it was made, all that crazy detail."

"Do you still have it?" I asked. My heart stepped up a gear. Could it be this easy?

Harry Feathers shook his head. "I sold it. Mom made me wait until I was twenty-one because she said that's what Grandpa had wanted. We had a valuation, then another one because my dad reckoned the first guy didn't know what he was talking about. We were back in England by then. The second guy advised us to sell the carriages separately – he said we'd get more money that way. If he was right or not I have no idea, but that's what we did. I got just over £7,000 for it. I used the money as a deposit on my first apartment."

"So that would have been seven, eight years ago?"

"About that, yes."

"Can you remember who handled the sale?"

"Not a clue." He swilled the remains of his JD around the bottom of the glass. "What are you, anyhow? Some kind of model train nut?"

"I'm a lawyer," I said. (I knew this would get his back up and it did.) "I'm here on behalf of a client."

"You're not trying to accuse me of anything are you? Because I can assure you I have nothing to hide."

"It's nothing like that." I smiled, and sipped my drink, trying to show him that I meant well, even though my initial dislike for him had increased rather. "My client believes that particular model might have belonged to him once. Before your grandfather owned it, I mean. He's trying to trace its whereabouts, to buy it back, if possible. I was hoping you might be able to help me with that, that's all."

"I'm sorry. I wish I could, but I can't." He shook his head decisively. "I don't have a clue what happened to it after we sold it. It could be anywhere." He leaned back in his seat, tapping the base of his glass against the marble bar top. He appeared to have relaxed somewhat. "I'll tell you something, though. The thing gave me the willies."

"The willies?"

"Yeah. All those little people inside. They reminded me of that kids' TV show, you know, *The Borrowers*? Those creepy little faces, all watching you. I was glad to see the back of it."

I smiled and laughed, and so did he, then we finished our drinks and went our separate ways.

I could describe my search for 'Hazel' GB5BEL0X1/37/3H in minute detail – the dead ends, the unanswered letters, the bounced emails – but that would be tedious, so I'll stick to the short version. I started in the usual way, with a Google search for 'Barstein' and then the train's serial number. Most of what came up turned out to be irrelevant (it's the internet), but after a day spent clicking back and forth between links I finally tracked down a reference to GB5BEL0X1/37/4V – 'Vera', in other words, the other centre car, the carriage that would have been hooked up to the rear of Guppy's 'Hazel'. It was on a forum about limited edition locos – someone calling themselves Choodunnit happened to mention that a friend of his had recently purchased a Barstein model 'Vera'.

Needless to say it cleaned him out, quipped Choodunnit. *He's barely been out of the house since.*

I sent a message via Choodunnit's online contact form, and after a pointless and tiresome misunderstanding – the resulting exchange meandered on for several days – about Choodunnit's friend's right to remain anonymous, I was able to wrest free the information that GB5BEL0X1/37/4V 'Vera' had been purchased privately from a dealer in Oldham. Two days after that he sent me the name of said dealer by snail mail: G. Wheeler's. Ordinarily I would have just telephoned, but I'd never come across G. Wheeler's before and felt curious about what they might have in stock. Also I fancied getting out of London for the day. I took the train up to Manchester straight from work, spent the night in a B&B (The Railway Inn, of course, in Greenfield – the food was excellent) and went in search of G. Wheeler's the following morning.

G. Wheeler turned out to be a woman, Gillian Wheeler. There still aren't so many of us lady train nuts around, so meeting one of our number is always interesting and fun. Gill was fiftyish, maybe sixtyish, and had spent the first half of her adult life as an Oxford academic. She came north to take over G. Wheeler's when her father (George) retired.

"I must have been mad, really," she said. "My colleagues certainly thought so. But I couldn't bear to see the place close down."

George Wheeler had opened his model shop just after the war. It was a good shop, full of quirky surprises and a few genuinely rare models, all of them in lovely condition. I browsed for a while, earmarked one or two items I knew I'd have customers for the moment I advertised them, plus a weathered-finish London Midland parcels van for myself (I have a weakness for non-passenger coaching stock) that I couldn't resist. Once I'd finished looking around I went to find Gill. She filled me in on the latest developments in the Oldham Loop Metrolink saga (still behind schedule, but finally getting there) and then I asked her if she remembered selling the Barstein 'Vera'.

"Of course," she said at once. "That was just after Dad died. Some bloke in Rochdale paid £2,000 for her. I cleared quite a few outstanding bills with that sale."

I nodded. All of this was true, but none of it was new to me. "Do you happen to remember where you bought her originally?"

"I didn't. She was one of Dad's. I don't like 'I' gauge particularly, not even Barstein. It's wonderful craftsmanship of course, but it's very clunky. A good layout should be all about movement if you ask me, not decoration. That's the engineer in me talking, I suppose, but what do I know? Those things are as rare as hens' teeth, and they do sell."

She fetched a ledger out from under the counter, a monstrous black thing that looked about a hundred years old. Its heavily scuffed binding bulged with loose invoice papers and torn-off memos. "Let's have a look, then," Gill said. She began paging back from the end, stopping every few seconds to push her hair back from her face or to resettle her glasses higher up the bridge of her nose. "This is it," she said at last, stabbing at one of the entries with her right index finger. "He bought the two named centre carriages, 'Vera' and 'Hazel'. At auction through Stainforth's, in '05, separate lots. It looks like the train was split up deliberately. I wonder why?"

"Don't some people say you get more profit that way?" I said. I was trying to sound unexcited, non-committal, which was pretty difficult given that I was a mere five seconds away from finding out what had happened to Vivian Guppy's missing 'Hazel'.

"Pfff," said Gill. "In the long run, perhaps, but not always. Personally I can't stand greedy people."

An image came to my mind, Harry Feathers, swilling Jack Daniels and glancing nervously at his fake Rolex. "Do you know who bought 'Hazel'?" I asked.

"A friend of my ex-husband," Gill Wheeler answered without hesitation. "It was a works thing. A retirement gift for a colleague." She laid a scrap of paper inside the ledger to hold her place. "I can call Swain, if you want me to, get the bloke's number?"

"Swain?"

"My husband's name is Raymond, but I used to call him Swain. One of those jokes that refused to let go, even when it was long past its sell-by date. We're still friends though, it's not a problem. Would you like me to call him?"

I said that if she could it would be most helpful.

"'Hazel' was the buffet car, wasn't she?" Gill Wheeler extracted an ancient Nokia from the drawer beneath the till and hit the dial key.

"That's right," I said. Gill turned towards me then. There was an odd look on her face, and for a moment I felt certain she was about to tell me something. Then the phone was picked up at the other end and the moment passed.

"Hello, Lynn," Gillian Wheeler spoke brightly into the phone's hidden microphone. "Could I have a quick word with Swain, do you think?"

She made a face, and I smiled.

I think that was the moment we became friends.

Swain's friend Peter bought 'Hazel' on behalf of his company (Moore's Tiles, in Macclesfield) as a retirement gift for Gareth Jeffries, who had run Moore's Tiles's front office for thirty years.

Everyone in the company (some sixty strong at the time, though there have since been cutbacks) made a donation.

'Hazel' took pride of place in Gareth's home office until the day he died (of a massive coronary) in 2009.

Gareth's wife Judy sold the family home and moved to a pleasant seaside bungalow in Hythe, near Romney in Kent, where her daughter lived.

For reasons of space, more than half the contents of the Macclesfield house – including some one-hundred-and-twenty model railway engines and a serious amount of track – had to be sold.

"I felt awful, getting rid of Gareth's trains, they were so much a part of him," Judy confided when I finally spoke to her on the telephone. "But there just isn't room for them here. And I think Gareth would have liked to think of them giving pleasure to someone, don't you? What's the good of them being packed in boxes in the garage?"

I agreed that Gareth would. Apart from anything else, the damp atmosphere of a garage will often rust a loco's delicate circuitry.

The trains were sold off as a job lot to a local dealer. Judy Jeffries couldn't remember what they were called.

"The guy's name was definitely Billy," Judy Jeffries's daughter called through from the kitchen. "I remember that."

The information, as I'm sure you can imagine, didn't exactly thrill me. I'd been involved in the search for six months by then, and I was getting impatient. The 'Billy' lead (if you can call that a lead) took me nowhere, and I was just resigning myself to placing an advert in the trade monthlies (always a last resort for me – once people know you're looking they push the price up) when out of the blue I received a phone call from Gillian Wheeler.

"That 'Hazel' you were looking for," she said. "She's turned up again. Do you want me to grab her for you?"

"You're an angel."

"Not last time I looked," Gill said. "But I think I can get you a pretty good deal."

It seemed that 'Hazel' GB5BEL0X1/37/3H had come into the possession of a man named Simon Sayers who'd spent the last thirty years of his life inside a mental hospital. I was to discover two things about Sayers: 1) that the only thing he seemed to care about in life was his model railway layout and 2) that he had recently committed suicide by throwing himself from a momentarily unguarded window of the hospital library. I felt a little chill go through me when I heard that. Probably it was just that I'd let the quest for GB5BEL0X1/37/3H get out of proportion, but I couldn't shake the idea that Simon Sayers's acquisition of 'Hazel' and his suicide must be connected.

"Why did Sayers kill himself, do you know?" I asked Gill, when she called to tell me she'd secured the object of my desire. (At just shy of £2,000 she was right, that was an excellent deal.)

There was a short silence at the end of the line, then Gill told me she had no idea. "Just sick of it all, I suppose," she said. "Poor man." She sounded sad but also wary, like someone trying their luck with a lie they're pretty certain won't be believed. I didn't push the matter. Why would I? I didn't know Simon Sayers – never would now, either. I told Gill that if she'd hold 'Hazel' for me until the weekend I'd be free to come up to Manchester and collect her myself.

"I'd come tomorrow if I could, but there's too much on," I said.

"No need to worry, I'll send her FedEx," Gill said. "Can you give me the postcode? Hang on just a moment while I find a pen."

There was a thunk as she laid the phone aside and went to look for one. I waited, feeling disappointed and vaguely hurt. It would have been nice to see Gill again, to have a meal with her in the pub across the road from Wheeler's and swap stories about our wackier mutual acquaintances on the train forums. But it was obvious Gill would rather conclude our bit of business by courier service. Either a) she didn't want to see me or b) she wanted to get GB5BEL0X1/37/3H off her hands as quickly as possible.

Gill eventually came back on the line and I gave her my work postcode. When she'd finished taking it down, she asked me if I fancied coming up to Oldham the following weekend. "We could walk part of the Loop, if you're interested," she said. "I know a great place for lunch."

Definitely b) then.

This whole thing was getting seriously strange.

4: How I Came to Meet Tania Guppy and What She Told Me

I decided I should go and see Vivian. I'd been in touch with him regularly by email, keeping him up to speed with how the search was going, even sending him a couple of photos of the LMS parcels van I'd bought in Oldham (it was really very nice, and I knew Vivian would be interested) but I hadn't actually clapped eyes on him in person since my original visit. I thought he might be pleased to see me – I had some pretty major news for him, after all. Also, I had some questions. I thought it might be better – more productive – if I asked them to his face.

I could have phoned ahead but I didn't. I guess I wanted to catch him unawares. I arrived at his place around seven-thirty. It was chilly out. I remember thinking that autumn had arrived finally, that there would be no turning back from it. I rang the bell and waited, hunching my shoulders inside my coat against the cold. I was feeling nervous, I remember that, too. The one thing I hadn't reckoned on was him not being in.

The door was opened to me by a woman. Fair haired, my own age or close to it, frowning slightly as if annoyed at my intrusion into her evening. I recognised her at once – she was the woman in the painting above Vivian's mantelpiece. A moment later I realised she couldn't be, because that woman, Clairmont Guppy (Claire to her friends) was dead. Vivian had said so, I felt certain of it. Even if she wasn't, Clairmont Guppy would be old now. Faded and grey.

"Yes?" the woman said. "Can I help you?" She sounded impatient. I gawped at her, amazed at her likeness to a ghost, confused by her presence, still fazed by the fact, I suppose, that she wasn't Vivian.

"Is Vivian in?" I said at last. I wondered if I'd somehow rung the wrong doorbell by mistake. The woman's hair was scraped back from her face, held in place by two tortoiseshell combs. She was wearing jeans and a polo-necked jumper. On her feet she had on a pair of too-big tartan bedroom slippers, presumably Vivian's.

A hundred awkward images zoomed through my mind.

"I'm afraid not," the woman said. "It's his book group on Tuesdays. Can I take a message? I'm his sister."

I'm not sure if my mouth actually fell open, but it felt like it did. Suddenly I realised I was just standing there, looking like one of those weirdos who come to your door asking for a glass of water and end up murdering your entire family. (It happens. Look it up on Wikipedia.)

"Tania?" I said. It was an effort to form the word, a greater one to expel it. "I thought you were..." What, exactly? Dead? Abducted? Trapped inside the buffet car of a model railway train? Take your pick.

"Oh God," the woman sighed. "I thought he'd stopped all that. You'd better come in."

She made us coffee in Vivian's kitchen, wonderfully fragrant two-shot cappuccinos. She moved about briskly and with confidence, looking as if she owned the place, and this in spite of the shabby bedroom slippers, which really were awful, the kind you give your granddad for Christmas and that get sent straight to Oxfam.

"Vivian's fine, really. Or at least he is now, mostly. But what you have to understand is that he's not a normal person. He doesn't say a lot, but the things that go on inside his head can be really quite frightening. I don't suppose he told you, but he had a nervous breakdown when he was sixteen. A proper one, with doctors and straitjackets and everything. He spent a year in a private clinic. My dad almost went bankrupt because of it. It was a terrible time."

"What happened?" I said. I was feeling completely disoriented by now. The thing was, I liked Vivian. He came across as modest and quiet, interesting and obviously intelligent. In spite of his bizarre ideas he seemed like a nice person, basically. I saw no reason not to trust him. Talking to this woman behind his back felt like a betrayal.

But I had to know, you must see that. And this was my chance. The woman in front of me looked like Tania, moved and breathed as I imagined Tania would move and breathe. From Vivian's description of the fights they'd had when they were younger I found I could even recognise Tania in this woman's impatient, borderline bossy way of speaking.

Why would she say she was Tania if she wasn't? Why would she be here?

"Well, we're still not exactly sure," the woman replied. "Vivian always was a bit strange, even before that whole cinema business. Too sensitive for his own good, the doctors said. We were so close as kids, though. We grew apart a bit as we got older, but that's only natural really, isn't it? Only I think Vivian had problems with the idea of things changing. If there's one thing my brother hates, it's change. He's lived in this house all his life, you know."

"Yes, I know," I said. "What did you mean about the cinema?"

"It's hard to describe, really. We're still not entirely sure what happened. Viv and I often went to the pictures together, the old ABC on the Fulham Road usually – it's gone now. On the night this happened we'd been seeing *Amadeus*. When we came out I realised I'd left my bag in there, under the seat, so I went back inside. It took me a while to find the bag because I couldn't remember which row we'd been sitting in, then I decided I might as well pop to the loo as well while I was there, so I did. Anyway, all this must have taken a lot longer than I thought, because I ended up getting locked inside the building. I was pretty terrified when the lights went out, I can tell you. I sat down and cried for a bit, then blundered around in the dark trying to find a way out. It couldn't have happened these days, of course – I'd have set off the alarm system, but they didn't have anything like that then, so I was just trapped. After a while I managed to pull myself together. I reasoned that the absolute worst thing that could happen to me was that I would be stuck there till the following morning. I was inside, out of the cold, and at least there were toilets. I even managed to get to sleep in the end. I had another bit of a cry when I woke up the next day but I knew all I had to do was wait and I'd soon be found. It wasn't a nice experience, but I was never in danger. Only when I did get out, I found everyone was in a panic because of this story Vivian had made up about me being kidnapped. The doctors thought he probably felt guilty for leaving the cinema without me. People will say anything sometimes, rather than admit the truth. They told us he'd come out of it in the end, but he never quite did. What did he tell you?"

"He told me you'd been bewitched."

She put her hand to her mouth and then laughed. It was not a nice sound. Not nice at all. "You didn't believe him, did you?"

"Of course not," I answered quickly, too quickly perhaps, but I didn't like the way she had laughed. I didn't believe Vivian, that was true, but I believed *in* him. I also felt protective of him, I suppose. "I should be going," I said. I stared at the dirt-coloured froth at the bottom of my cup. Did I believe what this woman had told me? I didn't know. "Thanks for the coffee."

"You can wait, if you like. He'll be home by nine."

"Oh. No thanks. I need to get back."

"You never said what your message was?"

I shrugged. "Don't worry, I'll email him. It was just a work thing."

"Well, if you're sure. I'll see you out."

She led me back along the cream-painted hallway towards the front door. I wondered if she lived in the flat as well, or if she had her own place somewhere nearby. I wanted to like her, but I didn't. There was something stiff about her, something cold. I remembered the photo Vivian had shown me, the schoolgirl in the green pullover.

There had been a sweetness about her, a girl with wispy fair hair and a bashful half-smile who lived in a dream world of books and childish secrets.

This woman was slippery as chrome and just as hard.

There was a coat rack by the door. From one of its four brass hooks hung a furled pink umbrella with a polished oak handle.

On the hook beside it hung a black mackintosh. It looked expensive, Aquascutum perhaps, or Daks. It was a beautiful coat, the kind of garment that is always in fashion and lasts forever.

I felt a sudden and overwhelming instinct just to leave.

5: *What Happened in the End*

'Hazel' arrived the next day. I was on a conference call at the time, tying up the final loose ends in a property transaction – four-and-a-half months of tedious back-and-forth, and all over a run-of-the-mill basement flat in Catford. But that's the way it often goes with probate sales. I was dying to open the FedEx package but I had to content myself with just staring at it, squatting on top of the filing cabinet where Darren had placed it, beaming full-force 'open me' signals directly into my brain, all while having to listen to Hilary Blenkinsopp blather on interminably about security deposits. It was hard to concentrate.

I'd emailed Vivian Guppy the evening before, more or less as soon as I arrived home from my expedition to Parson's Green. I didn't mention that I'd called round, just that I'd heard from the dealer and that I hoped to be taking delivery of 'Hazel' in a day or two. I'd still not had a response from him, which was unusual – normally he replied to my emails within a couple of hours.

The most logical explanation was that he was embarrassed. Even if I hadn't told him I'd been to his house, his sister almost certainly would have. He would know that I *knew*, if you see what I mean, and looking at it logically my silence on the matter now would make it look even more as if I'd been spying on him. He was angry, probably – he had a right to be. The only way of restoring the balance would be for me to admit what I'd done, and ask the obvious question, or for him to reveal that he knew what I'd done, and explain to me what the hell was going on.

Either way it was tricky. Even trickier was the fact that I didn't believe my own story. I didn't believe the Tania woman *had* said anything to Vivian about my visit, for a start. Knowledge is power, and from what I'd seen of Vivian's sister, power was something she rather enjoyed. She would like the feeling of having one up on him, a little bomb she could drop when she chose and not before.

And there was something else too, something even more bizarre: by the time I got home to Streatham I was beginning to wonder if my meeting with Tania Guppy had even happened.

I'd spoken to someone, I knew that, but who was she really?

I kept thinking about that coat, that black mackintosh, and the more I thought about it the less happy I felt.

It sent chills up my spine.

I can't say why that was, only that is was so.

I managed to hold off from opening the package until after supper. I was starving when I got in. Also the damned conference call had given me a headache. I made myself an omelette, poured a glass of Chianti and plonked down in front of Channel 4 news. By eight o'clock I felt more or less human again. There was still no email from Vivian and I was beginning to feel worried about that, but first things first.

I opened the FedEx – very carefully – with a Stanley knife. Beneath the outer layer of corrugated cardboard was a layer of bubble wrap. Inside the bubble wrap was the shoebox-sized grey cardboard carton that contained my – or should I say Vivian's? – purchase. Gill had certainly packed 'Hazel' securely. Her original box was missing, of course, but with a train that's been split up that's par for the course.

To say that 'Hazel' GB5BEL0X1/37/3H was an object of great beauty does not adequately do her justice. The most accurate way I can think of to describe her is to say that she wasn't really like a model train at all. 'Hazel' was the real thing – it was our world that was wrong, an oversized realm of clumsiness and brute force, too blatant and too commonplace to aptly contain her.

I checked the enamelling, the exterior fixtures, the spring mechanism for the doors and windows, and found everything in perfect working order. 'Hazel' showed no signs of wear or tear or accident – you might easily have been convinced she was brand new. It was strange to think she'd been to the States and back, stranger still to think she was fifty years old.

I should explain that the windows of many Barstein trains are a special feature. Fitted with magnifying lenses instead of plain glass, they reveal the interior detailing of each carriage in far greater detail than would be visible otherwise, and grant to the viewer the sensation of actually being there, inside the railway car, as one of the passenger figures, to create a kind of diorama effect. I'd never come close enough to a Barstein train before to be able to test the effect for myself. Perhaps this goes some way to explaining why I found the experience of looking inside 'Hazel' so disconcerting. I'd seen a diorama before, years ago in an amusement arcade in Bexhill, a ballroom scene, complete with real lead crystal chandeliers, painted silk wallpaper and hand-stitched detail on the dresses of the dancers. I remember it was lit in a peculiar way, so that the tiny figures seemed to cast extra shadows, and (from certain angles, anyway) gave the illusion of movement. It was a fascinating object, and quite unnerving, but gazing into the interior of 'Hazel' GB5BEL0X1/37/3H was something else again.

It felt like being transported to another world. On an objective level I knew I was still in the upstairs room of my house where I keep my train layout – but on some other, more primitive level I felt much less sure. It was as if I'd tripped over in the street, then picked myself up only to discover that the whole of my surroundings had been transformed somehow in the interim.

A kind of imaginative concussion.

Have you ever been inside one of the old Pullman railway carriages? Train travel was different in those days, there was a grandeur to it, a sense of occasion. In these motorway-plagued, post-Beeching days, people have been brainwashed into thinking of train travel as a cramped, fraught and altogether *inconvenient* experience. In the days of Brunel, when civil engineering was a calling and the idea of a properly sustainable travel infrastructure was a prerequisite for progress, to go anywhere by train was to undertake a *voyage*.

The blue plush seats, the freshly vacuumed carpet, the swagged velvet curtains. The opulent lighting, sheening the polished rims of the champagne glasses. I heard the rustle of newspaper pages being turned, a quiet cough, the muted slam – I swear it! – of a compartment door being closed further down the train. The young soldier, sitting by the window at the end of the carriage, was smoking a cigarette and looking out upon the passing countryside. The ashtray on the table in front of him was already half full.

The young girl, at the table opposite, seemed absorbed in reading. She was young to be travelling alone, I thought. I glanced quickly along the carriage, hoping I might see evidence of an accompanying adult, some obvious parent or guardian, but there was only the young married couple, lost in each other and giggling over their champagne, the elderly theatre grandée busy with her newspaper. The child seemed calm, unworried by being alone, although in her pale features, the slightly hunched set of her shoulders there was perhaps something desolate about her.

It was growing dark outside. I hoped there was someone waiting to meet her at the end of her journey.

I gazed at her fixedly, astounded by the lifelike way her features had been painted, the detail that had been employed in her manufacture. Her blonde hair, done in two bunches, was remarkable. Almost certainly it was real human hair. One of the girl's tiny hands rested, palm downwards, on the Formica tabletop. I could see the blue veins beating in her skin, the tiny crease in the angle of her wrist, the pearlescent, palest pink of her fingernails.

I leaned over towards her, curious to see what she was reading. As she shifted in her seat the book's cover flipped up slightly and I saw it was *Chocky*.

I could see individual hairs, bright and clear as glass rods, sticking out from where her hair was parted at the nape of her neck.

I could hear the old familiar ratchety-*thump*, ratchety-*thump* of iron on steel as the train hammered its path along the rails towards Brighton.

I kept wondering what would happen if the girl happened to turn around and see me watching her.

I didn't sleep very well that night. I kept dreaming that it was I, not the child, who was being watched, and each time I awoke in the darkness I had the feeling that whoever had been watching me in my dream was still in the room with me.

I thought about calling Michael, but didn't. What did I imagine I was going to say?

I awoke fully just before six. I could have sworn someone had been ringing the doorbell, but by the time I put on my dressing gown and went down to see there was no one there.

I showered and dressed then switched on my computer. I was intending to send Vivian Guppy another email, telling him that 'Hazel' had been delivered and that I could arrange for her to be couriered over as soon as his account was settled. I was surprised to find an email from him, already waiting for me in my inbox. From the time-log, it had only just been sent.

Could we meet for coffee this morning? Your usual place?

There's a big, open-plan Italian cafe where I sometimes have breakfast. I like it because it overlooks the street, because it's always busy and therefore private and because the coffee is excellent. I go there three, perhaps four times a week.

The only way Vivian Guppy could have known this was if he'd been spying on me.

So he'd been spying on me, so what? I found the idea vaguely amusing. I certainly didn't have the energy to worry about it. I reckoned that if he was that good a spy he wouldn't need an answer to his email and so I didn't send him one. I just went to the cafe instead. Vivian was there before me. He had a pot of tea in front of him, and the smoked salmon and scrambled egg breakfast option.

"Marian," he said. He looked different somehow, almost dapper. Perhaps it was just that he had a new jacket on.

I ordered my coffee and then sat down.

"I'm sorry," Vivian said.

"Sorry for what?" My head was still muzzy from lack of sleep. I hoped they'd hurry up with the coffee. The coffee in that place is always scalding hot, just the way I like it. Plus it has a kick like a kangaroo on acid.

"The woman you spoke to," Vivian said. "She isn't my sister."

I was silent. Like I say, I just hadn't the energy. "She looks like her," I said finally. "She looks just like the woman in the painting."

"I know that, but she isn't," insisted Vivian. "I don't know who she is."

*

I once owned a book, a children's encyclopaedia of the universe, full of interesting facts on endangered animals and space rockets, intricate line drawings and six marvellous colour plates showing the internal organs of the human body. I loved that book, it remained with me all through my childhood, and yet when the time came for me finally to leave home after finishing university it was among the many mementoes and keepsakes and redundant toys I decided to get rid of. As far as I could see, I had outgrown the book. There was nothing more I felt it could teach me, and life moved on. I didn't miss it particularly, or even think about it. So it might seem strange to admit that when I came across a copy of it, years later in a second hand bookstore in Eastbourne, I bought it at once.

I knew that the chances of this being *my* copy were thousands to one, but the desire to take the book once more into my possession was overwhelming. When I did so the sense of homecoming, of *buying back time*, was so intense it brought tears to my eyes.

What was it I had bought, then? Not just the thing itself, not just the memories even, but the ghost of the person I had been when I first owned it.

All that hope.

All that not-knowing.

All that wide, blue future.

My heart aches to think of it. I still have that second copy of the encyclopaedia. It no longer holds the power it once did, but it reminds me of how I felt when I first came upon it, lodged in the bottom shelf of a second hand bookshop in Eastbourne, all those years of my past, still somehow intact.

I'm guessing that's something of how Vivian Guppy felt, when he first opened my FedEx parcel and saw 'Hazel'.

*

"I've had a long time to think about it," Vivian said. "I think the train is a nexus."

"A nexus?" I said doubtfully. I wasn't too sure what a nexus was, even. God, I was tired. It felt like I was suddenly starring in my very own episode of *The X Files*.

"We both had so much invested in that train, Tania and I. Emotionally, I mean. For Tania, 'Hazel' was the perfect idea of escape. For me, she was the perfect embodiment of the idea of perfection. Either way, we both concentrated so much energy on her that in the end she became – *charged*. Someone – some*thing* – homed in on that energy and used it to make its own escape, to cross over into our world. This creature, whatever it was, must have trapped Tania at the point of nexus and taken over her body. In my own way I became trapped too, searching for her. I want her back."

No, Vivian, you don't, I thought. You want back the person she was, the person you were. What you want is another chance at life. It's the same as me with my encyclopaedia, or like Uncle Clive, when he first came upstairs that time and found Michael and me, playing with his old model train set. Just for a while, he saw a world where the future hadn't happened yet. But it doesn't last.

"You've got to stop," I said to Vivian. I put out my hand, touched the tips of my fingers to his across the table top. I felt such pity for him. "Whatever happened, you have to let it go or it'll drive you mad."

"I know you can't believe me," he said. "But can we still be friends?"

"Of course we can," I said. It was easy to say that, because it was what I wanted, too. I also said I'd have 'Hazel' GB5BEL0X1/37/3H sent round to his place by DHL.

"But I haven't paid you yet," Vivian said.

"That's all right," I said. "I trust you."

It was true, I did. Also I wanted the thing out of the house.

What with one thing and another, I would be glad to see the back of it.

*

That black mackintosh, though. I know this sounds stupid, but I've never forgotten it.

It doesn't add up.

Platform Alteration: UK Ghost Trains

In was Dr Beeching's fault. Fault if you are a train operator anyway, irrelevant if you are just about anybody else – but if you are one of the few who loves poking into the obscure and quirky then it is one of the few things that you might be thanking the old axe-wielder for.

Apparently, it was after the infamous Beeching cuts and everybody was so pissed off with the whole thing that the UK parliament attempted to quieten things down with a few tweaks to the amorphous blur that is 'the way things are done', making it far harder to ever close railway lines. The result is that it is now such a difficult and expensive legal hassle to shut down a railway that it is often easier simply not to bother. Conversely though, it seems that in order for a line to be alive, one has to run a scheduled "revenue earning train" along it. This means that the poor train operators are stuck between the proverbial rock and the equally proverbial hard place. On the one hand, an agonising legal process, on the other a useless train that nobody wants. And often, it is actually the cheapest and easiest option to just keep running the absolute minimum number of services, which is something daft like one a week in one direction. Even if there is no call for them. Even if they are entirely empty. Even if they are not advertised anywhere. Even if there is no functioning station left for them to stop at.

Those are the ghost trains. Pointless, useless little regurgitations of bureaucracy – sad railway waifs condemned to an existence without meaning or reason. Sometimes they are run by ancient trains who only avoided the scrap heap to perform this last heart-breaking service. Sometimes they are just normal trains diverted from their usual route for this one minor break in the driver's routine. Usually they are empty . . . or are they?

There's the thing, of course. The irony is that if you have the right kind of interest, these obscure ghost trains are irresistibly fascinating. The rabid train nuts and explorers, or those just interested in a touch of the unusual or occluded, are only too keen to track them down. So sometimes these ghost trains are actually quite popular, precisely because they are useless. You will sometimes find little knots of enthusiasts waiting to greet them and ride down some stretch of track that most people wouldn't even begin to care about – maybe ride in some ancient carriage that is almost a museum piece or almost dead. So is that still useless and pointless? Or do both occasionally become self-defeating concepts?

Apparently there is at least one in London, my home city, though you certainly won't see it on the transport maps. One day I shall track it down . . .

DR

Last Train

Joel Lane

It was the mildest winter he'd ever known. There was no trace of frost on the black ground. Malcolm wondered if he'd dressed too warmly. But this was late afternoon; midnight would be another story. And he didn't really believe he'd find the fire. They'd probably demolished the bridge, taken up the disused track. In place of the ruins of his childhood, he'd probably find yuppie flats or a trading estate up there in the night. He was ready for madness, decay or death, but he wasn't ready for uniformed security guards. Still, he had to go.

Rose Road looked much the same as it had twenty years before, though the fire station had closed down. The house where he'd lived for most of his schooldays was still there, but it had been repainted pale blue. He remembered a black door. Opposite, there was now a car park. He stepped between the silent vehicles and looked upward in the fading light, through the wire-mesh fence to the steep bank. Was there still a way through? Yes, the fence was torn at one corner, with a gap he could crawl through. Which meant children still used it – either that, or Malcolm was seeing the memory rather than the reality. He did that a lot, according to Dr Fenn.

Beyond the crawl space, an empty concrete yard stretched from the fence to the back of a derelict house. Something dark was lying in the shadows by the mould-coated wall. It could be a kitten or a large rat; whatever, it was dead. A memory came to him vividly in that moment. In his last weeks of junior school, two girls had led him up here. They'd told him to look away and count to ten, then look back. When he'd turned round, they'd been dishevelled and red-faced. Again, they said. The second time, their white cotton knickers had been down to their knees. He'd been puzzled at the lack of any shape in what they showed him. They made him expose himself too, the first time he'd been hard.

All his teens had been about looking, not touching, and by the time he'd got close to anyone it had already stopped being real. Dr Fenn had told him the reason he felt so much guilt was that he associated sex with dreams, and was shocked when it had consequences in waking life. That came from being woken so many times by his parents' violence towards each other. The fight on the stairs, both of them falling together and carrying on in the hallway. The early alarm clock of screaming. Dr Fenn offered him these insights for all the world as if it made a fucking difference.

But he'd come back to find what he'd buried under the railway tunnel. Dr Fenn hadn't believed in that. He'd said Malcolm was remembering a dream, which was his way of saying *lying*. But Malcolm had only remembered about the fire when he was in the hospital. So if it wasn't real, it was Dr Fenn who'd put it in his head. The old man was madder than Malcolm anyway. It was he who'd told Malcolm about the Last. And for all his bullshit, he could be totally honest. Once he'd said: *It's easier to be depressed than mad. If you're depressed people give you support, they invite you to join their Facebook group. If you're mad people are afraid of you.*

There wasn't much light up here, away from the streetlamps. But a half-moon was out. He could see, or at least remember, the steps between the derelict houses that led up the bank. Nothing had changed. Malcolm fumbled in his coat pocket for his cigarettes and lighter. Another thing that had started here. The smoke felt raw in his lungs. He wondered if the lit cigarette was visible from a distance. *A lonely spark.* Its heat made the night seem colder as he climbed the steps and followed the steep path to the ridge. He could still feel the tracks under his feet.

This railway must have been disused for half a century or more. It had never carried passenger trains, only freight trains going to and from the quarries and furnaces. The ground was scattered with clinker, a blue-green translucent stone that was a waste product of glass-making. He'd kept a box of it as a child, looked at it by torchlight when he couldn't sleep. He'd imagined being a fossil, a hybrid of the living and the inert rock. His feet touched weathered sleepers across the tracks, embedded in the hard ground. Some of them were missing.

What Dr Fenn didn't understand was that Becky wasn't a signpost to his past. She'd shown him a way to his future. With her, everything had been new: cities, trains, music. He'd learned to live again. But the old fears had caught up with him when they began to argue. He couldn't be with her when she was raging, couldn't even look at her. After a bitter argument, he'd gone out and got drunk, ended up sleeping with a man from Tipton. He'd told her, and that had been the end of it. But she'd become obsessed with the idea that he'd infected her with some disease. It wasn't true, but she'd had test after test, called him every time she had a sore throat and screamed that he'd killed her. It would have been easier for him if she'd been right. Then, nobody really knew why, she'd stopped breathing.

And that was when they'd all come back. Everyone he'd forgotten, moved on from. Their voices came after him on the wind, until he realised there was no-one he hadn't let down, not even his family. He couldn't remember much of what had happened then. The rain had come in through the roof, into his head. Eventually there was the hospital, Dr Fenn, so many doctors. Had he been sectioned? It didn't make much difference once you were there. But he'd remembered the fire. The secret burial. He'd come back not to embrace the past but to set himself free.

It might have been a loose sleeper that tripped him up and sent him hard against the tracks. His hands jarred on broken stones. When he stood up, the distal side of his right hand felt icy cold, as if he'd dipped it in ground water. The last two fingers wouldn't move. He felt for a tissue and wrapped it carefully around the injured digits, holding them together and absorbing the blood he could feel on the chilly skin. Already the flesh was beginning to swell. He cradled his hands together and breathed on them, then felt himself laugh. In the last year he'd taken two overdoses, cut his left wrist, tried to starve himself. But given a minor injury, he was desperate to avoid harm.

The moon gleamed through a tissue of cloud like a cold sore. The nebula of streetlights in the distance was real, but up here on the track everything was a ghost: trees, brambles, fireweed. Malcolm adjusted his rucksack and wondered if the Last would be waiting in the tunnel. That was why people were disappearing, according to Dr Fenn. Not the police, not unpayable debts, not the suicides he kept saying he understood. It was the silent circle of watchers. The last twelve people left alive at the end of the world. And that was close enough for their ghosts to reach back and take us. So much for fucking science. He'd even warned Malcolm: *Don't touch them. Keep away. If you touch them, you're lost.*

Dr Fenn believed in drivel like that, but not in ghosts. For a year Malcolm had been afraid to sleep because of the dreams in which Becky was drowning, or trapped in a fire, and calling to him for help. He didn't move in case he got dragged into the same terrible death. Or in case she was faking and wanted to see him die. He'd woken shaking, tearful, appalled at himself. But Dr Fenn said it wasn't a ghost. It wasn't even about Becky: it was about his childhood, the fights he'd been unable to stop. There was no reason for him to feel guilty. And similar bullshit, a drip-feed of liquid excrement that trickled over him, session after session. He could still smell it.

The moon was fading and the trees were getting thicker, blocking out the distant lights. He knew he'd reached the tunnel more from the reek of damp stone than from any change in the shadows. Working clumsily with his left hand and right thumb, he flicked his lighter. At once, he was back in the past. The brick walls were streaked with mould. Thin spikes of lime hung down from the ceiling. A rat stirred in a heap of rags by the wall. Malcolm lit a cigarette and breathed smoke over his frozen hand. This was home. And then he realised that what he'd come to do, the digging, would be all but impossible due to the injury. He couldn't see himself coming back another time. Or even leaving this time.

It was colder here. The deep chill of stone. Malcolm shrugged off his rucksack and clawed it open, reaching for the garden trowel he'd bought in Wilkinson's that afternoon. He stood for a long time, trying to remember, then started to dig near the wall opposite the rags. The hard ground smelt faintly of ammonia. Digging left-handed was slow and painful, but he couldn't even hold the trowel in his right hand. The cigarette burned down; coughing hollowly, he lit another. Was the hole in the ground real or just memory? It was at least an hour before he uncovered the muddy bundle.

A rag from the local garage, wrapped around something not quite spherical. He rubbed at its uneven surface, not pure glass but clinker. What he could see inside was mostly smoke. But coiled within it, there were glimmers of fire: blood red, bruise violet, midnight blue. He raised the crystal and threw it as hard as he could against the wall. It exploded, spraying him with wet ashes. Coils of flame dissolved into the bricks. The memories echoed around him. They were nothing new. What Malcolm didn't recognise was the raw, seething reactions within him. The lost voices of fear, loneliness, grief, love.

It was done now. There was nothing left. The cold of the tunnel pushed him down and he fell onto the broken track, crying weakly. There was blood in his mouth. One hand ached from digging; the other felt icy. The cigarette burned out before its dull flame reached his lips. The taste of smoke faded. He curled up on the tracks and closed his eyes. But something wouldn't let him rest. It wasn't inside him, it was in the ground, and it took him a few moments to realise what it was. The track was vibrating.

Malcolm raised his head and looked back through the tunnel. Among the distant points of light, one was brighter than the others. Clutching his injured hand, he stood up and moved to one side of the track, pressing his back against the tunnel wall. The bricks too were vibrating now. The mingled smells of lime and urine almost made him retch. The light was closer now, a dull red glow as if the industrial buildings north of the tunnel were burning. He could hear the pounding of the engine. Close to the tunnel, the light stopped. There was silence.

He walked towards the train. A faint glow from the carriages made them visible: a small branch line passenger train of the kind that had been common when he was a child. There was no sign of anyone inside. Why had it stopped here? There were no guards, which encouraged him. It seemed important to be moving on. He stepped up to the nearest carriage door and opened it clumsily with his left hand, then stepped inside. No whistle blew, but the train slowly began to move into the tunnel. When it emerged from the other side, the half-light inside the carriage was unable to penetrate the dusty windows. Outside was only darkness. As his eyes adjusted, Malcolm realised that more than half of the carriage's seats were occupied. Nobody was moving. He peered at the nearest face – then, hastily, moved on to the next – and the one after that. All of the passengers had Becky's face.

They were wearing masks of plaster, or possibly stone. They appeared to be sleeping. He counted twelve passengers. With his left hand, which had become quite unsteady, Malcolm reached down to one of the still faces and felt for the edge, then ripped it to one side. Underneath was a crumpled rose of burnt newspaper that could have been used to start a bonfire. The air in the train was colder than it had been in the tunnel. Slowly, with no purpose other than a need for the truth, he knelt on the carriage floor and reached up with his injured hand to touch the ruined face.

The train shuddered on through the night.

Writer's Block

SJ Fowler

Driven mad by the sound of nearby locomotives in their squalid tenement flat, fighting with his wife, drunk, Paul Verlaine once threw their three-month-old son against a wall.

What has happened? It is life that has happened; and I am old. Said Louis Aragon, between Paris and Lyon, on the XG14.

If a train could paint a picture, his god would look like a train. Said Xenophanes.

Despite decades of self-analysis, Freud was forever so anxiety ridden about missing trains that he would arrive at a station as much as an hour ahead of time.

Joseph Beuys was a train driver in World War II.

Raymond Chandler lived with his mother until her death when he was thirty-five. And then almost immediately married a woman he had met on the tram, seventeen years older than he was.

Bruno Schulz was carrying home a loaf of bread when he was shot down in the street by the Gestapo near Drohobych train station.

Only a lunatic would dance when sober, said Cicero.

Impoverished and freezing, having ridden the rails back into the city, Gerard de Nerval hanged himself near a cheap Paris doss-house after no one responded to his late-night knock.

Ingenious nonsense, Isaac Newton dismissed poetry as.

Life is a long wait for a train that never comes

Thomas Hobbes was born prematurely when his mother became hysterical at the approach of the Spanish Armada.

Picasso, when told that Gertrude Stein did not look like her portrait: Never mind. She will.

TS Eliot was a virgin until his marriage at twenty-six. And possibly thereafter.

The tyranny of the ignoramuses is insurmountable and assured for all time. Said Einstein.

Act 2

Northern Line Tube Announcement

Anon

Good evening ladies and gentlemen, this is a northern line train to Kennington via Charing Cross. Our next stop will be Embankment. This is to advise you that there will be a short delay here while checks are carried out. Any passengers who boarded the train north of Archway are advised for your own safety to alight here before we cross the Thames. Thank you.

The Path of Garden Forks

Rhys Hughes

The title of this story is some sort of feeble pun on a famous text written by Jorge Luis Borges called 'The Garden of Forking Paths' that is usually cited as one of his best tales. That's what I believe anyway, but Flann von Ryan, the railway engineer who is the main protagonist of the exploit that follows, disagrees with my analysis. He says it's just a coincidence. Down on his allotment is where he can generally be found these days, so let's go there now and learn if he's right.

Flann retired from his career in disgust when one of his best ideas was rejected by the transport ministries of every government on the planet and his beautiful blueprints were savagely laughed at. He grudgingly realised he was wasting his energy and genius working for humans. Unluckily, no other species of employer was available at that point in time, so he simply gave up work to devote himself to his hobbies, of which the cultivation of edible plants is the most harmless.

His plot of land is small but productive. In a sentence or two you'll see that for yourself. Follow me through the gate and along the path but take care not to slip on the mud and impale yourself on the bamboo beanpoles. There he is, bending to turn the soil with the prongs of one of his garden forks. He has many spare forks lined up along this path, I don't know why the fork is his favourite tool, but communal allotment gardens are always full of eccentrics, so I never ask.

"Mr von Ryan, might you spare a moment?"

He stands slowly and puffs his cheeks and exhales condensation from his nostrils and I'm reminded of one of those steam trains powered by hot geysers instead of fossil fuels that the inspired engineer tried to sell to the Siberians a few years ago. Strange that the scheme wasn't successful! The geysers were carried safely on board in big bathtubs and there weren't any safety or efficiency issues, but it's often something as arbitrary as fashion that dictates technological progress.

"I'm quite preoccupied, to be honest," he replies.

"I do appreciate that, sir, but I brought the reader with me all this way to convincingly settle a dispute."

"Is it about the title of this story again?" he sighs.

"Yes, I'm afraid it is."

Shaking his head dolefully, Flann lays down his fork and stands like a scarecrow specially designed to scare off other scarecrows. His mouth is set in a grimace and his eyes betray a cumulative pain. Then I notice that his bare legs below the hemline of his shorts have turned black, not black with gangrene but some other way almost as bad, and I recoil in terror as he steps closer, a terror that objectively is rather mild but quite sufficient in the context of this paragraph.

"Ants," he explains. "My plot has been invaded."

His lower body is literally alive with ants, seething, pulsing and biting, tiny actors in an evil costume drama, irritating his skin like no fabric ever could, hundreds of ants in the shape of an awful pair of formic trousers, a garment of repentance that can't be flung, and when Flann reaches down to brush the nasty insects off with his hand he gains a dark glove as many ants jump over, while new ants rapidly climb up from the ground to repair the sudden gap like impish tailors.

He is the very sorry personification of itchiness. "That's a terrible thing to happen to a gardener," I shout.

And he doesn't disagree with my sentiment. "Indeed!"

"Have you tried any remedies?"

"For ants there are none," he replies impatiently.

"Are you quite sure? What about a chalk circle? I read somewhere that ants will never cross a circle marked out in chalk. Another solution might be the importation of an anteater."

"Our local climate is too wet for either!"

"Fair enough, but there's another creature in existence that's the doom of ants. Although called an antlion, it doesn't resemble a mermecolion in the slightest and in fact it's just the larval form of an insect that's a sort of lacewing. Antlions are also known as doodlebugs and they make traps by digging pits and lurking at the bottom. When an unlucky ant falls into the pit, the antlion soon devours him."

"What's a mermecolion?" Flann wonders.

"A mythic beast, half lion, half ant, half absurd fiction, and I apologise if those figures don't add up but it's not really my fault. Anyway, it seems you'll just have to suffer without any hope, because ants can't be defeated by any force in the universe, that's plain from your demeanour. What can possibly rid an allotment of ants? Nothing. That's the message I'm getting loud and clear from your stance and it's a fact you're much more clever in all subjects than I could ever be."

Flann sneers at that. "Are you being sarcastic?"

"No, I'm not," I reply honestly.

"Cleverer in *all* subjects?" Flann persists.

"Apart from the taxonomy of imaginary beings," I concede.

"I'd better learn fast," he sniffs.

"It's a pointless subject, don't bother," I say.

"Very well. Back to ants…"

Suddenly the reader speaks up. That's you, by the way, you out there. Yes, you. I'm not referring to an abstract figure with no more substance than the fictional characters in this tale, but to a flesh and blood person, the only solid lifeform in the vicinity. Don't attempt to hide and pretend you're not there. You betray your presence by sucking the words off this page into your mind and they make a noise when that happens, a gloopy sound, and I can hear it right now.

So I know you are there, even though I can't see out of the story. That is how you'll never evade your responsibility while I'm the narrator. With a superior sort of smile you say:

"You need to kill the queen, that's what."

Flann von Ryan narrows his eyes and licks his lips. "What?"

"To get rid of the ants," you add.

"Yes, I see," he comments.

"They have clearly established a nest somewhere in your plot and they probably regard your land as belonging to them now, so they are here to stay, and killing the workers won't make any difference at all. You must kill the queen. It's the only way."

I whistle through my teeth in amazement at your insight. "Superb! I'm sure that's the one viable tactic."

"Kill the queen?" echoes Flann ponderously.

"The only option, absolutely."

He rubs his chin and studies the ants on his legs. Then the ants on his hand that have transferred themselves to his chin because of that rub run across the rest of his face and he closes his eyes and opens them abruptly, using his eyelids to flick some of them off. But it's clear that soon he will be utterly covered in ants, that he'll turn into a statue of ants, that there'll ultimately be sufficient ants for them to cut him up into tiny pieces with their mandibles and take him home.

Back to the nest. Back to the queen. The queen that must die, I remind him, winking at you, the reader.

"I'll do that," he cries. "I'll really do it!"

After we have left, Flann staggers up the path to his shed, shaking off the ants as he goes, then he pulls off his clothes and uses them as mild whips to lash away the irritation of the acidic wounds on his flesh. Next he jerks open the shed door and lurches inside. A hurricane lamp suspended from a rafter on a chain illuminates the interior with a solitary candle, but it is the brightest candle in history, one of his own inventions, and no shadows find refuge in any corner. Not one.

In the exact centre of the room stands a wide table and on this table are the technical sketches of his ultimate innovation, the Infinite Train. It was this very project that was spurned by every government he took it to, but he has since refused to destroy the plans and occasionally consults them for nostalgic reasons. The Infinite Train is still a viable concept and one day it might be adopted by some futuristic regime. Then he should finally receive the real respect he deserves.

An ordinary train has a finite and easily measurable length and moves like a metallic sausage on a predetermined course along a track. When it reaches the end of the line it presumably turns back, either by reversing or by being rotated on a giant turntable. The Infinite Train isn't like that. The Infinite Train is a closed loop made of millions of carriages that run on a track that also forms a closed loop around the entire country so that every station lies somewhere along the loop.

Because I currently reside in Britain, allow me to use British locations in the following example of how an Infinite Train could work in practice. In a simple version, a single track might connect London, Bristol, Cardiff, Swansea, Wrexham, Liverpool, Lancaster, Carlisle, Glasgow, Inverness, Edinburgh, Sunderland, Leeds, Sheffield, Norwich, Ipswich and back to London. That's the loop the track would make and an Infinite Train would make an identical loop on top of it.

The loop that is the train would go round and round the loop that is the track, allowing any willing passenger to get on board at any point without needing to wait for the train to arrive, for how can it possibly *arrive* when it's already there and will always be already there? The only tricky part is the transition from solid ground to moving train or vice versa. A perilous jump is required for that, or as an alternative maybe rows of springboards and safety nets could be installed.

To render the journey even faster and more efficient, the Infinite Train actually carries its own conventional railway inside its carriages, for they are wide enough to easily accommodate a track that runs the entire length of the loop. On this track race orthodox electric locomotives, doubling the relative speed of a commuter who takes advantage of them. Eventually a second Infinite Train may replace these locomotives, with a third loop of railway line inside them, and so on.

Round and round in the same direction forever…

That's enough about that. Flann von Ryan turns over the piece of paper covered in the drawings of his most futile scheme to expose a blank side that he'll use to design a new project for the eradication of the ants in his allotment. He sets to work with a pencil. The candle burns to a stub, the moon rises over the silent gardens outside, the herb spiral he has been tending gleams in its beams. When he finally nods to himself at midnight there's no pencil left to throw down.

His plan seems perfect. He will devote the rest of the week to building a working prototype of the thing, but now he needs to sleep. He stands up and crosses the room to a trapdoor in the wooden floor. He raises this and descends a metal ladder to a secret underground platform where a sealed train of his own devising glides him smoothly down a vacuum tube to the basement of his own house, where he mounts another ladder and emerges in his cosy living room. On time too.

He moves into his kitchen and brews a soothing mug of herbal tea. His herb spiral provides him with all the herbs he might ever need, including coriander, dill, curry plant, lemon balm, sage, oregano, thyme, rosemary and lavender, but you don't really need to know that. Nor do I. He carries his tea up to his bedroom and sips it under the covers. He is too weary to clean his teeth or wash his feet. His bedroom was once his workroom but now it's a much more relaxing place.

Having moved all his tools and apparatus to his allotment shed, there's little on display to indicate that he was ever an engineer of rare skill. Just a model of the shed on his windowsill, in every way a perfect copy, with an interior exactly the same as the real one, full of scaled-down working representations of all his tools and apparatus, even including blueprints of the Infinite Train and a trapdoor in the floor that leads to a secret platform for a subterranean vacuum train.

If he can't sleep after an overly relaxing day with his vegetables, Flann von Ryan will occasionally get out of bed and tinker with the contents of this model shed, designing prototypes of prototypes that he can build the following day in his big shed. He's not sure the model shed came after the big one. Maybe the big shed was actually designed inside the model one? In that case, what's the model shed a model *of*? It's an enigma. Luckily an enigma makes a comfortable pillow.

He sleeps the deep sleep of any collection of words on a page. But he's sleepy, so his sleep is even deeper.

Have you seen the newspapers yet? The headlines are incredible. Yes, I'm talking to *you*, so don't sit there with a look on your face as if you've done nothing wrong. That innocent expression of yours won't fool anybody and you'll certainly get the full blame for what occurred. After all, you are the one who put the idea into his mind.

Yes, the police are coming right now but don't imagine that I'll be held responsible too. I'm the author and can rewrite the tale to provide an alibi, to prove I wasn't there when you concocted your treacherous plot. As for Flann von Ryan, he won't suffer either. He's just a character in a story and doesn't exist, whereas you are real.

There's a vast difference between those two conditions, so you're alone to face the brewing storm and it's going to be a huge one, mark my words, so I suggest you get out of that chair and start running now. I can't believe you're still there, still reading this sentence, instead of fleeing for your life and liberty. What's wrong with you?

It's as if these words have some hypnotic effect on you, as if you can't abandon them until they come to an end of their own accord. If that's the case, then maybe I can help you by breaking this sentence and ending the spell like this… What, you're still here! But why? The *police* are coming for you. Because of what happened.

What do you mean, you have no idea what I'm talking about? That's a very poor joke. You should be reading newspapers instead of this story and then you'd know. Always read the news first and fiction later. But as I have no choice other than to believe you, I may as well give you all the details. The event occurred yesterday.

Buckingham Palace was involved in a collision…

It was hit by *another* Buckingham Palace, an exact replica of the first, that came from nowhere at high speed. Someone must have laid invisible rails for the second palace to travel on.

When it collided with the original Buckingham Palace it smashed it to bits and came to rest in the same location, so it appeared to tourists that nothing had really happened other than a loud crash. When they blinked again and looked, the palace was there.

What a cunning trick! What a devious ruse!

The queen is no fool and ran out of her palace the moment she heard the sound of the oncoming building, so her atoms weren't dissipated by the mighty force of the impact and even her crown remained balanced on her head and utterly untarnished.

But then she stopped and turned around. Buckingham Palace was still there! The crash must have been a strange hallucination and it was clearly safe to go back inside and resume her normal regal life without reference to such a revolutionary scenario.

So that's what she did. She noticed nothing amiss as she trudged back up the stairs to her bedroom. To settle her nerves she pulled a silver cord that was connected to the servants' quarters. Footmen rapidly materialised in eager response to her summons.

She ordered a pot of tea and a large plate of scones with clotted cream and raspberry jam. She didn't say please or thank you. Queens don't need to have manners, everyone knows that, but she didn't get what she asked for. She had walked into a trap.

The footmen weren't really footmen but assassins in disguise and they cast off their livery and revealed themselves to be animated garden forks equipped with limited electronic intelligence. The queen raced down the red carpet of a hallway but they quickly caught up with her and then they stabbed and jabbed her to death.

Thus was treason committed in accord with Flann von Ryan's vision. It can be a messy vision sometimes.

And not just any old treason, but the high kind!

Yes, you'll be cast into the deepest dungeon for that, dear reader, and I doubt they'll even let even your skeleton out. Now there's a knocking on the door. Must be the police. As you still seem too lazy or blasé to get out of your chair, I'll open it for you.

Not the police after all. Flann von Ryan.

He has a complaint to make.

"I did exactly what you said and killed the queen but it didn't help my problem with ants at all," he says.

He waits for you to reply, but you don't utter a single word, so he adds angrily, "My allotment's still infested!"

"Come on, Mr von Ryan," I cry, grabbing his shoulder. "Let's get out of here pronto and save ourselves. The reader can bear the full brunt. He's just sitting there, the dullard!"

"Where shall we escape to?" Flann wonders.

"Beyond the end of this story, less than seven sentences away. We'll take a leap off the edge of the prose into the void, while this sap answers the door and gets bundled to jail."

"Sure, that's fine by me, I agree," comes the reply, but I never know if it issues from Flann or from you.

Together, we run and jump and get away…

But at no point along its entire length does this tale bear a resemblance to the famous Borges story. So Flann von Ryan was right in the very first paragraph and I was wrong. Damn!

149

Platform Alteration: The London Underground Mosquito

Did you know that the London Underground is home to unique life-forms that can no longer survive in the outside world? As you ride through those tunnels – or better still even walk through them if you are one of the few – that maybe doesn't seem such a faraway concept. It's a place that speaks to us on a very deep horror-movie sort of level – on the other side of those windows is a unique self-contained world and as spooky a place as you could find on the planet.

But hey – I am not kidding. There really is a unique and genetically distinct form of mosquito called the London Underground Mosquito. It is apparently found in other subway systems and city underworlds as far away as Japan and there is an outlandish theory that it spreads in cargoes of (damp) second hand tires. Its nearest relatives on the surface only attack birds, but this form has adapted to the only food source available in its world – us, and with the occasional rat thrown in. It might sound wild for anything so fragile to survive in those old tunnels continually blasted by gales of passing trains but if you think about it, the environment of the metro tunnels is relatively unchanging, with a constant influx of walking pray and nutrients blown through the dark. You couldn't make this up!

The world we live in is a strange place, and there are always remarkable new things in the most unexpected places – and the possibilities for life are just about endless. That's what the London Underground Mosquito reminds us.

DR

District to Upminster

by Marion Pitman

Sami had a theory, which he started explaining as we passed the barrier at Richmond.

"Speed," he said, "speed beyond a certain point isn't natural. It upsets the waves of reality."

"Upsets the what?"

"Reality is a construct. The intersection of time, space, magnetic fields and mental projection."

"What does that mean?"

He looked at me and sighed. "If I explained," he said, "would you understand?"

"Probably not."

The pigeon got on just before we started, and it pottered about, pecking rather inefficiently at discarded chips and kebabs on the unswept floor. I watched it for a bit, while Sami went on explaining his theory, despite his conviction that I wouldn't understand it.

"G. K. Chesterton," he said suddenly – well he probably didn't, it just swam suddenly up out of the stream of what he was saying, as something I'd heard before. "G. K. Chesterton, you told me once he wrote that it was a miracle that a train to Victoria actually went to Victoria."

"Well, yeah. I think he might have been exaggerating a bit – I mean in principle he regarded it as a miracle, but he probably wasn't that astonished when he got there." Or maybe he was just astonished to find he'd got on the right train. However.

"He was right," said Sami. "Every time a train gets where it's going, it's a victory for the human will over the forces of randomness."

"I suppose it is." I wasn't really thinking much about it, as I was distracted by looking out of the window, and thinking the station we were just leaving should have been Turnham Green and didn't look like it. I checked the map; maybe Turnham Green was closed. The map had been taken down. It was getting dark, so I couldn't see a lot outside once we'd left the station.

"We've passed the point at which the technology is controllable by human strength, you see."

"Have we? What point was that?" I was distracted again by two men behind me talking very loudly about the Test match.

"Some time in the twentieth century –"

Sami was drowned out by a large party of men in white robes, arguing loudly as they walked down the carriage. The lights dimmed as they got to the end, and I didn't see what happened to them. I was beginning to wonder if I'd had too much gin. The pigeon looked up at me, only it was a pied crow, and I was sure that hadn't been there before.

I looked out of the window again; a long level grassland stretched away from the track, and in the middle distance a large group of horsemen were galloping, keeping pace with the train. It didn't, somehow, look like Ravenscourt Park. At the end of the carriage two men were sitting, handcuffed together.

I said to Sami, "Where are we?"

"What?"

"Where are we? I mean what's the next station?"

He glanced at the window and said, "West Kensington. Look, are you listening?"

"Oh yes. But like you said, I don't really follow all of it. As far as I can understand it you're saying that the technology is now out of our control, and it could be doing anything. This train is no more likely to finish up at Upminster than at Ongar or Manchester Piccadilly or Gdansk."

He sighed. "I knew you'd oversimplify. You just don't do abstract, do you? It's always got to be a concrete example."

"That's the way I think. You know that."

The pied crow was now an ibis, and the window was obscured by people clinging to the outside of the train. It looked very hot out there, somehow. We went into a tunnel and all the lights went out. I thought very hard about Earl's Court. Sami went on talking. I closed my eyes and concentrated.

When I opened them again, we were pulling into a station; it was almost Earl's Court but not quite. A couple who looked just like Trevor Howard and Celia Johnson were standing beside the train, gazing into each other's eyes. I wasn't terribly surprised. The pigeon was back, though, looking a bit confused. I looked out again as we started; some of it was right, I saw the sign that says Tower Hill – Stops Here – Barking; and then I remembered they'd changed the indicators and it shouldn't have looked like that.

Gloucester Road seemed to be full of refugees, but it might have been an art installation. I didn't manage to notice South Ken because a fight broke out and a passing waiter dropped a tray of drinks on Sami's briefcase. He got angry about it without apparently noticing that drinks waiters on District Line trains were an unusual sight, to say the least. I wondered fleetingly if he carried the abstract thing too far. The carriage was very full, and there was a lot of jostling. Sloane Square is always dark anyway – could have been anywhere. I pinned my hopes to Victoria. I concentrated very hard, thinking about G. K. Chesterton, and the human will, and I probably prayed a bit too. I tried to picture Victoria Station, as it were, in essence, without too many details that I might get wrong. I concentrated on the pigeon being a pigeon, too. I found I had to keep pushing a picture of Isambard Kingdom Brunel out of my head.

My concentration was broken by Sami's elbow in my ribs – "Come on, this is Victoria, we get out here."

It looked all right, so far as I could tell. We were supposed to change and get the Victoria Line, but I said I'd got claustrophobia, and insisted on getting a bus. I was feeling a bit tired, and I wasn't sure I could keep us going to Oxford Circus.

I'm a bit worried about the man in the stovepipe hat I saw at the top of the escalator.

Wi-Fi Enabled Bakerloo Sunset

RD Hodkinson

Archduke Soupy van Brilliantine sits down on a cool metal bucket seat and wonders vaguely what he is doing on the northbound platform of Marylebone tube station.

He wonders, though less vaguely, whether the pressure on his skull is a result of alcoholic excess or of some physical contusion, and he wonders most specifically why he has lighted on 'Archduke Soupy van Brilliantine' when that is almost certainly not his name. At least, he hopes not.

He stifles a giggle and snorts it back in. He's been doing that a lot, he decides, giggling. He remembers nothing of his recent (or indeed his distant) past, but a good deal of giggling was involved he feels sure, and such expressions of incontinent glee are inappropriate to his predicament. His predicament, it appears, is parlous. He is in a fix. This is not a giggling matter, not at all. And yet, here comes another one, one he can't suppress, and Archduke Soupy blows a snotty bubble of mirth right there on the platform. Stop it Soupy, he thinks, stop it Soupy or whatever your name is, this is serious.

In a little more detail, the nature of the predicament facing Archduke Soupy van Brilliantine is this: he has no idea how he came to be on the northbound platform of the Bakerloo Line, no recollection of ever entering Marylebone Station and, more seriously, not a clue about anything that has happened to him in his life ever. Ever. No memory of falling asleep down here, no memory of waking up.

So, no laughing matter, then. In fact it is safe to say that, in all his 28 years on the planet, this is the most un-laughingest matter he ever… whoa there. What was that? Rewind Sparky.

28 years? Soupy is 28? Well, that's something – it's a start. Suddenly things are looking a bit brighter. Why don't we quit the giggling for a second and pause to consider the facts as we know them: here is a man in the prime of life, quite possibly the scion of a noble family and, insofar as it is possible to tell, in tolerably good health. The headache, all things considered, is likely to be a result of perfectly conventional young-aristocrat-style debauchery, Prince Harry – God bless him – having given young-aristocrat-style debauchery the shot in the arm it has so badly needed since the death of Queen Victoria. This is all good news, and for the first time Soupy feels he has a grip, a degree of self-control and he celebrates by daring to examine his clothing for the first time since coming to. An element of risk is involved here, a steady nerve required because they can tell a lot about a fellow can the old threads, so gently does it, Soupy. Downstairs first: a solid pair of brogues – leather soles – not new but not bad. Sober grey woollen trousers of a cut that defies generic classification, hence neither on the sartorial cutting edge nor actually unfashionable. Reassuring. A calf-length black wool coat that could be cleaner – the odd mud stain, a loose button – but is obviously of sound provenance. Expensive gear, slightly soiled knees: the attire of a young aristo in full debauch mode, surely.

Soupy giggles audibly again, and again he tries to shut himself the hell up, but too late. The sound that emerges is thin, forced and unconvincing. It falls flat to the platform, barely troubling the tunnel's prodigious echo. It is a lonely sound and it frightens Soupy. He is alone on a deserted underground station and he doesn't know why. Nice trousers are all very well, but he doesn't know what he will do when a train arrives. He doesn't even know whether he wants to *go* north on the northbound Bakerloo line. Does he want to go anywhere? Why doesn't he just leave? Why doesn't he *want* to leave?

Actually, Soupy may know the answer to that last part. He doesn't want to leave because this place makes him feel safe. It's the rails, he thinks, the certainties they offer; north or south, that's it. Those are your options: north, south, east or west, the occasional cross-town diagonal, choices, limited and prescriptive, laid out for you generations ago by men with bowler hats and large moustaches. You could really see it down here, the shining steel superstructure of the city, arterial, functional, essential, underpinning past and present, Edwardian and modern, Victorian and cyber-aged, the humming engineered solution to a crazed and riven metropolis. Who wouldn't feel safe down here? Who wouldn't, when push comes to shove, choose to hide down here?

This is how the thought occurs to Soupy that he might be down here hiding from something. It's not a comforting thought, it is a greasy, queasy kind of thought, and not as unfamiliar a thought as he might have hoped. Hiding from what? From whom? In truth, it is a thought that would rattle the stoutest chap, but Archduke Soupy knows what he must do to dispatch such a thought to the outer darkness, and he does it. He stands up briskly, takes some invigorating deep breaths and shakes his arms about in the accepted manner of a British man readying himself for decisive action. He strides a purposeful eight feet to the edge of the platform and a purposeful eight feet back again. He stretches a confident neck left and right to make a businesslike assessment of the cream and brown tiled décor and estimates, in a bold and assertive manner, the length of the platform as being no greater than 150 metres. Then he sits down again and admits that he has no idea what to do and, moreover, that he is shitting himself.

Still, standing up and striding about seems the only positive thing to do right now, the alternative being to sit still and shit oneself, so he is about to propel himself into some affirmative pacing – possibly accompanied by manly throat-clearing and harrumphing – when he catches sight of a dim figure at the far end of the platform. And he could swear it is Princess Pinky de Tootsie-Roll.

"Your Highness…" he almost calls out, but he catches the words just in time, because he knows that the sound would scare him some more, and because Princess Pinky has disappeared from view, perhaps into one of the platform's many exits end entrances, the obscure hodinterchanges and service tunnels common to all tube stations. Soupy does not feel up to exploring the occluded labyrinth, especially as he carries in his gut a troubling sense that Princess Pinky will not be at all pleased to see him. Whoever she is. Whoever *he* is.

So instead of pursuing his princess (his? that's a thought), Soupy continues his impression of manful activity, forcefully evacuating his upper respiratory tract and yawning the expansive yawn of the supremely self-assured, the sort of yawn Gordon of Khartoum must have yawned on that fateful morn, or General Wolfe on the Plains of Abraham. Down on the silver tracks he notes not Gordon's murderous Sudanese or the retreating French, but tube mice engaged in their usual business of scurrying and whatnot. Softening to their engaging presence but without slackening his newly adopted military resolve, he takes consolation from the workaday activities of the mice, from their lack of concern, their part in the natural order of things. He relaxes enough to allow himself a few moments' reflection on rodent ecologies in subterranean transport systems: why, for instance, does London have industrious little mice, sleek and appealing, while New York has rats that could drag a prop forward to his doom?

The observation calms and encourages Soupy, suggesting, as it does, that he may have first-hand experience of mass transit systems from around the globe, experience that would mark him as a well-travelled sort, perhaps even a man of means. His instinctive affection for the Bakerloo mouse over the New York rat might indicate, also, that he is a native Londoner, and it occurs to Soupy that, on the point of his nationality at least, a simple test might clarify the situation and add another level of substance to his ephemeral self. "Hello", he says, then more boldly "Hello. I am Archduke Soupy van Brilliantine and I am here to claim my birthright." The vowels that echo along the drab tiles are plump, round and pleased with themselves. Thank God, he thinks. Thank *God*. English.

Unless. Unless all accents sound unaccented to the ear of the speaker. I mean, wouldn't Americans do something about that nasal 'nang nang' noise they make if they could really hear themselves? Concerned, he tries again: "How now brown cow. The rain in Spain stays mainly on the plain." No, definitely English, but what kind of English? There's English and then there's English. There's the English of healthy ruddy-faced girls stomping about fields in Shropshire savouring the rub of tweed on thigh, the hearty suck of Wellington in cowpat. And then there's the English of the whippet-faced, crack-for-breakfast, lock-up full of stolen Beamer hubcaps proletarian scum. And although Soupy tacitly accepts that his prejudice in the matter suggests that he leans more toward the Shropshire cowpat crowd than the crack-whippet set, he clears his throat and puts his elocution to the test: "Cam on you 'ammerz! 'Ave 'im Psycho, do 'iz aynkles!" No, not right, that. So then: "Play up Cambridge! Heave, boys, heave!" Oh yes, much more the sort of thing, and with some relief Soupy places himself securely in the middle-to-upper rank of English society. Big relief, that, he has to admit. And he is about to begin a swift hands-only examination of his genitals to further firm-up details of race and ethnicity when he spots something that might offer all the answers. To everything. Because under the row of seats on which he has been sitting is a small, soft, black case in which, he instinctively knows, is a laptop, an infallible window on the world, on life, the universe and on Soupy himself. This is the information age, the answers are at hand, buzzing through the ether, bombarding him even down here: the age of the moon; Scarlet Johansson's cup size; the coefficient of linear expansion; the box score of the 1932 World Series and… and. His name. All the answers, so many answers that, standing there, he can actually feel their tide now, great energetic clouds of answers that swim about him, protons in a particle accelerator, a boiling soup of answers, a determined tsunami of empiricism. Thank Christ, he thinks, thank Christ for wi-fi. Hope the battery's charged.

And it is. The case unfolds and the lid of the chic little Mac flips open with an action reassuringly familiar to Soupy, his fingers instinctive in engaging the power button, in finding their habitual position over the keys, activating the bright screen, its ordered queues of electrons as logical and comforting as the steel rails of the Underground. This is Soupy's machine, no doubt about it, and he opens up his web browser to give material form to that maelstrom of answers, a circling galaxy so dense that it seems to make the still subterranean air move.

It does move. Something in the atmosphere shifts almost imperceptibly, but shifts enough to startle Soupy. There is a distant hum, an inaudible bass note and a movement across his skin – a train, not close, but somewhere, pushing pillars of stale, warm air through miles of inky tunnels and empty stations and stirring a page of discarded newspaper which lifts a languid corner in the draft, drawing Soupy's eye to the far end of the platform where a still, dark figure watches him.

Before he can even register surprise, someone closer laughs a tinny, abbreviated laugh and a flash of floral-print fabric disappears into a side tunnel. Princess Pinky, he is sure. And the other guy is familiar too. Familiar but suddenly gone, and Soupy stands up so quickly he almost spills his laptop. He wants to call out to Pinky and the other guy, wants to call them over, to normalise relations, but at the same time he wants them to be anywhere but here, anywhere at all and, again, he doesn't know why. So he stands dumb and stupid, goggling down an empty platform with the computer gripped at chest height, hands and feet insensible, jaw loose, bowels tight, and he listens. Listens really hard.

But the laughter has stopped and the only thing moving on the station is the air, shooed along by that far-off train, invisible but announcing its incremental progress through minute changes in air pressure, like an approaching storm head.

Still clenched and crazy-eyed, Soupy sits and tries to direct his attention to the laptop. "Nice trousers," he thinks, "good shoes, tube mice, tube mice…" and slowly his respiration slows and he registers that the Google homepage has opened up. Automatically he checks the bookmark bar at the top of the window. The BBC website is up there. OK. Gmail. To be expected. Wikipedia. All good, but nothing else, no magic key to his identity. Nonetheless Soupy finds himself morally buoyed and somewhat relieved by this bland menu of favoured sites. Nothing very helpful there, but the absence of paedofilth.com or wizardwars.tv or crochetworld.co.uk is a boost. It might just be – despite his current situation, despite the fact that his associates and acquaintances appear to be messing with his mind, that their presence invokes in him a very particular sense of dread – that despite all this, he may actually be a nice ordinary bloke who has done nothing to call down on himself this slightly biblical torment. He clicks on the Gmail tab but, as anticipated, he needs a user name and password to access his account. He has neither. Archduke something? Unlikely.

More movement down the platform as shifting air moves the stray newspaper and something pale and soundless enters his peripheral vision and disappears again. He looks but sees nothing except, perhaps, a stirring in the tunnel itself, something sensed rather than seen, gone now, and probably a mouse or a blown leaf of litter or a curling finger of that fog that has been getting everywhere. And Soupy remembers the fog. The fog and Princess Pinky in the fog, laughing and waving her voluminous sleeves in the dirty light, cutting vampiric poses. And the other guy in black, Tonto something, and the stiff in the cricket sweater who nobody invited sitting on the back of a park bench under a Victorian reproduction streetlamp, laughing at Pinky and doing what? Doing something but mainly laughing at Pinky as she dips in and out of the shadows beyond the sepia cone of light, dips in and out and sometimes falls over and laughs and gets up and falls over again and then doesn't get up. "Pinky…" breathes Soupy, but the word is cut short because at the end of the platform – no, closer than that – he sees a collapsed form, a strewn fabric heap, garish and discordant like the spilled contents of a charity shop. It is Princess Pinky and she can't get up.

He closes his eyes tight and inhales violently. He does it again and when he opens his eyes, collapsed Pinky, the debris of Pinky is gone. "Why don't I just leave?" he thinks but knowing as he thinks it that he can't navigate the tunnels, the blind corners, the clanking steam-age stairwells that stand between him and the street. "Why am even here?" he moans, knowing the answer, knowing now that he is hiding here, and not successfully.

The laptop is still gripped by both hands. He stares at it, at first without seeing it at all, then as the numbing black cloud begins to disperse ("nice trousers, good shoes…") he remembers that this alien object is his computer and that his computer does – must – hold the answers. He clicks on the tab that opens the BBC news website. The BBC has answers – David Attenborough, Jeremy Paxman, Simon Schama – authoritative conduits of truth, definitive inarguable truth, and like all Englishmen in times of crisis he turns to the BBC, home and beauty, mother's milk, Jackanory, Newsnight, the shipping forecast, and did those feet in ancient times…

The local ambience shifts again as the unseen train stirs the air, and Soupy becomes aware of another atmospheric layer imposing itself, quiet conversational voices in the connecting tunnels, voices swelling and dying, a broadcast from a badly tuned radio, dialogue caught on the wind. Pinky is speaking and so is Tonto – Big Chief Tonto Pees-in-Hot-Tub – and someone else, he thinks, the stiff maybe. In the cricket sweater.

He struggles to tune them out, bowing his head until the little computer screen fills the whole of his vision and he takes comfort in the machine's consoling hum, almost loud enough to exclude the sound of voices. Seeing no evil, hearing no evil he cups himself over the Mac, focusing on the BBC, gripping the glowing umbilical to the world above.

He opens the London news page hoping for an item on tube stations, on unexpected blackouts, mysteriously displaced persons. It's a funny town – there could be dozens of amnesiacs waking up on empty platforms, it could be the fashionable phenomenon *de jour*, a virus or a terrorist gas attack or global warming or something. Something to do with the fog. But the evidence of the local news page suggests that Soupy's predicament is unique or at least very bloody rare. There's lots of stuff about the fog of course, and the screamers, and the dead girl in the canal but nothing to do with perfectly blameless young men finding a blank slate where their memories should be, an epidemic of his hopeful imagination: tube station tabula rasa. There's none of that, and the worst of it, Soupy realises, is that he may not *be* that perfectly blameless young man after all, a thought that carries a heavy resonance. It rings a bell does that thought. It is a nasty thought, one he would rather not have, one so unsettling that it seems to inspire a physical manifestation, because despite holding his face so close to the screen that he can barely focus on the text, Soupy is aware of movement a few feet to his right. Without lifting his forehead from the lid of the laptop he turns a reluctant eye to the fallen form of Princess Pinky ten paces away, a nebula of collapsed swathes and jarring prints and textures. Only the hair, dirty blonde, braided and dreadlocked, is identifiable as belonging to the girl herself, but the clothes are unmistakable, and very slowly they begin to shift now, first disturbed by the train-shunted air (getting quite close, that train) and then rising on the struggling body inside, the hair lifting in listless stages from the dusty platform until Soupy can see a white and mottled brow, an unhealthy shade for skin, then cheek bones, an eye socket, sharper than they ought to be, and then the face of Princess Pinky, not the animated laughing face from the park bench or the flushed, excited face of better times, but one that is blue-veined, livid, spit-flecked, and looking at Soupy with a penetrating yellow-eyed hatred.

He has time to recognise the distant figure of Tonto, also rising from the platform and the stiff in the cricket sweater emerging from the northern tunnel entrance with a curious swimming motion before he closes his eyes and wills them gone. And they are. He flashes hot glances in both directions along the platform, and he is alone but for the breathy sub-bass of the oncoming train and the hollow chime of voices deep in the invisible tiled spaces behind.

He grips the laptop harder and pushes his forehead against the sharp lip of the lid until the pain registers as real, as physical and manageable. His breath is quick and shallow, his extremities numb. He senses that a sort of countdown is in operation, that his time and his options are finite and severely limited. He battles to restart his conscious brain, to join-up a few lonely archipelagos of rational thought and direct their focus toward the computer and on its precious intimations of life *up there*. How good it all looks, the real world, how wholesome, uncomplicated, life affirming – look! look how the economy is failing! See how the government is standing firm over public sector pensions, how Arsenal lose in Europe, the royals tour Sri Lanka, fog halts tubes and trains, dental floss causes cancer, concerns raised over Mars probe, union leader in benefits row, bodies in park man sought.

And there it is.

Bodies in Park Man. It is his name. His real name, the only operative name in the circumstances. He reads further and all their names are there, the names of Princess Pinky de Tootsie-Roll, of Big Chief Tonto Pees-in Hot-Tub, of the stiff in the cricket sweater who no-one invited and of Archduke Soupy van Brilliantine himself. But those names, the names their mothers gave them, don't matter now, because the only names that really matter down here right now and probably forever are Bodies in Park Man. And Bodies in Park. Plural.

It's all there on the BBC in emphatic sans serif: Bodies in Park Man Sought; Bodies in Park Man Leaves Scene; Bodies in Park Man, 28; Bodies in Park Man, known to police, previous convictions, Oxford educated, drugs offences, petty theft, surgeon father, family appeals; Bodies in Park Man. Him.

Bodies in Park. Them.

And then the other stuff not on the BBC: Princess Pinky in a nightclub; Princess Pinky naked on the beach at Brighton; Princess Pinky dressed as a cowgirl doing a line; shooting up, handing over the green, handing over the green to him, to Bodies in Park Man. And the pay-as-you-go phone calls, those coded communiqués that fooled no-one: Princess Pinky, your cupcakes are ready for icing; Big Chief Pees-in-Hot-Tub, the butter for your asparagus will be churned this evening; Princess, your muffins are baking; Big Chief, the buffalo are plentiful on the prairie tonight. The covert transactions, the packages handed over with a wink, a laugh, the zip-locked plastic bags, the foil raps, the gummy bear packets when things got tight, the good stuff, the barely cut stuff, the absolutely historic stuff, the okay stuff, the not-so-good stuff and the other stuff, the stuff from last night, the stuff in the park, gummy bear stuff at best, untested, new supply, cheap, cheap, cheap and him skint, skint, skint.

So, there. He is where he needs to be after all, down, down where the city begins and where the city ends. And he can feel the breath now, hot, soft and strong from the tunnel, cold, thin and regular from the three who stand beside him, unseen because Archduke Soupy has shut his eyes to the cruel immutability of the BBC, and he keeps his eyes closed as he locks the laptop and lets it slide to the floor, standing, feeling the whirr of charged particles, the competing pulses of answers that surround him, redundant and unwelcome now that he has more answers than he can handle. The heel of a solid brogue, a brogue with Hyde Park mud still clinging to the sole, crushes the computer lid as Soupy begins his slow walk toward the platform edge. The sound of the approaching train, actual mechanical sounds of wheel on track, of gears and loose body panels, can be heard over the rush of air, and Soupy is buffeted by eddies, by sooty vortices drawing down the smells of steam power and hot iron, ancient and unchanging even as he stands in the digitised midstream of the present, erect against the shrapnel of unwanted answers. The wind is the wind of Edwardian enterprise, of optimism and progress and as it grows stronger he opens his nostrils to its power and solidity, blocking out the white noise of the present day and the sibilants of the three who follow him to the edge of the northbound platform of the Bakerloo line at Marylebone Station, he, registering only the currents of an older, uncorrupted London and not the small, cold hand, insistent in the small of his back as first one foot and then the other slips over the concrete threshold, down, free at last of answers, and toward the consoling steel cradle, the pulverising bedrock of the city and into the uncontested darkness beneath the first northbound Bakerloo line train of the morning.

Platform Alteration: The DLR Shuffle

London's DLR is the scene of one of the politest yet most dramatic passenger confrontations in the entire world's transport network. It is a battle that takes place dozens of times every day, yet few visitors unfamiliar with the train will ever even notice.

This situation arises because of the glorious quirk of driverless trains – that the front seats have *forward looking windows* and you can sit there and imagine that you are actually driving it – fulfilling that almost universal childhood dream. The other quirk is that these driverless trains are very often driven after all, by some poor sod of a service agent who isn't even given an actual cabin and is thus reduced to sitting among the passengers operating a small control panel in a cabinet. No wonder they so often seem pissed off. But the upshot is *front right. Front right* – the seat you have to get and a seat worth fighting for.

Terminus stations are the key of course, since once the train is running and taking passengers, you might as well forget it. *Front Right* might as well be a million miles away. But at those stations where the train sweeps in, disgorges everybody and then waits patiently to reverse with a fresh load – that is the battleground. As you wait at Bank, or Lewisham, or Stratford, or some other terminus, you might notice a small knot of people all standing at a certain point near the end of the platform. Watch closer as the train arrives and you will see that the first set of doors lines up with them almost perfectly. They *know* you see.

The DLR shuffle is about very gently placing yourself in the best possible position, while using the classic British passion for personal space as a weapon. You edge a few inches closer to your opponent, still not looking at them in any way, and it becomes a battle of wills. You can sense the electricity in the air – the crackle of personal space being violated *just enough* to maybe edge that person away a few inches, but without ever breeching the impeccable British manners. Or alternately, you fail and are forced to retreat yourself.

I guarantee you will exchange no words with your opponent or opponents – you will just monitor them quietly out of the corner of your eye as you slowly shuffle around the platform, each seeking the most optimum position from which to launch your big push. Just as they will be monitoring you. In your head, you are trying calculate the distance between the train's nose and it's first set of doors, trying to edge just those precious few centimetres nearer than your opponents. As the train stops, politeness still rules the world of course, and you all wait with impeccable manners for people to disembark. At this point, it is as though someone with a starting gun is saying *on your marks, get set . . .*

And then, at the earliest possible polite moment, you are off! There is no running. No one shoves or pushes. This war is fought almost entirely based on one's positioning on the platform, so it is a game of skill and forethought (and luck) rather than violence. As you launch yourself forward, you feel that same exhilaration an athlete must feel as they leave the starting block. And very quickly, indeed almost instantly, you know whether your gambits and positioning have succeeded or doomed you to failure. You sail through the double doors of the train, aware of the position of every one of your opponents with meticulous clarity – and you casually stroll through the corridor and your arse plops comfortably into *front right*. You give a sigh of satisfaction as your opponents take the seat behind you or settle sheepishly somewhere else, further back in the train. The driver gives you a brief glance out of the corner of the eye – seen it all before. But you can take some satisfaction in knowing that you have mastered the DLR shuffle and won . . .

DR

Stratford International

David McGroarty

David McGroarty

ISLE OF DOGS, 1985

The boys were playing soldiers. There was a coarse dust drifting over the yard from the construction site next door and it worked its way into their clothes and throats and noses. They screwed up their faces. Some of the older kids made a big show of blowing out one nostril with an index finger pressed against the other. Owen Green, who reckoned he was the smallest if not the youngest, and did not know any of the other boys but his cousin David, rubbed his eyes when he thought no one was looking and tried not to cough.

It was not much of a game. A boy called Javed, who had a moustache and looked to Owen to be at least twelve, was the General, and the only rule appeared to be that whatever he told you to do, you did.

"Hey," he said to Owen. He turned to David: "Wossisname?"

"Owen."

"I call him Owie. Owie, you're on guard, bruv. The Russians are coming. Stand on that wall."

He pointed to what was in fact the leftovers of a wall, one of a small number of visible relics, remnants of the warehouse or packing house or factory that had once occupied the site. When Owen climbed the wall, even from a modest height of five feet or so, he could see the old building's floorplan scratched out across the surface of the yard – a blueprint in concrete and broken brick. Narrow runways of rotten vinyl marked the corridors; cracked tiles and twisted pipes, the bathrooms.

"You stay there," the General said. He called to his troops, "If he comes down without my permission, shoot him dead." And the boys ran off to conspire in a corner of the yard where some shattered ceramic had been bulldozed into a jagged heap.

Owen was relieved to be out of the game. The boys were all local, and said things like *nuffink* and *innit*, and everything was *nawha'amean*. He had only moved up to Millwall from Kent the week before, and not gladly. He hadn't understood what it meant when Mum told him they would be living with Grandad on the Isle of Dogs, but had found the name of the place obliquely unenticing. For him, Isle meant distance and isolation from comfort, and the Dogs quickly came to mean the shiny Dobermans that drooled at the gates of all the empty factories. Now he imagined that these wild children, whose parents never came looking for them, were the dogs, running across the bleak Isle in their pack, following General Javed. He felt more comfortable at a distance from them.

And he was glad to be out of the house, Grandad's damp terraced house that smelled forever of fried fish. He was glad to be out and away from Grandad and Mum, with either of whom he could happily spend his time alone, but never together. The place felt emptier when the three of them were at home than at any other time. The long silences ached in his gut. The air was full of waiting, like the family court had been. Like hospitals. David said Owen's mother was hanging on for Grandad to die. She shouted through the wall when the old man moaned in the night. One time he fell over and she wouldn't help him up, just sat on the settee and watched him wriggle on the floor. But she sent Owen out to play that afternoon with a grin while Grandad slept upstairs. She waved him off from the door like she would have done back in Sevenoaks and gave him no curfew. He thought he might stay out until six at least.

From the top of the wall, he could see over the fence into the site where they were building the new railway line. The construction was in evidence across the Isle of Dogs in the hoardings that bordered the streets and the pairs of concrete struts that poked up from behind them, but with a little height, Owen could see the scale of the thing. It was a brutal undertaking, dead straight and stopping for nothing. The line cut terraces in two, crossed parks and waterways. In places, the viaducts that would eventually hold the trains aloft were complete, and he had a sense of elevated vehicles gliding quietly over the rooftops of a futuristic landscape, a place of shining metal and sharp angles.

In the corner of the yard, from somewhere, an older boy had come among the little pack, his broken voice carrying over the younger children's pre-pubescent shrieking. Standing on his lookout on the wall, Owen could see only the youth's head, pink and shaved raw. Although he could not make out the words, he understood that the broken, faltering quality of whatever was being said meant trouble.

Spontaneously, the group dispersed, the smaller boys bursting like sparks away from the skinhead and scattering. Owen then observed three things in turn: his cousin, running towards him with a strained expression that was hard to interpret; the skinhead, his white vest, his thin arm and the long, ugly knife at the end of it; and the boy, Javed, kneeling prayer-like at the skinhead's side, his forehead resting, lightly, almost purposefully, in the centre of a dark red puddle on the concrete.

Owen ran. The top of the wall took him to the edge of the yard and he jumped over the fence and into the building site. He heard David calling to him from the other side of the fence, but he did not stop, did not look back, could not process anything except the urgency of getting away. Somewhere further along, the new line ran alongside the back of the estate where his grandfather – where he – lived. He only had to follow it.

He ran. The air was different behind the hoarding. There was a smell of wet stone, a clean smell. The dust was thicker; he felt it on his skin as he gained speed. And as he ran he found he did not want to stop, because there was no impediment, no barrier. He ran a perfect straight line between the pillars, beneath the viaduct, leapt puddles and ditches at speeds that were beyond expectation and belief. He could not stop. Everything that was not the line dissolved – the streets outside, the factories and the dogs. His feet no longer touched the earth. He was airborne. And the dust was everywhere.

ISLE OF DOGS, 2005

Owen boarded the Docklands Light Railway at Poplar depot and performed his checks. It was five in the morning and upon leaving the depot he found himself alone on the automated train, a passenger service agent with no passengers to serve – no cleaners, no cooks, no homeward-headed nightworkers – through several miles and several stations.

It was common enough, on an early shift, that he would ride alone, and he relished it. He would wake at ten-to-four in the flat in Millwall, leave his mother sleeping in Grandad's old room, eat his toast in the taxi – dismissing the cabbie's flaccid banter with a few well-placed grunts – and if he was lucky he could start work without having to speak to anyone at all.

This way he placated the little curled snake of panic that lived, day and night, in his gut. It was a well-practiced routine, refined over years, and it pushed the anxiety down until he reached his train. The depot was the danger zone. He could seldom avoid the banal interactions with colleagues that brought the acid into his throat. *Morning, Green. Cheer up, son. Might never 'appen.* They hated him: *Owen Green, freakshow, lives with his mum.* He learned to keep his face turned down, grunt his replies.

Here on the line, he was free from all of that. The platforms glided into alignment and out again. The sunlight, scattered by the skyscrapers, the windows, the water, entered the train a hundred different ways. He stood in the centre of the aisle at the front of the train, looking out, braced against the seat backs on either side, his eyes closed against the glare.

This is like heaven, he thought. *I'm dead here.*

He worked the whole network but this was his line. It was his line, and he knew its turns and contours. Through the steady force of repetition, the journey had worn a groove across his city, a route that his thoughts of the East End would always follow, over Poplar at height and speed, North then East, to Stratford. The streets around might as well not have been there.

There would have been an occasion – a single journey – upon which he passed by the old yard in Millwall and for the first time did not see the outline of a factory on the ground below and recall at once the curled form of the young man, bleeding into the dirt and dust. Certainly, he now sped by the spot six or seven times each day without giving it a thought. The yard had long since been torn up.

But when the empty train stopped dead on its track beside the flats that now occupied the lot, he knew at once where it had brought him. He glanced down, imagining the skinhead beneath the train on the back lawn of the block, looking up at him, squeezing his bloody knife, his lips moving, chanting silently.

The train hung in silence for a moment. There was a blast of static from the control panel by the doors. The sunlight had faded. A fine layer of dust coated the windows.

A human form sat on the front seat beside him: a figure, wrapped in dirty sheets from its feet to the top of its head so that there was nothing of the human to be seen other than its outline. He was unstartled by its presence – it seemed always to have been there, although he had no memory of seeing it. And he found he could hardly bear to look at it; it was like looking over the edge of a cliff. Vertigo. When he tried to take it in, to comprehend it, his footing failed him.

Instead, he spun and began to walk down the aisle away from the thing, but there was a sustained static roar from the control panel which stopped him in mid-step. There were sounds amongst the white noise: voices, laughter.

He turned again. "Is everything okay, Sir?" he said. He laughed at the absurdity of his own words – a strained *Ha!* The figure was in the aisle now and moving towards him, imperceptibly, like a distant ship whose movement only registers when looked at askew. Every glance at the window or floor brought the thing closer. By the time it was standing fully in front of him, Owen had surrendered to it. He could not look away, and did not try.

It stood. The top of what would have been its head was at the height of his chest. Its shrouds were hemp, linen, Paisley-patterned silk, all faded to the same murky shade of brown. It had no ask.

The windows of the car were now so coated in dust that the only light to penetrate was a dull orange and the sun was a cool disc in a corner of the front windscreen. Owen raised his hand to where the figure's face should have been and peeled away a strip of silk. The fabric came apart like it was rotten, though it was bone dry to the touch, and a puff of grey dust came up. He raised the other hand. Another layer, another cloud of dust, stone dust, coarse and dry. He stripped the thing down, tearing the fabric away in long ribbons. Some pieces came away to reveal pockets of powdered stone too dense to disperse in the air, which scattered over the floor and over his shoes. Before long, the thing less resembled a human than a pile of rags, and the dust was everywhere, inside the train and out, in Owen's hair and stinging his eyes and catching the back of his throat.

He felt the train jolt and begin to move again, but he couldn't escape the dust. It forced his eyes closed and then his throat. He curled over, still feeling the humps and turns of the track as he blacked out, still following the line in his mind.

It brought him to Stratford. Like a ghost on the rail, the train floated into the station at five-thirty with only him aboard. He opened his eyes and found himself on the floor in the aisle as the doors opened. Some commuters boarded and stood around him.

"You alright, mate?"

"Should I call an ambulance?"

The car was again flooded with sunlight. The floor was clean and slightly damp and smelling of bleach. He stood up, shook his head, and pushed through the bystanders and onto the platform, where he sat in the sun with his head in his hands, fighting nausea, until the train wheezed off again, back the way it came in.

The incident was reported. A concerned commuter, who had boarded the train at Stratford, told another passenger agent how she had found Owen kneeling, unconscious, in the aisle, his forehead resting gently on the floor. The account was filed, and sat in a supervisor's inbox until later the same week when trains beneath Paddington, Bloomsbury and Spitalfields, and a number 30 bus, were attacked by suicide bombers, and all reports of extraordinary incidents or unusual behaviour were sifted carefully by investigating officers. Closed circuit footage did not verify Owen's claim to have passed out, rather it showed him in the centre of the car mouthing the same unintelligible words repeatedly and drawing his finger across his throat before lowering himself carefully to the floor, as if under the order of some unseen authority. In the climate created by the attacks it was easier for the company, which had never liked him, to sack him as a potential threat to passengers, rather than (as they might have been forced before) to offer him any sort of support.

Owen told his mother that he had quit, and wanted to get a job in the City instead and to work his way up, but while she saw him on the job sites, eating toast and making enquiries between cups of tea, instead of going for interviews and meetings he went out and rode the driverless trains across the Isle of Dogs, always alone and always back to Stratford.

STRATFORD, 2012

The flow of people, of thought, of intention, had turned Eastbound. The rail routes, beneath the ground and on the ground and suspended in air, bore a hundred-thousand a day, all away from the city, to Stratford. Everyone came together there. They pressed their hands on the windows of their trains and snapped the Stadium, the Orbit and the Copperbox with their smartphones. They wrapped themselves in their national flags and, smiling, allowed themselves to be jostled by their fellow passengers, and squeezed and channelled into the Olympic Park. Each night they dispersed into surrounding England, but in the morning they came back to Stratford. Everything came together at Stratford.

Owen rode with them on his line several days a week, got off the train and stood like an island in the swelling crowd. He scanned the visitors' faces, listened in on their conversations. The city's topography had changed. The centre of gravity had shifted. He felt it. A bottle of wine and he would sit for hours at the side of the road and just watch the people move. He had nowhere else to go.

On the final day of the summer games, Owen sat by the track at Stratford International and looked at the high-speed trains that were coming through from Kent. They paused here, four every hour, before roaring off again. The yellow-nosed international trains from Europe did not stop, or even slow down. They sent the dust flying up as they powered through towards Central London.

He sat for most of the morning, and then it occurred to him that he had been waiting for something to happen, and it hadn't, so he left.

At Stratford Station, the train home was packed. He stood in the aisle, wedged himself between a Spanish family and a group of loud American students. The Spanish father put his foot on top of Owen's toes and one of his daughters was wailing, "*Estoy tan cansada!*"

As the imminent departure was announced, there was a scuffle behind Owen's back, one of the American men shouting, "My wallet, you little prick." Owen could not turn to see – there was no space to turn into – but he looked over his shoulder, straining his neck. He saw the American's face distorted by the pressure of a white-knuckled hand, the hand's heel under the American's jaw, skinny white fingers in his eyes and mouth. There was a teenaged boy in a tracksuit, whose hand it was, and whose face was distorted in a near-perfect reflection of the American's, the American's own broad, hairy hand pressed hard against his cheek. They stood like this, locked in a grim *pas-de-deux*, until another American student intervened, breaking the symmetry and shoving the teenager backwards towards the door.

In an instant, there was space on the train where before had been none. The passengers scattered away from the scuffle, falling into one another's laps and across the backs of seats. Owen found himself standing in the clear, and he saw the teenager reach into the elastic waistband of his trousers.

When Owen saw the knife in the boy's grip, he felt the air change, like stepping into the shade on a hot day. It was a crude thing, the kind of chef's knife that might be sold for a pound in a supermarket. The onlookers, for the most part, did not react. One or two parents picked their children up and held them to their chests. Many only looked on as though they were watching a performance. But Owen was transformed. There was a rushing in his face and neck, a sensation he hadn't felt since the afternoon he had run through the half-built railway cutting in Millwall as a boy. He imagined he could smell the wet concrete, and could feel the stone dust in the inner corners of his eyes.

And it occurred to Owen that the line had always been bringing him to Stratford, always to here and now, even twenty-two years ago – before they had finished building it – the line had been trying to deliver him here.

An alarm sounded; the doors were about to close. Just as he had in Millwall, Owen felt suddenly freed by the straightness of his course, the lack of impediment. He charged at the youth and pushed him backwards through the closing door. As the boy fell, he slashed with the knife, slicing through Owen's cotton shirt and across his wrist. The door shut between them. Owen fell against its inside. The boy hit the platform and sprang back up, throwing himself against the outside of the door, indignant and raging.

"You're dead," he mouthed, as the train pulled away. His face tight, eyes bulging, teeth bared like a dog: "You're dead!"

On board, a short burst of applause fizzled as the onlookers saw the state of Owen's arm. The Americans helped him to his feet, but he felt himself begin to black out and staggered to a vacated seat. His blood had soaked his shirt up to the elbow and the wound was starting to ache.

"You're alright," someone said. And they took his left hand and placed it firmly on his right wrist. "Press hard." Someone else was phoning for an ambulance. Owen rested his head against the window as the Olympic Stadium floated past.

The brownfields around the Stadium had been repurposed as an urban wetland. He had watched the landscape change over the course of a year or more. Where there had been wet clay and industrial debris, there were now waterways and tall grass, and dragonflies. In among the reeds, a dozen shrouded faceless figures, some up to their knees, some to their waists in the marsh water. They turned slowly where they stood, following the train, following Owen, as if they had eyes and were seeing him out of Stratford. He pressed his cheek against the window and watched them shrink into the distance until they were indistinguishable from the clumps of bulrushes.

There was an ambulance waiting at Bow Church, but he had begun to feel better and he stayed on the train, through Poplar, where the train hit the viaduct and took off, and lifted him up and over the Isle of Dogs.

The Cuts

Danny Rhodes

*'The industry must be of a size and pattern suited
to modern conditions and prospects'
- Harold Macmillan*

When Atkins boarded the train at Gaerwen he already knew what his report would contain. There could be no denying the state of things. He took out his pad and wrote a quick observational note, recording the scene before him; the empty platform; the unoccupied carriage; the obvious lack of usage. And he added a further note on the disrepair of the buildings; the general state of decay. It had been like that for much of the journey after Chester and it occurred to him that the people opposed to the changes might benefit from a few journeys such as this one, a few forays onto the branches and tendrils. It might alter their mind-set.

The weather didn't help. The North Wales coast had been fringed with cloud that grew heavier as he pressed further westward. When the previous train slipped in and out of the tunnels under Bangor the cloud dropped and darkened, threatening rain that came in squalls, dashing against the train's windows, restricting Atkins' view of the Menai Straits and depositing him in the grey misery of Gaerwen before he was fully prepared for his arrival. His enthusiasm for the trip and the job he'd been sent to do dampened then. The task could so easily have been carried out from the warmth of his London office. After all, he had the receipts and the figures from the survey. It was just the local protestations that had him in this godforsaken place, the need to show some willingness to listen, even if it were pretence.

Nobody boarded at Gaerwen. He was the only passenger as the train pulled out of the station and started its journey north towards Llangefni, moving from one inconsequential place to another. Atkins shifted in his seat, watched the blurred scenery slide by the window. He'd expected this part of the country to offer topography of hills and valleys. Instead the landscape was featureless, a rippled patchwork of fields bordered by hedgerows and narrow, puddled lanes. That would change of course. In places like this roads would replace rail. Busses would replace trains.

Atkins flicked open his briefcase and examined the contents, noticing Macmillan's statement at the top of the pile. All very well, but Macmillan didn't have to make journeys like this one. Macmillan didn't have to explain those prospects to men who had grown up attached to their engines in some neurological bond. And neither did Beeching. It was left instead to department people like him, 'characterless bureaucrats' as he'd not so fondly been described on so many occasions.

"If this engine dies, I die," a driver had blankly stated on his last sojourn into the furthest fronds. There had been no melodrama in the statement and Atkins had listened to the man believing it was entirely plausible. But these decisions had long since been made. He was not able to alter the course of things. And wasn't he part of something significant, something historic? Staring out of the train window he spotted the still visible scar of an old drover's road carving its way across the landscape. Or perhaps it was Roman, an echo of the past, a symbol of the ingenuity of mankind to keep bettering itself. They were making the country a healthier place, more viable, seeing beyond the thick foliage of raw emotion to the great vista beyond. They were visionaries really, the whole division.

Atkins didn't plan to spend long in Rhosgoch arguing these points, just the time it took to pay lip-service to the local pressure group, just as long as he needed to satisfy them nought had been decided, even when everything had been decided. Nothing on his trip so far had caused him to doubt the decision, and nothing would. There was some irony of course, that he'd made his visit on the very form of transport he was trimming, but he saw it as reassurance, a sign of solidarity, a demonstration that he had faith in the rail system even as he did his duty and lopped the branches away. This was a new beginning, the age of the motorcar. There was no value in turning a blind eye to progress.

And it wasn't all bad news. After the Gaerwen-Amlwch line he'd head south to inform those villages on the mid-Wales route that there would be no closures. The marginals had put paid to any pruning there. Such was politics.

The train juddered to a stop in Llangefni. Atkins stared through the window at yet another empty platform, at rainwater dripping from unkempt guttering, at weeds growing from cracks in the station walls. He made another note in his pad, stating how he could not think of a better example of why the cuts should be carried out than his experience on the Gaerwen-Amlwch route on this day of November 1963. It would make an excellent statement for the press. Should there be any press.

At least the weather was changing. As the train turned North-West, moving on a gentle arc, heading through the countryside, passing farms and smallholdings bordered by stonewalls, the sun broke through the cloud, forming bright patches on the fields. Atkins' mood lightened a touch. If the death-warrant for this route had been issued, and it had, he at least was experiencing its charms before the axe fell.

But the dullness returned as he approached his destination. The clouds rolled back in. The train entered a trough in the landscape, ran along the edge of a wide expanse of marshland. A heavy mist reared up beyond the window. Through the mist, Atkins found himself peering at a lunar landscape, at scarred and scraped earth, at heavy machinery shipwrecked in mud. He'd read about this. They were constructing a new reservoir and moving the road linking the coast to the centre of the island. Nothing as significant as the new roads springing up on the mainland of course, the magnificent motorway system that was transforming the lives of the populace, linking one metropolis to the next, delivering freedom of movement to the masses, encompassing all. Atkins already owned a car. He'd driven his wife up the new M1 just for the thrill of it. And it had been a thrill, getting his foot down on an empty stretch of freshly laid tarmac, stopping for lunch in one of the new state of the art service stations, showing Mrs Atkins the marvel of 20th Century progress, a truly harmonious event.

The mist dragged him back to his more pressing engagement, or more accurately, the smell of it. The mist carried a strange odour that infiltrated his nostrils. It was as if the very air itself was clogged and clotted with some curious decay. Atkins took his handkerchief from his top pocket and placed it over his nose. He was not used to the rich smells of the countryside. He stared through the vapour at the strange scene beyond the window, marvelling at the way a layer seemed to have been stripped away from the land, exposing scratched white bone beneath. But the machinery was motionless, the landscape deserted. Whatever hands had been busy on the site, they were not busy today, which was curious, with the day being a Tuesday and the time being just after two in the afternoon. Perhaps the smell had something to do with it. It was as disgusting an odour as he'd ever had the displeasure to experience. He couldn't imagine anybody working in it. And it seemed to accompany the mist because as the train entered the cutting before Rhosgoch station, the mist cleared and the stench dispersed too.

Atkins alighted from the train expecting to be greeted by the usual barrage of hand-painted hoardings and hurled accusations. Instead he found himself standing on an uninhabited platform. He stood quite still, aghast. As the train pulled away he checked his watch. He was bang on time. He looked up at the station clock to be sure, but the clock's hands were bent out of shape, the Roman numerals faded and fractured. Now Atkins noticed other things about the station, the flaking paint on the window frames, the missing segments of glass, birds' nests in the rusting ironwork of the roof. He could hardly believe the audacity of its proprietors. During this time of sweeping change he had visited over thirty branch lines facing the hatchet. In each and every case he'd stepped off trains to witness thriving, well kept (often pristine) amenities. In times of crisis and desperation, people were capable of such blind optimism and fakery. He'd listened politely to their speeches, took note of their concerns and returned to London confident he'd made the correct decision. They all seemed to forget he had the figures in his logbook. They all seemed to forget that in purely economic terms, their stations were a liability.

There was none of this at Rhosgoch, no pomp and ceremony, no eagerness to demonstrate what the figures flagrantly disproved. It unnerved Atkins a little, so much so that he remained on the platform until ten minutes after his agreed arrival time, convinced his hosts had been delayed by some unforeseen event, a broken down tractor for instance, a herd of sheep blocking a narrow country lane, an accident. He stood stock still on the platform, the mist hanging like a veil above the distant treeline, staring down at the rails and the weeds growing between the sleepers. In those few minutes, he almost thought he could see the weeds pushing themselves out of the earth.

When it was clear nobody was coming to greet him, Atkins picked up his briefcase and started along the platform towards the exit. He entered the lobby to notice the unmistakeable fragrance of incense burning on the ticket office counter. He was used to the smell of polish in station lobbies, and the musty odour often hidden behind it. He peered out of the open doorway in the direction of the village church, barely perceptible in the mist that had now enshrined the village. He found himself thinking about medieval miasmas, how people believed such bad air inflicted their victims with all manner of ailment and disease. For the first time, his feelings shifted from annoyance to discomfort. Something was clearly amiss in Rhosgoch. The yellowed timetables, the dusty office behind the counter, the dated posters advertising products from the previous decade all pointed towards absence, and yet someone must have lit the incense stick, somebody must have opened the little office and changed the date on the wooden block calendar sitting there.

Tuesday 16th November 1963.

Atkins felt himself growing irritable. Was this some carefully constructed ruse, a deliberate wasting of his time? Were his hosts playing a game with him, aiming to make their point in a way that might make the newspapers? Well they'd shot themselves in the foot. It would be two hours before the next train entered the station. He had little choice but to wait for it. Then he would leave this insignificant branch line to its decay, board the train back to Gaerwen, cross the straits to the mainland and head down the coast to Llanelli where an altogether more important battle was taking place.

Atkins stepped out of the station building. As he stared up the lane the mist rolled over him, enveloping him, causing him to cough. Such a curious taste. He pulled his handkerchief to his nose, started up the lane between the high hedgerows towards the church steeple where he imagined the village centre must be. The mist thickened with his every step. It clung to him.

He'd only walked a few paces when he spotted a figure in the lane. Surely this would be his host, eager to please now, keen to appease for his lateness. Except the figure in the mist didn't seem to be moving. It was stood in the middle of the lane, so still that Atkins wondered if it were some sort of obstruction placed in the lane and not a person after all. But it looked like a person. Its soft edged outline, the sloping shoulders and roundish head suggested a person.

Atkins called out, 'Hullo there?'

The figure didn't respond. It didn't move. Atkins gritted his teeth. He wasn't the type to be pestered by the strange behaviour of others. A man in his position had to expect to meet all sorts, meet them head on and face them down. It was one of his rules of leadership. Straightening himself, making himself as upright and forthcoming as he could manage, Atkins strode purposefully up the lane. He could now see that it was a man, a local for sure, dressed in wellington boots and the general get up of a farmworker.

But when he was ten feet away, Atkins stopped.

"Hullo," he called again, more inquisitive this time, more timid, offering himself to the man as a guest, offering subservience. The man still didn't react. His face seemed fully engaged in the scene around him, but his eyes didn't follow Atkins as he moved past, circling, circumventing, seeking out some answer to this latest peculiarity, a man who simply stared forward at a distant object on an invisible horizon as though he were peering at something that had once been and was no longer. The man was locked in mid-stride, one foot extended in front of the other, the rear foot resting on its toes, the front foot on its heel. The arms fell as arms fall when a man is walking. He seemed to be suspended in a moment. Atkins circled the man carefully, expecting him to move, to begin to laugh at his version of a practical joke.

But the man didn't laugh. He remained impeccably still, so still that Atkins started to wonder if he were standing beside a mannequin. Perhaps that was the joke, a mannequin placed in the middle of a lane to flummox the civil servant come to deliver his verdict on the railway. Ill thought out, ridiculous, pointless but somehow a demonstration of disobedience at those in authority choosing to put one hundred years of history to the saw.

Atkins raised his right hand to the man's face, moved in very close to him, his left hand still firmly pressed against the handkerchief. Subconsciously he had made a potential link between the strange smell in the air and the man standing in front of him. He touched the man's cheek. It was warm, supple, rough with stubble, exactly how a man's cheek ought to feel. He touched his own cheek. It felt exactly the same. Atkins felt a great desire to strike the man then, to push him to the floor, to do something to bring him out of his stupor, but he couldn't bring himself to go through with it. He stood looking at the man instead, waiting to see if he blinked. But the man didn't blink. He didn't do anything.

Atkins, in best practical fashion, decided his best course of action was to head up the slope into the village, to find somebody and inform them of his strange discovery. Perhaps the man was prone to seizures of some sort. *Le petit mal.* Perhaps the rest of the villagers knew how to help him. He walked up between the hedgerows; turning his head every few steps to check on the shape behind him as it softened in the mist, became the same grey silhouette he'd first seen from the bottom of the lane, more frightening from a distance, more unsettling in its motionlessness. The man remained perfectly still.

The mist continued to thicken, isolating Atkins and reducing his world to a cluster of blurred shapes, the stalwart silhouettes of dwellings that made up the village of Rhosgoch. A sad little place really, all the more tragic for the weather. He wandered haphazardly amongst them, his handkerchief pressed to his nose, searching for signs of life, locating none, until sallow lamplight appeared in the gloom ahead. He arced his way towards it, a curious moth, reached out to touch a damp stone wall, traced its outline to a doorway, saw the sign above it that signalled a public house.

The Locomotive. How apt. Perhaps here he'd find something of the welcome he was expecting, even if it was fuelled with disapproval, suspicion and anger.

Warm lighting within, a cosy atmosphere, a fire dying in the fireplace but clinging on, the same smell of incense he'd discovered in the station lobby. At first Atkins imagined the place to be empty, but then he noticed two figures sat at the bar, two men hunched over the polished oak.

But there were no sideways glances, no shifty eyes or glares of dissatisfaction as he emerged from the doorway. The men didn't move at all.

"Hello," said Atkins.

The men didn't respond. They simply gazed ahead of themselves. He could see their eyes in the bar mirror, exhibiting the far off stare of the intoxicated. Atkins stepped across the tiled floor, wondering at what point he was going to stop participating in this game of charades. But when he reached the bar he saw the men were stricken by the same condition as the villager in the lane, waxen figures in a museum display but real, human, pliable, trapped in some curious frieze. He stared about himself, at the dying fire rippling in the mirror, at his own furtive gaze, at the quaint décor, the oak beams, the black iron equine appendages, the tankards and spirit glasses. But were they quaint? Or were they out of place, remnants of a past, something been and gone. Were they like the railway line, no longer viable? Atkins pinched at the cheeks of the two drinkers. The men remained perfectly still, oblivious.

Behind the bar were a number of masks. Atkins eyed them darkly. Each had a long, protruding beak, a pair of round glass openings for eyes. Curious collectables, they were lined up in a row above the spirit bottles, five of them hanging from great six inch nails that had been driven into the solid beam supporting the upper storey of the building. At the end of the beam, where a door led into a backroom, Atkins spotted a further two nails. There were no masks hanging there.

Through the incense, Atkins imagined he could smell the faintest scent of the curious, bitter mist. He stood at the bar staring at the hanging masks and at the vacant nails. He raised the handkerchief to his nostrils once again. For the first time since his arrival in Rhosgoch, he started to fear for his safety. He considered heading into the back room, seeking out the source of the incense, continuing his search for some answers, but he retreated instead, retraced his hesitant steps across the tiled floor and back into the village, back into the mist.

It was thicker now, settling in layers amongst the buildings, pooling in recesses, a deeper yellow in those places. Atkins peered upwards to where the church steeple vanished into its folds. It was time to leave Rhosgoch, he decided, time to return to civilisation. He fought to orientate himself, to locate his route back to the station, recalling how he'd reached the pub door he was now nestled against, his body refusing to follow the instructions his mind was relaying. It took all of his fortitude, all of his years of civil obedience to pull himself away from the door and into the mist, tentatively stepping into the road in the direction he imagined the station to be located.

No sooner did he manage it than something moved in the mist ahead of him.

He was uncertain at first, convinced he'd imagined it, that the movement might have been nothing but the mist rolling and folding in on itself, thickening for a moment before dispersing. But no, there it was again, a shifting form, moving away from him, moving towards him. He couldn't quite be certain. It seemed to be shrouded in a flowing garment, a cloak perhaps. When it turned its head to one side Atkins spotted the curious beak like protrusion, the downward curved shape of it. The figure *was* moving in his direction, he could see that now, approaching him through the mist that swirled and eddied around it. It raised an arm, to point, to reach out, to grasp for him, he couldn't be sure.

Atkins retreated in small, shuffling footsteps, retreated with the unfettered horror of a child, his eyes fixed upon the swirling mist and the shape lurking within it, his hand pressed so hard against the handkerchief that he could taste his own blood on his tongue, until the backs of his thighs bumped against something cold. He wheeled about himself to see he was pressed against the stone wall bordering the churchyard, the looming structure of the church building above. As he fought for escape, he caught sight of another figure amongst the headstones, one dressed in the same curious flowing garments, the same terrifying mask. Atkins heard what might have been the rapid wording of a prayer, or a remedy, followed by skittish laughter and his own involuntary gasps as he tried to comprehend what was taking place here, what creatures he'd happened upon, what strange events were unfolding in a mist that enveloped its victims until they were smothered and frozen in a moment.

Atkins fled.

He set off at the fastest pace he dared, forcing his way through the mist, one arm extended to feel his way like a blind man, the other pressed against his handkerchief, wanting to look behind him to see if he was being pursued by the masked figures, not daring to take his eyes off the mist cloaked world in front of him. He bumped into something, flailed his arm and swung his briefcase at it, imagining it to be another of his pursuers, but it wasn't, it was another mannequin, frozen in time, stricken by the miasma, a woman this time, a woman carrying a placard. He didn't read it, didn't get an opportunity, because now he was trapped amongst a gathering of similarly transfixed bodies, five or six others, all of them carrying placards, all of them immovable structures that he had to barge and force his way between. As he did so, he lost his grip on his briefcase. No matter. He could not stop to look for it. When he was clear of the throng he dared to look behind him where, amongst the shadows, he saw the figures in the masks doing the same, clumsily chasing him down. He resolved that they must be men, as he was a man, but such understanding did not dilute his fear. Men were capable of terrible things in ordinary times. The situation in Rhosgoch was not ordinary. Something had occurred here, something catastrophic. Perhaps here in this godforsaken village, Atkins had stumbled upon the beginning of the end of the world.

He reached the top of the slope that led to the station, or at least he thought he did, it was difficult to know for certain. He tore down it as best a man could with one hand pressed to his nostrils and the other held in front of him for protection. He spotted the figure in the lane ahead, the man in wellingtons. He hadn't moved. Atkins barrelled past him, knocking the man over. The man fell like a ninepin. Atkins heard the snap of bone as his forearm splintered upon impact with the ground.

Atkins reached the station. He stood at the entrance for a moment, gasping for breath, turned to look back up the slope. The mist was dispersing, moving away from the lane and across the fields, thinning as it did so. He watched the man in the lane recover consciousness, struggle awkwardly to his feet. His arm dangled at the elbow, a useless appendage. As Atkins watched the man released a maniacal, tormented howl. Behind him a group of people emerged. The two cloaked and masked figures were at the front. Those behind were carrying placards daubed with incendiary messages about the government's plans to take away the railway. The group engulfed the man with the dangling arm and marched down the lane in the direction of the station. But they were not people, not really. They were dangerous, shuffling forms, inhabitants of a dying village, reduced to almost nothing. Atkins struggled with the station door, forced it open, tried with all his might to separate himself from the anguished cries, the agonised screams, the wails of melancholy and garbled prayers drifting along the lane in his direction. He had visions of dying in Rhosgoch along with the inhabitants, of disappearing into its folds never to surface again. He closed the doors behind him, dragged a trolley across the entrance to buy himself some time, pushed through the second set of doors onto the platform. One of the doors came away from its hinges, crashed to the ground at his feet. As he tried to make sense of that moment, Atkins saw the flaking paint on the door, the cracks in the platform, weeds pushing through the concrete. He looked over at the track, or the place where the track had once been, to see an overgrown mass of brambles instead, a section of bent and rusted rail, a rotten sleeper covered in moss. He wheeled about, staring at it all with an incredulous gaze. He saw the windowless frames of the waiting room, the shattered glass at his feet, the clock with no hands dangling from the broken roof, the sign that once read Rhosgoch now a faded and forlorn remnant of a forgotten time. If the station had been dishevelled when he arrived, it was now dilapidated.

Atkins dared to understand.

He realised the mist had settled over the station once more and that he'd not been breathing through the handkerchief. He'd let his guard down with the shock of what was before him. He heard a sound behind him. Two figures appeared at the far end of the platform, each cloaked and masked in the nightmarish get-up he'd seen in the village. One of them was carrying his briefcase.

When Atkins tried to turn his head to look for a place to run to, he realised he couldn't do so. When he tried to raise his hands to his eyes in order not to look at the strangers approaching him he couldn't do that either. As the mist started to lift, carrying his sanity with it, Atkins was forced to watch the figures remove their own masks, forced to understand for the first time what Beeching was guilty of. Each of them displayed the symptoms of a dying man; sunken eyes; drawn features; pale, grey, ghostlike skin. They might, in fact, have been walking corpses.

And Atkins understood.

An old type of darkness was coming, a darkness the country hadn't seen for a century. He'd helped deliver that darkness to Rhosgoch and Amlwch and a thousand other places in recent months. He was bound to the shadows that would seep into each and every one, bound to every lost soul who inhabited those places, bound by ignominious history. And if the people of Rhosgoch killed him on this station platform and strung his body from the rotting roof timbers or let him go it really didn't matter. It would be forever thus.

Sleepers

Christopher Harman

Factory? Power plant? Waterworks? Vince had said, chucking the apple-core away. Saying nothing, Rory had sat on a ledge of peat roofed with wiry grass and tightened his laces. In the haze of distant hills and under the egg yolk sun, the shape was an offending sight Vince's binoculars made larger but not much clearer. A residential block wouldn't have a gate as wide and half as high as itself. The gate, if that was what it had been, rose to a peak at the centre. Huge panels above it were partially obscured by an array of pipe work; there were traces of smoke from two or three poking above the roofline.

For a second or two Vince had been convinced the shape was the nearest in a row receding to greater obscurity. One such eye-sore would be indefensible, a whole row an outrage out here—up here. Maybe he'd been mistaken. Could physical fatigue, which sometimes caused him a slight blurriness of vision, create an illusory duplicating effect?

The edifice hadn't been on their route so would remain a mystery, which Vince had in any case been strongly disinclined to investigate further. But during the remaining miles of the walk that day its impingement amongst the undulations of those outriders of the Pennines had niggled, along with the problem with Rory. Gridling Bridge as dusk was falling embodied the failed promise of the six-day trek.

"Civilisation," Rory said. He sounded a degree more animated after a day of monosyllables and short-winded responses. Vince knew how the mood of one staff member could infect a whole team; his own Learning and Development department wasn't immune. He'd had to fight to stay positive today.

Vince looked down and across faded moorland to the town. In the shapeless shallow depression between hills it was a series of dark heaps, laced with evening mist and points and smears of muddy yellow sodium street lighting. He could make out a couple of smokeless mill chimneys.

"Prefer last night's civilisation," Vince said.

"That chocolate box village?" Rory said with a faint sneer. "Too quiet."

"Wish I could time all our stops with 'chocolate box villages,'" Vince said, a touch provocatively.

Rory didn't take the bait and argue his case. Enough for him to have re-established his lack of enthusiasm for the rural environment.

The stony path began to descend. Rory went first; the lightness of his step wasn't a marked contrast to his usual pace. His demeanour had been weary rather than his walking. He was stocky and strong; he looked like a hiker, but hills had never been an essential as they were for Vince, for whom they were an antidote to environs like Gridling Bridge. Vince noted stepped streets of terraced houses, broken necklaces of street lights, the elephantine pillars of a viaduct. A street-length of green tufts was probably a littered, turd-studded park. A pair of headlights moved at speed until they were out of town. You've got the right idea, Vince thought.

A high-hedged track took them low and opened out into allotments. Broken glass crunched underfoot, rusted hoes and spades lay abandoned. There were planted rows, strangled by weeds.

A ginnel entrance interrupted a variegated and mostly dilapidated assortment of rear fence panels. Unlit windows set in the black brick terrace looked onto dank and dark back yards. A forbidding boundary; once past it they were fully encompassed by the town. In their walking gear, Vince felt they were as likely as tigers. If they were unobserved, he was thankful for it.

Rory was looking from right to left. "Which way?"

"O.S maps don't give street names," Vince said.

An empty street. Rory rolled his eyes almost imperceptibly but Vince could see he was marginally happier having tarmac under his feet.

"We'll have to ask—" Vince looked towards an intersection, "—him." He walked quickly; the man might not be around long. For the moment the man was undecided as he pulled and pushed an upright structure loaded with luggage and on two small squeaking wheels. If he was a visitor Vince figured they might at least get a sympathetic hearing. There was too much luggage for one. Was he a coach driver who'd lost his way with his charges' belongings between coach park and hotel? But now Vince detected not so much anxiety as frivolity. The man appeared to be dancing with the trolley thing.

"Hello there!" Vince's voice echoed off house and shop fronts. The figure showed no sign of having heard. They were half way to him when he spun around, moved off sharply and disappeared around a corner.

Nobody was visible in any direction once they reached the intersection but Vince recognised a street name. A few houses in, another sign stuck out over the path—The Sleepers Hotel. Further along there were indications of similar establishments. Someone walked haltingly out of sight. He hadn't been pushing a luggage trolley. Vince figured the one who had been could have entered one of the bed-and-breakfasts or hotels—perhaps even the Sleepers.

In the entrance, Rory looked out over opposite rooftops to the dense grey wall of hills.

"They won't look like that in the morning," Vince said.

"Still be hills," Rory said.

"Three days done and dusted, only three to go." Vince's artificial brightness curdled inside him as Rory shouldered past the double doors.

They had slippers in their packs but hadn't previously felt compelled to wear them in the interests of not antagonising proprietors. Conditions had been dry for several weeks and their lightweight boots were clean-soled and barely distinguishable from brogues. They passed through an atrium between two sets of double doors and into a reception area. It was deserted; nobody at the desk. No sign of the trolley man. They went through into a lounge.

A woman vigorously trowelled coal from a bronze scuttle into a bright orange inferno contained within a narrow arched aperture above a stone hearth. At Vince's discreet cough she stood straight and turned a long, haughty and heated face towards them.

". . .you?" she said, the preceding "can I help" implicit more than heard in the shape of her thin lips. She'd addressed Rory and with an unblinking consideration of him, she moved a damp worm of hair off her brow. Vince was too settled, too married, to be chagrined—but he'd done the booking by phone and said so after introducing himself. "Mrs Coburn isn't it?" She looked him up and down and appeared briefly disinclined to admit it before she said, "Yes. If you'd care to follow me."

Back to the reception area where they signed a ledger of biblical solidity. "Your key. I'll have the boy send up your—things." A raised plucked eyebrow at their rucksacks. Hill walking was incorrigibly alien to the uninitiated.

"No need," Vince said. "Been carrying them all day. Stairs won't hurt."

The beds were set at right angles to each other along the walls. The radiator was tepidly warm. Bracketed to a wall was a television with a glass paunch.

"Cheap and cheerful," Vince said. The former adjective was true. "Did she say when dinner was?"

"She didn't," Rory said. "Anyway, I'll be giving it a miss. I'll grab a bite in a pub." That was too much for Vince. He'd seen Rory nibble at sandwiches and pork scratchings in pubs and tea rooms. "Be sensible Rory. Fresh air won't sustain you another day, let alone three to the finish."

"About that," Rory said, unpacking from the pristine red rucksack Vince had convinced him to buy years ago in the Army and Navy Stores. He sniffed a sock.

"I bet mine could finish the walk by themselves," Vince said. He didn't want Rory to expand on 'about that' just now and make an irrevocable decision. "I saw a launderette. Watching our tumbling togs'll be something to do." With a single breath of mordant laughter, he went to the window. Not a great choice, being cooped in here or wandering through a town he'd taken a dislike to at a distance and had yet to revise his opinion of. He noted a dark rectangle against russets and greys set in a comparative low point between the dark humps of the hills. As enigmatic in failing light as that similar shape had been in the mid-afternoon haze hundreds of feet higher than this.

Rory had joined him at the window. "There's at least one pub," he said. A curious lack of enthusiasm considering the Derby Arms across the railways lines from his house had become a second home.

A drunk staggered from lamppost to lamppost, each one an immobile dancing partner he either stopped to embrace or swung around one or more times. A vivid body-memory in Vince of making his way down the aisle of a rocking train decelerating towards his station. "I'd recommend less beer, more potato crisps," he said. The man's clothing swung on his frame. Hollows under his cheekbones, like adjacent toothless mouths. Hair like artfully arranged bristles of a yard broom.

They withdrew back into the room and drank dusty tasting complementary tea. Liquid in sachets had held nothing in common with milk but whiteness. On his mobile phone Vince told Emma the name of the town, the hotel and watched Rory's face for envy. Rory always brightened in Emma's presence; at home, he and Moira treated each other like stains on the wall, unsightly, liveable with, but generally to be ignored. Vince would have confided his misgivings about the trek had Rory been out of the room.

After ringing off, Vince said there was no need for them both to traipse down to the launderette. Generous of me, he thought, and Rory would benefit from resting before tomorrow's labours. Rory surprised him, saying he wanted to 'look around the town'. They packed items due for a wash into Vince's rucksack and left.

Locking the room, Vince listened in the corridor. Not a sound. No voices, no TV or radio. Outside, they set forth under a few salt stars in coal blackness. Chilly air, straight off the unseen hills; Vince wondered if Rory's tracksuit top was adequate; 'Leeds University' emblazoned across the chest would have been appropriate if he'd ever been there.

An ache in Vince's legs, used to grassy or peaty slopes, not hard unyielding flags. He kicked out through the advance party of a regiment of prematurely fallen autumn leaves, pattering and scraping to meet them.

Odd markings. He stamped on one, picked it up, showed it Rory. "Bus ticket," Vince said. "Better than that—rail," Rory said. The tickets hopped and fussed on their way, like the long train of a ceremonial garment.

They passed nobody, though there were people about. Vince heard a shuffling in a side alley. Crouched in a doorway, a man was pressing a dark-stained handkerchief to his forehead; he looked about to ask Rory a question before thinking better of it. Vince asked if he was 'OK' but he made no reply.

Behind the plate glass window of the launderette, the black 'O's of the three front-loader machines were like the potholes Vince's walking guide had warned of. Inside, he loaded a machine. He slid a coin into the slot and the machine rumbled to life. While Rory stood at the window, Vince sat in a plastic stack chair and traced tomorrow's route on his Ordnance Survey sheet. He became aware of Rory's reflection, coldly eyeing the map. "Want a look?" he said.

"Moorland isn't it? Then more moorland?"

Vince's smile at the pun failed to elicit one from Rory. "Steadier— fewer ups and downs."

Rory sat in one of the chairs. Vince wished he'd initiate some conversational nothing. In their silence the washing machine's grumbling mechanism made the plate glass tremble. The noise and vibration intensified and Vince couldn't be sure it was all down to the washing machine. Then with an abrupt lessening of volume, like a change of gear, it was as if a layer of sound had been removed. Vince would have got up to look out through the window, suspecting some retreating massive vehicle, had not a figure been standing outside, staring in, staring hard from under the peak of his cap—and at Rory. Rory was unaware of it; he seemed mesmerised by the churned contents of the washing machine.

Vince glared down into the contours on the map where the shape of the man persisted like a dark cairn. Why not enter if he thought he recognised Rory from somewhere? Vince glanced up, fierce—challenging the man to do just that.

Glinting eyes. Caped—and with a drastic slope on one side, as if his shoulder and a significant portion of the upper left side of his chest had been surgically removed—or obliterated in some unspeakable violence. From his neck a slender cylinder hung on a chain. His curiosity apparently satisfied, rather than escaping Vince's combative scrutiny, the man swung away and was gone.

Rory got up. "I'm going to look around," he said.

Vince considered advising against that, but he wasn't here to chaperone the man. And he'd been right not to draw Rory's attention to the one looking in. Evidently Rory hadn't been whoever the caped figure at first thought he was.

"OK. I'll see to this lot." Vince gestured at their tumbling clothes. "See you back at the hotel."

Rory left and Vince could stop pretending an interest in landmarks to look out for along the route tomorrow. He thought of the massive feature in the landscape today he hadn't attempted to identify on the map—and it wasn't as if it hadn't occurred to him to. Had he preferred it to be vaguely troubling rather than revealed as serving some ghastly industrial purpose that would have rendered it all the more ugly in its setting? More than that, he recognised a deeper unsettlement at the possibility of there being nothing on the map to shed light.

He'd make amends for that ridiculous qualm right now. Finding the approximate position where he and Rory had stopped for a break, he plotted the position of that far off corridor lined by spurs of hillside. Nothing—no water treatment works, no factory, no utilitarian residential block that might have belonged to a university or leisure group. A trick of the light? A mirage in the hazy uplands of northern England? No, just something erected hastily after the area had last been re-examined by the Ordnance Survey—and forever a mystery to Vince.

He shoved the map back into an outer pocket of his rucksack. No tabloid in sight left by some previous client. Imbecilic, the round full mouth of the washing machine with its suds like saliva. The cycle could take half an hour to complete. Nobody would interrupt it to steal their clothes— welcome to them if they did. The question of going on or abandoning the walk would be settled for them. He got up, lifted the empty sag of his rucksack and bore it by one strap out into the street.

He went in the direction Rory had gone. Where a choice of routes presented themselves, he took a narrow way, closed to traffic. The long, downward curve was lined by shops, most shuttered. Tiers of terrace houses rose over low office blocks. There were cracks of light around curtain edges. Most windows were unlit.

The narrow way ended, depositing him in a space of empty taxi ranks, a line of buses in an open-fronted depot. On a patch of grass before a building with a pillared portico there was a piece of municipal sculpture—three large iron wheels leaned against each other on the ground-plan of a triangle. Metal rods twisting up between the spokes represented vegetation—or maybe flames. Hideous, either way—and he wasn't one to automatically deride the kind of public art that council sub-committees gave the nod to.

A road swung left and upwards at a widening angle from the path he'd descended. There was a high metal fence from which scraps of posters dangled like bandages. From behind it a rhythmic rocking, as of some weighty structure—an attempt made to either topple or right it. Or perhaps neither as the voices he heard weren't effortful. Some property of the night air made laughter reedy, disembodied. Nothing drunken or nefarious to dissuade him from going forward to peer through the metals slats.

He was left not much wiser. A great open space of darkness with hints of parallel shallow trenches here and there, green smudges of vegetation, a peppering of yellow ragwort. To the left, warehouses with pitched roofs. A considerable distance further out, a stacking of terraced streets in a muddy miasma of sodium light.

He moved to where the fence was interrupted by a wide dark opening. Over it, parallel posts lacked the board which had presumably identified the place the tunnel delivered people to. Vince hesitated on the threshold until he'd ascertained the multiplying echoes of pattering steps were heading away in the direction he decided to follow.

After a bend, all made sense. The tunnel ended in a few railed steps dropping to a wide concourse. There were drifts of yellowing tickets. A bench seat was all frame and no slats to sit on. Two grooves between the platforms were filled with nettles. On the right a wooden bridge, weathered of most of its paint, crossed over the tracks—or rather where the tracks had been.

Low buildings on three sides; a former ticket office had broken grilled windows. In an adjoining room a single garment hung from a hook. Probably years since anyone had waited in the waiting room. Some steps led to a first floor of window frames lacking glass.

Vince rose up the steps of the bridge until he was at an elevation to realise the dark lake beyond the platforms was a dumping ground of railway detritus; sleepers, an uprooted length of track, twisted buffers like medieval instruments of torture. Farther off were dim shapes of rolling stock. A nearer example lay on its side. People contained within rocked the old style carriage, and there had to be a good number of them to do that.

They spoke in dry rasping voices, and went silent as the carriage settled to motionlessness, as if aware of a listener. They surely couldn't actually see from out of the shattered sky-facing windows the figure moving along the far platform towards the bridge. In fact, his measured pace suggested he'd no intention of reporting them.

Vince held himself taut as the man rose up the right-angled extension at the far end of the bridge. Turning onto the flat of the bridge proper, the man was lit by a suspended light that gave him a yellow, bloodless tinge, so that Vince didn't immediately recognise it was Rory. So much for fresh air and exercise, Vince thought. Rory walked slowly, looking at the floor until Vince spoke.

"This place has seen its day." Here and there, dirty yellow light casings glowed—for security purposes, Vince supposed, though he didn't feel secure.

Looking up with lustreless eyes, Rory showed no surprise at Vince's presence.

Realising Rory wasn't going to ask, Vince explained. "Got bored watching our gear get clean. Wandered for a bit and was passing here and heard voices. First since yours. The town's dead." He began to head down the steps. "Don't think we should linger. The folks in that overturned carriage could be trouble." Rory moved at half Vince's rate and stared down at the rustling greenery where trains had once ran.

When they were back down on the concourse, Vince said, "Did you see that bloke staring into the launderette? Wore a cape, peaked cap—had a whistle on a chain."

"Sounds like a railway worker. Should be here dressed like that."

"You're joking." Vince wished Rory would regain his capacity for jokes. "No staff around, no timetables. Oh, and no tracks. Place has been defunct God knows how long. Anyway I was saying about this guy. He was beady-eyeing you a good while, then buzzed off. Case of mistaken identity I suppose. Thing is—he was in a bad way. Big chunk of him missing— here." Vince tapped his shoulder.

Rory toe-ed a loose piece of clinker. "Time for me to go home." No interest in caped, partially dismantled strangers, this town, the walk. He'd caught Vince off-guard. Vince blurted out, "Home? Already?"

Home: the front half of a semi. Moira had the back. Meals prepared at different times in the shared kitchen. Rory lived off tuna forked straight out of tins. Moira did the same, Rory had revealed, "'cept she empties them onto willow pattern plates." She was rake thin, a heavy smoker. Daily she drove her Escort from car boot sales to bric-a-brac fairs to antique emporia. With his painting and decorating business gone bust, Rory stayed home, endlessly tinkering with his old Ford Capri.

"I suggest we discuss this over steak and chips."

Rory's shrug communicated that there was nothing to discuss. Vince ignored it. Rory needed to persevere. Vince knew from his leading council role in Learning and Development that nothing came easy. Rory cast a last gaze at the empty platforms before they entered the tunnel.

Out of the tunnel and heading up the hill, Rory didn't lag. Such was his passivity, Vince guessed he'd be persuaded to accompany him at least one more day. The forecast was for a continuation of the mild conditions. A steady slog in the three days ahead, but nothing too arduous.

A trundling of small wheels under a heavy load. Vince glanced through the opening into a paved court dominated by a structure of interlocking wooden planks. He halted Rory. "What the Hell's that?" If it was another piece of public art it was less slickly done than that wheel affair.

"Sleepers. They're cross-pieces from rail tracks."

"I can see what it's made from," Vince said, testy because it troubled him. Just then the trundling sound gained in clarity and the man appeared pushing the metal construct piled with bags. His feet flickered. He appeared to be dancing in a circuit around the construction.

"Him again," Vince said. "Pushing that . . ."

"It's a sack truck. They hump stuff around with them at railway stations."

"If you say so." And Vince was glad he had. Rory had sounded just a little more engaged naming things, though as laconic as ever. "Is that a peaked cap he's wearing? It is. Dressed like a railway porter—what's going on? Is it Dress Like a Railway Official Day or something?"

At one time, Rory might have smiled tolerantly. The 'porter' chap wasn't eliciting any laughs either at his high jinks. Nobody with him—a lone mental case. "Pour soul. All dressed up and nowhere to go."

And speaking of poor souls, Vince thought, as Rory walked on. Vince went to catch up.

Ahead, the narrow end of a cake-wedge building divided the road. They went left. In ground-floor windows people sat at tables, not talking, not eating—so must have been waiting for food. Then they were staring out as if they'd been synchronised to do so at the exact same instant when the next person or persons should pass by on the pavement. Vince stopped to confront their interest. The caped man had taught him to do that.

In the light of low-energy bulbs, pale skin set off a sorry collection of scars and bruises; some had surely necessitated stints in Accident and Emergency departments. Some injuries he had to look away from. Some conditions looked terminal. A hospital outing?

Another instance of Rory having a magnetism, in Gridling Bridge at least, which Vince was aware of lacking himself. Did something in Rory's drifting detached demeanour intrigue them—even amuse them? Their shoulders had begun to shake, but then so had his own. The walls and sign "The Railway Hotel" shook too.

Vince and Rory walked on. "I get the feeling this place could fall down a hole," Vince said.

"Yeah," Rory said, as if it would be of no consequence if it did.

Vince guessed a geological shift could be felt for miles—and in the approach to Gridling Bridge hadn't there been a gash of ice greys and emeralds in the hills, suggestive of an open-cast mine gone green with disuse? That could mean there were deep seams with rotted props.

Ahead was a church on a mound wrapped in a skirt of gravestones. A street circled it; over-stuffed and reeking wheely-bins stood sentry at every gate. On the far side of the church a café with nets half way up its windows promised 'no frills'.

Inside, the chalked menu concurred. They ordered and sat at a middle table in a single row that extended to the back. A frieze of hot water urn, cake display case, wicker dish of condiment sachets and the serving lady, who stared out at Rory from under a tottering edifice of piled creamy hair and through a wobbly line of smoke rising from her cigarette.

"My colleagues in Health and Safety would love that," Vince said, with a lean of his head in her direction. Rory didn't rise to the topic. Since the same council ended his painting and decorating contract he'd lambasted it at every opportunity. Those days were gone. He arranged two streaky bacon rashers end to end in a track bisecting his plate. Vince ate with gusto. His hunger finally satiated, he thought it time to speak plainly.

"You're body's been up in the hills, but your mind hasn't—you should give it a chance to."

"I have done."

Vince let that go. "You've lost weight." He'd tried for a positive slant in his tone; difficult as Rory looked underfed. A pallor; loose flesh at his jowls like stubbled unbaked pastry.

Cloud after cloud puffed up from a vent at the top of the urn. It was like the smoke stack of a train. It whistled piercingly and everyone looked. Vince nodded past Rory's shoulder. Rory turned.

A couple huddled at a table by the window.

"Not exactly love's young dream," Vince said. Her eyes were too large with large deltas of red veins at the corners. Her lips caught on her dry teeth when she smiled. Her partner's hands enclosed hers and the two pairs resembled a pile of sticks you could put a match to. At a gurgle behind him, Vince twisted in his seat to a sight hardly more palatable.

The man faced away at the back corner. An asymmetry of huge bumps and deep hollows under the thin material of the raincoat was suggestive of a distorted skeletal configuration, endured since birth or the result of some shattering subsequent injury. Rory's scraping chair had Vince turning back. "I'll fetch the stuff from the launderette," Rory said.

"OK. See you back at the hotel."

The woman behind the counter looked from Rory's full plate to Rory opening the clattering front door. Her piled hair shuddered like haystacks in a high wind. Her cigarette twitched, "Not eating—now there's a surprise."

"This town would stifle anyone's appetite," Vince said, and who cared if he offended? She cared. She swung around the hairpin end of the counter and bore down on him. No, it was Rory's plate she wanted. Vince clasped its edges. "No you don't. My appetite's fine. I can eat for two." The town rumbled as if in laughter. He ate quickly and left.

There were more people in the streets, though to describe the town as 'coming alive' wouldn't have been apt. He passed a man glued to the shadows in a shop doorway. A group with smooth faces and the gaits of infirm pensioners came out of the darkened Roxy Cinema. Vince thought the girl was playing hopscotch under the grocer's awning until he saw the fresh air beneath one hip required her to hop.

He stopped by a gate like a flattened birdcage. Grass, a drinking fountain, swings. A seated youth licked cigarette papers, toppled and lay on his side. Sharp cheekbones. Bony protuberances at his wrists and bare elbows. His dyed-blonde hair was spiked like needles without him wearing any polyester sweater to have generated static. His tee-shirt had scorch marks, presumably from his cigarettes or matches. Vince was ill-prepared to get lumbered with another non-coper. Let others provide succour, and there were more around to, though a pair close by coming into focus—a limping man and a grimacing woman who clutched her midriff—looked incapable.

Back at the hotel Vince was glad to be alone in the lounge. The thought of Rory's company up in their room held little appeal. The fire smouldered in the narrow arch of the fireplace; holding one hand with the other to the few pink coals stilled the tremor in both of them. A clink of glass.

At the bar, Mrs Coburn was placing glass tankards onto a tray. With an enquiring tilt of her head she acknowledged Vince. He asked for a double whisky and water. "Have one for yourself."

"I don't partake while on duty," she said, fixing his drink. When are you not thus occupied? he might have batted back, had her general manner invited such repartee. She placed a glass before him.

"Seen my friend pass through?" Vince sipped a smoky blend.

"Yes." A slightly pondering delivery as if Rory's return was not something she for one would confidently have counted upon. Vince was puzzling over this when a rumbling shook the floor. Hanging beer glasses 'tinked' against each other.

"What *is* that?" he said to forestall her signs of moving off.

"Heavy vehicle." Her eyes were weary, pained and stoical.

"Been a few this evening."

She took that as a statement not requiring an answer.

"Reminds me of a time longer ago than I care to contemplate." The whisky warmed and words slipped out of him. "Grandparents lived by a railway line. They never noticed—but we did when trains went by. Whole house rattled."

From her tight smile she either appreciated his little saunter into the past, or despised it. She went to the fire and began digging coal out of the coal scuttle and flinging it into the narrow aperture with a furious energy. Hot-faced, she went to the bar; forgetting her self- imposed stricture, she poured herself a generous measure of gin, ignoring the scraps of lemon in the glass dish. She tipped back her glass and half her drink was gone.

Vince thought the silence between them should end. "Been here long?"

"Since Matthew died. There he is." Matthew was behind her shoulder in a framed photograph amongst silver tankards. A man with a smudged brow and cheeks leaned out through the opening at the side of a steam engine. Grinning. Cap at a jaunty angle.

"Steam trains were his hobby—and a passion. He was a bank manager."

"Sorry to hear that—I mean about him passing on. Sudden was it?" On shaky ground. Nosy and sympathetic. Vince didn't evade difficult issues in those flip chart sessions he ran for the council. Tomorrow he'd be on the hills, forgotten by her, she by him.

A quick tip of her glass and all the gin was gone. "Yes, he was stoking the firebox. Dropped dead. Heart." Vince was unsure how to respond to this slippage of her frosty exterior. She was smiling past him as if someone she actually liked were just coming in. "I never stop expecting him to come through those doors."

Absurdly, Vince found himself jerking his head around to the lounge doors, where Rory happened to be entering at that moment. Mrs Coburn took this as an opportunity to absent herself from the lounge as if Vince were a package which could be safely passed on.

"Drink?" Vince said heavily.

"No thanks," Rory said.

"No? Yes, well I didn't think you would. Anyway, m'lady's gone— and so shall I . . . be, if that's the correct grammar." He stood and the floor trembled slightly underfoot. "Heavy vehicle," he said. A dull puzzlement on Rory's face. Vince moved across the lounge and hoped Rory wouldn't follow. His tired legs gave the floor a perceptible slope.

Size rather than content had been more of a consideration when he'd been choosing a book to pack in his rucksack. In their room, translating local dialect in the Book of Pennine Tales failed to distract Vince from a matter of crucial importance, which refused to clarify any more than the angular blot in the hills had. Furtive footsteps drew him to the window.

More restless than the ones casting them, shadows rippled across opposite house fronts.

He was in a mood for expecting the wall-mounted television not to work, and it didn't. As Rory walked in Vince didn't break off staring at the fuzz in the screen. Rory sat on his bed and did the same. Vince considered descending to the lounge again, not to spite Rory but out of sheer necessity. Noting the sensation of his heart beating was no way to spend an evening.

"We should ask Mrs Coburn about buses. Maybe I'll come with you. The hills from here lack a certain variety if truth be told."

Rory stared vacantly. No guarantee he could get home unaccompanied. What self-denial, what self-sacrifice, Vince thought with some bitterness. Emma would be proud. "And I'm not one for the old saw-bones—but maybe you should, you know, have a word."

Rory got up off the bed, faced the window a moment with its bobbing shadows, then was heading for the door. "Where are you . . .?" Rory was gone. Vince didn't think Rory had taken his advice as an insult; probably hadn't taken it in at all. It felt like a desperate measure extracting his mobile phone from his rucksack and ringing Rory's landline.

Moira's chimney flue voice answered and Vince came to the point quickly.

"I'm concerned about Rory."

"What's he done now?" A downward-stepping inflection; Rory a wayward relative. In the background someone was putting a valuation on a tea service. "He was talking about giving up the walk and now he's not talking much at all."

"Does he have to?" A rare defence of her husband.

"I've never known him as short as this of things to say for himself. He's deathly quiet most of the time."

"Wish he had been the night before he went off with you," she said. "Stumbled in at three in the morning, knocking things over—a right din. Woke me up. I shouted something down. 'Derby Arms!' he shouted back. 'They shut four hours ago,' I said. He said he'd taken a short cut across the railway line. 'More fool you then,' I said. One or two get killed every year trying that. There's a bridge half a mile off but some just can't be bothered."

Bickering; Rory must have had his fill of that. Moira was telling Vince not to take any nonsense when the television spoke. "Who's that?" she said, her voice like a blunt knife. "Television's on the blink," Vince said. "It's not five-star here." He drew the conversation quickly and awkwardly to a close and lay back on his bed and watched the screen. He'd seen similar displaying arrivals and departures in stations. What had the woman said behind Moira's advice? He waited. Announcements were usually repeated—and this was no exception.

Lemonade fizzed in the screen in time with each precisely enunciated syllable. "Please make your way to the station for the late service."

Vince sat up. The violence of his shuddering wasn't all down to him. The hotel shook. He left the room. An emptiness where his heart and lungs had been. He had to guard against becoming like Rory.

She was wiping pristine tables in the dining room.

"Late service?" he said.

Refolding her J-cloth gave her time to prepare her reply. "Yes. It'll be here soon. They're drawn to it. Trains take. This one gives back."

Vince gripped handfuls of his hair. At his expression, which should have frightened her, she merely looked sad and superior. She resumed wiping a table top. "It's not here for the likes of you and me. I suggest you go back to your room."

Vince shoved his way out through the hotel's doors. The street was deserted. He turned left, the way the walkers had gone. The woman was off her head—and he'd seen for himself the condition of the station. So had Rory. He wanted to go home and nothing at the station was going to facilitate that. There would be no arrival at Gridling Bridge Station tonight, nor any other night. So where would Rory have gone to?

A trundling as of small wheels bumping over cracks in a pavement took Vince back to his and Rory's arrival. The 'porter' might have noticed Rory within the past ten minutes, *everyone* here noticed Rory. Vince ran over a cobbled thoroughfare and came out before a factory covered in graffiti. There was a cinder car park to the side of it. Hoses rotted before the empty gape of a fire station. There was a stepped yard alongside a school comprising nothing but red-brick extensions. Low-rise residential blocks farther off. Further still, a wide staircase of terraced streets faded by a light mist. Not sight nor sound of the porter fellow—Vince was looking in every direction when the rumbling made the road surface seethe.

Vince held steady as he became aware of massive dark blocks moving behind distant crumbling housing stock. They could have been carved from solidified black smoke, and were the height of roof guttering. Now they were nearer, and he saw they were marked by odd gleams as of shining jet in a general matt dullness of coal.

Vince tottered at the sight lumbering across the edge of the car park. The engine was almost the height of the carriages it pulled. A cattle guard affair was like the closed gates of an asylum. Above it was a windowless iron mask veined with vertical pipes which bent back at the top to merge in a Medusa tangle with twenty yards or so of exposed engine parts directly behind. Pipes of varying thickness were twisted upwards and blew smoke at the stars. Pistons punched and gleaming black rods linking the monstrous wheels rose and fell. Valves spewed rusty liquids or milky steam. Other apertures oozed blood reds and honey golds. In deep interstices fires glowed. There was black smoke—here drifting, there in violent spurting jets. No window or other indication of cabin space in the bizarre mechanical complexity; Vince wondered wildly if the thing drove itself.

With the engine passing from sight, the gargantuan carriages pulled behind offered no relief. They were near identical. If they weren't containers, they were monoliths which in another place others might kneel and worship before. Massive chains linking them swung and clashed together. There were myriad squeals and groans.

Moments passed and the moving panorama showed no signs of ending. He feared the rearward carriage could be as remote as the engine now must be. He pressed the heels of his hands to his eyes and wondered if all of this was happening behind them. This train didn't belong out in the real world. Even a real train a third its size couldn't just slip along trackless ways between buildings and back yards.

He opened his eyes. The train was palpably present. It displaced air which thrummed around it. But then suddenly, without any warning, a carriage had none following behind. A final carriage—*a final carriage*. It felt like a reprieve. The last carriage vanished behind the factory. A deep rumble and tintinnabulation of dangling metals remained, then these too dispersed, leaving a silence that breathed a testament to the scale and mystery of what had gone by.

Vince had to share his astonishment. Talk would generate explanations. His attempts to merely describe would surely awake Rory from his listlessness. But Rory wasn't here. Somebody else was.

It would be even better if the man at the street end had seen the train for himself. If Vince hadn't already witnessed the odd behaviour, evident now, at earlier points of the evening he might have suspected the sight had driven the man mad moments before. Having experienced the train himself, Vince knew nothing else would ever faze him. He could deal with this uncertain borderline between eccentricity and insanity. And in any case there were worse afflictions than thinking you were a railway porter on the streets of a town without a functioning railway station. Maybe seeing an impossible train was one?

The man was gradually working his way nearer. He'd have been within arm's reach sooner were it not for his twirling, his light-footed dancing backwards and forwards with the loaded sack truck. The man had gone to some trouble with the peaked cap, the dusty black uniform with tarnished brass buttons. His own belongings, piled to his own height on the toe plate? It was becoming apparent they were in a desperately poor condition; faded, torn; loose threads trailed for several feet; there were coppery stains, yellow stains; a bass relief of markings looked fungal. It occurred to Vince the man was a genuine former railway porter driven to madness as well as penury by redundancy. If that were the case, his misfortunes hadn't ended there.

Vince crouched in the shadow of a wall, tried to silence his breathing. Unthinkable, advancing out into the sulphurous light to make himself visible to the man. And would he have been? Or heard. There was no guarantee that sight wasn't possible from cracks in that swollen blackened remnant of a face. The tissue paper twists of his ears might yet hear. Vince covered his nose and mouth with a hand—the luggage piled on the toe-plate stank of dry old meat—or the man did. Vince gagged soundlessly.

The porter had drawn level. Vince closed his eyes as if that might cover himself more comprehensively in the shadow of the wall. He heard shoe-soles twinkling between and to each side of the little wheels. He was bursting to breathe by the time the dainty complex steps had passed by.

He and Rory had to escape from the town. He shuddered to think that had Rory been present the porter might have interrupted his jaunty progress. It was clear to Vince that he himself was about as visible to the porter as he had been to so many others this evening. The same couldn't be said for Rory.

Following the porter at a distance, Vince felt as noteworthy as his shadow sneaking across shops fronts. Two or three times he saw others heading in the same general direction. He could guess where. If not curiosity, then dead-eyed passivity might have carried Rory along with them. He had to make sure Rory wasn't amongst the number whose voices he could hear.

The rumble again he knew was the train. It adhered to no earthly properties of time and motion. An indeterminate phenomenon, arriving from disparate directions. It could just as well not have appeared to him in the hills. Even now, he doubted anyone had accurately predicted when it would arrive at the trackless station. But that was where it would stop.

The porter was dancing with greater animation, legs kicking alternately to each side of the sack truck. Then, tipping it back, he made a tight turn into the slope of a side road. Vince followed a moment later, saw at the bottom of the hill the black mouth of the station entrance.

It took no noticeable effort to control the sack truck on the steeper incline; the feet pattered as deftly as ever about the small squeaking wheels. A moment later the porter tipped the trolley back towards him and executed a sharp left-turn into the tunnel entrance.

On the tunnel's threshold, Vince hesitated until squeaks of small wheels had merged into those of scuttling vermin. Setting forth, his shadow leaned ahead of him, then past the bend it pooled uncertainly before shrinking back as the wan light grew ahead.

The concourse was full, as was the wooden bridge linking the platforms. Everyone faced the same way. Walking between them he glanced one way then the other, surreptitiously at first, wincing at dead flesh, scar tissue of old mutilations, smashed teeth, facial geographies realigned where not completely obliterated, flesh skimmed clear of red bones, brown bones protruding like the prows of model ships. No reactions to his scrutiny, no focused stares, no glints of envious hatred at his clear skin, his intactness.

Children were less beholden to the great emptiness beyond the platforms. A couple ran around the broken motionless obstacles. As they dodged and swung and scampered nearer, Vince kept still, shut his eyes against the sight of their glistening faces, encrusted with slick rubies and red threads. Then they were gone and he could continue forward, searching, and with a growing sense of futility.

No space was unoccupied. The shallow trenches between the platforms were all full. The occupants of the nearer one were oblivious of the great bushes of nettles they shared the space with. Though the light was as abstemious as the flesh faces were clad in, Vince had soon convinced himself Rory wasn't amongst their number. So still, they were; the nettles showed more animation. There rustling became more agitated; no reflexive jerks of hands as nettles surely stung.

Vince felt a dry chill wind, it barged amongst the watchers, ruffling stiff hair, plucking at loose-fitting garments, collars, hems, scarves. The rumbling was everywhere. It jumbled his insides. Voices imitated it, rather than communicate dread or wonder to immediate neighbours. An alertness, a straightening of posture in those capable. A slow sway of bodies on the farther platforms and in the populous gaps between.

Vince stared as fixedly as the one next to him, who had no eyelids to blink with, as the monstrous engine came into view from the left. The towering carriages followed, each linked by a massive encrusted chain to the one before and behind. Under-parts clanged and sparked.

Vince had lost count of the number of carriages that had passed out of sight in the interstices between warehouses to the right when the whole collection came to a halt. He couldn't conjecture how many more carriages were yet to reveal themselves.

An unobstructed view of three complete carriages now. The flank the central one presented was like a huge iron screen in a condition of extreme rust, the process of oxidisation making for a scabbed texture.

Gazes had converged on a figure clambering athletically onto a short length of running board protruding out a good four feet above the level of the farthest platform. Vince recognised him. The caped man stared out as intensely as he'd stared through the window of the launderette. Vince was expecting him to make an announcement when a vertical fissure appeared and widened as a hitherto unnoticeable component slid into the body of the carriage.

A doorway, though positioned too high for anyone to enter with ease. Vince began to think some extraordinary person was about to appear from the blackness and these present were all anxious to see it or listen to what it might have to say to them.

Nothing like that. A general surge forwards, arms of those nearest reaching. The caped man stooped, braced to lift. His one bulky shoulder more than adequately compensated for the absence on the other side. His arm stretched low and grabbed a withered hand, one of many shaking for attention. An easeful lift propelled a bag of bones upwards and through the dark doorway. A forest of drably sleeved thin arms sought the same assistance. The man stooped again, grabbed another hand and again an insubstantial shape was soaring upwards, to be consumed by the black rectangular mouth.

Several more were pulled aboard as Vince watched aghast. Space vacated by those gone into the train was immediately filled by figures with a desperate mute need.

His gaze sharpened on a raised arm. The hand grasped at nothing as yet. A puce sleeve in the prevailing beiges, duns and greys. The wearer was briefly knocked to one side by someone equally single-minded and Vince glimpsed words—'Leeds University'. Rory had never been there—and where did he hope to go now?

Vince shouted Rory's name and bodies sucked in the sound. Rory turned his head, slack-mouthed and briefly aware of something beyond his need to be singled out by the caped man. He turned and reached up again, revealing inches of flaccid waist, and even at this distance the yawning meaty gashes appeared of mortal significance. Not so much *when* Rory had sustained the injuries locked into Vince's thoughts as *how* he'd was surviving them. Looking at those around him, Vince couldn't imagine anything inside the carriage that might cure or fix their chronic physical impairments, and he doubted that was what they sought in any case. So what did they want?

He lunged forward a few feet—stopped.

A fingertip contact, then a definitive grab onto Rory's hand and he was lifted upwards, his stockiness now manikin-light. All so fast, so routine—as if Rory had been just one item in a mass of sentient luggage. No chance for a last look at what he was leaving—jerked into the black opening, gone.

Vince's groan threatened to split him apart. Even were he to succeed in fighting his way through the hordes to the carriage, what would he do? Shout? Make appeal to the caped man? If he were to raise his hand and be chosen, lifted, what would he find inside and would there be a means to escape again, with or without Rory?

The carriage was no place for him. For Rory it must have been since the moment he'd sustained that terrible injury. He recalled Moira's complaint. It had been a costly shortcut across those unlit railway tracks.

Vince watched as dozens more were hauled up into the train. Figures brushed and bumped by him. How much longer before he'd be the only one remaining? And if he should find himself before the carriage would he take the reaching hand, if offered, in the need to understand?

An academic question. He wouldn't be taken.

And he wouldn't be alone when the train departed.

The caped man was standing straight. The many stretched up arms fell back to scrawny flanks. No cries of frustration or disappointment. A sliding panel reduced the black opening to a crack, then there was no hint in the scabbed surface that there had ever been a way in.

The man put the tips of his circled finger and thumb to his lips. A glint of silver and a single silvery piercing tone. He jumped lightly from the plate and into the midst of those who would have to wait until another time.

A clanking from way up the line. Successive clashes as great chains took up slack and huge weights shifted forward. The first carriage in complete view on the right shuddered, then moved a few inches. The enormous chain linking it to the central carriage lifted. Tension briefly before the central carriage with its new cargo moved with a grinding of its massive wheels. The following carriage jerked in turn and then the three were in motion together, dragging the ones as yet unseen into sight one by one.

Minutes of staring before there was a final carriage. Massively, it too moved out of sight. The clanking and rattling, the wheezes and breaths as from monstrous iron lungs lessened in the night, became nothing.

An atmosphere of resignation as figures dispersed—back to the tunnel, or out into the black lake with its decrepit abandoned rolling stock half-drowned in darkness. Last of all the porter with his sack truck of luggage danced off into the tunnel, and Vince was alone.

His phone rang as if from a distance. For some reason, the real world hadn't ceased turning. For a moment he feared Rory had awakened to the realisation of some terrible and irrevocable fate and would be begging for rescue.

It was Moira. "Can I speak to him?" Grudging concern—maybe a little guilt.

Vince said, "You can't. He's not here."

Seconds of silence in which Moira must have expected a fuller response. Her dry smoky voice came through decisively, "I'll come and collect him. You can carry on with your walk." She blew out into her receiver. "He's going to have to shake himself up."

"I've just said—he's not here. You're too late."

"Where is he?"

"On the train."

Platform Alteration: The DUMB Network

Driving trains is a dream job for many. The romance is still there at some level even as trains develop more and more into cattle carts where efficiency is far more important than comfort or any kind of romance. Maybe you dream of driving a tube train, becoming one of the few who keeps the city going as you hurtle through hallucinatory tunnels. Maybe you want to pilot a bullet train even, which feels like a guided fighter jet as it barrels down its sleek undulating track. Or maybe . . . well, how about a subterranean rail network travelled by maglev trains at multiple thousands of miles per hour . . .

Make the right career choices, and maybe you can. For *it exists!!* Nobody knows about it. The evidence is shaky at best. But *it exists*! The tunnels span the continental United States and beyond, drilled by special nuclear-powered TBMs that *melt* their way through the ground covering several miles a day. Nobody knows about them either, but they also *exist*. They connect the deadly secret and hidden underground military bases and bunkers that everyone knows are scattered across the United States.

Your approach to conspiracy theories all boils down to how much you trust the government of course. Whichever government you happen to have the misfortune to be stuck under. For just about anyone who thinks and asks questions, that very quickly becomes *not very much* and you soon start to get that nagging feeling that there is more than just incompetency, discord, self-interest and carelessness going on. There has to be malice and hidden agendas, surely? You wonder what secrets they have, for you can bet your rosy pink arse they have plenty – and it's an open question which is more paranoid, them or you. We humanity couldn't possibly fuck up this royally without a malevolent motives to help us – could we?

And hey – in the face of that, horror stories of secret alien contact and evil experiments, in places so deep and dark and secret that the surface world seems like just a memory maybe don't seem so daft – do they? The DUMBS – Deep Underground Military Bases – in the USA somehow seem almost inevitable.

Don't they?

And of course, such an evil underworld would need a transport network and yet again the humble train arises to fill a need . . .

It is not my place here to get into a long discussion of conspiracy theories and the forces that generate them, but I would ask two things: 1) What is it in human nature that makes us want so desperately to believe the least likely but most spectacular? And 2) Just why do governments seem to go out of their way to promote this sense of paranoia and uncertainty? Is that in itself a conspiracy theory? A conspiracy theory about conspiracy theories?

My head hurts!

If conspiracy theories truly teach us anything, it is the horrific scale of the dislocation that has taken place within our species – and how little power we actually have to shape our world.

I wouldn't mind driving one of those trains though . . .

DR

Escape on a Train

Steve Rasnic Tem

"That town is burning down," Carter says to the stranger sitting across from him.

But the stranger seems not to have heard him. He pulls the spread of newspaper even closer to his face, as if wanting to give his closest scrutiny to some account of murder and mayhem. Or perhaps it's because the train rocks and bucks so severely the stranger has to grip his newspaper all the tighter, drawing it closer to his face. Carter was never very good at physics, but he thinks that's what might occur. He studies the whiteness of the stranger's knuckles against the outside of the paper, trying to gauge by this whiteness just how many foot-pounds of pressure the stranger must be applying. At any moment, Carter expects to see the paper split in half from the forces being applied to each end. But then, luckily, the stranger has selected a tabloid-style paper to read, which Carter imagines must be somewhat sturdier than the larger size. So perhaps the stranger's reading matter is safe after all.

"That town? Outside the window? The one the train is passing? It appears to be burning down."

Still no answer. Carter gazes out the window, wondering at the length of time that has elapsed since the burning town first appeared in the train window, puzzled that the train still has not completely passed it. It makes little sense to him, since the town is small (soon to be even smaller) and the train, he is told, moving very fast.

Of course, the train doesn't appear to be moving all that quickly, at least from where he's sitting. He vaguely remembers that there are a number of physical laws specifically concerning moving trains and their relationships to those observers on the train and those observers off the train, say, watching the whole thing – the fire, in this case – from a grassy knoll nearby. But Carter can remember the specifics of none of them. Perhaps there's even a law concerning the relationship of a moving train to the burning town it is attempting to pass – and seemingly unable to pass with any speed – and the observer on the train attempting to interest a stranger into also becoming an observer. He wonders how the concept of 'witnessing' figures into this physical equation. Also the concepts of 'responsibility' and 'guilt'.

Outside the train window the small town – just a few buildings isolated out on the prairie where only a train might pass – continues to burn. Carter presses his nose against the glass and imagines he can feel the intense heat on the other side, outside the confines of this swift-moving train. The small town continues to burn and suddenly he is in pain and when he removes his nose from the glass a small patch of skin from the tip remains, adhering to the hot glass.

Even though the town is some distance away he can observe what is happening there with remarkable detail. An old-fashioned red fire engine is moving between the burning buildings, dragging its ancient canvas hose which is also on fire. Carter thinks the age of the fire equipment would be a problem in any case and now the hose is on fire, and the engine is in fact aiding the spread of the fire by dragging this burning hose through the streets. He wonders if anyone has warned the driver. On closer examination he observes that the man behind the wheel in the open cab, the man in the yellow slicker and black fireman's helmet, is also on fire, his torso and head and upraised arms a long tapering flame like that of a candle.

And yet he knows this is impossible. He knows one cannot possibly see such detail from a moving train. It is that lack of connection, of specific, closely-observed detail, he suspects, which makes travel by rail so attractive in the first place.

Here and there Carter can see open windows like dark mouths and hollow eye sockets within the flaming structures, and burning human beings – women, men, small children – transfixed in these dark openings, their own mouths and eye sockets opening wide with darkness. And it is all impossible, he thinks. Such observations from a moving train are impossible. Such pain must surely be impossible. Suddenly he wishes the train would go faster, much much faster so that it might pull away from the town.

"There are children, children burning up in that town," he insists, staring at the stranger's raised newspaper. On the exposed front page there are articles concerning murder, earthquakes, and arson. The headline reads: FATHER ABANDONS FAMILY: THREE FEARED DEAD. In exasperation, Carter grabs the man's left hand and pulls it down, separating the stranger from his paper. "Can't you see? That town's on fire! People, children are dying!"

The stranger glances out the window, then shrugs. "We're on the train," he says. "There's nothing we can do." Then, amazingly, the stranger grins.

Carter stares at the man. Then he touches the hot glass, pulling it away before his fingers can burn. "Children are burning like cotton! Their faces melting like a cheap plastic doll's!"

The stranger puts his paper full of murder and mayhem aside. "That's very unfortunate," he says. "But we're on the train, you see, moving past the town. The town remains still, an immobile location. It's physically impossible for us to do anything to help those people."

"But they'll die!"

"They're already dead," the stranger says. "There's nothing for us to do. We're on the train, they're on the land, the still, unmoving land. We're removed from them by sheer speed." And again the stranger grins, as if in the pleasure of his explanation.

Carter stares at the man. "And by time, too, I suppose."

The stranger nods. "Precisely."

"Because speed and time are somehow related," Carter continues. "I was never good in physics, but I believe that's true. Time and speed are related. On the train we're removed from them by time, and speed."

"And state of mind," the grinning stranger says. "For the people in the town are wrapped up in their present, workaday lives. We are living on the train, in the future, or toward a future, on a train headed for a destination. Their world could not be more separate from ours."

"So we have no responsibility toward them," Carter says.

"None whatsoever," the stranger replies. "It's simple physics."

It takes a long time for the town to burn to the ground, but not so long, Carter imagines, relative to the average train schedule. The window is still warm to the touch for hours after the town has been reduced to embers.

That night Carter finds it difficult to sleep on the train. The irregular clicking of the rails, the rocking of the sleeping car, the periodic tappings at his window probe into and irritate his sleep. The window tappings are particularly bothersome. Each time he hears them he rises out of the seats which have been converted into a bed and goes to the glass, pressing his face to the glass first on one side and then the other in order to look as far as possible down the length of the train. He sees nothing. He speculates on possible causes: gravel thrown up by the wheels, the slap of branches which have not been trimmed back, grit carried by the wind. The window tappings continue all night long, but he never sees anything. In the morning he discovers hundreds of round, slightly greasy spots on the glass.

There is but one empty seat in the dining car, across from the stranger from the day before.

"May I?" Carter asks, gesturing toward the seat.

"Of course," the stranger replies. "Feeling better than yesterday?"

Carter studies the menu. "Mostly. Some . . . trouble sleeping. That's all, though."

"Glad to hear it." The stranger grins, absentmindedly taps the folded newspaper on the table. Carter wonders if he has already read it, or if he is now feeling anxious to read it. He hopes the man has already read the paper; he doesn't think he could stand it if the man picked up a paper again. He isn't sure why.

Carter can just make out the small headlines showing on the folded portion: MAN KILLS WIFE, CHILDREN, SELF and PLANE FEARED LOST and HUNDREDS DIE IN FIRE. He turns to the train window. Out in a field is an impossible vision: a man in overalls is beating a young boy – his son? – with a piece of timber.

"So, are you married?" The stranger speaks so quietly Carter at first isn't sure the man has actually spoken, or if he's imagined the question.

"Yes . . . yes I am." Outside the train, the man in overhauls raises the timber higher with each swing as he beats the boy.

"Children?"

"Two. A boy five, a girl eleven." Is that correct? Suddenly Carter isn't so sure. Outside the train, the little boy's mouth stretches wider and wider in silent agony.

"But they're not travelling with you?"

Carter stares at the man, trying to measure his expression. "Why would you ask me such a question?"

"Just being friendly," the stranger says.

"You think I don't care? You think I'm like those fathers you read about in that damn paper of yours!"

"Just being friendly," the man says again, seemingly unaffected by Carter's outburst.

"You should save your worries for kids like him." Carter gestures toward the violent scene being enacted outside the window.

They both stare at the boy and his father. The boy's mouth now stretches impossibly far in his attempt to adequately express his pain. "Most unfortunate," the stranger says.

"We have to do something," Carter says. "Here we are sitting comfortably in our speeding train, and a child is being beaten. We have to do something."

"But I explained all this yesterday," the stranger says. "We're on the train, removed from that child by time and speed. There's nothing we can do." And again, the stranger grins.

"There must be something we can do," Carter says.

"Nothing. Relax. There's nothing either of us can do."

"That boy'll be destroyed. If not physically, certainly mentally . . ."

"That's his present. We live in the future, on the train. We cannot reach him."

Carter slumps back in his chair. "This was supposed to be relaxing. Like a vacation."

"Then enjoy yourself," the grinning stranger says. "You're riding the most modern of passenger trains. Shattering time and distance. The old life is gone – this is your new life, your destiny."

After the stranger leaves, Carter puts his ear against the glass pane. He can hear the boy's screams fading in the distance. And yet he knows it is impossible to hear such sounds from a moving train.

When night comes he sleeps no better. The rails click and the cars rock, and a tapping that begins at dusk continues through the night. The train passes through open countryside with only a few houses, scattered here and there, but in each house at least one window glows with light. And behind each glowing window Carter knows there is some happiness he cannot share, or perhaps some tragedy he cannot prevent.

A face rises suddenly into the glass, glowing like one of those distant windows. Carter stares hard at this face, but once he realizes that it is his son's face, it disappears, swept away by the wind created by the fast-moving train.

"Somebody has to save him," Carter mumbles aloud. But he is on a speeding train, and can do nothing.

Night passes, and then the day, and then night comes around again. He sees the grinning stranger now and then: in the dining car, the lounge, passing through on his way somewhere else. He's afraid to speak to him: afraid of all the questions, the too-easy, yet perfect, excuses. In the landscape outside his train window the impossible occurs: murders are committed, avalanches bury skiers, children are abandoned and ignored, houses burn down. And there is nothing he can do. It is impossible for him to do anything. He has made his escape on the train; their lives could not be more separate. He has left his responsibilities behind on the station platform.

Night passes to day again and the tappings continue at his window. He wonders if they merely want to gain his attention, or if they in fact want to escape their present situation and board the train.

Eventually it seems as if it is the train standing still, and the land, the people enacting their little dramas, rushing past, flooding his senses, leaving him behind.

"You asked about my children," Carter says one morning to the stranger. "Well, I left them behind. Abandoned my wife, and them."

"That's all in the past now," the stranger replies. "You're on this train, now."

"I couldn't support them; I kept losing jobs. I was never a very good father, or husband."

"Look out the window," the stranger says.

In the valley below them a swift-moving river has improbably left its banks and is pushing houses, cars, livestock, all rapidly down its path.

Carter can see the smooth fish-shapes of human bodies tumbling in the flood. The train, of course, is safe, on a bridge high above the valley.

"We can't do anything," Carter says.

"Correct. You have no responsibility. That is another life. You have escaped." The stranger grins so fiercely Carter is surprised the man is able to get the words out.

"It was best that I leave."

"Of course." The stranger thumbs through a week's accumulation of newspapers. Carter can make out only pieces of the headlines: HUNDREDS DIE . . . MAN JUMPS . . . 23 INJURED WHEN . . . CHILD ABUSE ON . . . CANCER UNDER . . . FIGHTING CONTINUES . . . WAR DECLARED BETWEEN . . . ESCAPEE FOUND . . .

"Anyway, I was never very good in emergencies."

"Of course – few of us are," the grinning stranger says. "Few of us are responsible. But you're on the train, now. Its speed is beyond anything you've ever known before. It splits time and space. Its destinations lie in the future, another dimension entirely. Those other people, the ones outside the train, are merely lost messages coded into the winds, and the dry dust which disintegrate as the train pushes through their world. They cannot reach you. They cannot hold you responsible."

"But a witness? Doesn't a witness have some responsibilities?"

"This is the modern era. An era of media, media faster than any train. We are all witnesses. We are born into witnessing."

Carter continues his escape on the train. Rails click and cars rock, his wife and children tap and kiss the window, but he will not look at them. He will not feel guilty. And every day, unthinkably, people die outside his window, towns burn, children starve, planes plow nose-first into the ground alongside the tracks, and all the pleading voices are readily accessible to him. All he has to do is press his ear against the glass. Day rolls over into night and the seemingly endless night turns slowly into day.

Outside his train window he sees his wife and children caught out in an open field, a tornado like a man's anger ripping up the ground around them. Stones are picked up by the fierce winds and hurled like bullets at his family. Branches become spears. Odd bits of debris become flying shrapnel. He watches as his wife covers their children with her own body. He watches as the blouse across her back begins to tear into bloody strips. He watches as his children's clothes are plastered to their bodies by drenching rains. He moves closer to the glass, and he watches.

And as the impossible scene with his family continues, as his unlikely family is tortured and dies, he waits for the stranger to come and sit across from him. He's eager to hear whatever the stranger has to say.

Choice

Charles Wilkinson

Now there is little to distinguish one day from the next, not even the spice of disappointment, I suppose I must set it all down. Time is what you make of it here. Although most of the countryside in these parts is flat, the bungalow sits at the top of a rise and has a good view of the sodden fields that surround it. There are no stone walls, which would surely have sunk into the soft wet earth long ago, and such boundaries as exist are marked by low straggling hedges that remain leafless throughout the year. The leaden pools and slow-running streams criss-crossing the landscape are perhaps the most notable features of the area. Apart from the mud.

I can't remember exactly how I found the bungalow, but coming here was my choice. For some months, I had been living near the coast in a small town with white buildings and pretty wrought iron balconies in the Regency style. A place that I had been told had much to commend it. My apartment overlooked a shingled beach, a marina and the arc of a bay that was often filled with the masts and white sails of small boats. Having pale skin of the type that burns too easily, I had long avoided the glare of the midday sun. And so it was early in the afternoon when I walked on the promenade above the beach and noticed a wave – quite an insignificant one, I thought at first – that seemed to foam, as if its crest were coming to the boil. At the same instant, I felt a vicious scalding in my left eye, which was followed by the conviction that infinitesimal specks of moisture on my eyeball had evaporated, leaving the raw dry surface sensitive to every gust of wind.

The week afterwards the world became too bright. The sun seared the surface of the white buildings, turned every breaker to a shower of white-hot metal. However, it was, perhaps, the little unexpected coruscations, those for which it was impossible to prepare by shutting one's eyes, that caused the greatest distress: the light catching the chrome on a red sports car as it flashed down the coast road; the blade in the turning mirror; the sun-dance on the stony beach; the long line of thin white waves turning to wires pulled through the brain. I spent more and more time in my bedroom, with the curtains drawn. It was during these long hours alone that I came to realise how few friends I had found. It was true that the women were beautiful, but self-consciously so. And then the men. Wasn't their laughter too loud and their manner condescending? Though perhaps it was the way they dressed that made me find their company uncongenial. Every garment was immaculately cut, but weren't the colours just a shade too sharp, even corrosive: the acid yellow that stung the eye; the vibrant reds that bled beyond the fabric; the bilious greens?

A week later and the white town, the sea and its knives, the unremitting intensity of the sky's daily blue – all became intolerable to me. Even my one consolation … I won't call it a hobby, and certainly not a game … could not change the light.

Now I live at the bungalow. It's an unprepossessing place, with a flat roof and walls that once must have been cream, but which I sense are a dirty grey-brown, the colour of scum on a tea cup. It is impossible to open the windows. The front door has a portico that is out of proportion with the rest of the house. I did not at first notice that the bungalow, when viewed from the road, leans slightly to the left, as if it were about to slither down the slope. Either the builder failed to level the ground on which it stands or the foundations on one side have begun to sink. To reach it, you must climb a winding muddy track pockmarked with holes that are filled with water. There are traces of the gravel that covered it in more prosperous days.

It must have been about mid-day when the man arrived. Although the sun is almost never visible in this country, its position is suggested by a faint patch on the sky, just lighter than the unmoving grey ribs of clouds around it; sometimes, at about noon, the wet fields gain a strange, leaden luminosity, a response perhaps to the dim and distant light that plays upon them. Although I noticed him when he was almost at the bottom of the slope, and thus not clearly visible, I knew he was a man from the way that he walked with his legs too far apart and his slightly rolling gait. I did not go towards him, but waited calmly for him to reach the summit. It was some time before I could see him distinctly. A small wiry fellow, he had something of the jockey about him. He was wearing trousers, which were streaked with the dark mud that had been thrown up during his climb, and a leather cap. He was singing to himself, but I could only just make out the words: 'blood', 'wounds' and what sounded like 'lairs' or 'fears.'

"Are yer coming out?" he said.

"What?"

His eyes were black and moist, like those of a dog.

"I said … are yer coming out to play?"

The inhabitants of the town near the coast had many faults, but at least they were never culpable of this sort of lunacy.

"I have no idea what you mean."

For a moment he affected to ignore me. I could see him peering around as if he were looking for someone in a game of hide-and-seek.

"I know this place," he said at last.

"Do you indeed," I replied flatly.

"That's right." He nodded to himself, reminiscing. "Many a barney."

"I'm sorry," I replied. "I have simply no idea what you are talking about."

"Fight all night, they did." He laughed. "Up and down the stairs, up and down the stairs." He shook his head, almost disbelieving at the memory of it.

This was such nonsense that I did not feel obliged to respond. Then suddenly he was holding something I believed to be brown and saw to be small, between his first and second two fingers; it had an excremental gleam and was attached to a string. A conker.

"Come on then. Bring it out, bring it out!"

When he saw that I had no intention of obliging him, he raised his weapon and flicked his wrist. The conker struck my jacket with a dull thud. If I were capable of feeling embarrassment, I would have felt it at that moment. Then he made the mistake of looking up, meeting my eye. Very firmly, and without making a movement of any sort, I began to push him back. Inside myself, I withdrew all vestige of interest in him. He took several paces backwards, then turned as if to go, before once again swinging round to face me. As I stared at him, I felt only a far off disgust at this man beseeching for boyish companionship. And then he was walking away down the long slope. Once or twice, when I berated him under my breath, he lost his footing and fell, slipping and sliding on his back, leaving a smooth track of mud in his wake. Then finally he was up and climbing the five-barred gate. I made a last push with every ounce of my vision and he ran and stumbled up the road until he was out of sight.

I thought it quite possible that Holder was living at the bungalow before I came here. There appeared to be no other explanation for the manner of his arrival. Yesterday I found him standing proprietorially in the largest room in the house. He was wearing a tweed jacket, a v-necked sweater, a tie and a pair of shorts. Black stubble covered his chin. Afterwards I discovered that all the doors and windows were locked, and since there was no sign of a forced entry, I could only assume he must have a key. I was shocked to see him standing there, with his hands in his pockets and completely at ease, looking around as if he was considering where to put his furniture. If he felt any surprise at my arrival, he did not let it show.

"Who are you?" I said.

He turned towards me slowly. He had an oval face, a long, disapproving nose and eyes that I realised must be the same pale shade as diluted blue disinfectant. For a moment, he studied me evenly before turning away to continue his inspection of the room.

"Where on earth have you sprung from?" This time there was indignation in my voice. Nothing stirred in the grey light that matched the unmoving cloudscape that could be seen from the windows. Only once since my arrival had I seen the sun; it was as pale as spirit and hurt my eyes no more than the moon.

"It should fit in here, don't you think?" he said at last.

"What?"

"My model railway, of course."

"I know there's nothing in this room at this moment, but that does not mean to say that I had no plans to furnish it."

He looked at me without emotion. "And where have you come from?"

"The coast."

"Ah, the coast!" I thought you looked as if you hadn't been here for long."

"Perhaps not. But I just want to say there was no one living in this bungalow when I arrived and…"

"Not really the flatlands type, are you?"

"What do mean by that?"

"Exactly what the normal sense of those words suggest. Anyway, what's your game?"

"My game? I have no game. I'm not up to anything. All I want to point out is that when I chose to come to this bungalow I did so because I have a decided preference for my own company and no intention of sharing…"

"No, no, your game … chess, drafts, poker?"

"It's no game", I said, "no game at all."

He shrugged and then went over to an old leather suitcase, which he unlocked.

Although it often looks if it will rain, I have never seen it do so, and yet the ruts in the path leading up to the house and the furrows in the muddy fields were filled with standing water. Was the moisture rising from the ground - or did it only rain at night?

"You've met him, of course." He took out a length of track, several figures in black uniforms, and a herd of tiny cows.

"Who?"

"Pengevil, the boy with the conker."

"The idiot who's always singing to himself?"

"Yes."

"I know who you mean. But he's hardly a boy. He must be well over thirty."

"He was a boy when he came here."

Now Holder put a shining black engine on the track and attached several carriages. In another minute or two he had added a station with platforms, a stationmaster and a little man holding a flag.

"Do you want to help?" he said. The suitcase must have been a great deal larger than it appeared from the outside because he had found himself a small forest and at least three fields.

"Not really."

He arranged the cows in one of his fields and then turned his attention to the track. It was not long before he had the train running through a mountain gorge and then past a lake.

"I hope you're going to put all this stuff away once you've finished with it," I said.

Although he had been kneeling down in order to place a tunnel just beyond a bend in the track, Holder stood up and looked at me once again. The earlier neutrality of his gaze had been replaced by evident distaste. I felt a sudden thrust on my chest, and took several unsteady paces backwards, as if he had pushed me, which could not have been the case since he was holding the tunnel and a signal box in both hands. For a moment, I stood my ground, but in spite of every effort to return his antipathy I could not prevent myself from being steered towards the door; it was as if two invisible hands on my shoulders were now complementing the palm of pressure on my breastbone, which was steadily driving me in a direction that I had no wish to take.

Last night was the first time that I heard them since coming to live in the bungalow. It was just after midnight when I awoke. The building was suffused with a strange light I unaccountably knew to be purple. I think that I had already heard their cries and racing footsteps in my dreams for when I at last became fully conscious I was standing by the door and peering out. I did not have to wait for long before I saw a figure at the end of the corridor. It was waving thin arms, as if trying to beat off some aerial attacker, and screaming as it came, half running and half skidding, towards me. Once it had drawn level, I saw it was a boy of about twelve or thirteen. His mouth was wide open and he appeared not to see me as he rushed past. Although he was soon gone, losing control of his legs and then bouncing off a wall in terror, before careering out of sight down the passageway that leads to the kitchens, I was able to form an impression of matted hair and a tender, claw-ripped face patched with blood – I thought I saw the ghost of its colour below the cheekbones; his clothes were no more than rags. This boy was soon followed by another of about the same age, running silently and at great speed. His shirt had been torn wide open to reveal a dark wound just below his chest. He too failed to notice me. This time I followed him down to the end of the corridor and along the passageway. I was just in time to see his bare legs as he took the stairs that lead to…

The stairs? This was a bungalow. And yet for an instant I could have sworn that I knew where they were headed. And could I not hear, even now, the sound of their footsteps ringing out above me? There was a second of silence followed by a terrible scream and what seemed like the thud of bodies against the wall, interspersed with the crack of a head or an elbow against stone. Then there they were, tumbling down the last flight, locked in combat; though now the first boy must somehow have succeeded in surprising his enemy for he had him in a headlock and his fingers were working their way into the open wound. I was just about to intervene when suddenly they were both on their feet and off. The boy with the torn shirt was the first to reach the corner, and this time it was his companion in mayhem who was in pursuit.

I decided not to follow, but instead made my way back to the stairs. Even though the light was dim in that part of the building, I understood, rather than saw, that unlike the wall, which was made of stone, the steps had been formed out of some red-brown material. Clay? When touched, it crumbled, leaving a dry mark on my hand. I remembered the words that I had heard Pengevil reciting in a curious sing-song: *They fight all night and the blood from their wounds forms the stairs.*

From the portico, we can see the grey fields of the flatlands laid out in front of us. There are days when the landscape in the middle distance seems almost indistinguishable from the sky, where a rim of faint light around a cloud's edge suggests the course of one of our many streams, all of them sluggish, the shade of tarnished silver. In the foreground, we have the muddy slopes of the hill on which the bungalow sits. Now that I have been here for some time, I've noticed a line of rotten wooden stumps. I suspect they are the only visible remnants of a fence that is being sucked into the ground. There are a few shapes that are less easy to identify, although from the way they glimmer dully on the days when the patch of light that is the withdrawn sun is just perceptible, I believe they are made of metal. Holder has told me this is evidence of the submerged farm machinery that lies all around us.

Pengevil is once again at the bottom of the path that leads up to the bungalow. He is moving his arms about in a way that leads me to believe he is playing conkers with an imaginary opponent. We do not care for him, Holder and I, and it is this lack of love that keeps him at a distance. Yet we cannot always be vigilant. If we become too preoccupied with our own concerns, Holder with his model railway and I with my … I was going to say game, but of course it is not a game. As I was telling you, it is best if we do not become absorbed with our own activities to the exclusion of all else, for then Pengevil will once again attempt to climb to the hill and enter the bungalow. One feature that has been greatly in our favour is that the path is slowly opening like a wound that has not been stitched. I believe it will soon become impassable.

Even though I have closed the front door, I can hear the sound of Holder's train eternally on its track. Although I was loath to allow him possession of the living-room, I have been forced to concede defeat. There is no doubt that there is a force within him that is superior to anything that I am or was. Nevertheless, it is to our credit that for the moment we have overcome our mutual antipathy to the extent of co-operating in the matter of Pengevil. Holder has also succeeded in easing my fears about the two boys. The only explanation, he argues, is that there is a house on the site that is now also occupied by the bungalow. The quality of the light in this place is worse than ours; for instance, he has pointed out that it was not actually possible for us to see that the stairs of blood are red, although, of course, we know this to be true. We are free, he said, and we will not join them in their gaudy games unless we wish to do so.

Pengevil, I am pleased to see, is now walking away from the hill. He has undoubtedly noticed me standing under the portico and realised that for the time being there will be no point in attempting an ascent. I walk back into the house and through the living-room. The black train is going past the forest, past the field with the cows in it, through the gorge, along the side of the lake, into the tunnel and out of the other side.

"Why do you never stop at the station?" I ask.

"Because then the journey would be over."

"No, it wouldn't," I counter. "You could pick up some passengers and then go on."

Of course, he knows exactly why I have asked him this. If the train stops, then there will be, if only for an instant, some respite from the ceaseless sound of the engine, something close to the silence I came here for.

"Just get used to it," he snaps, "there's nothing you can do."

Some shadow of the emotion that was anger rises in me.

"Don't you think that all this is really not very suitable in a grown man? And why do you have to wear short trousers?"

"And why should I answer someone who's dressed as a cowboy?"

Then suddenly there is Pengevil, beating at the window, his face muddy, his dog eyes shiny with child-like excitement.

Holder and I exchange a glance.

"Shall we go outside?" he says.

"I think that would be a very good idea."

As soon as he sees us, he zigzags forwards, waving his conker on its string.

"Play, play," he says.

"Perhaps," Holder replies, "but first you're going to have to play one of our games."

"A very good game," I say, conceding the point. Of course, it's essentially a solitary activity, but there's no harm in letting someone else join in occasionally.

"And I wants to see them, I does. They fight all night and the blood from their wounds forms the stairs." He laughs and shakes his head.

"Not now," says Holder, "there's something that you're going to have to do for us first."

I take a bullet from my belt and then draw my weapon from its holster. My gun looks as shiny as anything can look around here. I break it, load, snap it shut and then *spin, spin.*

Holder explains. "One in six. Really very good odds. And thrilling too. If you win, I promise you'll feel as if you're almost alive."

Pengevil takes the gun and puts it to the side of his head.

"No, no, in your mouth," says Holder. Then he looks at me. No friendship there, just the half-joy of collusion.

Even though we are outside, I can still hear the sound of the train, the faint changes to rhythm and pitch as it rounds the corner, the moment of its barely audible passage through the tunnel. I imagine the cows, motionless in the field; the passengers eternally waiting on the platform.

There is a moment before Pengevil gets the angle right. We watch as the top of his skull lifts off. God punishes no one. It is our choice: this place, the company of the damned dead. And as for the blood, I won't say that I see it as red, but it has the closest thing to colour we will ever know here.

Act 3

Embankmen

Gavin Salisbury

I found a girl dead once
outside my hole – a body
snagged in hawthorn,
like a fresh bud
lost in blossom.
Maybe she fell from a train,
maybe thrown:
I didn't look too close.

(Long before you
had to come and dig
down the bank,
in the days when lads explored
in gangs – and almost unearthed
me on occasion.)

What did I do?
I ground in and waited; still
heard the pain when they found her
and took her away.

As I clawed my path
out again, famished,
I saw this patch of blackness
hooked among the haw flowers.
Could have been hers?
It was a cold enough night
for gloves, that's for certain.

Wait a minute – quiet.
Don't gabble over the rumble:

even after all this time I must
put my hands against the earth
if I can when they go over.
They soothe my buried bones,
especially the freight trains,
that men like us could delve in
and unload ourselves in another place.

No, the boy hasn't been again
since you last came round.
I don't know that he will now,
though he's surely another
burrowing creature

deep down. I was going to ask him
to live here with me as my own,
you know, to talk to
and look after. We could hunt
for clothes along the old lines, and deer
in the in-between spaces.

And then I wouldn't need *you* any more,
would I, you old fake?
And I could stop
digging out next door, unless
he happened to want it
when he got older,
needing a hole of his own.

Will he come back?
Oh, shut up
with your silence!
you're less real than *I* am
so leave me alone.

Just give me another
train on my hands,
the drip of diesel
on my head to fuel my dreams.

Sunday Relatives

Douglas Thompson

As a treat to himself, Doctor Hugo Wiseman locked his office door and set up his train set. On Sundays most of the other staff were home with their families, but his were so far away in time and space, they didn't seem worth the bother anymore. Becoming the director of a mental asylum is a peculiar sort of attainment in life, but not without its consolations. Who was there to question his eccentric hobby in this far-flung location? —So long as he indulged it outside official office hours.

At first the beautiful scenery here had enchanted him, reminding him of childhood holidays, and on his short drive home across the peninsula every evening he had sometimes fantasised that he was returning home to a wife and children rather than just a housekeeper and an ageing Doberman. He took out his favourite engine and tender now: a 1:72 scale replica of the Coronation Scot, a futuristic flagship in its time, now an eccentric figurehead of a lost avenue of history: the age of steam superseded by diesel, electric, and other forms of universal boredom.

He had subtly altered the manufacturer's track for the trains: taking off the plastic sleepers and nailing the rails directly instead, down into the dado rails that topped off the antique oak panelling around the room at waist-height. Train rails and dado rails. Neat. Thus their existence, let alone their function, was not apparent to any of Wiseman's visitors. Not that he received any of the patients in here. But his fellow doctors and occasional orderlies and nurses: they were gossips enough. The locking of the door wasn't paranoid, however. This was required in order to complete the circuit: an ingenious flap of wooden shelf which could be hinged down across the door to rest on its handle, allowing the circuit to be completed and the trains to start running, right around the room.

His walk-in cupboard, which he had finally had to ban Mrs MacAteer from cleaning, was his main station and landscape diorama. It had taken him months, perhaps a year, to construct in his spare time, and could still have done with a few additions. Why not do all this at the privacy of his own house? He was circumspect enough to understand how other people might find all this childish. But beyond that locked door, in the mournful white corridors, he knew there lay several dozen examples of the more harmful obsessions that the human mind can become fixed upon. Next to that, that private zoo of the human capacity for self-torment, his every thought and action, even these eccentric ones, felt reassuringly normal. Indeed, perhaps there was a relationship, a deeper balance. Like a temple to order and miniature perfection, his train set kept the asylum at bay, in his mind at least.

There was something deeply reassuring in the miniature landscape with its tunnels and bridges. Farmhouses and sheep. Vintage motorcars poised in eternal deference at the closed gates of level crossings. And the station with its multiple platforms and points, criss-crossing rails, overarching vaults in dusty Perspex and imitation-steel girders painted green. The little advertising posters, the tobacconist's kiosk, the artificially aged walls of brick, bearing witness to imaginary years of locomotive smoke and grime. Here was order, timetables, routine, all bastions against the great demon, whatever that was. Wasn't Wiseman entitled, just once, in this one case (meaning himself), to pass up the opportunity for deeper analysis?

Like a sore tooth, or a scab one has been instructed not to scratch, it was always there, just out of sight in the shadows of his consciousness. Of course, he know this demon was probably the void, the silence of loneliness, but worse than that: a sort of chaos and madness of undefined time, empty days, the boredom that should be freedom but that always feels like a prison in the end. Yes, life is full of such ironies. The sane and solitary man, free of all bindings of family and love, ought to be the most free of all creatures in the world, and yet through God's terrible strait-jacket of loneliness, finds himself in chains in a cell made of invisible walls. —No less captive than all the poor souls who mutter all night within an asylum, intoxicated by morphine and the smells of disinfectant. But order, routine, the reassuring rattle and murmur of trains stands against all that, ushers us out with a gleaming fresh ticket to somewhere.

Wiseman sighed wistfully with his chin on his hands then leaned down close above the tracks to watch the 3.15 from East Coker come rumbling in to stop at platform three. Meanwhile the 3.25 to Golders Green came rattling around what he had dubbed East Brae. A fine little row of farm-workers' cottages at the foot of a long field over near the side of the cupboard closest to the light switch. This reminded him of his aunt's house in Bavaria which he had often visited as a child, while the station terminus reminded him of his student days in Oxford. There had been a girl then hadn't there? Some girl, a distant memory now, even her face was blurred to him, her smell (of all things) almost easier to call to mind.

As he stared through the tiny darkened windows into the carriages, he found he was there again. Ensconced on those seats, full of youth and expectation. That fabric on the seats: how he'd forgotten, impossibly old-fashioned things, but there they were again clear as day now in front of him. And that smell of paper tickets and… what? It was impossible to expand upon it. The smell of trains, of travel, of hope.

The carriage jolted slightly, then gently got under way. A few of his fellow passengers glanced outside. That feeling in the pit of the stomach, a flutter, of movement, of suspension. Yes, that was it. On a train, a man is ageless and without responsibilities, tireless and deathless. Everyday life with its burdens and trials is lifted, put aside, indefinitely postponed. The rhythm of the rails is like a lullaby, comforting as the movement of our mother's bodies while we were still inside the womb. The destination is never quite known. The glimpses we get of backyards and gardens and lanes: voyeuristic, placing no obligation upon us to interact or judge. They seem to each embody a hundred thousand alternatives to our own lives, threads not yet grasped, other ways to brighter futures.

Strange perspectives, odd angles of views, these fleeting railway carriage glimpses. Even the grubbiest of suburban squares and hedgerowed avenues, from such a standpoint, seem sweet and grandiose. Like death, or some kind of dreamlike afterlife: a train journey leads us on a magical cross-section cut through the world we thought we knew, revealing to us that in fact we knew nothing, a blissful revelation. So many lives side by side in harmony, in dissonance, pregnant with possibility, each a path we want to take. If these are beautiful, we see by extension that we might be also. –That our place on the vast grain and fabric of life is sacred and privileged and necessary.

Wiseman looks down at his hands and finds that their skin looks strangely younger, the veins less pronounced. He glances up, going through a tunnel now, briefly. He catches his reflection in the darkened glass. He's nineteen again, his balding pate replaced by that dancing mop of dark brown hair he recalls always getting in his eyes. He recognises and remembers his old clothes like long-lost friends. The dark green great-coat with brass buttons, his red paisley-print shirt, tackety boots, student outfit. And his haversack. Did somebody steal it in the end? For now, it is still there by his side, with something in it. Something bulging, preposterous… is it? It can't be. The embarrassment. Flowers for Clarissa (*that* was her name!). Doesn't he realise she will dump him soon, after she meets Kevin from Plaistow? He stands up in the swaying carriage, thinking he spies somebody he knows through the porthole doors, the connecting corridor. He strides forward to enter the next carriage. Could it be? That resemblance…

It is himself he sees, seated in the next carriage, in suit and tie. A young junior doctor studying in London, attached to King's College, nose buried so deep in his medical text books that he is in constant danger of missing his stop. Wiseman sits down opposite himself in curiosity, in awe, looking over at the older man. He catches the eye of a middle-aged woman sitting next to the older Wiseman, and wonders if she can see the resemblance, eyes flicking briefly between the two of them. Probably not. He'd love to ask, but nobody ever dares to break the customary walls of silence on commuter trains. He'd like to nudge his own leg, tap his own foot, catch his own glance, but something stops him, locks him in tentative fear. The train slows as the next station approaches and the older Wiseman glances up in surprise, caught off guard, panics, fumbling his book away into his briefcase in bungling haste, reaches for his raincoat and dashes out.

Wiseman half-follows him towards the door, then looks after him through an open window, wistful as the train moves on. The back of himself hurrying off to his busy life. Oh, if only he knew, all the jolts and shocks in store. That unfortunate affair with Mrs Radcliffe. The misdiagnosis of that neurotic seamstress from Spittalfields that nearly got him censured. What station did he get off at to meet Clarissa anyway? He turns away from the window, wondering. Wasn't it a flat in Clapham she stayed in at the end? These ludicrous flowers he's still clutching. He walks to the next carriage, curious to see what he'll find.

He sees them and smiles, approaches, sits down in wonder in front of them, a seat thankfully left clear. It is his mother, sweet mother, so young, what age must she be, thirty two? And there by her side, feet dangling, little sandals and shorts and socks: himself as a four-year-old boy. He catches Mother's eyes for a second, but she politely looks away. Not recognising him of course. Not even a family resemblance, or one she hasn't yet imagined seeing in its mature incarnation. But he fares better with the boy. Bored and restless, little Hugo's eyes roam all over the carriage, alighting at last on the smiling young clown of a man sitting opposite him, who is sliding his flowers from his haversack now, one by one, like a magic trick. Lifting them like glowing gold now, their petals translucent in the yellow light from the dusty windows. With a flourish he hands one to the child as he smiles sweetly to the mother, his mother to be, or has been, as it were. And little Hugo is turning to look up at Mama to check if it is OK for him to accept. Of course, never out-stay your welcome. Wiseman stands and bows, the gift delivered. How much more trusting and friendly people were back then, no muttering behind your back about perverts and child molesters.

As he approaches the next carriage, they enter a particularly long dark tunnel. Damn, he curses, he always forgets this bit of the journey until it is upon him. Stumbling out into the next carriage, he thinks at first that a light bulb has failed, a circuit shorted, then an icy chill comes over him. The claustrophobic smell of sweat and fear and death. Hands of strangers reach up to his face, chest, searching his features like the pleading blind. He knows with a terrible lurching in his stomach where this is and calls out for his mother over the closely-packed bodies and bobbing heads. People curse him in strange accents as he pushes and grapples through the sea of acrid flesh. He thinks he hears, he does: his mother's voice, then his father's also, calling back, calling out his name. He pushes. A few people try to punch, lunge at him in anger, but he keeps fighting on.

As he pushes through, each of his flowers is torn from his shivering hands, one by one, the petals scattering and falling to the floor. He leaves a trail of smeared yellow pollen and green stems across the heaving darkness of human despair. In the end he has only one left, clutched in his first, a pathetic, strangled little bloom.

When he reaches them, he sees that this tunnel will never end, and that the only light here is moonlight through the tiny gaps in the wooden slats of the wagon doors. It is bitterly cold now, the night wind hurtling through, at least taking some of the smells of urine and excrement and terror with it. Mama, papa. In their best Sunday suits and hats and their pitiful little suitcases. Oh let them recognise him at last. Let him be known and knowable to them. Grant him this last respite, a chance to say farewell. Herr and Frau Weissmann. Their dark eyes watch him, gleaming with moonlight. Eyes adjusting to the shade, he sees their tender smiles amid their tears, of melancholy and of joy. To see their only son again, who they gave all their savings to smuggle to Switzerland, to London. Sacrificing, martyring themselves so that he might live. How to say goodbye, or whatever needed to be said, by a child too young to understand. Outside in the dark, the soldiers bark like dogs as the train slows down. The anger, the indignity, indignation. He beats his hand against the wood slats and prises two of them a little further apart and cries out for help for them, desperate to save them. But they look on, shaking their heads in slow resignation.

As the train turns a corner, the half-moon comes into view, and blinking, incredulous, Wiseman sees that it is a huge face, illuminated from one side by the daylight from high windows on a Sunday afternoon. —A doctor reaching down his enormous hand and lifting this whole carriage off its rails, bringing it up and out of the tunnel into bright daylight…

Wiseman examined the model carriages and goods vans and reassured himself that really there was nothing inside, not too much dust, not even a spider. It was getting late now. He tidied his train set away and disconnected the electrics, lifted the drawbridge from across the door and unlocked it. He donned his white coat and, checking his pocket-watch, set out into the sanitised corridors for his four o' clock stroll.

The late shift of nurses would be back on soon and the patients would get their trip down to the back gardens, closely supervised. The lucky, or well-behaved ones. Midsummer, the rain clouds of the morning banished, it might do them all a great deal of good.

On a sudden impulse, Wiseman took the keys to Miss Empson's cell and let her out himself, taking her arm and ambling with her along the corridors, escorting her down to the gardens, so she'd have an extra fifteen minutes of peace before the others came down.

Audrey Empson hadn't said much in thirty years, since a bomb had hit the tenement she lived in, killed her two children in front of her. Some unfortunate incidents afterwards with knives and passing strangers. To this day she only got to eat with a plastic spoon. Her gaze was often fixed on the far horizon, a wistful smile on her lips as if recalling happier times, precious memories. Sometimes Wiseman would just talk quietly away in front of her, about himself or the time of day, like dictating his own diary. And sometimes he could have sworn he saw her smile a little more at this, rocking slowly on her chair, as if soothed or comforted. Perhaps conversations were just noises after all. Dolphins and monkeys and crows were all chatting to each other all the time. Were we really supposed to believe that they were all saying something meaningful? Maybe in the end it was only about being there, calling out in the dark, just checking, knowing that someone was nearby and was kind, was listening.

Audrey and Doctor Wiseman sat side by side on the dark green-painted wooden bench in the garden, between the peonies and the chrysanthemums with the neatly mowed lawn in front of them, all immaculately maintained by Walter Simmons, the slow-witted giant from the village, who always wore the same old blue boiler suit. The July sunlight falling on both their faces, dappled by the shadows of leaves, reminding Wiseman at least, but both of them he devoutly hoped; of childhood summers. One day Audrey would talk, Wiseman was sure, and come to her senses again and ask to be released. At least he liked to imagine it. No doubt she wouldn't know where to begin, how to start over, where to pick up the last thread of her interrupted existence. Perhaps it would have to start with a train journey back to the locale of her old life, back to civilisation, the noisy city. In the meantime, here was a peaceful place to wait.

Yes, maybe that was it. This was all just a station, a station platform. Maybe to Audrey: everyone's voices were like echoing distant Tannoy announcements that never quite seemed to be referring to her. The ticket clutched so tightly in her fist, long out of season. But sometimes it was nice to be becalmed, in a sanctuary like this. When she was ready, Wiseman liked to imagine that he might travel with her. Back to the world. It was a long time since he'd travelled on a real train.

Platform Alteration: The Necropolis Railway that Was and the Sewage Railway that Wasn't

Apparently, way back in the late 1850s when London was getting increasingly desperate about choking on its own shit, some bright spark made the suggestion of using the railway to get rid of it – to run a dedicated service of sewerage trains out of the city. The plan was rejected – apparently rather quickly – and London went on to dig the city's first sewer system instead . . . but there is something rather nice about the thought process going on here. If there's a problem, don't worry – the railway can fix it.

Even though the dedicated shit trains never materialised, the railway did get the chance to fix something else, if anything even more dramatically and at roughly the same time – when the London Necropolis Railway opened. And yes, that is exactly what you think it is. Given the extreme crowding in the London cemeteries, something urgently had to be done with the city's dead bodies? And what was the solution? The marvel of the age to the rescue, of course! The result was a special railway terminal near Waterloo and a regular service of dedicated trains directly to a massive new out-of-town cemetery, offering one-way 'coffin tickets' for, well, up to 60 dead to travel in dedicated 'hearse vans' while the passengers rode in standard passenger coaches. The cemetery was carefully equipped with not one but two stations – one for Anglicans and one for Nonconformists (everybody else basically). Indeed, the entire system was carefully partitioned in both religion and class to prevent both mourners and corpses from different social backgrounds mixing.

The seal of the company could hardly be more dramatic:

They didn't mess around the subject back then it seems.

Funeral trains are a thing of the past now of course – though we still have some weird trains travelling our rails - weedkiller trains and, rubbish trains to distant out-of-town landfills – even nuclear waste trains. It is hard to imagine funeral trains running through London's crowded transport network today. Likewise the dedicated shit railway in the sense the Victorians briefly imagined it. In the world of might-have-been though, I think they would HAVE to have their own dedicated tunnels deep below the city – and there must be a few story possibilities in both those concepts!

DR

The Engineered Soul

Jet McDonald

I am Charles Monkface and this is my stand. There being no room on Sclater Street, I take myself to Brick Lane and set my stall outside The George. The publican, Billings, is fierce with gout but he sees my worth for ale and I keep my ground.

The illiterates do not buy my Railway papers but they listen to me speak for some coins in the hat. And so, there being little else to occupy a good mind, I read the journals and give them a summary.

I have a whistle made of two wooden barrels so that when I blow it makes the noise of an engine and I have timed it such that when the Express from Liverpool Street passés it shakes the beams of the ale house. The illiterates do not favour committees, they do not understand wigs and law but they know the rails are paved with gold and the viaducts with fame.

"Tell us of Mr Hudson," they shout. As if the chairman of the Midland were a Napoleon, as if I bring news of a battle from the front, as it advances with its iron and sleepers through their lives.

*

I build a shack outside The George. I have raised some poles from the table and back to the public house and nailed planks to the sides and top. Billings supplies me with pie and ale and rents the table to my right to a doctorer of shoes and to my left, a maker of toy mice. The mice move on rails on a wooden board by means of a rod. It is a poor man's train.

The shoe doctorer buys old footwear, patches them with paper and sells them 'warranted'. They stand a few weeks wear but go to pieces in the wet. His customers hobble past and swing their broken heals at him. He tries to force entry into my shack by pulling at the planks near the paving, but I will not have it. My stall is my chapel, a confessional in which I must immerse myself for the day's oration.

The gentry have read in the Railway Courier and the East London Gazette that I have spirit guidance from the navvies, that I know which company will offer the greatest return. Not one to obstruct the channels of finance, I have affixed a sign to my shack.

Charles Monkface Seer of The Railway.

Sometimes when I do not remember what Mr Hudson of the Midland announced to the directors of the East Counties, I let my spirit guide me to that assertion. "The stock of tomorrow," I declare, "is the prophecy of today," and the gentry tap their canes, write in their pocketbooks, cast a glance at each other and check their pocket fobs as the engine leaves Liverpool Street and rumbles through Shoreditch to the East.

I no longer eat with Billings in The George. I must separate myself from such worldly matters. It is not enough to talk of railways but of the ways the rail makes us and so I read the natural philosophers. To this end, I have hammered shelves into my shack and stacked them with books from the market. To prevent theft I have fitted iron rails to the outside and then planks to these. I have the works of Leibniz, Descartes and Spinoza within and the railway without. I do not leave the shack and I live off Monday's fruit from the Sunday market. And yet still the crowds come and I sell my foresight for a shilling. They listen rapt and I shape their minds to eternity.

"The seat of the soul lies not in earthly physic but vaporous steam!" I say as they wave their shares above their heads.

"But what of Mr Hudson. Is he to have The Great Northern?"

"Think not of Mr Hudson," I say, "but of the Pineal of the brain. For as a train enters a tunnel, so the spirit enters the body through the hemispheres. The Great Eastern will run not to Anglia but through your inner eye into your eternal conscience. The body is the locomotive of your passage through mortal life and it is only in the vapour of the heavens that you will reach your station."

I spend my shillings on the pineal glands of cadavers. I know a harlot who knows a vagabond who knows a mortician. One must slice between the hemispheres with a cheese wire and remove the glands from the mid brain with a fruit spoon. I have put them in jars with a little gin and put the jars between the books of philosophy, which I have arranged in order so I might better reach them. With one hand on my hammer, one hand on a book, and the pineal glands gazing inward, I fathom the transports of the eternal realm. And yet still they pester me with their infernal shares.

"What of The London and North Western? Will it have the Carlisle line?"

I nail the shutters shut and leave a small slot through which food and water and paper may pass. They post two shillings and a railway share and I write on their bill and return it through the hole.

There are three kinds of gentry. Those who think I am a medium, those who believe me cousin to a clerk in the Railway Committees and those who would have me chained in Bethlem. These last wipe their nose and post handkerchiefs through the slot.

I am prone to fits and the blood in my mouth has the taste of iron. Billings says I suffer from lack of pie and he will fetch a physician. I explain through the slot that I am near the plane for which pie is no longer needed. The fits are but the eternal realm's rejection of the physical vase that holds it and must not be dissipated but controlled. As the steam of the engine is forced to the piston, so the humors of the body must be channelled to the inner eye. To this end I build a wooden cage around my body so that I might be held, so that the fits might reach the gauge of spiritual transport.

Billings says I have the railway melancholia, an inverse of the mania. He says I should be bled by a barber and taken to The London Hospital. I tell him I am not for healing but for immortal life.

I fold myself into a shipping box and with my right hand I nail a plank over the palm of the left. I squeeze my head through an iron collar and push my free hand onto a nail pointing inward. I stare at the pineal glands I have arranged about me, close my eyes and look within.

Billings and the mouse maker organise a subscription for my funeral. There are horses with silver and feathers, pall bearers with batons, a mute with a wand and a pauper girl swinging a lantern. They do not bother with a coffin and use the shipping box into which I am fastened. They seal it with pitch, fix it with brass and sink it on a carriage of ivy.

My spiritual engine floats above, with pipe and boiler, piston and pump; it is faint in outline but bold in design. I stoke it with darkness, great lumps of black hewn from the dusk.

As my earthly carriage meets the Shoreditch station, I release the brake on my eternal soul, slip over the cortege and join the rails of the Great Eastern line. The ostrich feathers of the horses break in the draft, the mute screams and the lantern is blown to a smoking wick.

The Engineered Soul is an 'E' Class locomotive. It travels through eternity at one remove from reality. It flies above earthly locomotives while following the rails of reality below. It goes from the Midland line to York, then the Northern line back down to London, then the North Western to Edinburgh.

We take on passengers from the minds of the passengers on the train beneath us. We travel through the nervous rails of their brain to their pineal gland. The rhythms of their mind must be singular and regular, with vocations of unerring repetition. And so our passengers are clerks of the docks, tailors, laundry wringers; the journeymen of Empire.

Their spirits join The Engineered Soul, leaving their body chained to the machine of earthly locomotion. And then we steam to the next brain and the next, travelling onwards through the railways and onwards through the minds they contain.

The souls of the passengers sit one behind the other in The Engineered Soul and are in dialogue with those in front and with those behind – we have a great conversation that has no beginning and no end and reports back and forth along the train. And as we take on more souls the carriage grows longer, so extended that it begins to cross itself, as it weaves above the national rail like a snake crossing its tail. We speak not only with the passengers behind or in front but with those we pass as our carriages cross the carriages that precede us. We form a new mind, a composite of all it contains, with its own junctions and signals and spokes, an ever-fleeting self made up of the conversations of the industrial soul.

The physical railway spreads across England, Scotland and Wales, the companies merging and dividing but always extending and, as it advances, The Engineered Soul grows too, inviting souls to meet the souls on board. The railway is nationalised and so then too are our carriages, married into an Albion of travel. Until, with parliamentary decree, the 'British Rail' is cropped, its branch lines snapped like twigs from the trunk, the Beeching of a tree, and the government closes its purse. Like a winter pruning this only serves to set us free and I wrench The Engineered Soul from its roots. As I do so, the mirror of the rail network we have been following unpins itself from its destitute template and sits up. The tip of the soultrack reaches hundreds of miles into the earth's atmosphere. It claws at the heavens like the unfastened rails of a roller-coaster.

I take The Engineered Soul to its tip, fly off the end, and make a coil around the world. We wind around the equator and then at higher and higher latitudes until, somewhere over the Russian Steppes, we come across another train, its ghost outline approaching like a magic lantern from Asia. I blow my whistle, draw alongside and find the driver to be a withered man with a long black beard and a bullet hole in his forehead.

"We are two million souls," says Rasputin as he puffs smoke from the hole, "*The Sickle Express*; a million Siberians from the camps and peasants from the Russian steppes. Be careful where you roll, the clouds are spies."

He accelerates from us with his million-tailed engine, its steam pink like blood in saliva.

I untangle the Engineered Soul and swing west across the Atlantic only to meet a train with a bulbous chimney and a snow plough that carves the clouds like pastry. I draw alongside the pot-bellied driver and his pot-bellied nose.

"PT Barnum," he says, "and *The Tom Thumb Express*. Got a million Okies and freaks. Go find your own sky." He leaves a trail that glows yellow and red like the arc of a fairground ride.

I pull The Engineered Soul round and steam back to England where I must settle for Europe. But here I meet a shambolic engine, *The Drunken Bateau*, with a blue eyed boy called Rimbaud.

"I have a million foul-mouthed soldiers," says Rimbaud, "and they bow to no one." The boy flicks lice from his hair and his drunken soldiers hurl insults at our clerks as the carriages overlap. His wheels leave trails like cart ruts in the champagne sky.

But before we can settle into the regional networks, discover our own place in the companies of the planetary soul, we have incursions from pure white Japanese bullet trains filled with car workers, sooty Indian sleepers rammed with sweat-shoppers and the rusting hulks of Chinese transcontinentals stuffed with circuit board stampers. Every time a new space is negotiated, another competitor emerges. We can no longer defend and partition the sky and instead must tangle and join. We nationalise and then internationalise the companies of the soul and the chatter of our passengers spans countries, cultures and ages as trains weave back and forth between their tracks. We make a mesh of carriages that travels around the planet like an ever-spinning gyroscope, a railway of the global mind, streaked with colour and language, a brain scooped from the skull and strung with fire and magnetism.

Tangula   Ticlio   Condor   Galera

        Jiangkedong   Pikes Peak   Jungfraujoch

        Ghum   Ooty   Shimla

Mount Washington   Pattipola   Nobeyama

Ahju   Abramovo   Finse   Snowden

        Kubova   Chujeon   Ais Gill

        Skitube   Dent   Joginder Nadar

*

They throw clods of earth on the box at my burial. Billings tosses a railway share that sways back and forth in the cold air before it lands on the lid like a leaf. They do not hear me rapping on the wood, they do not hear the underground train that tunnels beneath the cemetery like a dream. But I can hear it knocking. I can hear it chattering on the tracks.

Stratford,

Romford,

Chelmsford,

Colchester,

Ipswich,

Beelings,

Woodbridge,

Melton,

Wickham,

Yox,

Darsham,

Blyth,

Brampton,

Beccles,

Lothing,

and

Lowestoft,

to the sea.

Didcotts

John Greenwood

When I was offered the opportunity – although that word implies an element of choice absent in this as in all my work activities – to travel abroad on behalf of my employer, I greeted it as a means of respite from my bitch of a wife and the two moronic adolescents I had apparently fathered by her. A memo from my supervisor informed me that I had been chosen to visit Zolnay, the capital of Bandrika, and once there to contact a regional manager in the Ministry of Transport, with the object of selling computer terminals to be installed in his departmental offices.

Included in the envelope along with the mimeographed memo were a company chequebook for my expenses, a pocket Bandrikan dictionary and phrasebook, and a smaller envelope containing train tickets. My attention was immediately drawn to the largest of these: a rectangle of stiff taupe printed in the blocky and unattractive Bandrikan script, with which I had as little familiarity as I did with the spoken language. The proportions of the ticket were not quite a square. I found this a dissatisfying shape. I could read the prices and dates alone, from which I gathered that I was to spend two weeks away from home.

Unusually, I was to travel alone. I queried this decision with my supervisor.

"The rest of the team are already away on sales trips, or else sick, or incompetent. It's unfortunate, but unavoidable," was his reply.

"I thought it was company policy not to send reps abroad alone, both for their own safety and to protect the interests of the company," I said.

Although the expression on my supervisor's face did not change (it rarely did), something in his manner altered. "You were specifically chosen for this task," he said. "Do you have doubts about your capacity to fulfil it?"

"I asked only in order to ascertain whether the company's policy has been revised, and if so whether the Staff Handbook should be updated to reflect this. Also," I continued, the thought having only just occurred to me, "to confirm that my activities will be fully covered by the company's insurance."

There was a brief hesitation, which my supervisor masked by clearing his throat. "It goes without saying that all necessary legal precautions have been taken care of," he said. "I don't know how widely you have travelled, but let me assure you that Bandrika is not a third-world country, albeit less technologically developed that its neighbours. Provided you conduct yourself in accordance with the expectations of the company, you have no more reason to fear mishap in Bandrika than you would on the company's premises."

From his reassurance I concluded that I would not be covered by the company's insurance policy should I find myself a victim of crime while abroad.

"As to the Staff Handbook, editorial decisions are beyond your remit. I would draw your attention to page sixteen, which states that, as circumstances demand, any of the policies set down therein may be revised, suspended or repealed without notice. Perhaps you should take the opportunity of your journey to re-familiarise yourself with this section."

My supervisor stood up from his desk and extended his hand to me, indicating the end of our interview. I understood that his words were both a commendation for my years of unexceptionable service, and an implied threat that I should not take this sales trip as an opportunity to indulge in louche behaviour. I could not imagine how the company would be able to monitor my conduct, and as far as I understood this was the main reason why sales reps were always sent abroad in groups. There was a potential career advantage in ratting out one's colleagues. That alone provided a sharp disincentive to employees wishing to satiate abnormal appetites beyond the surveillance of family and friends.

On reflection, I understood that my assignment was doubly insulting. Firstly, the task of selling computer terminals to the government of Bandrika was so routine that it could easily be accomplished by a single rep. Secondly, from the pool of available staff I alone lacked the energy and initiative to discover the routes to excess and dissipation Bandrika had to offer. Such had been the thinking of my superiors. I was, after all, a family man of 52 with slim prospects of further promotion and a pension I was anxious to safeguard. All of this only increased my determination to do something while abroad. Of necessity it would be something undetectable, at least by those who had a vested interest in exposing me, my colleagues and my wife for example.

Ensconced in a seat which had been reserved for me and to which I was entitled by law, watching through the window as the tracks branched out of the station, divided and recombined: this was the last time I can recall feeling a sense of peace, however misconstrued. Until we reached open country, I watched the scenery keenly, taking a particular interest in the narrow, winter-soiled back gardens of terraced houses, the rooftops and attic flats which from the elevation of bridges I could peer down into. Removed from them by steel and glass and speed, I could stare brazenly at the little figures going about their enigmatic, but no doubt wholly mundane, business.

Pleasant experiences pall with time and repetition. As we left the city behind, my homeland resolved itself, after interludes of suburban housing, of retail parks and industrial estates, into a series of waterlogged grey-green fields, interspersed with black fringes of copses and gnarled hedgerows. Even the Bandrikan dictionary and phrasebook were a more effective distraction than this turgid landscape, but I had little appetite for concentration.

The Bandrikan language and script are unique in bearing no resemblance to the systems of any of its closest neighbours; of this fact its speakers are childishly proud. Spoken nowhere outside its own borders, I had little enough reason to apply myself. Nor did I anticipate any serious difficulties in negotiating a deal. The events I relate took place during the infancy of the computer industry, and the products I sold on behalf of my company were still exotically futuristic. As a tool for conducting business they were an absurd waste of time, and incomprehensible to all but a few hobbyists. With most client companies I had only to identify the employee with enthusiasm for these toys for my negotiations to run smoothly. If my supervisor's information was correct, the chief engineer within the Department of Transport had written to us on his own initiative, requesting a demonstration of our products. More than likely I was the first man ever to bring a computer terminal into the territory of Bandrika. Language would not present a formidable barrier here. But that was a day away.

Our train did not stop at the border and nobody demanded to see my papers. It was only when I saw the Bandrikan letters on a road sign that I understood where we were. Black trees infested Bandrika without hindrance. They marched down the hills to flank the railway line. Every few miles a break in the trees flashed past, through which one might catch a glimpse of a dismal hovel, a clearing, or an oppressive path leading into the gloom.

Bandrika had its share of grey stubble fields, thatched farmhouses and corrugated steel outbuildings. These insignificant settlements fought for what little space they had against the encroachment of the surrounding forest. More frequently we were hard up against an uninterrupted line of black trunks, and only by craning my neck at the window could I see that the sky was still overcast and colourless. The trees did their best to deny us even this weak light.

We passed through towns with squat apartment blocks in weather-stained concrete, strung about with washing lines, roofs thick with aerials, spreading according to no obvious plan. They rather depressed me. These places could amount to nothing more than regrettable accidents. Preoccupied by their inscrutably foreign tasks, the people were no better. They crossed roads in taciturn masses, tended market stalls, or stood motionless on bridges and railway embankments. Markedly Bandrikan in appearance, these tiny human figures alarmed me. It seemed impossible that I would soon leave my speeding cocoon and go out amongst these people. The nearer we drew to the capital city, the greater was my dread and nausea at the thought of it.

Every time the train stopped at one of these towns, I was afflicted by a minor crescendo of anxiety lest Bandrikan passengers intrude on my privacy. Several did, always to ask the same question: "Where is the ticket inspector?"

This was one of the few phrases I had learned from my phrasebook, as was the answer, "I'm sorry, I don't know." They would mutter some words of apology or irritation in Bandrikan, before closing my compartment door, to my relief. But I began to worry that I had neglected an important obligation. If it was my responsibility to track down the ticket inspector and have my ticket validated, then I might find myself in breach of Bandrika's regulations. My phrasebook contained no clues, and I could not bring myself to vacate the compartment, which might be claimed by others in my absence. I sat tight. If I had broken the rules, I would simply have to plead ignorance on account of my foreignness. The thought brought me little comfort, and the solitude I had enjoyed until now was marred by worry.

As we waited at one station, I observed a puzzling incident. Two men alighted from my carriage. From their dress I judged them both Bandrikan. The one was greying, authoritative and sported a bristling white moustache. The younger man was shabby, sunken-cheeked, harassed. An altercation took place, thankfully silenced by the glass, but I saw the younger man pleading with outstretched hands. In a minute, half a dozen Bandrikan railway officials emerged from the ticket office and were called over to intervene. After an explanation from the man in the moustache, two of the officials each laid a hand on the young man's shoulders. They marched him away towards the ticket office, laughing as he made some urgent plea. The official at the head of the group opened the door with a mock bow and, as they jostled to enter the building, the man at the back of the group lifted a boot and delivered a solid kick to the passenger's backside, not quite knocking him off his feet but propelling him into the dark interior. The gentleman on the platform appeared satisfied and boarded the train again. No sooner had he done so than it heaved into motion.

A moment later the same man opened the door to my compartment. He did not ask the whereabouts of the ticket inspector, but instead made a great fuss of hoisting a large briefcase onto the overhead luggage rack and hanging up his overcoat and cane on one of the hooks provided. When he had finally got himself settled on the upholstery directly opposite me, he hitched up his trousers by the knees, stretched his short, hairy fingers on his lap, and moistened his lips as if in preparation for a lengthy exchange.

"How are you enjoying your visit to Bandrika?" he asked in my own language, grinning with the yard-brush moustache.

It was around dusk. The edge of the forest was so close, the trees so densely packed, and the train traveling at such a speed that I could distinguish only a blurred, repeating pattern of black marks against the softer black of the forest depths. My greatest desire was to turn away, to rest my forehead against the cold glass and lose myself in contemplation of the silent trees. I had long bored of looking at them, but now that it was no longer possible without giving offence, I longed to.

"Very much, although I have only just arrived," I said, speaking the first two words in broken Bandrikan conned from my phrasebook.

"You speak Bandrikan?" asked the gentleman, repeating the question in my own language with a smile of generous condescension.

"A little," I was able to stammer, exhausting my stock of Bandrikan phrases.

The man performed a little mime of applause. "Excellent," he said. "Your pronunciation is impeccable."

I smiled and nodded, beginning to understand the rules of his game. We were to exchange compliments as a means of establishing the dominant party. Already I was at a disadvantage.

"If only I could acquire a vocabulary to match yours," I said. I would have liked to have asked what had happened to the man at the previous station, but our conversation would not yet admit so direct a question. "Are all Bandrikans so cultured?" I asked instead.

He waved away the suggestion. "Many years ago I was fortunate enough to study at your famous university. As a man of business, your language is one of my tools, and like any tool it must be regularly whetted and oiled. Whenever I meet a gentleman traveller such as yourself, I am always eager, if you will forgive a mixed metaphor, to indulge in a little sparring."

Before I had a chance to digest this peacockery, he asked, "Tell me, what do you think of our Forest of Bandrika?"

"I think it is very beautiful," I said. "Beautiful and mysterious." It was not true. Had I been ejected from the train into that forest, I would have died from exposure before the morning without having found anything in the least beautiful or mysterious about the process. Nevertheless, compared to spending the night in conversation with the man sitting opposite, that prospect had an attraction for me.

"Beautiful and mysterious, you think?" he said, making a face. "Well, such aesthetic considerations are the luxury of the tourist. From my point of view, it is all an unpardonable waste of space which has been holding back the development of Bandrika for hundreds of years. I would burn down the whole lot, all except for a little patch, just a couple of square miles, which I would preserve as a botanical garden. Yes, torch all the rest, and use the land to grow soya beans. Just as soon as it stops raining for long enough to light a match, which, by happy coincidence, is about the length of our Bandrikan summer. What? You don't believe me?"

I guessed that I was not the first to be treated to this little comic monologue.

"I believe you all right," I said. "But what sort of place would you find yourself in once you'd chopped down all the trees?"

"Burned them," the man corrected me. "There would be no benefit in felling them for timber. This endemic species of conifer has no practical use. But to answer your question, we would find ourselves in a great tabula rasa of a country. Think of it: the opportunity for a fresh start! Of course, we would expose some oddities in the process."

"Oddities?"

"There are all kinds of hermits and degenerate little communities hiding away out there," he said, scowling through the rain-flecked glass at the rushing ribbon of black trunks. "From time to time my work brings me into contact with these manifestations, these residual elements from Bandrikan prehistory, inbred, uncivilised..." He drifted into a brown study for a few moments before recovering. "But I am forgetting my manners. We are not yet introduced."

We introduced ourselves. I have forgotten his name. It seemed a typical Bandrikan name. That is as much as I can remember, as I thought his moustache and flourishing eyebrows and ear hair typical.

I explained my purpose in coming to Bandrika and my work in general terms, a subject which never failed to bore, but in which my companion took a riveted interest. He asked to see brochures and instruction manuals (the computer terminal itself was packed in Styrofoam in the luggage van).

"Yes, yes!" he cried, slapping the glossy pages on his lap. "This is exactly what Bandrika needs! Sweep away all the old inefficiencies! Onto the scrap heap with the lot of them. I've been saying it for years. Put one of these screens on every government desk in Zolnay and we'll soon see these forests cleared, all the way to the borders."

"They are useful for keeping track of accounts," I concurred.

"But don't expect any of those useless sons of bitches in Transport to see the justice of your cause."

My companion gave me the name of a friend of his, a senior accountant in the department – "one of the few good eggs in that rotten basket". I was assured that this friend could open doors. "Are you sure you have got the name? Let me write it down for you."

While he wrote on the back of his business card, we stopped at another identical two line station in whitewashed concrete, lit by fluorescent tubes in wire mesh cages. Baskets of geraniums hung from the ceiling and vending machines had been placed every few metres along the platform.

"Surely these fellows can't all be so rotten," I said. "Everything seems to run so smoothly."

He handed me the card with the name and business address of his friend in both Bandrikan script and transcribed into my own writing.

"All this is thanks to President Zol," he said. "He would turn in his grave if he could see what these lazy bastards have done to his great work. They are not worthy to wear the uniforms he designed!"

My companion lapsed into a morose silence, and I did not know how to respond. Within moments, I heard the guard slamming all the heavy doors satisfyingly shut, and we felt the engine straining. Soon we plunged back into the unvarying darkness of the forest. Our compartment door slid open, and in a sonorous *basso profundo*, I heard the Bandrikan words for "tickets please".

The ticket inspector wore silver piping around the brim of his hat, silver-fringed epaulettes, and gleaming metal insignia of the Bandrikan railway sewn into his jacket. Ginger mutton-chop whiskers underlined the dignity of his office.

In ritual silence, the ticket inspector examined both sides of my thick rectangle of card, before reaching down to a leather pouch at his waist for a brass ticket puncher. The largest and most elaborate of such devices I had seen, it incorporated cogs, wheels, rods, levers and buttons inlaid with mother-of-pearl such as one might expect to find on a saxophone. I was reminded of an orrery I had once seen in a museum as a child, and also of an instrument of torture I had observed in different circumstances. For an unaccountably long time the inspector looked me over while fixing the settings on his device. With some dexterous manipulation of the controls, the ticket was punched, and handed back to me with gravitas. Having performed the same service for my companion, the ticket inspector inclined his head to us and glided backwards out of the compartment.

As soon as the compartment door had closed, my companion fell to his hands and knees and scrabbled about on the dusty floorboards until he found a tiny, irregular cardboard shape. Seated again, he fitted the sliver back into the hole in his ticket. "The three-headed griffin," he observed. "I always get the griffin. President Zol's personal emblem. Symbolises loyalty to the Republic. Quite common."

With an expression of mingled relief and disappointment he replaced the ticket in his wallet before asking, "May I ask what you received?"

By my feet I found the tiny shape of a creature like a squid or a cuttlefish. I handed the sliver to my companion, who held it delicately between thumb and forefinger before the electric lamp above his seat.

"Quite exquisite!" he said. "I have never seen the like! I did wonder what type you would be assigned, being a foreigner."

I examined the corresponding hole in my ticket, wondering how many different shapes could be produced by the ticket inspector's device.

"What does it mean?" I asked.

He shook his head, his attention still rapt by the tiny, tentacled silhouette. "I cannot say... a profound mystery," he said, followed by some murmured words of Bandrikan before he emerged from his reverie. "I mean to say, I must confess to the possession of a hobby, and like most hobbies, to the outsider mine must appear trivial to the point of absurdity," He smiled urbanely, quite in control of himself again.

"Not at all," I countered. "I take it that you are a collector of these..."

"The word you are looking for is 'didcott'," he said. "In my language as well as yours. A little cultural borrowing, for which we Bandrikans are grateful."

"Would you like to keep it?" I asked.

"You are kind," he said, pocketing the item, "both for your generosity and your understanding of an old man's eccentricities..."

"I would gladly exchange it for a small favour," I interrupted. He had already assumed possession of my didcott, and to demand it back would have been awkward, but I pressed on. "Simply to answer a question that has been bothering me since we met."

"What little information I possess is at your disposal, but I must warn you that I do not know quite everything about my beloved Bandrika."

"The question is not about Bandrika, but about you."

"My favourite subject!"

"What happened to the man on the platform at Dravka?"

"That man? I'm afraid you will have to be a little more specific," said my friend, shaking his head.

"The man who was arrested, or at least taken away by the railway officials. You had an argument with him. What had he done?"

"I cannot recall any such argument. Are you sure you did not mistake me for somebody else? Or rather, somebody else for me?"

"I'm sure," I said. "They hauled him off into the station building. You don't remember seeing that? Just before you got on the train?"

My companion stared out of the window. The forest had given way to the same species of unambitious, squat apartment blocks I was now familiar with. It was past midnight, but the streets were crowded with Bandrikans wrapped in oddly padded overcoats and headscarves, trundling their shopping trolleys amongst illuminated market stalls, glumly inspecting the piles of alien produce.

"Two minutes from our destination," said my companion, checking his watch, "and exactly on time."

I felt a pang of dread, a hollow feeling in my stomach, at the prospect of leaving the warm compartment and being thrust out into this foreign night, among these faces. My companion began hauling his suitcase down, but I remained seated.

"You are alighting with me here at Zolnay, yes?" he asked, buttoning his overcoat. "We'll need to hurry – this is not the terminus. Once we're out of the station I can help you to find a decent hotel."

I shook my head and smiled. "I'm afraid I must say goodbye to you here." I stood and tried to shake his hand, but he was not ready to accept my explanation.

"Not Zolnay? But the Department of Transport has its offices here."

"My journey will be a little longer than expected," I said.

The man looked astonished. "So where will you get off? Morsken?"

"Yes, at Morsken," I said. "I have relatives there, quite distant relatives on my father's side. I promised him that I would look them up. It's been many years..."

"Relatives in Morsken!" The man tapped his cane on the carriage floor as though I had made a good joke. "I know Morsken well! I don't doubt you will have a very interesting time, and be back in the capital on the first available train. Well, you have my card. It has been a pleasure to make your acquaintance. I will be disappointed if you do not call on me. I will show you my collection of didcotts, where your contribution will take pride of place."

I smiled and nodded. "I will look forward to it."

"I hope that we will become firm friends."

I assured him that we would, though it cost me some effort to keep a straight face while I watched him leave the train and wave to me through the window. Men of our age and position neither sought nor encountered friends. What I meant, and I assumed my companion was clear-sighted enough to understand, was that we hoped to find one another useful. I had no need of friendship. What I required for the remainder of my life was to be left in peace to satisfy certain undimmed appetites while arranging to minimise their unpleasant consequences.

Dozens of Bandrikans were crowding onto the train; there was no hope of my keeping the compartment to myself. The ticket inspector had alighted here, and was gravely passing his ticket-punching device to an identically uniformed colleague. The two men were interrupted by my "friend", who pointed with his cane at something further down the train, beyond my view. The inspectors listened attentively, and both were at pains to shake hands with the gentleman before he left, waving to me as he strode towards the ticket barrier. I waved back, relieved to be rid of him, but still curious about his identity, and the extent of his power over his fellow countrymen. Was he employed by the Bandrikan National Railway Company? His business card, printed in Bandrikan script, was no help to me.

In contemplating this I was avoiding a more pressing issue: I had not alighted at Zolnay as I should have done, and while the train was still waiting to leave I was sitting motionless, with my coat and briefcase stuffed into the overhead rack. Bandrikan passengers were still handing over luggage, exchanging parting words and kisses. If I got up this second and grabbed my things, could I force my way through the oncoming crowds and get to the doors before the train pulled away? I tensed, ready to stand. There was the old bang, bang, bang as the guard moved up the train, slamming the doors. They would not yet be locked. A large, noisy Bandrikan family appeared in the doorway of my compartment, and seeing that I was alone, began to take over the remaining empty seats, the adults smiling shyly at me, the children gawping brazenly. Did I still have time? The only reason I had lied to the gentleman was to avoid his company. By now he would be clear of the station. A muscle in my leg twitched. The next thing I felt was the shudder of the engine vibrating through the floor. The guard blew his whistle and we were in motion. We passed a pile of luggage at the end of the platform, which a gang of porters were loading onto trolleys. Near the edge of the pile sat the plastic crate containing my computer terminal. A moment later we entered a tunnel.

Boisterous though they were, the Bandrikan family made no attempt to communicate with me. While we rumbled through the outskirts of Zolnay, they pointed out landmarks to one another. Once the black trees took over, they unpacked large baskets of food: mysterious pies, unrecognisable fruit, things on sticks resembling the pupae of large insects. I rested my forehead against the cold glass, closed my eyes, and tried to imagine Morsken. This was not how I had imagined my act of transgression, and while I was still surprised at the decision, I told myself that I could excuse myself by playing the ignorant foreigner. All could be put right at the cost of a little humiliation. As an employee and as a husband, this was a price I was used to paying. As the train began to labour up through the mountain passes I drifted into sleep, consoling myself with images of the debaucheries that Morsken might hold in store.

A Bandrikan voice woke me: "Tickets please!" The family went first, and it took longer than I expected for the inspector to study each passenger in turn, decide and then calibrate the shape of their punch hole. Bandrikan railway etiquette apparently demanded that the slips of card not be retrieved from the floor until the inspector had withdrawn. The family sat in expectant silence while I handed over my ticket and prepared to express my confusion: I had fallen asleep and missed my stop. I could not even read the names of the stations. How foolish of me! The inspector's face darkened when he read the ticket. I smiled helplessly and reminded myself that Bandrika was not a third world country; I had no more reason to fear mishap here than I would in my own office. My supervisor had assured me of this, but my supervisor had been wrong before, and had lied to me before.

I had expected some hard looks and words. I was prepared for them. I did not expect to be hauled to my feet and dragged into the corridor. I was not prepared for my arm to be twisted up painfully behind my back and marched down the length of the train, being yelled at in Bandrikan the whole time.

Every time I tried to speak, the inspector twisted my arms a little further, and shouted over my words. I recognized only the word "didcott". By the time we had reached the rear carriage, I had stopped complaining. The passengers in the second-class carriages, in the open seating, gawped unashamedly as we passed. I was shoved into the luggage van, and the door was bolted from the other side.

A dull caged bulb on the far wall held the van in a yellow gloom. There was no heating. It was noisier in here than in the first-class compartment – the walls were thinner and vibrated more in sympathy with the wheels and the rails. Sprawled amongst the crates and suitcases was an unshaven young man with a thin, crooked cigarette dangling from his lower lip. His hands were crossed behind his head as though he was just settling down for a nap, or had just been woken from one, but I judged this attitude, like the crooked cigarette, an affectation. He was dressed in the costume of a Bandrikan peasant, but on him it seemed almost fancy dress. His greeting was to jerk his chin up. He looked at me from the depths of his distressed floppy cap.

I took a moment to assess my surroundings, rub my shoulder where the ticket inspector had hurt me, then chose a sturdy-looking crate and sat down, tucking my cold hands into the sleeves of my jacket. The young man and I were sat too close together for my liking, but there was no getting away from him. I thought I could smell his feet.

"Hello," I said to him in Bandrikan.

Again, that little jerking up of the chin. "You are foreign," he said, in my language, his pronunciation very approximate. I gave him, in a very simplified form, a brief explanation of my circumstances. I hoped he could provide some information about what treatment to expect in Morsken, but from his reply it was doubtful whether he had understood anything I'd said.

"So – a foreigner!" he laughed. "And no ticket!"

I couldn't feel the thick rectangle in my inside pocket. I pointed to the locked door behind me. "Gone," I explained. "He took it." The man barely registered this, and I wondered whether he might have fallen asleep or was on drugs. We sat in silence for a longish moment, watching the crates and suitcases vibrating gently against one another to the rhythm of the train.

From out of his stupor, the man said, "Didcott?"

"I gave it away," I said ruefully. "Do you think that might be important? Not to the ticket inspector though. To a different man, another passenger. He told me he was a collector."

I wondered for a moment whether he was another collector trying to wheedle me out of my cuttlefish. Was the whole country addicted to collecting these things?

The man scrunched his eyes then tried to open them wide. "Didcott?" he asked.

"No didcott."

"No didcott?"

"No. No didcott. I have no didcott."

The man sat up and pulled his ridiculous hat off, leaning in close to me. I realised that it was not his feet I could smell, it was his breath.

"All you foreigners have no didcotts?" he asked. He was about to burst out laughing in my face, as though I had admitted that all my countrymen had three bollocks.

"How the fuck should I know?" I said.

He did laugh, but not maliciously, I think. He slapped me on the knee. "That's good!" he said. "Very good! Fuck you know! Fuck I know!"

I tried to smile back. I had taken him for a student, slumming it in peasant gear and hitching free rides around Bandrika, but now I was inclined to the view that he was a man of smaller intelligence – perhaps, given that open, guileless laugh, mentally subnormal. Still, I thought, he might prove of some use.

"Are you travelling alone?" I asked.

"I go with my brother, but he is gone. No ticket."

So that was the man who had been taken off at Dravka. "You?" I asked. "You have a ticket?"

He shook his head firmly. "No money."

"Didcott?"

No longer looking me in the eye, he sighed, "Yes, yes." From inside the band of his hat, he produced a transparent plastic container, like a flat pill case the size of a coin. He struck a cigarette lighter so I could see his didcott trapped within: the silhouette of a seated cat. "Look, cat," he said, pointing. He repeated the word in his own language, "You say 'cat'?"

"Yes, that's right," I replied. "Cat. So what happened to the ticket?"

He snatched the little box back and tucked it safely into the hat band. "Ticket gone, many years ago. My mother...my mother, many, many years ago. One time I was so small." he grinned and held out his palm to the height of a little boy. "Very small. My mother she took me on the train..." He stopped speaking and looked down, his hat covering his face, and from a small, choking sound I understood, to my disgust, that he was crying. I endured this without comment, until a shriek of metal interrupted his sobs. The train was braking.

The young man clamped his hat more firmly onto his head, and put his ear to the door.

"Morsken?" I asked.

All trace of his former grief had been replaced with a wolfish grin. "No," he said. "No Morsken. Never again, Morsken."

There were mysterious shouts and whistles from the corridor and, it seemed to me, from outside. Then a sound of twisting and snapping metal, and the door of the luggage van was hauled open. A lamp flashed blinding beams around, making wild shadows jump up from the crates. There were happy shouts of greeting. I saw three pinched, unwashed faces framed by heavy hoods, two burly, bearded men and a woman with a sharp nose reddened by cold. Gusts of freezing air swirled into the van, and I remembered that I had left my coat in the luggage rack. The young man leapt down onto the tracks and hugged the woman. She had tears in her eyes. The man beckoned to me.

In a lifetime dedicated to the maintenance of a certain tolerable position of financial security, I have learned something about decisions. Decisions left to others are usually made badly, and lead to irritation. Decisions made by oneself are usually made equally badly, and lead to regret. It is simply a matter of taste as to whether one prefers to foster resentment against oneself or against others. I don't remember making a decision to leave the train. I remember my tan brogues landing in a dark puddle on the side of the track. They immediately began to let in water. A heavy cloak was draped over my suit jacket. I half-slid half-fell down a mud-slicked embankment in the darkness. Rough, urgent hands dragged me into the deeper night of the forest.

We jogged in single file through the trees, two ahead of me, two behind me, through the dawn, until I thought I might stop to throw up. The woman kicked me in the shin. "Not here," she said. "The dogs will find us."

"Who are we running from?" I asked between retches, my hands on my knees.

The woman called the others back, and they discussed me in Bandrikan. The young man from the train slapped me on the back until she stopped him. Then the two of them had a little spat, until a decision was taken, and the three men crashed off into the undergrowth, while the woman and I followed behind at a slower pace. "My husband will go ahead to start the car," she told me. But we must not be slow. Soon it will be daylight. We must get away."

"Away from whom?" I asked unhappily.

"From the railway. Do you know nothing at all?"

"Nothing at all!" I said. I tried to sound cheerfully equanimous, but I was given a sharp look for my trouble. She didn't altogether trust me, but enough to tell me her name, which I have forgotten. It wasn't Helen of course – it was some inelegant Bandrikan name – but I'll call her Helen for the sake of the story. And her husband, the scruffy young man I had judged mentally deficient, we will call Peter. Of the two bearded men, one was very old, older than me – Tom is as good a name as any. The other wore glasses and barely spoke or made eye contact. Simon will do. There was probably something wrong with him too, although I assumed that they were all in one way or another avoiding reality.

If there was a path, I could not see it. We were weaving through a maze of grey, mossy tree trunks. The forest floor squelched like a sponge. At each step cold water streamed through the broguing to keep my feet numb.

When the first, distant peal of barking reached us, I tried to convince myself that I was mistaken. When it came again, nearer, and from a different direction, I looked to Helen for reassurance, but there was none.

"Please hurry," she said, taking a hold of my upper arm and trying to force us into a run. I knew then that I should not have left the luggage van, should have got off the train in Zolnay as my ticket had instructed. It had been a mistake to accept this assignment, given what I knew about the company's indifference to the safety of its employees. It would be tedious to relate the extent of my regrets as I stumbled through clinging wet mist, my breath failing me. And it was then, as I sensed Helen's fear and became infected with it, that I began to lose control of myself. If she didn't think we could make it to safety, then there was no hope for me.

"Don't look back," she said, pulling fiercely on my sleeve. But as we pushed through a marshy clearing I did look back at the receding tree line, expecting at any moment to see bobbing heads, panting tongues teeth bared ready for me, covering the distance in a few exhilarating bounds. My feet found a root under the shallow water, and I found myself on my hands and knees, pine needles floating around the drenched sleeves of my suit jacket. My wristwatch was ruined. Two sets of arms hoisted me upright. I saw a steep gravel track behind the next line of trees: a loggers' road. "Just a little farther," said Helen, and kept repeating it until we crested the brow of a slope, and there on the other side was a jeep with its motor idling.

The others were jubilant as we bounced around in the back of the jeep. The old man, Tom, was driving us down the hill at a frightening speed. Helen and Peter hugged fiercely and talked with great urgency in Bandrikan. Perhaps they were discussing the possible fate of Peter's brother. Finding it tedious to listen to, I interrupted: "What did you do?"

Peter and Helen exchanged glances "We stopped the train," said Helen.

"How?"

She shrugged. "That tree was going to block the line sooner or later anyway. We helped it."

The driver called sharply in Bandrikan over his shoulder, and Helen argued back with him. Bending to look out of the windscreen, it seemed remarkable that we had been hurtling along a straight road for such a time, and yet the view remained the same. Two lines of solemn grey firs receded to the horizon.

Helen and Peter were arguing with the two bearded men in the front. I guessed that Helen and Peter were taking my side. Helen turned to me. "My husband says you already destroyed your didcott?"

"Not destroyed. Given away."

She had a wondering look that was quite appealing. "To whom?"

"A man I met on the train. He said he collected them." I found the business card in my wallet and handed it to her.

It had begun to irritate me that conversation in this country always came round to the same topic. "Is it really of any importance?" I said. "These little cardboard animals?"

The woman with the cold-reddened nose smiled a little. "No, not at all. It shouldn't matter in the slightest! That's what all this is about, what we're trying to achieve!"

She was looking at me with what I fancied was admiration. The pity was I did not know what I had done to deserve it. When she handed the business card back to me, I tossed it out of the open window with what I hoped was an air of insouciance.

Simon, in the passenger seat, had turned on the radio and was listening to what sounded like the news headlines. He held up a finger to quiet us, and a second later they all cheered. Peter banged his fist against the metal roof of the vehicle.

"Your train arrived in Morsken seventeen minutes late," Helen translated for me, grinning like an idiot.

I tried to shrug, but Peter leapt forward and grabbed me in a bear hug. "Mister No-Didcott, a very lucky man!" he yelled in my ear. "Lucky for us, yes!"

Before I could extricate myself the jeep lurched off the road onto a dirt track. Peter and I were nearly thrown onto our backs. "We are home now," he shouted, yanking me back upright as Tom manoeuvred the jeep into a breeze-block garage.

Home was a ruined cottage with a tree growing up through the middle of it, and a stagnant, midge-infested pool behind it. An ancient peasant couple with half a dozen teeth between them owned the place. I gathered that the train saboteurs were merely house guests, but this was one of many things that were never explained. It was futile to ask why anyone would make their home in that dank wilderness. The ancient couple seemed as much a part of the forest as the millipedes munching through the leaf litter and the stinking wild garlic thriving on the banks of the pond. They knew not one word of my language, and even my attempts to greet them in simple Bandrikan went unacknowledged. Probably imbeciles, possibly brother and sister, they spoke some gummy, spittle-fuelled archaic dialect of their own. The rest of the gang treated them with deference and referred to them as "The Old Mother and Father". For their part, the Old Parents were oblivious to our presence.

I have said that a tree grew up through the house. It may have been rather that a series of walls, lean-tos, roofs and balconies had been botched onto the trunk of a mature tree. I can tell you nothing about the genus of the tree, apart from that it was unlike the grey conifers that dominated everywhere else. Three storeys high, but as crooked as the spines of the Old Mother and Father, it was thoroughly infested with ivies, mosses, lichens, insects and small mammals. My pillow was regularly fouled with squirrel droppings. Earwigs writhed in the sink. When I brushed against the wall, I found a green powdery print on my shoulder. Sometimes, out of a silent moment, a pigeon would emerge frantically from a recess, flap around in our faces and slam itself against the window panes until we managed to chase it out. Every ceiling leaked and every curtain and bedspread was damp to the touch. I stayed in bed, or by the fire, and did as little as I could get away with.

Soon after we arrived, they sat me down in a study, its walls lined with mouldering books, and questioned me. I never understood whether this was meant as an initiation into the cell or the interrogation of a suspected enemy agent. I suspected they themselves did not know. Everybody gathered for the ritual humiliation. Old Tom seemed to be in charge of the proceedings. He sat behind a little card table, while the rest of them stood, leaning against the bookcases, arms folded, assessing my performance. Tom spoke only Bandrikan, and his questions, taken from a dog-eared old pamphlet, had to be translated by Helen, sometimes with the aid of an ancient bilingual dictionary whose leaves were stuck together and bloomed with gaudy moulds.

"Are you now, or have you ever been, an employee, subcontractor, volunteer or supporter of the Bandrikan National Railway Company?"

"No." It might have been a lie. I was, after all, here on business to sell computers to the Department of Transport. For all I knew the terminals would be employed to gather data on lunatics like these. A flat denial seemed safer and simpler.

Tom ran a ponderous finger down to the next question. As he spoke, Helen riffled through her disintegrating dictionary.

"Does your urine stream turn cloudy on the new moon?"

"Are you sure that is the question you meant to ask?" I said.

"Please answer yes or no."

"Could I just check something in your dictionary?"

"No."

It went on all morning.

"Do you cut your own hair?"

"Do the hairs on your back form the shape of an arrowhead or an onion?"

"How many times should a sugar sachet be shaken before opening? Please answer separately for white and brown."

Those intense, underfed faces told me that levity would not be welcomed.

By the end of the morning I had resigned myself to supplying random answers, whatever the consequences.

"Did you have an uncle or other male relative (other than your father) who habitually shook his sugar sachets in a way that was conspicuous or remarked upon?"

"Yes."

"If so, how many times, on average, were they shaken?"

"Not at all so, on average, zero."

The answers were recorded on a long, printed form.

"Was your earliest memory of cats frightening or benign?"

"Frightening."

"Have you ever, to your knowledge, been exposed to any form of industrial radiation?"

"No."

"If asked to design a tea service, what colour would predominate?"

"Maroon."

"Please indicate the colour on the attached chart."

I put my finger on the turquoise slice of a colour wheel.

"As a child, were you ever punished after being caught masturbating?"

"No."

"And as an adult?"

"No."

"Finally, what didcott were you assigned?"

"I haven't got one," I sighed. "I told you before, I gave it away."

"You'll have to draw a picture of your didcott on the back of the form."

I did my best to trace the outline of a squid, which was received with something like awe.

"You're sure it looks like this?" Helen's face, in a certain light, could have been described as still haunted by its former beauty.

I nodded.

Peter was the first to break the silence with a wild laugh. "No didcott, no ticket!" he yelped, slapping me on the shoulder. The others conferred in Bandrikan, then the old man stood, gathered his papers and left the room without a word.

"So what now?" I asked.

"The results are..." Helen consulted her dictionary one last time. "Collated," was the word she was looking for.

The collation took two weeks. Tom barely emerged from his room during this time, and the others were sworn to secrecy until the old man reached his conclusions. Was I a hostage? I didn't think any of them would prevent me from leaving; there was nowhere to go. If I had been determined I would have hunted out the key to their jeep, but I had no idea which direction to take, nor how much fuel there was in the tank. I was a little curious to learn the results of Tom's labours, and my didcott revelation had made me such an object of fascination with Helen that my curiosity began to extend into other areas. I wondered how old she was. A decade younger than me? That wasn't excessive. But she might have been younger – living as they did would age anyone.

One dank morning, lit half-heartedly by a winter sun, I was out with her collecting bits of firewood on the other side of the pond. I asked her how long the collation would take.

"In a complex case, weeks," she said.

"And am I a complex case?"

She brushed a wisp of hair from her face and gave me a quizzical smile. "I couldn't say, I'm no expert. It's certainly very unusual. I've not seen one like it."

"What will happen once the results are in? Shot as a spy?" I was trying to sound facetious.

"I hope not." She might have smiled, but I could read nothing from it.

"So why here?" I pointed at the crumbling masonry pierced by bare tree limbs. It looked like the corpse of a house, the branches and twigs the grave mould consuming it.

"Nobody bothers us," she said.

"I'm not surprised. But who are you worried about? The railway police?"

"Maybe."

"Is that who you think I am?"

"Maybe."

We had wandered away from the edge of the pond. There was a low fence, greened by frilly lichens, which I tried to climb over, but found the top bar crumbling away in my hand.

"We shouldn't go so far from the house," said Helen, but she followed me all the same. Through the trees I had caught sight of a rocky outcrop and had an impulse to explore further.

"Says who? Old Tom?" I called over my shoulder.

"I don't know why you call him that. He's not much older than you."

That stung a little. I crashed vigorously through a rhododendron bush. "But it's so much prettier here," I said, beckoning.

A rock wall jutted from the forest floor, and a little further on became an overhang. From the ledge above, a gnarled juniper poked out across the sky. The rain, which had been little more than a falling mist since dawn, put on a spurt of effort, and we sheltered under the bare rock. It was not quite a cave behind us, and we looked out over another rolling expanse of timber, unbroken by any road or house.

"You're right, it is pretty here," she said, hugging herself inside her overcoat. It wasn't really all that pretty: the same old trees, only we could see more of them.

We stood in silence watching puddles ripple on the bare earth, before she said, "We had better go back."

I made a disappointed face. "What harm are we doing?"

She pointed to a black speck that had been quietly tainting the blank sky.

"They can't see us from that distance," I said. "Even if they could, we'd be more easily spotted out in the open."

She acquiesced with a shrug.

We watched the chopper, but it didn't seem to be getting any closer. "So you just skulk about in that house all day – doing what?" I asked.

"I told you I can't discuss that."

"No, of course. Not until my results have been collated."

"I go for long walks, when it doesn't rain. Sometimes I come out here, just to look around at all this beauty."

"On your own?"

"My husband has other interests."

"You surprise me. I myself am drawn to beauty."

I leaned in a little closer, as though avoiding a persistent drip, but she averted her gaze to the rippling puddles. "There is more to life than chasing after what is pleasant," she said.

"Blowing up trains, for example?"

"I meant being true to yourself."

Her naivety was almost enchanting. I took a stab in the dark. "You don't think I'm being true to my squiddy nature? What about your husband – is he authentically feline?"

I knew I had hit a nerve. "I hate all that fucking garbage! We will never be free until we have burnt all of these bits of paper. It's just so childish!"

"You never told me what shape your own didcott is," I said.

"I burnt it last night. Now I am nothing, nobody."

She had a fierce, exhilarated look that I found arousing. "Two nobodies together," I said. "Why need we fear helicopters? There's literally nobody here for them to find."

That got half a smile. "And your husband?" I asked, knowing the answer. "He has burnt his too?"

"He is thinking about it. He feels more of an attachment."

"It was given to him by his mother, if I remember. I suppose some people value other things more than freedom. But who am I to judge? I'm just a foreigner, and a squid to boot. At least I was for about two minutes."

Helen held out a palm. "It isn't raining so hard, and the helicopter has gone. Come on, I know a shortcut back to the house."

It wasn't a shortcut. Helen led me up a natural staircase in the rock, which brought us out onto a bluff, for once treeless. A narrow path twisted down to the forest floor, where the laughably dismal roofs of the house emerged from the treetops. The view from here took in even more of the unrelieved countryside. The least intelligent group of rebels would have built a lookout here, but these people were playing at rebellion. For a few strides, the ground ended sharply on one side of the path, and we looked down into a lonely dell full of shadows and rampant ivy.

"Be careful," said Helen, her hand on my arm. "Nobody from the house would hear your screams."

"But you'd come and rescue me."

"Again? Once was enough."

I laughed but she didn't join in.

"Have you warned the others about this?" I asked, as we shuffled across the loose rocks, holding onto shaky branches.

"I'm the only one who knows about it."

Once she'd reached a safe foothold, she reached out for my hand and pulled me across. By the time I had found my footing we were almost pressed against one another.

"That makes two of us," I said.

Approaching the house, I looked up and found Old Tom's solemn face looking down at me from the other side of a window. My wave went unanswered. "There he is, beavering away," I said. "What can be taking so long?"

"He's calculating your soul," Helen said.

I shuddered. "Rather him than me."

In our absence a family of foxes had taken over my bedroom. Two cubs were worrying the pillow. The bitch looked up as I hesitated in the doorway, then lay her head back down on her paws, keeping her eyes on me. I retreated into the hall and collided with the Old Mother, who was waiting silently with a saucer of milk full of stale bread crusts. She shuffled past me and, bending with evident pain, placed the offering in the middle of a disintegrating rag rug. The cubs stopped wrestling for a moment, ears pricked, waiting on our departure. As she shut the door, the crone showed me her black and yellow smile.

"I'll find another bedroom," I said.

I tossed the neglected mops and buckets from a broom cupboard into what used to be a vegetable garden. The mattress was inches too wide and bent up at the sides. I could open the door no more than a crack to squeeze my belly inside, and once shut, it was dark as nightmares.

On the other side of a partition wall slept Helen and Peter. I wondered whether I would find their proximity queasy or arousing. I needn't have worried. They screamed at one another in Bandrikan until I heard Peter slam the bedroom door with enough emotion to shake the walls of my den. I thought briefly of my family. My wife and I had not argued like that for years. For us there was so little at stake any more. She'd be annoyed that I hadn't phoned her from Zolnay, but only out of habit, and now that I was here, it no longer mattered what she thought. I had an unassailable alibi. The nearest telephone might have been a hundred miles away. I doubted if the children had even noticed my absence. It occurred to me that I was in the only room in the house with no draughts. There was nothing for me to do but sleep.

I didn't remember what I dreamt, but on waking I heard a voice that had been smuggled over from the other side of sleep. Whether it was my father's voice, or my supervisor's, or that of some other authority figure from a lifetime of subservience, I couldn't make out. But what the voice said was quite clear. "What the fuck do you think you're doing here?" it asked. The answer took a while coming, and when it did it was so obvious I almost laughed out loud at my own stupidity: I was here to sell. I was a salesman.

I hadn't always been. As a young man, conversations with women left me suicidally mortified. There would follow a mental action-replay in which every lame joke, scrap of false modesty and pitiful bid for approval was held up to the light for me to regret at my leisure. But all that changed when I joined the company. "Before every conversation with a client, know what you want to get out of it, and what you are prepared to do to get it," the Staff Handbook pithily commanded. I soon realised that this procedure could be applied beyond negotiating the sale of computer terminals, into every facet of human interaction.

I followed the philosophy of the Staff Handbook, and life became tolerable. It allowed me to cohabit with my wife and children without the exhausting rounds of introspection and recrimination that had spoiled earlier relationships. It opened the doors to promotion within the company. I was not employee of the month material. I knew what would be expected of me, and wasn't prepared for such self-sacrifice. I had been an adequate salesman. I still was.

Now I was selling a product that was undeniably shop-worn. Paunchy, greying skin, bagged eyes, thinning hair – there was a lengthening list of shortcomings. Not that she was exactly fresh off the production line herself – years of this squalid existence had taken some of the shine off. For her, it was a seller's market, but I had added value: an exotic, didcottless foreigner. That was the angle to push: I was neither squid nor cat nor griffin, but a man true to myself, in Helen's words.

I'd barely formulated my plan when the object of my contemplation knocked on the broom cupboard door.

"I come in here with you?"

Peter looked so bedraggled that I wondered whether he had spent the night with the foxes.

"Sit down. Leave the door open, though," I said.

Peter squatted in a hangover posture, palms massaging his eyelids. "My wife hates me."

"I see," I said, nodding sagely. Language barriers have their uses.

"Burning didcott – this is very hard!"

"Yes. Your mother gave it to you, didn't she?"

"Yes, my mother…" There were the predicted tears, but this time I welcomed the snuffling, even when he wiped his nose on the bed sheet. He was softening up.

"What now? You tell me! What now?"

"Why don't you come out for a walk," I suggested.

I like to think I would have gone through with it. Whether Helen would have kept her end of the bargain is hard to say. Now that I think back, I can't say for certain whether I did sleep with her or not. I have an image in mind of her naked body: hardly any tits, ribs sticking out, longish white legs. But that might just be one of my fantasies. She's probably dead now, so it doesn't matter one way or the other. Peter too, but at the time he was still very much alive, and rather in the way. I managed to get him as far as the shaky cliff-top path.

"This place is no good. Very dangerous place," he was saying.

Perhaps I was waiting for the right moment, but a good salesman makes the right moment; he doesn't wait for it to fall in his lap. As I said, I was only ever an adequate salesman. I put it down to incompetence, rather than a sudden blossoming of scruples, that I didn't shove him into the abyss before we heard Helen shouting to us from the house.

I grabbed hold of his sleeve and asked him what the matter was. Peter turned and laughed in that foolish, trusting way. "She says you steal the car! I say no – you are here with me."

When we gathered in Tom's study, it was Simon who failed to turn up.

"A spy for the railway?" I asked.

Helen had her back to me, facing the little window that overlooked the empty garage and the fresh tyre tracks leading off into the trees.

"It appears so," she said. Peter took her hand, and she put her head on his shoulder. It looked like our deal was off.

"Did he take anything of importance?" I asked, assuming that there was nothing in the house worth taking. Who could want Tom's questionnaires, except as proof of the insanity that reigned here?

"Only our location," said Helen. Her face had sagged and lost its colour – I wondered what I'd ever seen in her.

Tom was busy dragging tatty box files from the shelves behind him. He spoke crossly to Helen and Peter. "He says we must burn all of these papers," Helen translated, "before they find us."

I nodded noncommittally, unsure what this had to do with me anymore. Once the authorities arrived, I would be repatriated just as soon as I could prove my nationality.

"What about calculating my soul? Did he ever get to the bottom of that one?"

Some more Bandrikan went back and forth.

"He says you're not really a squid at all," Helen told me.

"I'm very glad to hear it. But if not a squid, then what?"

"You're nothing at all, don't you see? People are full of contradictions, never one thing or the other. Every person who answers the questions is one more freed from the tyranny."

"Tyranny?"

"The mental tyranny of the railway."

It struck me as a remarkably facile conclusion.

"Perhaps it is hard for you, as a foreigner, to understand," Helen said stiffly.

They began to hump the boxes of useless paperwork down the stairs and into the garden, where they made a smoky bonfire of it all. As dusk fell and the last of the papers curled into ash, Peter took the little Perspex disk from his hat band and dropped it into the glowing embers where it flared briefly before shrivelling to nothing. Through the smoke I could see Helen gripping his hand tightly.

It took another two days for the chopper to reappear. I watched through the window of the locked study as it descended on the garden, the rotor blades blowing up a storm of leaves and garbage. The whole sorry mess of a house vibrated, as if the helicopter were a surgical instrument come to remove a tumorous growth from the landscape.

A few thuds and screams and barked orders in Bandrikan reached me before Helen and Peter were marched out in handcuffs and pushed to the ground in the shadow of the helicopter. I watched Peter trying to shuffle over to be nearer his wife, until one of the soldiers saw his little game and put a stop to it with his boot. They brought Tom out on a stretcher. From the way they dumped him on the ground I wouldn't have put money on him surviving the flight. The Old Mother, her face black with blood, didn't warrant a stretcher. I don't know what happened to the Old Father. All were pushed or dragged aboard.

I had steeled myself for a certain amount of brusqueness from these functionaries, before they understood that I was the wronged party in this silly business. I had not anticipated seeing the chopper take off again. Left alone in that place, I had a moment of blind panic. I thundered down the stairs and out of the front door, shouting and waving my arms at the shrinking silhouette. When a hand tapped me on the shoulder, I did not at once recognize the genial, moustached face before me.

"No spare seats in the 'copter, I'm afraid," he said, shaking my hand warmly. "But if you will accept a rather less glamorous substitute, we can offer you a lift back to the train station at Morsken."

Behind him, Simon sat grinning at the wheel of our jeep. He looked like a man who had every expectation of promotion. On the way back to Morsken, my old friend from the train offered some partial explanations.

"We've found your electronic gizmo. I have it safely locked up in the staff room at Zolnay Station," he said.

Out of politeness I asked him whether he had ever operated one before.

"Programming the human being is more my line. But we have a chap in signalling who's very keen. We let him have a go on your device. I do hope you don't mind. He's already got it doing some amusing little things."

In the circumstances I could hardly object, although it rankled to think of some greasy-fingered engineer tinkering with my demonstration model.

"Is there anywhere to stay at Morsken?" I asked. "I could do with getting cleaned up before I get back to work."

The gentleman translated this into Bandrikan for the benefit of Simon, and they both laughed. I smiled, waiting to be let in on the joke.

"There's nothing at Morsken but a prison camp. It's the terminus. The prison came first, then the railway, but if you read Zol's autobiography you can see how it was all conceived as a piece. This was the first line President Zol ever drove through the Bandrikan forest. A marvel of social planning." We had been bumping along the loggers' road at a hell of a pace – Simon was a less cautious driver than Tom.

"We will put you straight onto a train back to Zolnay," he continued. "First class, courtesy of the Bandrikan Department of Transport. After all, we are in your debt."

"Are you?"

"That business card of mine was giving us a very clear signal until its battery gave out. Never put too much faith in technology. Our chauffeur here did the rest."

"Is that where they're being taken? To Morsken?" I asked.

"Yes, but they won't be getting on any more trains in a hurry. They're at the terminus now."

"And what happens at the terminus?" I asked.

He stroked his chin for a moment and smoothed down the sides of his moustache as he contemplated the monotonous rhythm of trees. "Some are rehabilitated eventually, allowed to earn the price of a third-class passage to the closest branch station. But your little gang? I don't fancy their chances. I know their kind. No backbone."

We left the familiar gravel road now, and joined a two lane asphalted highway. We seemed to be the only vehicle on the road that day. The trees were thinning out, and there were patches of field and sheep-cropped hills on the horizon.

I decided to put an answer to something that had been puzzling me. "How did you know I wouldn't get off at Zolnay?"

Instead of answering, the gentleman took out his wallet. "Hold out your hand," he demanded.

"I don't understand."

"Not being Bandrikan, you can be forgiven for that. Without this, you weren't likely to do much of anything on your own initiative." He tipped the tiny template of a squid into my palm. "A souvenir of Bandrika," he said. "Rest assured, I took good care of it. You're free to get on with your life."

"You have no objections to my contacting the Department of Transport?"

"That's all settled," he said patting my arm. "We'll quite happily buy as many of those little television screens as you can ship over."

Morsken Station was a vast, bustling industrial affair. I didn't see the prison camp – they had built it some distance from the passenger lounge for reasons of taste. The journey back to the capital was uneventful, and we were met on the platform by a man in the plum and copper uniform of the signalling department. He shook my hand with genuine pleasure.

"He says he's been teaching some of the other lads about your box of tricks," said my companion."

I was surprised to learn this. The manual had not yet been translated into Bandrikan. We were led through a long corridor bristling with giant levers of greased brass, and into a staffroom that stank of old tobacco, where a gang of signalmen were gathered round the tiny screen of my demonstration model. A gangly youth was hacking away at the keyboard at tremendous speed. I peered over his shoulder, trying to read his code, but it vanished when he ran the program, to be replaced by a black and white graphic: a crude, pixelated rendition of a naked woman with cartoon bosoms ballooning outwards. The men around me cheered and whistled, and I glanced down to see that the youth at the keyboard had his flies open, and was masturbating furiously with one hand under the table.

Platform Alteration: The Little Carriage to North Korea

So – what's the longest journey you can actually take on a train? In the UK, it's probably the Penzance to Aberdeen service or, with a change, Penzance to Thurso. That was pretty grand – until the Channel Tunnel opened. I would stick my neck out a bit and say that the Channel Tunnel was one of the most profound things to happen to this little country in a long time, because in some strange way it connected us in ways that no plane or boat ever can. It truly does mean that you could get on board your train at some little British village and get off – where? Almost anywhere! The rail network is a bit fragmented of course. Even leaving aside oceans, you can't take the train to Africa or India without a gap of some kind. But you can make plenty of other connections. Bodø in the far north of Norway, anyone? Tbilisi maybe? Deep in the deserts of Iran? From London, you only have to change trains 3 times and you are in Beijing, you know that? A few more connections and you are in Lhasa or Ho Chi Min City. That involves riding the longest train ride of all of course – the Trans-Siberian – but Beijing is still not the longest. The Trans-Siberian has another rather stranger destination, taken in just a single carriage, that is handed around from train to train like a parcel, eventually taking you all the way to Pyongyang, North Korea. It's true that it's a rough and wild journey – and involves security that makes even a landing at JFK or Heathrow pale into insignificance in both oppressive atmosphere and inefficiency. But imagine it – London to North Korea. Now that's a train journey!

Whether these mega-journeys have any real place in the world aside from as a curiosity maybe depends on a redefinition of both time and travel – and as we are slowly waking up to just what is sustainable and what isn't, it is a redefinition that we may have to make eventually. Travel has by and large become an ordeal that must be got out of the way as quickly as possible – we accept crowded conditions and miserable treatment from transport companies and border officials with remarkably little fuss. But I have a vision of the middle-distant future where the race to ever-increase speed has collapsed – where we are forced to accept slower and more efficient modes of transport fuelled by whatever we can gather from the world. And in my fantasy, that slowing down comes with a forcing back towards other values: the romance of travel where we are no longer prepared to tolerate sardine cans on wheels/wings and glowering officials. Maybe this is just me of course, letting my own passions dictate possible futures – but I also have to ask, why not?

Other gaps in the world's rail network may also close in the future. China recently announced the wild scheme of a high speed rail link . . . to London via India. Who knows whether that will ever come to anything, but we can but hope. Fantasies also exist to build a connection between Siberia and Alaska across the Bering Strait, and on into the USA. Not impossible. The US blathers on about access to Siberian oil, but in my head I just see one of the last big gaps closing. If that ever came to pass, the journey could be even longer. London to New York anyone? The long way round? *Welcome aboard the 12:00 departure from London St Pancras to Seattle and San Francisco, calling at . . .*

DR

The Keeper

Andrew Coulthard

Between patches of grainy, black fog I sense a relentless momentum. Suddenly everything is intense and immediate again: the clank of couplers, the bogies' rhythmic thump on the rails and the more distant thudding of the engine all overlaid by a soft burble of passenger conversation. The scents of oil, steam, coal and putrefying blood surround me.

I don't know how I came to be here or even how any of this is possible. I only wanted to help free the young man from his Dark Keeper.

My vision clears a little. The passengers are the least distinct; I can scarcely perceive them at all nor they me. But that is good, for they mustn't see me. So far I've stayed one step ahead, as the Conductor told me I must, but exhaustion isn't far off and with it the moment when I must sleep and, inevitably, fall.

Outside all is darkness, but from time to time we draw to a halt at some terrible destination along these cursed tracks, each station a milestone in an odyssey of madness…

"Please, please…"

Another beggar! Vogel Maddox stopped in her tracks, she was tired. She'd slept badly troubled by that dream again, the one in which she was returning from a long journey only to find the city blighted with pestilence. She wasn't normally a big dreamer, recalling the odd snatch of weirdness once in a while, but these last few weeks…

The beggars were everywhere this winter and they weren't just the usual rogue's gallery of wasters and addicts either. This lot all looked alike; tanned, dark heavy-lidded eyes and black hair; squatting outside supermarkets and by ATMs with their paper cups and their little chants.

"Please, please."

She didn't give money; a policy decision made years ago when she'd been a poor student, but there was something about these people which, if anything, made her even less inclined to be charitable than usual. She'd heard from an acquaintance in the police that they came in teams from parts of Eastern Europe often renting an apartment in some rundown suburb. There were street musicians too who plagued the underground or acted as a diversion for gangs of pickpockets in the busy central shopping districts. According to her friend, the bosses usually ran prostitutes in the apartment during the days while their people were out working the city.

"Please?"

Vogel turned into the entrance to the Abstiegstrasse underground station and was immediately confronted by another beggar. Uncannily, this one looked almost exactly like the one outside. Perhaps they were family.

It wasn't rush-hour but the platforms were crowded. Vogel chewed her lip – lots of other people hoping to beat the crowds and do a bit of last minute shopping, just like her. She toyed with the idea of going home again, but there were things she needed. Two minutes until the next train.

Music arose from somewhere further down the platform. She winced. Accordion and another instrument she couldn't identify. They were playing some traditional eastern tune or other. She glanced at those around her, their sullen features mirroring her own deepening displeasure. A man was forcing his way through the crowds towards her, dark hair flecked with grey, tanned skin, dark eyes, waving his paper cup before him:

"Please, please, for music!"

The train burst from the tunnel in an explosion of sound and the crowds surged forward. The man with the cup vanished in the rush.

Vogel fought her way aboard the packed train. As the doors closed, a strange non-silence of mass breathing settled over the passengers and they strained against the motion of the train, swaying into one another, always off balance yet never in any danger of falling.

"Thank you, thank you!" When the music began a collective groan ran through the carriage; a different duo this time. They must have been on the train already.

Vogel swallowed, her head was spinning. The air on the train was bad and she was too warm in her winter clothes. How many stations to the centre? She glanced at the overhead map. Eight. No she couldn't take eight stations of this; she'd get off and walk at the next stop, wherever it was.

Vogel stumbled out onto the platform, the only person alighting at...where was she? *Hinterhafen?* One of the old dockside stops; she could probably have picked a better place. The doors snapped shut behind her, mercifully cutting off the music and the train's electric engines hummed into life propelling it from the station at gathering speed.

Vogel shivered her breath fogging on cold air that smelled of dirt and stale urine. Underground stations were generally quite warm and clean, but not this place. The platform was very rundown too, the walls a patchwork of missing tiles. She puzzled over a sign sprayed with graffiti. Only one exit as far as she could make out, at least it was close, but did she really want to walk into town from here; the docks could be difficult to get out of. She glanced at the notice board. It was blank for a time and then a new message appeared:

Temporary suspension of service due to power failure on the Eastern Line. Delays to all central underground traffic. Next train due at this station in 25 minutes.

"Oh great!" she moaned.

The murmur of voices caused her to glance down the platform to the opposite end. Two men were sitting on a bench, one clutching a squeezebox concertina. She took in their worn clothes, tanned skin and dark hair at a glance; *unbelievable!* The men had noticed her too; one pointed in her direction and then leaned close to his companion to say something. Then they got up and started walking towards her. Vogel's heart skipped a beat. As she turned towards the exit, they began to run.

Footsteps clattered on the iron stairs behind her. She hurried up the last flight and out into a deserted ticket hall. On the pavement outside she nearly stepped on a huddle of blankets perched on a carpet of newspapers.

"Please, please..."

She had to get out of sight and quickly. Vogel sprinted away, selecting her route at random. She darted down first one side street then another through a gridiron of nineteenth century brick buildings their windows smashed and boarded up.

As she entered a third street she spied the waterfront at the far end, the harbour beyond lost in fog. Vogel glanced over her shoulder but saw no signs of the men. Maybe she'd given them the slip?

She stopped, panting as she caught her breath and then began a slow walk towards the water. Moments later she emerged at a dilapidated wharf, which was in an even poorer state than the adjacent streets. Vogel shivered despite her mad dash, taking in the filth and ruin progress had left in its wake.

Hinterhafen was one of those blighted urban nooks where you could never be fully at ease, always suspecting that you were being observed. The whole area was probably swarming with just-out-of-sight rats and junkies. She shuddered again, glancing over her shoulder. If she was honest, part of her was drawn to such places in a way, though what she considered her better nature found them repellent, of course. There was the feeling that great chunks of the city's corpus had been relinquished into the hands of the darker metropolitan soul and that if left untended its corruption would spread. They really ought to bulldoze the whole place and build something new.

The wharf was littered with unlikely junk: sodden paper and rags of card, shattered wooden crates and pallets, an upturned desk, a heap of mattresses and a rusted bike frame that someone had fished from the harbour. Parallel to the water's edge, sunken orange-brown rails ran through the worn cobbles where goods trains once trundled to deliver and receive freight from old-time break-bulk cargo ships. Just past the point where Vogel had emerged, the stone waterside was crowned by a massive grey-brown riveted structure, once a crane mounting, but now more like a brutalist enigma striped with graffiti. Beyond that, huge iron and glass sheds loomed, their upper edges indistinct in the foggy air.

A figure appeared from the direction of the sheds, picking his way over wasteland and rubble and clambering onto the crane mounting. His appearance was so sudden and unexpected that Vogel froze, at first quite unable to take in what she was seeing or the fact that the newcomer was completely naked.

"What on earth...not swimming in this weather, surely?" she breathed.

Lithe and strong, his body had the effortless beauty of the young. Then she registered his deep tan, heavy-lidded dark eyes and glossy black hair. He had to be one of them. The young man paused, noticing her for the first time but apparently unfazed by the fact he was observed. Briefly their eyes met and Vogel found herself gazing into wells of melancholy and despair. And then he was gone.

She heard the splash before she even realised he was no longer there. Had he been holding something? All she could see were those dark eyes and then she thought she understood.

"*No!*"

Vogel was clambering up the metal skeleton, scuffing her fingers and bruising her shins. Out on the end of the outermost pylon she stared into the black waters. She could see him, an indistinct form, pale against the dark waters, sinking rapidly from view. Before she could even reflect her jacket was off and she was plunging into the icy darkness.

Later when they were both back on land, huddled and shivering at the foot of one of the huge sheds, she couldn't say how she had done it. She was shocked. Everything had gone too fast. What had possessed her? She wasn't usually impulsive like this.

"You not save me," the young man said, through chattering teeth.

Vogel turned to regard him. He was sitting in a puddle, his trembling arms clutched around his knees. Blood was running from lacerations on his forehead and a gash in his side. She wanted to scream at him, to tell him he was a fool and that he should go to hell. But all she could think of was his beauty and the sadness in his eyes.

"Life is...precious. It's all we have. I don't know what your problem is, but you're too young to give up yet," she admonished. But even she couldn't escape the lack of conviction in her voice, which sounded like that of an uninspired and mildly disapproving parent.

"Life *not* precious, I *not* free. I *slave*. My life will never be good. You cannot save me," the young man snarled and looked away from her.

"But why? Nobody has to be a slave these days, not here in this country. Why can't you be saved?"

"Because of Keeper. He own me, he own family. We his property. Can never get away, never be free."

Vogel covered her face with her hands, suddenly ashamed. *Of course, they're here without permits and unable to go to the authorities. If they do they'll be deported back to wherever they come from and the gangsters who brought them here will punish them.* She'd heard about that kind of thing too.

"Look I'm sorry. Really, I am. You're cold and bleeding, I want to help you. Where are your people?"

"You want help me? Go on train. There you help."

"Train? Do you mean the underground?" she asked softly.

"No, train here in shed," he said indicating the wall behind him. Vogel thought she understood. There must be some old goods wagons left from when this place was still in use. Was that where the rest of his people were living?

"Okay, I'll fetch someone," she promised.

She hurried around the building and discovered a shadowy goods entrance, the doors long gone.

"Hello? Is anybody in there?" she called. The place felt deserted. She took a few nervous steps into the loading area. "Hello?"

There was a strange odour inside the building, not just the usual ones of rot and damp, but something fouler. Vogel forced herself to continue over piles of rubble dotted with the shrivelled rust-coloured skeletons of dead plants. This couldn't be right; nobody had been in here for years.

A dark shape shot out from a crack in the rubble and bolted past her with a screech. Vogel yelped, stumbled, fell. She sat heavily on a pile of broken timbers, her eyes searching the shadows for signs of danger.

Must've been a cat... She let her pulse settle and tried to laugh at herself; just a cat. *Stupid!*

She passed on through a series of abandoned offices, each completely empty, the walls streaked with mildew and dirt, the floors deep in crumbled plaster and other mouldering rubbish. Each step brought with it a greater sense of unease.

She was just about to turn back when she came upon a narrow, windowless space, like a short corridor. At the far end, an odd-looking door opened onto bright daylight, but most of the passage was very dark. There was a faint droning sound.

A fly buzzed by her face as she entered the corridor; *late in the year for insects.* She batted it aside, intent on the doorway and the light ahead.

The opening formed a rough archway and had clearly been created since the building fell into disuse. Vogel approached slowly, the hairs on her arms and neck rising as she drew closer. *Who could have made this, and how? It looks almost as if a giant cutting tool has sliced straight through both brick and plaster.* Flies danced about her face.

There were heaps of rags on the floor around the arch making her think at once of the forgotten corpses of homeless people. *Don't look at them, just in case!* She trained her eyes upwards, picking out graffiti about the edges of the archway, latching onto the crude forms as a welcome distraction from the decay at her feet. Most eye-catching was a fly of giant size beneath which the artist had sprayed a lengthy, stylised tag that she couldn't quite make out, but that read something like: *Baaldhubaab.*

A sudden noise caused her to freeze. From behind her came sounds like stealthy footfalls. Her heart gave a jolt and she plunged out through the veil of flying insects emerging into a huge, bright space.

She'd been expecting to come out on the other side of the building. The first thing she saw, however, was the train: eight gleaming passenger carriages, their lacquered coachwork reminiscent of classical early twentieth century rolling stock, the windows as dark as night. At the platform's end, a massive black locomotive leaked steam, hissing softly.

Vogel paused in open-mouthed confusion. She was standing on a broad station platform bordered by a single track and not some simple warehouse siding either. Above her head a roof of glass and iron ran the length of the shed to the open far end, from which silver rails led off into the fog. In stark contrast to the rest of the building, everything here was clean, well-ordered and in good repair.

I've never heard of anything like this here. Must be the home to a historical railway society of some sort.

Between strands of white vapour she spied a pair of legs standing close to the engine.

"Excuse me!" she called. A tall figure in a well-pressed uniform stepped into view, his face in shadow beneath the peak of an attendant's cap.

"Madam?" he called.

Vogel dashed toward him.

"Sorry, I was looking for some help. A man's been hurt. Is this some sort of enthusiasts' run or something?

"*Enthusiasts*, Madam?" The Attendant seemed puzzled.

"Yes, I mean this isn't the regular railway, is it? Are you some sort of, I don't know, special, private association?"

"Well, yes, I suppose you could say that. You seem to be rather wet, Madam; can I be of any assistance?"

"That's what I was talking about, a young man. He fell into the water, hurt himself..."

"A *young man*, you say, I wondered why we'd stopped here. Right, well in that case you'd better come aboard," the Attendant replied. For a moment he seemed excited, though he quickly regained his composure again. "Here you go," he said stepping smartly past the coal tender and indicating a short flight of steps leading into the first carriage.

"Why do I need to do that, is there a doctor on the train?" Vogel wondered, hesitating before clambering up the steps.

"Oh, almost certainly, Madam," the Attendant replied and ushered her up into the carriage.

As soon as she crossed the threshold into the train it shuddered into motion and Vogel lost all sense of where she was or how she'd come to be there. Her mind was choking on thick slurries of grainy darkness, and movement became an effort, like wading through a blend of grit and syrup. The more she struggled the more her feet and body sank into its viscous depths.

"Tickets please!"

Vogel came to in a grey plush window seat. Next to her a man in an old style suit and trilby was speaking animatedly to a smiling couple sitting opposite. She listened briefly, but couldn't make out what they were saying.

"Tickets please, Madam!"

The Conductor leaned toward her, a tall, gaunt figure dressed in a dark uniform similar to that of the Attendant. Above a square jaw and pale, bony cheeks, his eyes were no more than dark hollows.

"Sorry, but I'm not actually supposed to be here and I'm afraid I don't have one," Vogel said. She was sinking into her seat and struggled to straighten herself up with little success, a most disconcerting experience, like being a small child on an oversized cushion.

"I see Madam," the Conductor said reaching out for her hand as her legs vanished from view.

"What's happening?" she shrilled in alarm.

The Conductor wrenched hard, and the seat slowly released her.

"What's wrong with the seat?" she asked, allowing herself to be helped to her feet.

"You'll have to keep moving Madam; this train isn't for your kind."

"What do you mean *my kind*, I don't understand," but her feet were already sinking into the carriage floor.

"Come along, let's walk together," the Conductor said setting off ahead without looking to see if she was following.

"You shouldn't be aboard here. You're too heavy. If you sit or stand still, you'll sink right through and the Keeper alone knows where you'll end up then."

"Too heavy? You mean I'm heavier than...than that man over there," Vogel asked indicating a corpulent passenger asleep in his seat. "That makes no sense."

"No I'm sure it doesn't. But you have to keep moving, walking, whatever. The energy released by the movement of your denser body will keep you buoyant and stop you slipping through. The only time you can rest a little is when the train's slowing down or stationary. Oh, and don't go bothering the paying passengers, they can't see you very well, but the more they do the quicker you'll fall through."

"This is crazy, completely...I don't believe it," Vogel protested, still hurrying to keep up as the Conductor passed from one carriage to the next.

"Yes, I know, but as you yourself said, you shouldn't be here," the Conductor replied.

"Look, I'll get off as soon as I can, I promise. You will be stopping won't you?" she asked.

"Next stop will be in about ten minutes Madam," he said consulting his watch.

"Good. That should still be somewhere in the city, right?"

"In the city...Madam, this is a pan-temporal European connection. Before you alighted we'd just come from the siege of Magdeburg. Our next scheduled stop is the Kessel on the Volga. I really don't think you'll want to get off there."

"The *Volga*? But that's in...now wait a minute; don't try it on with me. And how come you can see me and talk to me but I don't fall through the train faster the way you said I would?"

"Firstly, I am not a passenger and secondly, have you seen me at rest for more than a second or two yet, Madam? You might say I have a similar problem to yours," the Conductor explained with a cold smile.

Vogel's head was spinning; this was all simply too much. A surge of pressure was building inside her that she felt certain was going to end in disaster. She needed to concentrate, but someone close by was speaking in a pathetic high-pitched voice, blurting out silly questions. With a start she realised it was her.

"But how was I even able to get on? ...I didn't come from the siege of wherever it was. I came from Hinterhafen...Hinterhafen you understand."

"Only the Keeper knows the answers to questions like that, Madam."

"Well, am I the only non-paying passenger you've ever had or have other people who shouldn't be here climbed aboard?

"It does happen, though given our route I'm not sure how. It's all very unfortunate."

"What became of the others?"

"Some I didn't get to in time, others wouldn't listen. They fell through the train."

"Is that it?"

"The Keeper did find out about a few," the Conductor admitted.

"And?"

"They either became his possessions and were sent off to work for him..."

"Or?"

"...he destroyed them."

"Does that mean you got on here by accident too?"

"The train personnel are the property of the Keeper, Madam. He's the reason we're here."

"But I don't understand. You just said that..."

"It was very long ago, Madam. If you must know, I really can't remember. Now if you'll excuse me, I have to keep on." And he stepped smartly away into the next carriage and was gone.

Vogel's first thought was to follow him, but the train began to slow and many of the muted passengers around her seemed to be preparing for departure. She stepped out into the space by the carriage doors and leant out of the open window, performing a slow series of shuffling mini-steps in the hope that such movement would suffice to keep her from sinking.

Outside night had fallen, snow lay thick on the ground and a freezing wind was buffeting the train. In the light from the carriage windows, Vogel caught glimpses of ragged columns of men, some bearing weapons. Soldiers, she supposed, though they didn't seem to be wearing any sort of recognisable uniform. In fact they were dressed more like beggars, their heads, hands and feet swathed in blankets and strips of cloth. The patter of small arms fire came to her on the biting wind.

The train slowed further and Vogel abandoned her shuffle, though she still checked her feet every few seconds to ensure they hadn't vanished into the floor. They passed a high barbed-wire fence, beyond which the ground was littered with prone human forms. Those she could see at close range were emaciated, pale and hollow-eyed. Many were dead, the windborne snow drifting over their frozen remains. She realised that she must be witnessing some kind of major disaster yet she felt completely detached, as if she were watching from a great distance in time and space.

The train ground to a standstill and the carriage door swung open of itself. Directly outside a small group of ragged men were huddled together, their ruined frames shaking as they dipped their heads into the centre of the circle formed by their bodies.

Are they praying?

Slightly afraid and yet drawn towards the group Vogel clambered halfway down from the carriage just as the distant horizon erupted in great pulsing flashes. Seconds later a series of nearby shell-bursts illuminated the scene with the starkness of daylight and she saw the corpse in their midst. The shivering men pawed at its gaping abdomen, tearing out pieces of half-frozen offal with blackened fingers. One turned to regard her, his eyes pits of despair.

"Please," he moaned.

Vogel fled back into the carriage straight into the Conductor.

"Not leaving us then, Madam?" he inquired.

"Those men, did you see them?" she panted. Almost as soon as she'd spoken the carriage door slammed shut and the train lurched into motion.

"I've been speaking to the Attendant about you," the Conductor continued as if nothing were amiss. "He tells me you boarded the train with a specific purpose in mind. Why didn't you say?" Something in his manner suggested he was struggling to maintain his composure.

Vogel was shaking. "What *was* that place? Who did that to those men?"

"Yes, I know, horrible and none of our other stations are very much better either I'm afraid. This world does appear to be rather blighted. We do our best to ignore it when we can, but sometimes you simply can't look away, can you?"

Vogel didn't answer him. All she could think of was the men feasting on their fallen comrade.

"Look, if what my colleague said was true, you might, just might be able to help us. I have to keep calm. No good getting flustered, that will only draw his gaze down on us. Shall we walk a little, Madam? The train is picking up speed now and I fear you are slipping away from us again." The Conductor set off through the carriage at a brisk pace and Vogel, after the briefest hesitation, dragged her feet from the viscous floor and took up position behind him again.

"So, we have to get this clear, what was it you said to the Attendant?" he asked over his shoulder.

"Do you mean the man I talked to on the platform?"

"Yes."

"I'm not sure it's important now, there was a young man. It was in another place, where I got aboard, a city that isn't anything like your last stop."

"Well, that depends on who you are and what you choose to see. Anyway, what was it about the young man, Madam?" the Conductor pressed.

"I don't know really. He'd been hurt. I wanted to help him," Vogel said.

"So you wanted to help this young man?"

"Yes. That's why I boarded the train in the first place. The Attendant said I would be able to get help if I came aboard."

"Good, that's very good. Did you touch the young man in any way?"

"Well of course. I rescued him from drowning."

"Ah, in that case the Keeper probably knows of you. Still, that might not matter, not if we're lucky."

"What do you mean?"

"The young man is one of the Keeper's many, many servants. We all are. And we are *bound* to him in numerous ways. Our minds still belong to us in part and are not altogether transparent to his gaze, but we form a physical extension of him through which he senses the world. To an extent he feels what we feel, but there are so many of us that he tends only to dwell upon the extremes. Should we suffer great pain or pleasure for example or if our emotions become inflamed in other ways, then his gaze is drawn directly to us and we suffer his fullest attention."

Frowning, Vogel recalled the Attendant's strange reaction to her on the platform and how he seemed to stifle his excitement.

"Tell me," the Conductor continued, "did the Attendant touch you...no wait, I did when I pulled you from the seat. Damn. First the young man then me; that means he likely knows you're aboard. What a pity, he's going to be looking for you now and that rather forces our hand..."

"I really don't think I understand all this," Vogel interrupted.

"No, of course not. Look, one very important question: do you still want to help the young man?"

Vogel nodded, bewildered.

"Good. Now quickly, in here where nobody will be able to hear us," he said indicating a narrow wooden door, which seemed to have appeared from nowhere.

They entered a cramped office space with a tiny desk and two chairs. The Conductor stepped smartly behind the desk with practised movements and opened a drawer. Vogel began jogging on the spot.

"You don't need to do that in here. Even the Keeper recognises the fact that we must be still sometimes," the Conductor said indicating the other chair. Vogel sat down, her eyes trained on her feet and the floor.

"I think you need to meet the Keeper," the Conductor continued.

"He's actually on this train?" Vogel asked, her voice rising in alarm.

"Yes, it's his train. His carriage is at the rear, the very last one."

"But isn't he dangerous?"

"Yes Madam, very."

"Then I don't know if I really want to..."

"But you do still want to assist the young man?"

"Yes, of course, but under the circumstances I think I ought to help myself first," Vogel protested, angrily.

"If you took care of the Keeper, you would free us all and end this journey through madness once and for all."

"But what do I have to do?"

"You will need this," the Conductor said offering her a revolver from his desk.

"What? What for?"

"For the Keeper of course."

"You want me to *kill* him?" Vogel asked, horrified.

"Of course, Madam or help us to at least, what did you suppose?"

"No, no I can't, sorry, not that," she said shaking her head and getting up. A bell was ringing somewhere in her head and the scene before her was becoming indistinct as if grainy darkness were seeping into her eyes. Her gorge rose.

"If you want to help your young man, this is the only way," the Conductor insisted.

The air around Vogel thickened further and ragged shadows swam between them, with a texture that rasped against her skin. "Why do I have to do this? If you want rid of him so badly you should do it yourself!" she pleaded. In addition to the bell, somewhere beyond the shifting shadows a woman was screaming.

"Madam, like the young man we are *bound* to the Keeper, his *servants*. We are quite simply not capable of so direct and overt an action..." the conductor's voice was fading.

"No!" Vogel, mouthed the word but heard no sound. She forced her way through the turgid air and out of the little compartment to the carriage beyond. At first she knew only the need to keep moving and struggled along the aisle, darkness closing about her until the pain of aching muscles was all that encroached upon her torpor. But just when she was sure that she would fall into unconsciousness the train's strange interior materialised about her and she was back, stumbling from one carriage to the next, determined to explore every inch of her unlikely prison, from the conductor's office to the Keeper's compartment.

Finally the screaming stopped.

Weary hours passed as she wandered further and further, looking for anything or anyone that might offer clues to escape. All manner of people seemed to be aboard the train, many from distant points in history, but nothing about them suggested to her that she should risk their full attention. Eventually she lost count of the carriages she'd traversed, knowing only that she must have passed through far more than the eight that had been visible from the platform in Hinterhafen. Perhaps there was no real end to the train once you were aboard?

No end and no escape. What next? Retrace my steps, I suppose. At least I know of one landmark in the other direction by which I can orient myself: the Conductor's office.

To her dismay, however, the moment she turned about the passengers around her shifted and changed, becoming different people altogether. She heard that bell again, faintly at first. It was followed by a woman, sobbing and muttering. Hurrying back the way she'd come, she failed to recognise a single person and after further weary trudging her throat was parched and her belly growling with hunger. She had to find somewhere to rest soon or she was done for.

The train began to slow. Just as before, it seemed that many passengers were preparing to leave. Vogel didn't think she could face another destination like the Kessel, so once she judged the train to be moving sufficiently slowly she flopped down in the nearest empty seat and closed her eyes, praying they would remain stationary long enough for her to regain some strength. But the darkness behind her eyelids was full of ice and starving men and rest eluded her. She abandoned her efforts and pressed her face to the window. Perhaps this station would prove better than the last despite what the Conductor had told her.

The windows were caked in grime making visibility poor. From what she could see they were in a landscape of looming shapes and shadows, through which the sky shone in scattered fragments; a forest perhaps? As her eyes began to adjust she picked out indistinct patches of slow-moving murk against the darker background. A muffled shout went up and a series of blinding flashes erupted directly outside her window accompanied by thunderous percussions. Vogel recoiled, half-blinded. Then the screaming began and she closed her eyes, jamming her hands over her ears.

It didn't help. Sobbing and shouting filled her head. Vogel lashed out, kicking and punching at the floor, window and surrounding seats. In a chorus of anguish, her own screams joined those within until, exhausted at last, she grew silent and listless.

A soft touch on her arm roused her. It was the Conductor.

"The train will shortly depart. You look tired. Would you care to return to my office to rest a while?"

"Is it far?" she wondered in a tiny voice.

"My office is wherever I need it to be," he told her.

Vogel let herself be led to the end of the carriage where the Conductor unlocked the tiny wooden door.

"I was looking high and low for this and yet somehow missed it when I passed by," she murmured.

"That's because it wasn't here at the time," he said ushering her over the threshold.

Vogel flopped down in the waiting chair and fell asleep.

She was floating through a landscape of forests and corpses, dreaming of coffee, which she could smell on the icy wind. When she came to she was hunched in her seat in the little office, wrapped in a thick blanket. She sat up, massaging the stiffness from her shoulders and arms. Before her on the table, a chipped enamel mug of something hot sent curls of steam into the air. The revolver and six rounds lay beside it.

She was about to reach for the pistol when the door opened and the Conductor returned, squeezing behind his desk and into the seat opposite.

"Drink. It will make you feel better," he suggested indicating the mug.

Vogel did as she was bidden, relishing the hot coffee as it burnt the tip of her tongue and warmed her insides.

"I'd like to apologise for my poor attempts at explaining earlier. The reality of the Keeper is hard to grasp even for one like me who has known it for many years."

Vogel sipped her coffee and nodded. "Try me," she said.

"He possesses many souls. Few are happy about this state of affairs. So we resist in such ways as we can, but we cannot be hasty or passionate in our attempts or he will know which of us he must crush. We are his *web*, a network of interlocking beings, scattered wide through time and place. Any battle to overthrow him must be played out in that web; between us and within us. You are not part of the mesh of souls. He knows of you, but can only sense you through physical contact with us.

"And that means I can walk right up to him and kill him?" Vogel asked her eyes on the pistol again.

"Well, he's not altogether easy to take unawares. You could distract him, however. Your presence and this gun will cause him to focus all his attentions on you, briefly. While that occurs we will rise up."

"And what will happen to me when he realises what's really going on?"

"Once begun, it will all go quickly."

"How quickly?"

"Madam, I am not sure, but it is the only way. If you would help your young man or indeed any of us, and if you would escape from this train without falling into his possession, then it must be done."

Vogel sighed. She ought to protest, shout, throw her cup or something. But she couldn't summon the energy to do any of those things. And if she didn't go along with him, what were her choices?

"At the station in Hinterhafen, I counted only eight carriages, yet I've wandered your train for what feels like days, without finding the end of it. You said he was in the last carriage, so how will I get there?"

"You need this," the Conductor said throwing her a small key.

Vogel caught the tiny piece of grey metal. "But how will this help me find him? Unlock his door, yes, but a key is not a map, it won't..."

"Haven't you noticed? This train doesn't work the same way as the world you're used to. Don't try to figure it out, just take my word for it. With that in your possession, you'll have no difficulty getting to the back of the train," he said.

Vogel drained the last of the coffee and nodded. "And this," she said indicating the pistol. "There truly is no other way?"

The Conductor's grim face clouded further and he shook his head. "Take care of the Keeper and we will all be released, including your young man. Oh and another thing, if he tries to engage you in conversation, resist. Make no concessions to him."

Vogel marched toward the rear of the train, fully prepared for a long haul. This time, however, she passed through only four carriages before coming to a fifth, at the entrance to which was a locked wooden door. In the centre of the door a brass plaque read:

Private
No admittance

She drew the pistol in one trembling hand and placed the key into the lock with the other, turning it with a sharp click. The sound was so loud that she was sure anyone inside must have heard it and would be ready for her.

Her fingers brushed the polished door handle and the door swung open almost of itself revealing a shadowy carriage that was one long empty space. She took in the scene in a single glance: at the far end of the carriage was a large dark-wood desk behind which sat a hooded figure in a black lounge suit; he wore a thick white shirt beneath his jacket and golden cufflinks glinted at his wrists.

He must be able to see me. I should shoot, but it's too far away. I'll miss, I know I will.

Vogel stepped into the carriage and the door swung to behind her. In her head a man's voice said: "No going back now."

Was that my mind or the Keeper speaking? A fly buzzed past her.

She began the long walk, revolver held before her in both hands. The floor of the Keeper's compartment was carpeted in thick black pile which muffled all sound and the walls between curtained windows were hung with gold picture frames. As she proceeded she couldn't help glancing at the gilt-framed pictures. They were black and white mortuary photographs all of the same young man she'd saved in Hinterhafen, the cause of death different in each picture.

A fly settled on her hand, her eyes flickered from the pictures to the insect and then to the still figure behind the desk. Her fingers twitched and the fly was gone.

Focus on the Keeper!

When she reached the desk she paused, trembling; the figure before her had not moved since she'd entered the carriage. Was he even breathing? She couldn't tell. The hood was an eyeless black cloth bag, like the sort condemned prisoners used to wear to the gallows. Perhaps that was why he hadn't reacted to her presence?

"Why are you here?" The words rustled softly through her head like a breeze through fallen leaves. "Tell me, traveller, what brings you to me?"

An image of the young man falling into the harbour flashed through her mind.

"Ah. So you would save *him*. But you cannot, for he is bound to me."

Vogel squeezed the trigger; the revolver bucked in her hand, its report deafening. The bullet smashed through the back of the Keeper's chair and on through the rear wall of the carriage, but the Keeper was gone.

Vogel was kicking and thrashing, the freezing water numbing her face and hands. She had the young man in her grasp and was struggling to wrench him up out of the shadows, but he fought her, squirming from her grip and forcing his way downward.

The vision faded. She spun around. A man in a suit and hood was standing at the far end of the carriage by the door.

How did he get there, is he escaping? No he's completely still.

Vogel raised the pistol and fired again. The man vanished and her bullet punched a hole through the door. Muffled screams and shouting rose faintly from the carriage beyond.

The train had stopped and she was dashing through the stationary carriages, her feet pounding down the aisles. Swarthy-skinned musicians were battling their way aboard, beating aside pickets of uniformed station staff who sought to block their way and overwhelming the hysterical passengers who attempted to drag them off again.

"Missed!"

The voice was beside her. Vogel turned towards it, fired, but yet again there was nobody there. She spun about and discovered her adversary halfway between the desk and the door.

"Three bullets gone, already; *be careful, be careful, be careful!*" she hissed to herself. Teeth clenched she forced her feet toward him, revolver level before her. *You mustn't miss!*

Another report and he was gone. She turned, glimpsed his tall form through a haze of gun smoke, fired...missed.

Beggars swarmed over the locomotive, tearing at the valves and pipes. The Fireman wielded his shovel, the Driver a wrench but within moments they vanished beneath the sheer weight of numbers.

Vogel was in the centre of the carriage facing the desk and rear wall, but the Keeper was nowhere to be seen. She stifled a sob. *Only one bullet left.* Then something cold like mist enveloped her and her vision led her down twisting corridors through space and time. All across the cosmos, beings were locked in battle for release. Down one thread of sight she glimpsed the young man's struggle beneath the murky waters of Hinterhafen while from another she spied the Conductor and Attendant riding at the head of a great paupers' army. The Conductor's voice rang out over the din of battle:

"The train is ours! Quickly, we must relieve her; she holds him at bay, but she is almost out of time and bullets."

Then the vision faded and the weird twisting web of the Keeper's empire vanished. He remained close, however, a chill cloying presence of shadow and fog.

Dazed and half-blinded after the glimpse into his realm Vogel floundered about, waving the pistol at shadows.

"If you would *truly* save him, then you must take his place! Do you accept that?" This time the voice was immediately behind her. Vogel rounded on him, pressing the barrel into the centre of his chest.

The Conductor cried out to his followers from what seemed a great distance: *He's trying to entrap her!* But Vogel's senses were scrambled and his words could not reach her. For an instant the strange flowing vision paths opened up around her again permitting her a glimpse of him storming the Keeper's door, his heart and mind bright beacons of passion, connecting many worlds.

So this is victory; strange then that his face looks so anguished.

The Conductor was still shouting, perhaps to her, but the world outside the Keeper's carriage had grown silent and his lips were moving too fast for her to read them.

"Do you *accept* that?" the Keeper asked again from somewhere deeper within.

"Yes," she sighed.

This time when she squeezed the trigger he was hurled from his feet, a smoking hole in his heart. He hit the floor with a thud that sent a shudder through the train. The lights flickered, went out for a few heartbeats then came on again. Vogel felt faint. Her chest was covered in blood. Surely it was the Keeper's and yet the stain was spreading.

A great clamour of shrieking and groaning went up around her. Pieces of the carriage walls and ceiling fell away to reveal starless darkness without and the body on the carpet began to collapse, its suit disintegrating into rags. She knelt down, tugging at the drawstrings which held the deflating hood in place and her mouth filled with blood. When she wrenched the cloth away all she found within was an oval mirror, cracked from side to side, and reflected in it her own pale face staring back at her.

The lights went out and the train crumbled into fragments of shadow, smoke and glittering flame. The roar of its demise rushed in to fill every corner of the universe before fading to silence. And then she was falling, all strength leaving her in the icy cold. Somewhere above in a fractured window of light, Vogel could still make out the lithe figure standing at the water's edge, but as she sank deeper even that faded.

Not All Trains Crash

Steven Pirie

Ruth puts an ear against the track. It's November, and there's a hint of frost to bite her cheek. She feels the rust upon the line rasp her skin. Ruth shivers at the distant rumble of the trains. From here, in front of the old, abandoned signalling box, with its roof torn and its levers bent like arthritic fingers, she can sense every train upon every line. She hears the whine of the high speed express and the steady rumble of the goods wagon's shunter. She hears the creak of cooling brakes on the carriages at the platforms far away, and the slam of the doors when the people are off. She feels the clunk of a million points changing lines.

"What do you hear?" says Laura, Ruth's sister. "Will the trains come back today?"

"Not today," says Ruth. She stands and stares along the weed-covered track. The line is straight and disappears into a distant tunnel. There's no light beyond its crumbling arch.

"Your cheek is bleeding," says Laura. "It's red like when Father beat us."

"It's nothing." Ruth rubs a finger across her cheek. *Did Father beat them?* "It's just the rust from the line."

"Will the trains ever come back?"

Ruth grins; she doesn't think they will. "Soon, they'll come back soon."

"Good," says Laura. "I want to watch them crash."

"Not all trains crash."

"They don't?"

"Only some of them."

School is held at the rear of the carriage—the *communal area* as Mr Peterson, the old Guard, calls it. The car is split between six first class compartments on a corridor and the open-plan second class seating at the rear. It's certainly the largest open area, even if the last two windows look out under the wet mud of the pond.

Ruth sits, head in hands, lost to half-sleep. She's oblivious to the murmur of the others—of Laura, and Charlotte, the rich, fat girl with the pearl worth more than Ruth's world, and the two German boys—twins, Ruth thinks, whose names she's never quite known, and whose fractured legs have never quite healed. Ruth's startled awake as to the front, raised by the gentle slope of the carriage, Mr Peterson slams time-torn books down upon the table.

"Tuesday," says Mr Peterson. "Tuesday, children, is History."

Ruth groans. The only history Mr Peterson knows is that of the railways. Today they'll learn timetables again, the ledgers of ghostly trains that no longer even run. She'd rather be anywhere but here. She's fifteen, and has been so for as long as she can remember—this is no place for a girl of that age, hidden away in a stinking, muddied railway carriage lost to a tangle of foliage. She should be out finding her way in the world. Were it not for little Laura, Ruth thinks she might leave.

Mr Peterson coughs. "Now then," he says. "Who can remember where we left off last week? Did we get as far as the 06:15 from Paddington to Great Malvern, stopping at all stations bar Pershore (closed for platform repairs)?"

Laura raises her hand. "Mr Peterson?"

"What is it, child?"

"I'd like to learn about *our train*."

"Yes, tell us *our* story," says Charlotte. "Did *we* stop at all stations?"

"Were there leaves on the line?" says one of the German boys.

Mr Peterson grunts and hands out the dusty books from the table. "Turn to page twenty-two, children, the 06:15 from Paddington to Great Malvern. Now, Laura, please begin reading from the departure."

"But, Mr Peterson…"

"From the departure, if you please."

It's almost pleasant in the clearing, later, when the afternoon sun has chased away the early frosts. Ruth sits on the embankment, watching wisps of steam rising from the dark top of the carriage roof. At the front, still coupled, Mr Peterson's Guard's Brake Van sits level on solid ground and is probably the only reason the carriage has not sank down further into the pond. Sometimes Ruth wishes it had sunk. Maybe then they'd all be like the dead skeletons that wash up each time the pond floods.

Dead skeletons? Ruth pauses at that thought—what else could they be but dead? She shivers, because it hurts that if she ponders those skeletons she should also consider what the others are—what is Laura, Mr Peterson, Mrs Oates and Captain Stevens?—what is… *Ruth?*

She thinks back to that fateful day—a wet Wednesday in March, she's sure; a platform full of cheering soldiers just back from the newly-won war—but it's hard because the day is shrouded by steam billowing from the great locomotive at train's end, and her ears ring to its shrill whistle. She holds Laura's hand, because Mother's busy shoving suitcases on to the train, and there's a man who's not Father helping her. He has his hand around Mother's waist as he does so. He wears a golden bracelet. It's inscribed *Tom and Ruth*, which is odd because Ruth is Mother's name, too, and Mother has a pendant inscribed *Ruth and Tom*. Ruth chokes at the sudden realisation of who Tom was, partly because she wonders how she could have been so naïve not to have known, but mainly because one of the skeletons lost to the mud at the carriage's rear has a gold bracelet, too.

And Laura had skipped aboard the train, young and trusting and carefree, pulling Ruth after her in her eagerness to get to… where on Earth were they going? Ruth glances up at the clearing with its rusted line and broken carriage, its signal box all broken windows and peeling wood. All stations to… *where?* Surely not here? The split tree that bore the brunt of the carriage's impact still points downward into the pond water. Around it thorns and brambles and nettles run wild. And the other trees are closing in, raising a canopy across Ruth's world, so even in summer the sun shines through less each season and the carriage is darker inside. Captain Stevens said he'd take a chainsaw to those boughs, but there was no chainsaw and no axe, and when the Captain tried to pull back each branch, Ruth saw his shocked face as his hands passed right through leaf and twig as if they weren't there.

That night, when all were asleep, Ruth had climbed quietly on top of the carriage and reached out herself for the trees. *Ghosts*, she'd whispered, *either these trees are ghosts or we are ghosts. Surely there's more than one world, here. Now, if only I knew which world I should be in.*

Ruth reaches to one side for a stone. It feels angular and heavy and *real* in her grasp. She throws it out across the pond. It disappears below the surface but makes no sound. There are no ripples where it breaks the water. When she looks down, the same stone could be back at her side. A trick of the mind, surely, because there are lots of such stones on the embankment. Ruth sighs, no, it's all quite possibly a trick of the mind. All of it.

There's a treat every Tuesday evening. Mr Peterson is on the line, bounding about as usual trying to muster everyone into a group. Behind him, beyond the overgrown tunnel in the distance, the sun is setting.

"Hurry, Mrs Oates," he says. "We don't want to miss it now, do we?"

Mrs Oates is fat and old. She's half her head missing and the other half clearly lumbers because of it. It's all Mr Peterson can do to get her lined up in the right direction. Captain Stevens is already striding down the line toward the verdant tunnel. The German twins drag themselves along after him, their twisted legs all but useless for walking. Laura pulls Ruth by the hand, and Charlotte is fashionably late behind.

As Ruth nears the tunnel it gets harder to push forward. There's a force against them she feels as a cold wind upon her brow. The fear of it dries her lips. It swirls dust in the tunnel, flashed gold and brown by the setting sun beyond, until Ruth feels the tunnel itself is on fire. As far as Ruth knows, it could be Hell.

"Nearly there," says Mr Peterson.

Ruth feels Laura's grip tighten. She smiles down at her sister. "Don't be frightened. We'll just look through; we're not going inside."

"Sometimes, I think I want to go inside," says Laura.

Ruth pauses. So does she, oh, so does she. But Ruth's afraid there's nothing for them on the other side. She means *nothing*, not nothing; in a world of twisted reality there's a vast difference. And that fire looks real enough—even Captain Stevens won't venture into the tunnel and he'd gone *over the top* in the trenches. If Laura screamed and burned in those flames Ruth would never forgive herself.

"Now why would we want to do that?" says Ruth.

Laura smiles. "I want to see Mother again."

Ruth pauses once more. She bites her lip. "Do you think that's where Mother is?"

"I've looked everywhere else."

Ruth pulls Laura close. A final push into the flames and it could be over quickly, perhaps. A moment's agony for an eternity's peace? Besides, she's been this close to death already, even if she won't yet accept the vague memory of being thrown about the carriage as it tumbled down from the rails to the pond that wet Wednesday in March was somehow real.

"I've looked everywhere, too," says Ruth. "But, you know, I'm not sure I'm ready to go into the tunnel just yet. I'd like to learn about *our train*, too. And we still have each other, eh?"

There's a rumble beyond the tunnel. The sound is muffled as if from a world away. The distant horizon shimmers blue-green and unfocussed, but in the middle distance where the line meets *the points*, the rail is *silver-bright* not *rust-blind* like that below Ruth's feet.

"It's coming, everyone," says Mr Peterson. Captain Stevens raises his military issue binoculars. Mrs Oates stares with her one good eye. "Don't blink or you'll miss it."

"I hope we'll always have each other," says Laura.

Beyond the tunnel, the train streaks past. It's sleek and new and bullet fast, and the people behind its tinted windows are blurred and unreal. Ruth wonders if to them she looks the same; ethereal and waiflike like as she peers out at them through the disused branch line tunnel. Do any of them even notice her? It's clear they didn't come looking for her on that Wednesday in March. Why else would they still be there?

The train is gone. Its roar is Doppler shifted as it passes all too briefly upon its way. All that's left is the fading rumble on the line below their feet.

"Most excellent," says Mr Peterson. "It's good to see all is well with the world. Onward home!"

As one they turn and walk back along their track.

No one speaks.

No one ever does this close to the *real* world.

Ruth wakes early, Wednesday morning. Something is different nearby, she feels it as keenly as she feels the multitude of trains running on the main line beyond the tunnel and *the points*. Someone is out there.

Ruth dresses quickly. She slides open the first class compartment door, slowly so as not to wake the sleeping Laura. No sense in worrying Laura until Ruth knows just what is happening outside. It's what Mother would do.

Outside, the clearing smells of early-morning musk. No dawn birds sing, but then none ever have. To the east, the blush of dawn deepens the red rust on the line. There's only one hundred yards of rail here before the sharp, right-hand bend, but it's always been the most difficult for Ruth to explore. One day, she's promised herself, she'll push against the winds that force her back and peer round that bend. But if the tunnel leads to her future, surely this stretch of line is to her past. It's a past Ruth's never quite sure she wants to embrace.

Ruth kneels and presses her ear against the line. *All* the trains she hears are behind her, to the west beyond the tunnel and *the points*. She doesn't remember ever hearing anything from the east and the right-hand bend.

Ruth shudders and stands quickly. That's not quite true. In her mind, she tugs upon a memory. It's one of a host of memories she's long since quietened, ones she'd thought locked away forever. Occasionally, when there's something odd about the clearing, she can't help touching this dark place, and those memories are sharp and vivid, and they push and shove and fight to be let loose.

It's going too fast!

Ruth thinks she hears the train coming. But its wheels shriek against the rail, and the signalman's running past her down the line, his red flags snapping in the wind. There are people screaming, because in her mind Ruth is back in the carriage, lurching as it rounds the bend too fast. She looks through the window across the curve to where she now stands, sees herself from both ends as the locomotive is thrown from the tracks. The signalman makes no sound as he is crushed. Odd, that, because she's sure he'd cry out. Steam billows from the upturned wheels of the engine. There's fire, and the stench of burning flesh.

Ruth shakes her head. She's never been beyond this memory. She walks onward toward the bend. There is no train, but the wind rises to push against her. Where the embankment looms, the weeds are thick and rough against her skin. Ruth thinks she hears distant voices. There's the roar of machines.

She reaches the bend in the track. The wind is so strong that Ruth can barely breathe; so strong that should she let go of the weeds surely she'd tumble all the way back to the carriage; so strong that it might lift her skyward and she'll fly straight into the fires within the western tunnel.

Slowly, fearfully, she peers beyond the curve. Her eyes sting with salt tears. The rail runs straight for half a mile before disappearing under another tunnel. Ruth squints into the morning sun. In the distance, in what she thinks must be more of the *real* world, dust rises into the dawn haze. Ruth gasps. There are men working upon the line. She wonders at their machines; great mechanical arms that reach down and pluck at the track. They're taking the line away, and they're heading Ruth's way.

There's an emergency meeting in the school carriage. All are there, even the odd half-people that Ruth has seen come and go—ghosts within ghosts— folk so badly damaged by *the crash* they barely know they're there. Ruth shivers—is she finally ready to acknowledge *the crash* happened?

Mr Peterson frowns. "Nonsense," he says. "Why would they be taking the line away, child? The railway is expanding, not contracting. Soon, there'll be nowhere in the land that will be without its branch line. It's common sense."

Ruth can't help but doubt him. As far as she can tell, the last train to rumble down this line was their own, and she knows now it had taken the bend too fast. Had the brakes failed or had Mr Peterson in the brake van *messed up?* She tastes the acrid smoke in her mouth. Once more she's caught in the corridor of the first class section, looking back as the rear of the carriage sinks down into the mud of the pond. There are people down there, crying out, trapped in their seats, drowning. There's Mother, and Mr Thompson—Uncle Ted, Mother had said, though Ruth had caught them kissing, and Uncle Ted was flushed and breathless, and he kept his hand pressed against his lap like he was hiding something. His other hand rested on Mother's knee. It was the night Father had screamed and beat them all and thrown them out into the street, as though somehow Ruth and Laura were responsible, too. At the time, Ruth felt she surely was.

"There are no more trains, Mr Peterson," says Ruth.

Mr Peterson looks up sharply. Ruth thinks Mr Peterson might argue, but instead he shakes his head slowly. He suddenly looks very old.

"The line is dead," says Ruth. "And I think when the line is gone we will go too." She holds Laura's hand as she speaks. Ruth sighs; perhaps it's time they did move on. "Tell us the story of *our train*, Mr Peterson. The time has come to tell us what happened all those years ago."

For an age, Mr Peterson doesn't move. All in the carriage stare silently to the front. Even the *half-folk* are fleeting-still.

"They can't blame me." Mr Peterson stands. He lurches, and barely catches himself against one of the vertical hand rails, as if since he began talking his legs have aged the sixty-eight years they'd languished in this pocket of *no-time*.

Ruth feels it too. She knows speaking out loud the phrase *all those years ago* is significant. It was all she could do to force the words over her dried lips. Yet in doing so she feels closer to reality than ever she has. Time rushing in weighs heavily upon Ruth's shoulders. It's the same wind at the tunnel, the same that pushes her back at the bend. She's no longer fifteen years of age. She's seventy-eight, even if the last sixty-three of those years she's spent denying she's dead.

"This wasn't my route, see," says Mr Peterson. "My route was the 12:00 King's Cross to Leeds, calling at Grantham and Doncaster. I was only drafted in to cover this run through sickness."

Now that Ruth thinks of it, Uncle Ted was always *popping round* when Father worked nights. Even Mrs Hodgson at the corner shop had talked scathingly of it to Mrs Blunt, when Ruth was in buying ha'penny Blacks Jacks and Swizzles on the Tuesday before that fateful Wednesday. Perhaps she'd still been gossiping later when Father called in for his Woodbines. It was maybe why Father did not go straight home that day but went to the pub first. Ruth touches her cheek—she had only ever seen her Father lash out when he was drunk.

"I wasn't sure of the line," says Mr Peterson. "I mixed up the bend with the shallower one to come beyond the tunnel. I only gave a little of the brakes, why wouldn't I?"

Pack the bags, girls, Mother had said. Her eyes were rheumy with tears. She was breathless running here and there gathering clothes. *Running too fast, too fast!* Ruth could tell she had one ear cocked for Father coming home. *We're going away for a while.* She never said *for ever*.

"And when the bend came, and the carriages lurched, it was too late for anything but prayer. What could I do?"

That night, with the moon silver-high, Ruth paces her world. She walks barefoot upon the line. The steel is painfully cold against her feet, and each grain of rust is its own mountain peak. She walks eastward toward the bend, reading the history of the line as she goes. Each train that thundered by has left its mark upon the rail. She feels the weight of every engine, of every carriage, of every passenger on every seat. She shares their hopes and fears and loves and losses. Ruth touches the spirit of every driver and guard. Father was an engine driver, man and boy, and he'd often told of how each driver leaves a little of his soul to the railways.

Maybe that's why they're all still there in the clearing. With the thrill of the ride, perhaps it's easy for the railway to grab a little of the spirit when you're not looking. Perhaps it never lets go.

The wind as Ruth approaches the bend is light. The truth from the afternoon's discussion has pushed her *this* close to reality, so there's little potential difference now between her world and the *real* world beyond. She rounds the bend and stops, staring into the middle distance and the eastern tunnel. She can walk further, she knows, perhaps right up to where the line is ripped up and the men still work under their lights. Ruth wonders if she did so, would they see her?

She pushes forward. The lights hurt her eyes, but she sees no shadow behind her. With each step she feels weakened, diluted, lessened. The rail feels less substantial beneath her feet, until for all Ruth knows she could be walking on air.

At the final rail, she pauses. One more step and she will be away from the railway. But it feels wrong. It feels if she takes that step she'll fade away. She no longer has any business in this world. Her time here has passed.

Ruth turns and moves back to their carriage. It seems slight in the moonlight, or perhaps it too is already fading away. Ruth climbs inside and wakes Laura.

"It's time to go," Ruth says. Laura blinks up at her confused. "Get dressed. We've stayed here too long."

"Where are we going?"

Ruth brushes Laura's cheek. "I don't know, but it will be a better place than here."

Together, in the moonlight, they walk hand-in-hand towards the western tunnel. There's no wind to force them back. There are no fires swirling inside. Instead, at its far end is warmth and light.

"Will we see Mother in there?" says Laura.

"Yes," she says. "I'm sure we will. Come, it's time to go."

"I'm frightened."

"Me too. Ready?"

Ruth draws breath and steps forward into the tunnel. What she felt, who can tell?

There is a postscript to this story: These are big men that reclaim the lines. It's heavy work, and if they're not big men when they start it's true they are when they finish. But they tell of a tunnel, at the end of a branch line that just after the war saw the most horrific of accidents, where none of them are big enough to walk without forming a tear in their eye.

"It's the sound of a little girl singing," they say.

"It's just a trick of the wind," others say. "It's nothing more than the wind in the weeds." But they wipe their eye just the same.

"No, it's a little girl singing sweetly, whilst sitting warm in the lap of her mother."

The Turning Track

Matt Joiner and Rosanne Rabinowitz

Clutching his lover's manuscript, Edwin made his way to the train station. He dragged his feet through the piles of leaves on the empty road. When he was a kid, he loved shuffling through autumn leaves. He found it comforting now.

The crunch and swish of the leaves under his feet was the loudest thing in his ears. He was alone on this road, a half-hour walk from the terminus of the streetcar line. He'd been the only passenger by the time he arrived at that last stop.

While he walked, Edwin looked around for signs… of what, he couldn't say. Charles had written: "*There are verges in our world that the Train might have seeded with flowers grown in the silt of sleep.*"

He looked beneath his feet, at the roadside. There were dandelions gone to seed, lifting their heads from cracks in the concrete. He saw buddleia in all shades of purple; bindweed vines winding through rusted barbed-wire fencing, their shrivelled morning blossoms closed tight.

He searched among these common weeds for a sign of difference.

Charles had sketched some flora found on the sidings travelled by the Train. A plump-leaved orange-flowering succulent, a spiked black thistle, white blossoms with markings that gave them clock faces, wild orchids with red lascivious tongues.

But perhaps Charles didn't only mean *flowers*. He could have meant many things. The passage of the Train would pull on the air, pull on the fabric of space and leave something behind, or change some very familiar element.

The road was deserted, but showed signs of previous use. There were buildings that could have been warehouses, with doors open and windows blank.

He looked up in the sky. What shadow had just fluttered across it?

He stopped in the forecourt of an abandoned petrol station. He wasn't sure what drew him to it. Something odd about the pumps? They were old, but… He walked closer and picked up a dangling nozzle.

Yes! The end of the nozzle opened into a brass flower, reminding him of an ancient gramophone. That thing wouldn't service any known vehicle.

Edwin took out his camera, fumbled with the flash and took a photo.

"I'm doing this for you, Charles," he whispered to himself. "Though it scares the bejesus out of me."

Charles, Edwin noted, would use stronger language. Charles used to swear like the proverbial sailor and gently poked fun at Edwin's more refined manners. Charles' potty-mouth didn't rule out flights of poetry, though. He had also written: *This train is not for everyone, but its tracks stitch together many dreams.*

"OK, Charles," Edwin added. "It scares the *shit* out of me. Like you said, this train's not for everyone. I won't get on the thing, you hear? I told you I wouldn't. Of course, I wasn't expecting it would actually… arrive. And I won't believe that until I see it choo-chooing up the track. But if it does, I promise you I'll have a gander. A good *fucking* gander."

But you have a ticket. Edwin could imagine Charles arguing. *Someone sent you a ticket. What I wouldn't give for that!*

And Edwin answered: maybe that ticket was meant for *you*, and I don't belong on that train at all.

Edwin carried the ticket, as he had for over a year, in the money-belt tied around his waist, a relic from his grandfather's days in India when he lived in fear of getting robbed by 'natives'. Edwin never had any use for this item until the ticket arrived. He didn't really expect anyone would try to steal it from him, but he just needed to know where it was at all times. He needed to keep it safe.

The ticket came in the post at the height of summer last year. Edwin had just returned from the office, tired from a long day and a sweaty ride on the streetcar. He was feeling drained and sad, wishing things the way they once were.

Charles would break off work in his study and welcome Edwin home with a cold drink. Usually it would be beer, but on a hot day Charles might offer him home-made lemonade in a tall glass half-filled with ice. Charles used to fuss over Edwin's health, telling him to look after himself while he was young so he wouldn't end up with a dodgy heart. This meant days without drink, and without meat. Charles had some funny ideas, but Edwin went along with them.

But on that day, Charles had been dead for a month. Edwin's flat was just as he left it. The only sound was the hum of the fridge, its motor starting up and stopping with a weary gasp and heartbroken sigh. *I know how you feel,* he had thought. Then tears came to Edwin's eyes. *It's one thing to address myself to my late boyfriend. Another to start talking to a clapped out old fridge. Get a grip, Edwin.*

Edwin bent down to pick up the post without much interest. Those brown envelopes all looked like they contained bills.

As he dumped the envelopes on the table, one caught his eye. This one was brown too, but a rich brown that reminded him of fertile garden soil.

He turned it over. No return address. No postmark. But he recognised the insignia on the front of the envelope: a stylised train track twisted to form an infinity symbol or a Mobius strip. The symbol was raised and embossed, appearing three-dimensional. Edwin traced the symbol with the tip of his finger. Charles, of course, claimed that the train existed in many more dimensions than three. The same symbol – what was the word Charles used for it? *Lemniscate.* The symbol was *in* the ticket, running much deeper than mere paper should allow.

Edwin put the pump to his ear. Perhaps he heard a rushing sound, coming from a distance he couldn't imagine. Perhaps he was only hearing the wind that stirred the weeds and made a loose shutter bang.

He'd allotted time to explore the route, but he should be moving on. He started walking again, carrying on over a gentle rise. On the other side of the rise a single streetlamp shed just enough light to let him find his way. A violet moth flew in a circle around the light.

And at the end of the road: the station.

Edwin hadn't been expecting Grand Central Station, not after all his research. But the station itself didn't look like much, moss-blotched brick and smeared windows. It could have been a rural station that became stranded at the edges of a city after it expanded, then contracted for reasons involving the economy and trade. As the city receded it left behind these inbetween places, like beached flotsam after an ebb tide. The station sported those fussy flowerboxes that looked best in a cottage garden, though Edwin couldn't make out much of what grew in them.

There was a town-hall sized clock over the entrance, as if rushing commuters had once looked up there to check the time. It could have once been a landmark where people arranged to meet.

He was surprised that the big clock told the correct time, and the hands moved as they should.

Edwin opened his jacket and examined his ticket. He checked the time on the ticket and on his watch, as well as the clock. He was early. There was time to explore, and he also had a book to read while waiting. *The* book. Charles had given it a working title: *The Turning Track*. He hefted it in his hands. He'd like to think he knew it by heart, and in a sense he did. But every time he looked at it, he saw something different in the familiar sentences.

A dense grove of trees surrounded the station. *Catalpa*, Charles had called that kind of tree. They were a favourite of Charles, those big shady trees with tiers of small orchid-like blossoms. But Edwin wasn't so sure. Those exotic June blossoms always seemed dusty and wan, as if it was a struggle to flower in their city. And when the fallen flowers covered the pavement and parkland paths, their sweet scent made his eyes water.

As he came closer Edwin saw that the trees were in full flower, even as they shed their autumn leaves. As he walked beneath them, the flowers began to cast subtle light onto the station. He stopped. Charles didn't write about *this*. He chuckled at the thought that he was one up on Charles, until he remembered that he would never get to rib him or tease him. They would never even get to quarrel again. He even missed their quarrels.

The light from the flowers brought a buried memory with it: a single light on the landing at boarding school.

There was a scent of damp, a hint of musk. A steady drip of water. Before entering the station, he inspected the window box near the door. Black ivy flowed out of the window boxes and over the walls. He stroked a leaf. It had a texture like leather, thick stems like cartilage.

The station itself was deep in shadow, broken by flower-glimmer from the windows and a dim glow behind gingham curtains at the station office. He saw a flare of light from the platform, as if someone had lit a match. Then the tip of a burning cigarette.

In one way he was glad to have company, but he also bristled at the thought someone else could invade a territory that he and Charles alone had shared. And who could be in that office?

He heard the strike of a match again, and the repeated *miaow* of a cat. It reminded Edwin of Charles' cat searching the house for him and letting loose heartbreaking pleas.

He tried to avoid cats. They got to him these days, ever since he had to put Sophie down.

Miaow. Ignore the cat, move on. He had work to do.

So he left the ivy alone and stepped inside the station.

A woman in her thirties sat on the bench. She appeared wren-like and freckled in the thin light of the catalpa trees coming through the window just above her. She wore a cheap trench coat and beret. Beside her was a scuffed beige suitcase – and a carrier containing the complaining cat.

"I will *not* give you my ticket," she was saying. "I will not even sell it to you. I don't care how much money you say you have." Her voice grew shrill, then softened when she tried to soothe her pet. "Oh don't fret, you'll like it where we're going."

"You sure about that?"

A gaunt woman of about forty, black hair growing out of a severe crop, paced back and forth in front of the woman with the cat. She wore only a thin cardigan and a grey frock that might have been a fashionable party dress twenty years ago. It was a skimpy outfit for an autumn night, but she didn't appear to feel the cold.

She discarded a cigarette butt and speared it under her stiletto heel.

"That animal does like to whinge," she added with a curl of her lip. She took a gold case out of the pocket of her cardy and drew out another cigarette.

The young woman put sheltering arms around the cat carrier. "You'd complain too if you were put in a box. But it can't be helped. He'll be happy once we arrive."

"How the hell do you know? You don't even know where this train is going. Maybe they *eat* cats there."

Then she turned to Edwin. "And who are you?"

Edwin offered his hand. She ignored it. "I'm Edwin Brookes. I've been making a study of the Train, carrying on the work of Charles Bell, who died last year."

"Charles Bell? I've heard of him. Some kind of professor, been on the radio?"

"If you're referring to the anthropologist Charles Bell, that's correct."

"And if I recall, he was considered a right crackpot."

"His theories were controversial, but one person's crackpot is another person's font of knowledge." Edwin smiled, not really fazed at the woman's attitude towards his late lover. He was used to it. In this case, it was best to meet sarcasm with greater sarcasm. While he was hopeless at sport, he could certainly hold his own with a bit of verbal tussle.

And given that this woman liked the sound of her own voice, she could in fact provide some useful information. How *would* she know about the Train?

The quiet one with the cat might prove more difficult to draw out. He recognised her protective stance, how she hunched over her cat basket. She was protecting much more than her pet, perhaps some hidden core of herself. He could bet she was bullied when young. He recognised that stance because he once held himself the same way.

"I'm Carla." The gaunt woman finally flung her name at him.

Edwin sat down on the bench next to the younger woman. He nodded at her, then peered in at a long-haired black cat with a triangle of white at its chest, a large and imposing animal. The cat's orange eyes indicated Persian ancestry, but it had the robust build of a common moggie.

A far cry from Sophie, a petite shorthaired tortoise-shell.

He had nothing against cats, really. They just upset him sometimes.

Edwin poked a finger through the grate and offered the animal a tentative scratch of its head. The cat quieted, and rubbed its head against Edwin's finger.

This prompted the younger woman to introduce herself as Emily and her cat as Fintan.

"So Edwin, do you have a ticket?" Carla appraised him, head titled to one side.

"No," said Edwin, without thinking. Drat. He did have one, which he wasn't planning to use. It shouldn't go to waste, should it? Give it to this woman? But maybe he *would* want to hop on the train in the future, and he should keep hold of it.

Before he went anywhere he must publish Charles' book. And Edwin needed to add *proof*. He had to do this before he could move on. Charles would certainly want him to 'move on', but he never realised how hard it could be. The daft old bastard. Charles hadn't a clue how hard it would be to live without him.

Edwin hated deception. He'd been lied to as a child, and he vowed he wouldn't do that to other people. But that lie had just slipped over his lips before he could stop it.

"I'm studying the Train. Charles Bell started a book about that Train, which I plan to complete."

So now he *had* told the truth, more about it than he'd told anyone. "And what about you, Carla? What brings you here?"

Carla sat down on the bench, leaving a gap between herself and Edwin and Emily.

"That train took my death from me, and it left me stranded in this life," she said. "It owes me. So this time I'll get *on* it, not *under* it. You see, some years ago I was aiming to jump under the 18.05 express. But that train was late, and *this* train came along instead."

It took a while for Edwin to assimilate this last statement. Emily studiously stroked her cat through the grate. Fintan's purr swelled in the silence.

Carla scratched at her left wrist, then her right. The full sleeves of her cardy rode up, showing the trackmarks of scars on her wrist. She saw where Edwin was looking, and chuckled. "Oh yes, I tried to kill myself again, many times. Didn't work. It was that train, I tell you! Do you know my scars itch when the train is anywhere near me?"

Edwin looked down the tracks, where leaves drifted in deep piles on the sidings. There was no sign of a train, but then the indicator lit up.

Next train was due in twenty minutes. The infinity symbol appeared next to this announcement, in case there was any doubt *which* train it would be.

"But you *can't* have my ticket," interrupted Emily. "You say that train owes you, but *I* owe you nothing. That ticket came to *me*. I've grown up hearing that train. It rattled my walls as it passed, though I never lived near a railway. That ticket is mine."

"Shut up about your ticket. I'll get on anyway. Haven't you ever travelled without a ticket, miss goody two-shoes? I bet you haven't."

"But you said you had money. So what do you need to do that for?"

"For the fun of it. For the thrill. I shoplifted too. Don't anymore, because clothes don't matter now. Bet you've done nothing like that. Always dotted your i's and crossed your t's. So I'll get on without a ticket. See what happens."

A scraping sound from the station office interrupted Carla. They all turned around as the door opened and a figure emerged, holding a lantern.

"Good evening, passengers!" The man's voice rasped as if rusted and not used very often. He walked along the platform towards them, holding his lantern higher. It showed him in its flickering light, a scrawny young man with a scrubby red beard, clad in a railwayman's cap and a uniform too small for him. Despite his thin build, the faded tunic was stretched across his chest with half the buttons left undone to accommodate him.

"You... Do you work here?" Edwin asked.

The young man scratched his face. It brought to mind the way Carla had scratched at the scars on her wrists.

"I live here." He gave a nod towards the office. "But I intend to work for the Train, just as my grandfather did."

Edwin peered at the man's uniform in the dim light, the insignia on his cap and the badges on his jacket. *Yes.* He reached for his pouch under his shirt, so he could take out his ticket to compare the markings. Then he remembered what he'd told Carla. He couldn't reveal himself as a liar if he wanted to keep the trust of these people. But he *knew*. That insignia, that Mobius strip of train tracks, was the same as the one on the envelope and the ticket in his money-belt.

"Yeah, this uniform's pretty smart," the thin man wheezed. "I found it in my parents' attic, with a wage slip bearing the name of Stephen Henning, my grandfather. I was named after him. Seemed right to carry on his work."

Carla cleared her throat. "So what was on this wages slip? How much did your grandfather get paid?"

"That, madame, is confidential. A company secret. And the rewards of this position involve much more than money," replied Henning.

"Nothing matters more than money. If you've had it, then lost it, then no one can tell you any different," said Carla. "What do you know? You're just an old bum in an even older uniform."

Maybe the man's mad but there's no need to be cruel, Edwin thought. Carla reminded him of the kids who made his life miserable in boarding school, boys who later traded their school blazers for military khaki.

But Henning didn't seem offended by Carla's comment. He adjusted his cap and shuffled off towards his office singing to himself: *"I asked my captain for the time of day, said he throwed his watch away."*

Carla began another round of pacing, moving further down the platform. The cat was quiet now. Edwin looked in the carrier, and Fintan met his gaze with a weary dignity.

Nothing like Sophie, really. Small and sprightly, Sophie had seemed much younger than her venerable seventeen years. But after Charles died she wasted, sickened and suffered no matter what Edwin tried to do for her. Finally, the vet suggested that the most caring thing Edwin could do was put her down.

Edwin had followed the vet's instructions. And after he saw to ending Sophie's life, Edwin came close to ending his own. Then he looked at the ticket… again, and again. And he looked at Charles' book, which had been untouched since Charles last worked on it. Edwin couldn't leave it unfinished and unknown. He had to let others see the beauty of Charles' work, and help them understand those mysterious tracks that run like threads or veins of ore through the layers of the cosmos.

Fintan began to complain again. "Oh, I don't know what's got into him. He's travelled in that basket before without making a fuss," said Emily.

"He's picked up on our mood. He knows this isn't an ordinary train."

Emily nodded and smiled. This was the first time he saw her smile. It made him smile too.

"It's wonderful to be with someone who knows about the Train," she said. "A lot of people think I'm mad because of it. I didn't even talk about it with them, but they knew. At work, I always did my job and typed perfect letters, but they were always telling me off for my mind being 'elsewhere'. The other girls in the typing pool tried to be nice but they just didn't know what to say to me. And that Train... it rattled my room wherever I lived. Other people heard it and they thought I was doing something to make all the noise. I've gone through quite a few landlords."

"I used to live with Charles Bell." Damn, he'd meant to say 'used to know'! "I have his book with me. I'll show it to you if you want."

"Oh yes! Please... I didn't know such a thing existed."

"You won't find it in a library. It's not finished. That's my job."

He opened the folder containing the manuscript and turned to a page showing sketches of the Train. He turned it so the paper would catch the tree-light.

"Oh, but this is the one I dream about," Emily exclaimed. "It's a great steam train. There are compartments where you can sleep and dream some more. I once had a dream where I dreamed I was dreaming on the train. Funny, that! The bumps of the track lulled me into sleep. I heard the names of stations being called. Some were familiar, like Horseberry. Others were Wanderstone, Mycta, Seeksome, Mercatrix, Ariantini..." Emily's voice rose as she recited the names of the stations.

Edwin began writing them down.

"So what are you babbling about now!" Carla exclaimed. "I could hear you from the other end of the station. Not such a quiet little mouse now, are you?"

Emily visibly quaked under Carla's gaze. And Edwin wanted to shake her as much as he wanted to punch Carla to shut her up.

Stop that, Emily! Don't you see you're worth ten of her?

Edwin had probably been just as pathetic when he was younger. Or worse. How Charles had put up with him in those early days, he'd never know.

If Charles had to deal with an obvious bully like this, he wouldn't confront them directly. He'd distract them, use their illusions of importance to his advantage. Or more to the point, to the advantage of his work.

Edwin cleared his throat. "Carla, you're the only one of us who has actually seen this train. So what are your impressions?" He made his voice calm and neutral, like a newsreader.

"You mean, I saw this train before it ran me over? Perhaps I'll take it from the bottom, sweetie. Remember, I was waiting for the ordinary express train. I was teetering on the edge of the platform, then this *thing* appeared. It was sleek, like a submarine. But it was high, like it was a double-decker, but with more levels than that. There was an open platform in that station, so I don't know how it will fit in *here*.

"It had little windows, like ship windows. There was a jolt, something like weight passing over me, a rush of darkness and ghost-light. And just before I went under, I saw two people gazing down at me from one of those windows. Who the hell were they? And where did this train come from? Perhaps I had a moment of regret that I'd never find out. There was no clue in the faces at the window. They were a blur... I thought it was the speed of the train or the tears in my eyes. But no, I really think those faces *were* a blur."

Carla's voice had lost its stridency. Held by her story, she'd forgotten to harass Emily.

"Tears?" Edwin prompted.

"Yes, I was a shell filled with tears. Or I was until that damned train ran me over. I looked fine on the outside. Just a few scrapes and sprains, no breaks anybody else could see. But that train flattened me in other ways. Years of weeping burst out and now I don't even have tears I can call my own."

Edwin nodded. He didn't know what to say to that. But best to keep her talking. "And what about those faces you saw?" That detail intrigued him. The train shifted, curved around the dimensions it rode. The people in it must do the same.

"What about them? Did I take a picture? No way," said Carla. "Not when a train the size of an ocean liner was barrelling down those tracks.

And I was thinking: 'Take me!' So it took me, then spat me out." Her voice turned wistful, her shoulders slumped. She looked lost, the way Edwin felt after Charles' death.

This left Edwin unmoved. When he was a child, he saw school bullies, torturers in the making, break down and cry too. A relative who died, a beloved pet. He'd heard the bluster of a tough guy dissolve in the racking cry of an abandoned child. A marshmallow heart one day, a bunched fist the next; sentimentality didn't pull any punches.

"There's a hollow inside me," she said. "I wouldn't have it grow."

"Like carrying a child and losing it," Edwin murmured.

He'd only been thinking aloud. He did not expect Carla to round on him. She snapped, "It's nothing like that at all. How the hell would you know?"

Then she smiled in a toothy, dangerous way. "You ever been inside, Edwin? I know, you're a good boy. You and your Mad Professor. But even good boys get put away somewhere if they misbehave *just a little bit*. Could be the bin, could be prison. And I was basically a good girl in those days, but did that matter? They put me away, and there I stayed for many years."

"Carla, I'm sorry you had a rough time, but what's that got to do with Edwin?" Emily interrupted.

Emily was only trying to be helpful, but Edwin felt cold dread run in his veins. Had Carla guessed about him and Charles? *How did she know? Did it show?* But he was just an average-looking chap. He and Charles never went to bars, never wore pinkie-rings. They never joined a club; they only loved each other.

No, he *wouldn't* let her intimidate him. He was the one asking questions. "Carla," he began. "Why were you…"

"Christ, look who's here again," muttered Carla. "Still singing. Will someone shut him up?"

"The engine passed at six o'clock, the cab passed at nine…" Henning was waving his lantern as he walked towards them. This time he wore tickertape looped around his neck like a silk scarf. His tunic was now buttoned up tight.

"Hello passengers. I've just received word of a delay."

"Delay? That takes the biscuit. Yeah, what could possibly delay *the* Train? Leaves on the line?"

Henning touched the bill of his cap to her. "In fact… yes, ma'am." He peered at the tape. "Blank leaves on the rail. The Train may be delayed some time. I'll keep you updated, never fear."

"Batshit crazy," Carla scoffed. But Henning only raised his eyebrow.

"I think that's in the job description," he said mildly. "Now, if you'll excuse me." He went back to his office.

Thwarted, she began to kick through the leaves on the platform. "Leaves on the line," she muttered. "Crazy."

Pot and kettle, thought Edwin. But perhaps Carla had a point.

Emily touched his arm. "I tried to stop the Train. Maybe someone has succeeded."

"How?"

"I've heard it *everywhere* I've ever lived, in the walls, under the floor. The wheels mostly, sometimes its whistle. But always just passing through. I figured if I could find it a station, it would stop long enough for me to get on. So I went through junk shops, looking for pictures. Newspaper clippings, postcards, old books; anything that looked right. Here…"

She took out an envelope from her coat. Edwin thought she was offering him a fan of cards at first, but they turned out to be photographs of old stations, in colour, sepia, black-and-white, with pinholes at the corners. The stations themselves were as varied; some cathedrals in iron and glass and others little more than a shed at the side of the track, or brick stubs shawled with weeds. On the back of each picture she had written a name. Edwin recognised some as the dream-stations Emily had told him about.

"I stuck these up on the walls. Surely one of them would be on the Line. So I waited and waited, kept my suitcase packed under the bed. Every time the walls started shaking, I'd think, *this is it.* I watched every station to be safe. I knew how it would be, the smell of coal in my room, one of the pictures filling up with steam; I'd reach *through* somehow, and I'd be on the right side of the paper, ready to board." She laughed in embarrassment.

Edwin thought, *You don't have to laugh at yourself, not about this.*

"Sounds mad, doesn't it?"

"It's no madder than anything in here." Edwin touched the book.

Emily smiled at him. "No, but the Train never came to me. I kept moving on, room to room, putting up new pictures. I was passing through too, I suppose."

He had an image of her, in hotel rooms and bedsits, always gazing up at the unchanging stations, never giving up hope.

"Until one night, a few weeks ago," Emily said. "I came back from work and there was the ticket tucked into one of the frames. I knew at once where it had come from. The symbol in your book, the one on Henning's jacket – it's watermarked in the paper."

Edwin felt a flush of pride at that – *his* book! But honesty made him say: "It's Charles' book really. He died suddenly, and I owe it to him to finish it. I'm just following in his footsteps." He found himself wiping his eyes. *Carla complains she doesn't have any tears left...* he could certainly lend her a few of those, if not his ticket. He thought he'd finished with the tears, but they kept coming.

Emily looked him in the eye. "Charles wasn't just your *friend*, was he?"

He sagged, suddenly very tired and wondering what the hell he was doing. He could be put in prison for the wrong answer... in other words, the *right* answer. But if he encounters this Train with Emily, even boarding it with her, they needed to trust each other.

"No, he wasn't just my friend. Call it a labour of love, if you like. He's gone and this is the best I can do by him."

Now he felt better for telling the truth.

"Here..." Emily thrust her pictures at Edwin. "If they'll help with the book, you're welcome to them. I don't think I'll need them much longer." She took his hands. "I think he'd be proud of you."

Edwin smiled weakly. "I'm not so sure. I do have a ticket, but I might be scared to use it. Or I just can't decide. I keep asking myself what Charles would want me to do, and I still don't have an answer."

She pulled away. "You said you didn't have a ticket."

"I said that to Carla because I wanted to decide in the end. But really, all I want to do is *see* the Train. Charles never got the chance. But this isn't just for him. Somebody's got to stay and bear witness. How many people have seen or heard the Train and think they're mad? They didn't have anybody to help them understand. If I finish the book, then they're not alone any more. If I use the ticket, nobody speaks up for them. I thought the ticket was meant for Charles, you see, but it came too late. Hell, he'd *jump* on board if he was here. I could never do that. I'm too bloody cowardly to be passenger material."

There you go Charles – there's the truth. Hope you liked it.

"I'm scared too," Emily said. "I've spent all my life waiting. I don't even know where I'm going to end up. But I'm going to board, regardless. What will you do with the ticket?"

"Well, I could use it as evidence…" Edwin looked down the platform. Carla was rooting through the litter, as if she might find her stolen death under the leaves. "Or I could give it away. She needs it more than I do."

"Don't! I'm not going to share a carriage with that woman. Don't tell me you believe her?"

"I don't trust her, no. It doesn't mean I disbelieve her." Edwin thumbed through the manuscript. "There are people in here who saw the Train in the sky, made up of storm clouds and stars. You've dreamed of it as an old engine. Carla's Train was some kind of Leviathan, and God knows how I'll see it. Charles didn't know what to call it."

He closed his eyes and recited, "*How are we to classify the Train, then – ghost, god, machine, organic? Like all the old tales, it shifts shape depending on the teller. 'Train' itself seems too small a word to contain the thing; but all we have are words.*"

"That's pretty," Carla said behind him. "Maybe he could explain this, too."

She dropped a shredded glove into his lap. It might have been made of latex or lace, but it was too wrinkled to tell. It slid off him and whispered to the ground, translucent in the station lights.

"There's more like that back there." Carla nodded back at the leaf-drift. "Except most of that's not even leaves; they're goddamn *tickets*. Expired ones, of course. Rags. And this. Go on, pick it up."

"She's playing games with you," Emily said. "Don't rise to it."

"Mouse, you're boring me. Shut up. I'm talking to Mister Scholar here. What are you waiting for?"

Reluctantly, Edwin bent down. The glove was slippery and brittle to the touch, fine as an insect's wing. *Shake hands,* he thought, and wanted to be sick. "It's skin," he said.

Carla grinned. "Yeah. Look at it closely, you'll see lines and prints, probably enough to identify the poor schmuck. There was this, too." From her cardigan she brought out what looked like half a mask. She lifted the flaking thing up to her face and peered through an eyehole. Edwin heard Emily retching.

"We weren't the first passengers here," Carla went on, "and look what happened to them. There's probably a whole carriage-load of fucking *peel* back there. Anything like that in your book, sweetie?"

Through the taste of bile, Edwin said, "Nothing at all." He threw the 'glove' at Carla, who casually folded it away. "It felt old. Like snakeskin, did you notice?"

"Well, it's not. You could've read a future from that palm. Short one, obviously. We need answers." Carla pulled a razor from her sleeve; a big old-fashioned cut-throat blade. "It's time we had a proper word with the Thin Controller."

Emily plucked at Edwin's sleeve. "Don't go with her," she said in his ear.

Carla shot them a glance. "Oh, Mouse, Mouse, there's only one person I seriously tried to kill. And I had that taken from me. Keep behind me if you're that scared. I think *I'm* safe. Don't know about you."

She flicked the razor open and led them back into the station.

There was little in what Henning might have called his office; a sleeping bag and camping stove in the corner, a desk with a few books, his cap on top of them, and a mass of red-printed tape. Henning was stooped, coughing into a bandanna. When he looked up, his beard had turned darker, almost crimson.

"There's still a delay…"

Carla threw the skins in his face. "Update us on this one. Maybe you could give us another song. *The Butcher's Blues*?"

"Oh, *that*. Most of this accumulated before I started working here."

"But you know, don't you? Or is that another Company secret?"

Another fit of coughs shook Henning. Edwin tried to pull Carla away. "He's in no fit state to answer you."

"Fit or not, he can tell us. You can take notes, scholar-boy."

Machinery clicked somewhere in the room. Henning grew still. He wiped blood from his mouth. "Nobody dies here," he said at last. "But some people need to shed their old skins before they can board."

Like snakes, just as I said, thought Edwin. Carla snarled, "Don't fob me off with that crap."

Henning steepled his fingers. "I saw it happen once, just after I took up my place. It shook me, like it shakes you now. But I've read up on it since. The Train changes its shape for us. Seems only fair that we should return the favour."

It sounded like a quote from *The Turning Track.* There was, suddenly, something of Charles in the man behind the desk; a tattered magus surrounded by gazetteers and timetables. Edwin shivered, and Henning smiled at him.

"You're as bad as the scholar," Carla said.

"*All change here,*" Henning sang. "Doesn't have to be in the flesh." He tapped his forehead. "Here, does just as well. Nobody who ever looked upon the Train went away unmarked. Why, ma'am, you should know that yourself. Being immortal and all."

Carla turned white. "I want that back. I want my death where it belongs. Who gave you the fucking right to steal that from me?"

"Begging your pardon, but had you ever wondered if it wasn't yours to begin with? See, I'm not good with all this philosophy, I'm just a railwayman. But the Train takes freight as well as passengers."

She snarled, and the razor flickered out at Henning's face.

Edwin and Emily grabbed Carla's arms. She writhed, strong considering she was so thin. "I'll cut you as well, Mouse..." She rammed her elbow into Edwin's ribs. His eyes watered but he held onto her wrist until she cursed and threw down the blade.

Henning had not flinched at all. He merely got out of his chair and picked up the razor, admiring the mother-of-pearl handle before folding away the blade and offering it back to Carla.

"*Don't* give it back," said Emily. "My God, are you mad?"

Carla snatched the razor back.

"It's served its purpose, Madame."

Carla glared at him, saying nothing. She scratched at her scarred wrists.

"You carved a map you'd never lose. Good enough to follow the Train a ways, but it doesn't just use scars. There are leys and nerves; networks you and I will never see." Henning's voice was soft and sad. "I've changed too, but I won't be working the Line. It seems this is my station."

He opened his tunic and pulled up his clotted shirt. There was a machine rooted in his pigeon chest; dark metal wheels oscillating, oiled with mucus, a roll of veined paper feeding itself into the stuttering printer: destinations, lines, times stamped out in runes of blood and lymph. Cables and metallic fronds meandered through his thin skin. "Will you look at that," he said in pained awe. "I think it's taking at last. And your Train is almost due."

He tucked his shirt back in and beamed at the dumbstruck passengers. "I'm a true Company man now."

Edwin managed to speak at last. "So who is this Company? Everything I've heard about the Train, there's no mention of them." And he also wanted to ask: *Who would condemn you to that? Make that a condition of employment?*

But the simple pride in Henning's face stopped him. It was the expression of a man getting the job he had always wanted. Edwin envied him for that, despite the grisly growth on his chest. "Don't worry about the Company," said Henning. "Every effort will be made to ensure your journey is comfortable. As long as you take a certain degree of initiative, you'll be a satisfied customer."

"You should collaborate with this guy," Carla said to Edwin. "The Human Tickertape speaks your fate; make a mint at sideshows." She jammed a cigarette into her sneer; used the match-light to examine her scars. "You're welcome to each other." Still scratching, she left the office. The click of her heels was lost in echo.

"Thank God for that," said Emily, looking closely at Henning as he sat back down in his chair and glanced at the book he'd been reading.

She cleared her throat. "And what of us? Do *we* change as well?"

"I'm an employee. This…" He tapped his chest. "This is part of the uniform. There's still time for you to decide." He consulted a fob-watch. "A few minutes yet."

Emily bit her lip. "We'll take our chances." And when Edwin started, she quickly added, "Fintan and me."

"And you, sir?"

"I don't know. There's the manuscript… Who'll edit it? Who'll publish it?" Edwin raked fingers through his hair.

"These things find a way." Henning nodded. He closed his book and turned it so the spine faced them. The bronze green leather was scuffed and split; it might only have been the undependable light that made the words left on the spine come and go: *ING TRACK – BELL BROOKES GRIFFIN.*

Edwin reached out a trembling hand. The names sank into the leather. "I don't know anyone called Griffin," he whispered. "That's a fake, isn't it?" He made sure his own manuscript was under his arm.

Henning gently pushed his book just out of reach. "No, sir. It's a possibility. Best not touch it. It hasn't found all its authors yet."

A fresh coil of tape juddered out from beneath Henning's shirt. "Ah, too much talking on the job. Excuse me…" He reached for his cap and lantern.

Emily plucked at Edwin's sleeve. "We need to go, *now.* Can't you feel the Train? It's coming now."

"What?" But he felt the floor vibrate beneath his feet.

He let Emily drag him out to the platform, to the bench where Fintan waited.

There were too many echoes, the sense of *space* behind him. The station had begun to change. Edwin knew it, but he would not look back. This was it; he could only face forward. His heart clenched. He wondered if this was the transformation Henning spoke about.

The ground was shaking now. A wind blew down the track, making leaves, tickets, sloughed skins dance. It smelled of oil and steam and spice, fallen apples on the ground gone mushy and brown. It brought the scent of every autumn that had ever been. It made Edwin's eyes water but he stared downrail, unwilling to blink.

He hardly felt Emily's hand in his as she pulled him closer to the tracks, ready for the Train's arrival. She was laughing.

He saw Carla driven back, thrown down, her face disbelieving. She got up, fought against the wind like a bad mime. *It doesn't want you,* he thought. Carla got close enough to the platform edge to grab Emily's coat and pull her back. She shoved the younger woman against the wall.

"It won't take me," Carla said. "If I had a ticket, it wouldn't matter. C'mon, Mouse… you don't need it. You're young, you'll get another chance. What's a dream compared to everything I've lost?" She began to rifle through the pockets of Emily's trenchcoat.

Emily bucked against her, cursing. In a moment, Edwin knew, Carla would turn out the contents of the suitcase, going over everything, even Fintan in his box, until the ticket was in her hand. And he was back at school again, watching the bullies spill his life on the floor.

It filled him with rage. Carla believed she was *entitled* to take Emily's ticket. Despite years locked up, she still believed she could lay claim to anything and treat anyone as she pleased.

It had taken him years to learn how to stand up to people like that, years to know his worth. Charles had helped him; now he had to help Emily. Rather than wrestle with a crazy woman again, Edwin had a better idea...

He put his folder down on the bench and fumbled in his money-belt, then held up a ticket. "Carla!" He had to shout, straining his voice against those of the wind; they were changing all the time, modulating between whistles and horns and the call of an owl in a deep forest. The thin woman glared at him.

"Leave her alone. I've got a ticket too. You can take mine, just let her go."

Carla grinned. "You *lied*. I wouldn't have given you credit, sweetie. Alright then." She pushed Emily away.

"That's yours by right," Emily called. "Don't give it away."

"The journey's not worth this," Edwin said. He held the ticket high. Carla was snatching for it. He smiled – and let go. The wind took the ticket from his hand.

She howled and dived after it, straight onto the track. She got up, rummaging through the debris between the tracks. Then she lifted her bloodied face.

She brandished the ticket in crooked fingers, kissed it. Then she looked at it, and blanched.

"This is a fucking *streetcar* ticket!"

Edwin felt a terrible glee, but it was momentary. Whatever else Carla shouted at him was now drowned in a noise like syncopated thunder.

The indicator started flashing in a semaphore rhythm. On, off, on.

ALL STATIONS. ALL STATIONS.

There was a great darkness running down the rails towards them, studded with lights, as if the night itself was pulling into the station. And Edwin realised that Carla was making no move back to the platform.

"Get off the line, Carla! I'm sorry, I'll give you the real ticket. Just get off the line!"

Carla shot him a look of disgust. She stood up, dropped the streetcar ticket, and turned to face the Train. In the last moment, she spread her arms: to ward it off or embrace it.

With all the noise, he thought he heard her shriek: "Two strikes, you're out!"

Two hits by the Train, or was she screaming about his second lie?

"No, Carla, no!"

Emily glanced at Carla, shrugged, then turned her eyes towards the Train. Her face was illuminated. "It's everything I thought it would be… and much more."

The Train filled the station. It bellowed clouds of steam. There were whole landscapes in there, valleys, mountains, hills. The profiles of cities and forests boiled up as he watched; he could never map them all. Easier to turn his eyes downrail to ordinary land, desolate tracks where leaves and old tickets drifted along with the discarded skins. Yet even here there was a warping and tug on the landscape.

ALL STATIONS. *Click.* ALL STATIONS.

The Train pulled in with a volley of sparks and steel. He saw many Trains, arriving as one: industrial husks with magma hearts; genteel engines of brass and enamel; chitinous bullets and shaped storms; worms with carriages wired howdah-like to their backs. He saw much more than these, layers and layers with no end or centre. After a moment he had to pull his gaze back before he was lost forever.

"I asked my captain for the time of day… he said he throwed his watch away."

Edwin's work on the manuscript had given him the ability to see more aspects of the Train, but the study would only ever be a scratch on the surface. How had he ever thought a camera could capture this? The thing was glorious.

And it rolled right over Carla.

She went down without a sound.

"Dear Christ," he whispered. First a liar, now he had blood on his hands. If this was the transformation wrought by the Train, he wanted no part of it.

Emily grabbed his shoulder. "Come on Edwin, she'll be alright. The bitch is immortal, isn't she?"

Bitch. That didn't sound like Emily. But the woman at his side didn't *look* like the Emily he had met such a short time ago. Her face was transfigured, eyes bright. It was hard to tell where her breath ended and the Train's began. She was totally ruthless.

Emily has already sloughed herself, he realised. Layers of mind that trapped her in fear and timidity… all gone.

"Come on Edwin, get your things. Forget about her. We have to go. The Train will stop soon." She picked up her cat and her bag.

The Train stopped in a grinding of gears that sent shivers through him. It subsided with a steamy sigh.

The doors didn't open straight away. That would give him some time to think...

"Edwin, stop dithering!" Emily scolded.

"Emily, I am a born ditherer. Literally. I was born two weeks late, as if I couldn't decide whether to stay in the womb or take a chance in the big outside. My mother had to have her labour induced. Or so she tells me. I can't remember a thing."

"Edwin!" But he saw Emily was laughing. If she had changed, at least she had retained a sense of humour.

Finally, the doors to the train slid open with a whisper and a drawn-out hiss. Light spilled out of the Train's darkness, but Edwin couldn't see who or what was inside.

Then he heard a familiar voice. "Edwin! Hop on, will you?" And when he looked up, he met the eyes of Charles peering down from an upper window.

"Charles! It's Charles! He's at a window upstairs."

Emily only nodded. Perhaps she was humouring him. Or she thought she was being kind. *But Charles is dead*, Edwin thought. *You held him as he died.*

Charles beckoned.

He didn't look like a ghost. His cheeks were ruddy with good health or perhaps a glass or two of red wine. His face had always been thin but now the hollows of illness were gone. His hair was lush again, down to the collar. Edwin had nagged him about getting it cut many times. In return

Charles had gently poked Edwin in the stomach. "You should lose a few inches too, Ed." It became a long-running joke for them.

Edwin couldn't dither any longer. This time, he was pulling Emily towards the Train. "OK, I'm coming. Let's go!" And they rushed through the doors of the Train to stumble inside, with Fintan protesting at his rough ride.

A dog sitting near the luggage rack looked up. A birdcage was hooked to a passenger strap; the parrot inside squawked out a curse. Emily wasn't the only passenger to bring a pet. Edwin couldn't do anything except laugh. Oh, Charles would find this funny.

He had to find Charles. Where the hell is he?

Inside, the Train looked surprisingly normal. Passengers filled the seats. At first glance, they seemed like the passengers on any train. Perhaps many were people he didn't see about much in his town; people of African or Asian or Mediterranean origin. All ages.

But there was a shimmering to the edges of surfaces and objects, as if they masked a different state of things. And if he looked at his surroundings in another way, the right way, he would see layers unfold, surfaces invert. He thought of the Train's approach, the many shapes he saw lurking behind the first form to arrive.

"Alright, mate? Looking for anyone?" A sharp-faced little man with blond hair in rat's tails glanced up from his fiddle. The instrument was budding, breaking out into spruce needles and maple leaves.

Edwin only looked for one face. "Charles, I have to find Charles."

"Let's find seats first and get settled," said Emily. "I need to give Fintan some food and water. Then we can explore, and you can find your *friend*. I look forward to meeting him."

"You look forward to meeting Charles? You're not just humouring a madman seeing ghosts?"

"Mad? You told me nothing could be madder than anything in your book. So I'm saying…"

The *book*. He'd left it on the bench. He was so excited about seeing Charles in that window that he'd left *The Turning Track* behind. Charles wouldn't forgive him for that. He couldn't forgive himself.

"Emily, I forgot the book. I have to get it. The train's not left yet. I can get off and…"

"No, you can't. You can't get off. You may never be able to get back on. You *can't*."

"Listen to the lady, mate. She talks sense," the fiddle-player said. "You won't forgive yourself if you miss this train." He gave them a pointed glance. "And if you hold us up much longer, neither will I. I'm late enough as it is." He went back to pruning the violin, throwing foliage to the floor.

Did everyone know his business on here?

Any thought of jumping off and on was cancelled by sudden vibrations beneath Edwin's feet. The Train must be ready to go. It had rolled over Carla, and now it was rolling on.

"Edwin, we'll find seats upstairs. We're heading in the right direction. You said you saw Charles at an upstairs window."

Didn't Emily see Charles at the window? Had he been imagining it after all?

Emily led him up the spiralling stairs, stopping at the first level. They walked along a passage and found a compartment with some space. This was more opulent than the first carriage Edwin had seen, with deep velveteen seats and chandeliers with sinuous branches. An older couple sat on one side of the compartment, and a little girl sat near the window. She seemed to be on her own, though she was waving at someone on the platform. Edwin noticed a cardboard tag tied to her wrist, with felt-tip pen writing on it. She held something like a balloon on a string, but by rights it should have swam under water, undulating and shedding blue light.

The couple nodded at Emily and Edwin. They were dressed for a wedding, but perhaps the marriage had taken place in a sideshow. His morning coat had been cut to accommodate the sleeping twin fused to his shoulder; under the woman's lace dress, every inch writhed with tattoos like a kaleidoscope. The child smiled at Fintan, but ignored Emily and Edwin. Ha, when he was a boy he'd preferred animals to people too.

"Let me make more room," said the woman. She pulled something closer to her, something semi-transparent and dry. She handled it as if it was fragile, and she was very fond of it.

That couldn't be…

"Yes, dear, it's my old skin. Though I was glad to get it off, I still want to keep it." She held it up as if it was a dress she planned to try on. "I'll never fit back in but I can't just throw it away, can I?"

While he'd been sickened by the skin found on the tracks, this didn't bother him.

The woman smiled, then folded the skin into her handbag. "So where's yours? You didn't leave it behind, did you?"

"I *did* leave something behind," admitted Edwin. "I'm still upset about it. But…"

The vibration coming from the base of Train grew louder. Edwin felt it leach into his bones. It was beginning to alarm him, but Fintan began purring along with it.

Emily took him out of the box and he settled on her lap, looking twice the size that Edwin had imagined. He fluffed his fur out and slitted his eyes in feline ecstasy. His purring filled the compartment, taking on the rhythm of a powerful motor. A sound of grit and machinery, reminding Edwin of the factory where he used to work as a clerk. Fintan's sides drew in and out with the noise like a bellows. Edwin remembered the device growing out of Henning's chest; could some machine be taking root in the cat?

The juddering grew, as if spurred by Fintan's purr. Then an answering vibration and blast of static came from above.

Edwin realised this was the Train's tannoy, brass horns like the thing he'd found growing at the petrol station. Garbled tongues came through the static, an avalanche of language. Then more familiar words: "Attention passengers. We're sorry to inform you that the Train is delayed again due to leaves on the line."

"What? No body under the Train?" Edwin blurted this out. The old man raised an eyebrow.

"We had that before, bodies on the line. It doesn't take long to deal with *that*. But those leaves… We were stopped just down the line for that." He shook both his heads. "Leaves… Cause no end of trouble."

The grinding below increased rather than diminished after the announcement. Then the Train began moving backwards.

The little girl kicked the seat with exasperation.

"Why's it going backwards?" Edwin was already assuming his companions were seasoned travellers on this train bound for 'all stations'.

"Dunno. It's not done that before," said the little girl. "I've been on this train a long time and all. I'm going to see my grandma." She wriggled her fingers in the belly of her balloon. "Been promised a whole shoal of these for my birthday."

"I'll go see what's going on, and I'll see if I can find Charles," Edwin told the others.

Outside the compartment, he walked along a central aisle that led to the front of the Train. Carla had compared the Train to an ocean liner, and he saw that it was holding a shape similar to that at the moment. He could walk along the aisle to an area that broadened out like the prow of a ship. He joined others looking out of the window.

As the Train drew backwards, he saw pages from his book – Charles' book – uncovered on the tracks. He must've left the folder unfastened after he showed the manuscript to Emily.

A lump came to his throat. The centre to his life had fallen out of it once again. And if he could find Charles – what would he tell him? And if Charles was truly dead in the world of the Train as well as his own, he would still be letting him down.

Then there was a movement just on the edge of his sight, from under the train. He saw a cardigan, now in tatters with track marks and bloodstains. The grey party dress torn. Carla herself, jagged but still in one piece, crawled along on the tracks. She stood up and jerked along in an unsteady walk.

Carla picked up a page, studied it for a moment. Then she looked back at the train and a new expression crossed her face. A grin, a gleam of fascination.

Edwin had seen a similar look in the mirror when he retired after a good night's work on *The Turning Track*.

As Carla picked up stray sheets of paper, Henning came out of his office streaming more ticker-tape. He bent and extended a hand to help Carla climb back on the platform. Then she picked up the folder with the rest of the book and added the rescued pages.

As the train started to move forward again, Carla suddenly looked up and waved at Edwin, then left the station with the manuscript held to her chest.

The Train took on speed, and the world beyond the glass became a smear. Stars snail-tracked the night. Edwin thought of leaves, pages on the line, and the Train-beat sounded to him like the clatter of typewriter keys.

Then the Train shuddered under his feet. "Switchback!" came the cry from the window. He rushed back to see the night pull itself inside out and the track torque into a thousand silver lines. They were high above *everything*. Edwin's ears popped; his stomach flipped as if he was on a rollercoaster.

Paper rustled. The fiddle-player was behind him, offering a bag and a sympathetic look. "Try a lozenge," he said. "It'll help with the vertigo. That first view does it to everyone." Numb, Edwin took one; it tasted like a pear drop but left a heat like brandy.

"Where do we go now?" he said.

The fiddler shrugged. "It's all stations, matey. Your choice. But wasn't there someone you wanted to find?" He poked a thumb towards the wrought-iron staircase before he slouched off.

Edwin put his hand on the bannister. The iron was cold, his breath turned to feathers. Somewhere above him Charles was waiting: he *had* to be. A year apart, what might have passed? Perhaps Charles had changed, as they all must change. Would he still be the Charles he loved… and would Charles accept any changes in Edwin?

"Best foot forward," Edwin told himself. Slowly at first, then rushing like a child, he went to look for his lover.

Author Biographies

Nina Allan is a bit of a train junkie and always has been. She gets a great deal of enjoyment from perusing railway timetables, studying Network route maps and acquiring books with titles like Metro Systems of the World. She still hasn't relinquished her ambition to visit every stop on the London Underground and has always secretly wanted to be a station announcer. 'Vivian Guppy and the Brighton Belle' was partly inspired by a real Hornby Dublo 69567 which was originally given to Christopher Priest by his good friend Lawrence James and now stands on Nina's writing desk in Hastings. Nina's previous publications include the story collections A Thread of Truth and The Silver Wind, both from Eibonvale Press, and more recent works include the novella Spin and the story cycle Stardust, both published this year from TTA Press and PS Publishing respectively. Nina's biggest train pipe-dream is to ride the Trans-Siberian Railway from Moscow to Vladivostok.

Allen Ashley is an award-winning editor, author, poet, songwriter and writing tutor. He has recently rejoined the indie rock band The False Dots as vocalist and lyricist. He currently co-hosts a regular jazz and poetry event in Enfield called "The Sunday Edition". He runs several writing groups across north London including the very successful Clockhouse London Writers. Get in touch with Allen on allenashley-writer@hotmail.co.uk, check his next jazz gig at www.dugdalecentre.co.uk or go to his website at www.allenashley.com.

When not writing, **Andrew Coulthard** spends much of his time floundering in the cracks between worlds. He mainly does this in Stockholm where he also coaches business professionals in English and communication skills. From time to time he also indulges in a spot of translation for good measure. Andrew has recently completed a short story cycle that is also a novel, and is now working on the illustrations.

SJ Fowler (1983) is the author of four poetry collections. He has had poetry commissioned by the Tate Britain and the London Sinfonietta, and has featured in over 100 poetry publications. He is poetry editor of 3am magazine, Lyrikline and the Maintenant interview series. www.sjfowlerpoetry.com www.maintenant.co.uk

Daniella Geary is currently a mature student of Behavioural Psychology at the University of London, enjoying a second life now that her two kids have left home. She has always dabbled privately in poetry and philosophy. She has had short stories published in Eibonvale Press' Where Are We Going anthology and in 'Fur-Lined Ghettos' Magazine.

John Greenwood is the co-editor of *Theaker's Quarterly Fiction*, where most of his previously published writing can be found online. His major influences are books he has heard of but may never get round to reading. He runs a small bookshop in Birmingham, England.

Christopher Harman began his working life with a summer stint as an agricultural labourer uprooting turnips. He subsequently worked in the Lancashire Record Office before embarking on a series of jobs in public libraries. He has lived in Lancashire all his life and currently resides in Preston.

Since his first story in 1992, his work has appeared in magazines such as Ghosts and Scholars, Supernatural Tales, Dark Horizons, New Genre, All Hallows and Postscripts, and also in books such as Acquainted with the Night, Shades of Darkness, Strange Tales from Tartarus, Unfit for Eden, Terror Tales of the Cotswold and Terror Tales of East Anglia.
In 2012 his story Quis Est Iste was the winning entry in the Ghosts and Scholars short story competition; it went on to appear in The Ghosts and Scholars Book Of Shadows from Sarob Press, which is also due to bring out a collection of his stories.

"Sleepers" isn't Christopher Harman's first story to feature trains. He has an interest in railways as depicted in films and television especially where they provide a mysterious and dynamic aspect to the rural landscape; a particular favourite is Lawrence Gordon Clark's adaptation of Charles Dickens' The Signalman.

RD Hodkinson was born in East Yorkshire in 1965. He moved to London as an undergraduate and has remained ever since, working as a journalist and editor. He lives with his wife and innumerable children in a decaying Georgian property hard by the moldering remains of the capital's medieval dead. From time to time this arrangement may have an effect on his writing.

Andrew Hook's most interesting train journey was from Arequipa to Cusco in Peru. The train broke down several times during the lengthy scheduled journey and his toilet paper ran out halfway. He has also stood for seven hours immediately adjacent to the toilet on a packed train from Surin to Bangkok, and has also made the mistake of boarding a train to Liverpool Lime Street instead of London Liverpool Street. When writing fiction, he is luckier, with over 100 short stories sold including recent appearances in Black Static, PostScripts, and the Eibonvale anthology "Where Are We Going?". A collection of short stories co-written with Allen Ashley, the editor of that anthology, titled "Slow Motion Wars" will be published this summer.

John Howard was born in London, brought up in the Chilterns, and has been an adopted Brummie for more years than he believes possible. His short stories have been published in anthologies and the collections *The Silver Voices* (2010) and *Secret Europe* (jointly with Mark Valentine, 2012). The majority of John's fiction has central and eastern European settings, with several set in the previously unknown city of Sternbergstadt/Sárihegy/Steaua de Munte, the 'eighth of Transylvania's seven fortress towns'. *The Defeat of Grief* (2010) is a novella set in Steaua de Munte and the real Black Sea resort of Balcic/Balchik; *Numbered as Sand or the Stars* (2012) attempts a 'secret history' of inter-war Hungary.

"To the Anhalt Station" is one of the stories resulting from John's visits to Berlin. He feels at home there: clearly he has an affinity for sprawling cities with little if any obvious beauty but which have fascinating and often dark histories and where it pays to keep your eyes and ears open. He has not yet succeeded in getting himself lost on the Berlin equivalent of the Tube.

Forthcoming books are *The Emperor's Pavement* – a Berlin 'daybook'; and the collections *Cities and Thrones and Powers* and *Written by Daylight*.

Rhys Hughes was born in 1966 but can't remember the first time he travelled on a train. Maybe it was when he was three years old. That's just a guess. He has, however, travelled all over Europe on trains, in adult form. He has written many stories about trains, usually featuring an engineer called Kingdom Noisette who is half-human and half-locomotive. But the story in this anthology is his own favourite among his train stories. He insists that the concept of the 'Infinite Train' is perfectly viable and he thinks someone should build one. The idea came to him while he was lying in bed. He often lies in bed. "My femur is made of cheese!" is an example of one of these lies.

Mat Joiner is a member of Birmingham Writers' Group; his stories and poems have troubled the pages of *Never Again, Not One Of Us, Sein Und Werden,* and *Strange Horizons*. He plays the Omnichord, haunts charity bookshops and canals, and enjoys real ale, flippancy, and photosynthesis.

Joel Lane lives in Birmingham, England. His publications in the weird fiction genre include four short story collections, *The Earth Wire, The Lost District, The Terrible Changes* and *Where Furnaces Burn* – the latter a book of supernatural crime stories set in the West Midlands – as well as a novella, *The Witnesses Are Gone*. A booklet of his short crime stories, *Do Not Pass Go*, was published in 2011. His articles on classic weird fiction writers have appeared in *Wormwood, Foundation, Supernatural Tales* and elsewhere. The setting of 'Last Train' is a real place, though it may no longer be quite as described in the story.

Jet McDonald is a writer, musician and storyteller. His first novel "Automatic Safe Dog" is published by Eibonvale Press. He once faked a Young Persons Railcard. He reckons he could still get away with it now with some hair dye and a laminator. www.jetmcdonald.com

David McGroarty grew up in a suburb of Glasgow. When he was seven, he went to bed aboard a sleeping car outside of Paris and woke in the Spanish Pyrenees. He now lives and works in London, and occasionally takes the sleeper back to Scotland, with expectations of waking up in the mountains. He can be found online at www.davidmcgroarty.net

Steven Pirie lives north of Crewe Junction but south of the Carlisle Interchange. He has a brake van and one carriage now nearly sixteen years of age. He's (just) old enough to remember a mammoth eighteen hour steam-hauled journey to the far tip of Scotland. Oddly, he can't remember the journey back. Steve's fiction has been published in ticket offices all over the world. First Class may be found at www.stevenpirie.com

Marion Pitman is a Londoner exiled to Reading, and has no car, no television, no cats and no money. Most of the time she'd rather be in New Zealand or Zimbabwe. She comes from a long line of people who never threw anything away, and it shows. If she won the lottery she would avoid winter altogether, and watch a lot more cricket and rugby. She wishes someone would publish one of her novels.

She has had short fiction published in 19 and 3SF, Wildstacks and Estronomicon, and in anthologies from Sphere, Fontana, Hutchinson, Creeping Hemlock, Elastic Press, Ash Tree, Mortbury, Eibonvale Press, and NewCon Press, and upcoming from Alchemy Press and Fringeworks. She also writes poetry, which has appeared in various places, most recently in Sein und Werden and Unspoken Water.

Rosanne Rabinowitz's previous rail-oriented fiction includes „In the Pines", a novella about train wrecks, teenage angst, the Jersey Devil and weird physics, which appeared in the award-winning anthology The Elastic Book of Music. An earlier story, "Fugitive Spirit" (published by The Third Alternative) featured border crossings, forged identities and hauntings in a tale inspired by train journeys across Eastern Europe in 1990.

Rosanne lives in South London and works at a variety of occupations – including the occasional occupation of the local town hall. Her novella Helen's Story has recently been released by PS Publishing. Other work in print includes contributions to The Monster Book for Girls and Never Again: Weird Fiction Against Racism and Fascism - which gave rise to her auspicious meeting in cyberspace with co-author Mat Joiner.
For more information visit: rosannerabinowitz.wordpress.com

Danny Rhodes is the writer of the contemporary novels Asboville and Soldier Boy. His most recent short fiction will appear in Crimewave 12 (TTA Press) and The Christmas Ghost Story Annual 2013 (Spectral Press). He lives and writes in Kent where he also masquerades as the children's novelist Dan Street. Visit his website at http://www.dannyrhodes.net/ or his pseudonym's website at http://www.danstreetwriter.com/.

As well as writing poetry and stories, often with fantastical elements, **Gavin Salisbury** makes surreal miniature installations using figures and toys of different scales. His first novel, Conduit, was published in 2012. For more details of Gavin's writing and art please look in at http://gavin-salisbury.com.

Steve Rasnic Tem's latest collection is *Onion Songs* (Chomu), to be followed up by *Celestial Inventories* (ChiZine) in August. In November NewCon Press will be publishing his first all science fiction collection *Twember*.

As well as numerous short stories in magazines and anthologies, **Douglas Thompson** is the author of seven novels: "Ultrameta" (2009), and "Sylvow" (2010) both from Eibonvale Press, "Apoidea" (2011) from The Exaggerated Press, "Mechagnosis" from Dog Horn (2012), "Entanglement" from Elsewhen Press (2012), and "Volwys" and "Freasdal" from Dog Horn and Acair Publishing respectively, due in late 2013/early 2014. http://douglasthompson.wordpress.com/

Aliya Whiteley lives in West Sussex and writes in any direction she fancies. Her fantasy short stories have been collected together by Dog Horn Publishing in the book 'Witchcraft in the Harem' and her first two comic novels were published by Macmillan. You can find her website at http://aliyawhiteley.wordpress.com/

Charles Wilkinson: born Birmingham, United Kingdom. Publications: The Snowman and Other Poems (Iron Press, 1978) and The Pain Tree and Other Stories (London Magazine Editions, 2000). His stories have appeared in Best Short Stories 1990 (Heinemann), Best English Short Stories 2 (Norton), Midwinter Mysteries (Little, Brown), The Unthology (Unthank Books), *London Magazine* and in genre magazines such as *Supernatural Tales* and *Theaker's Quarterly Fiction*. A pamphlet of his poems is forthcoming from Flarestack (Birmingham, U.K.) and a short story is scheduled for publication in *Sacrum Regnum*.